THE LATITUDE SERIES BOOK 2

ORENDA

The Latitude Series Book 2

ORENDA

T.S. Simons

4 Horsemen Publications, Inc.

DEDICATION

For Anja and Markus

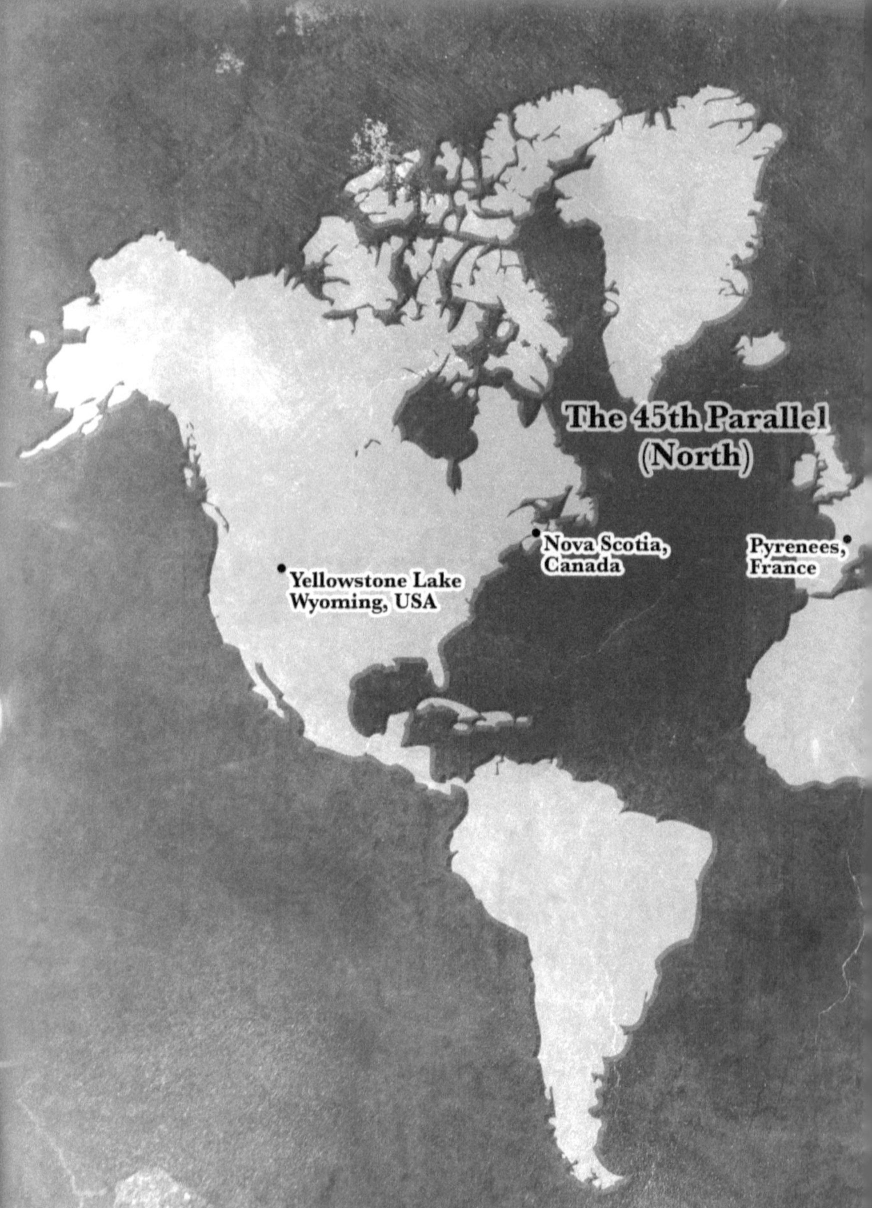

The 45th Parallel
(North)
Yellowstone Lake
Wyoming, USA
Nova Scotia,
Canada
Pyrenees,
France

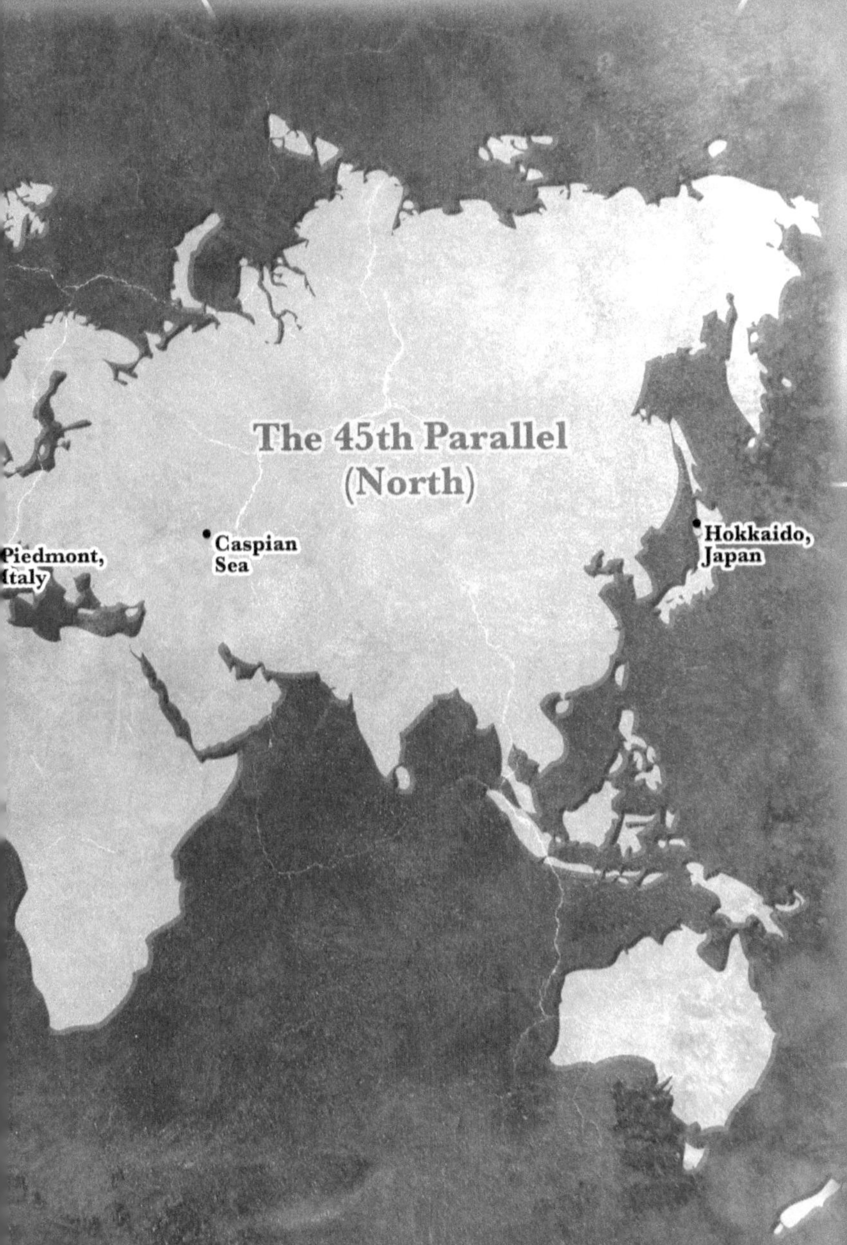

The 45th Parallel
(North)
Piedmont,
Italy
Caspian
Sea
Hokkaido,
Japan

CONTENTS

ACKNOWLEDGEMENTS

ONCE AGAIN, I FIND myself with so many people to thank that I can't list them all. Family and friends who continue to support me and my books. Without you, these books would never have been published. Thank you.

My love, thank you for doing life with me. While our home is a zoo most days, when we fall into bed together each night, still a team despite the madness, you make me the happiest girl in the world. Thank you for the coffee, cooking, chats, and endless support and hugs. Without you, I couldn't write, work, or achieve half of what I do. I love you.

CHAPTER 1

THE UNEVEN ANCIENT STONE of Dun Carloway broch pressed into our backs, making me shiver slightly from the cold it radiated. His arm slipped around my waist as we snuggled close and gazed over the roaring gray ocean beyond, white caps smashing onto the beach below. The ominous dark clouds rolled overhead in a stream of fluffy ribbons, but we pressed together, safe under the Lewis dome. From the small gasps, I knew Gio was entranced, taking in the colorful landscape, mesmerized by the wildflowers dancing along the cliff edge, gazing across the sea to lands far away, and I leaned into him. As the freezing air pierced us through the dome's fabric, I dropped my head to his shoulder, my dark hair falling in a fan across his chest.

"So, do you like my home?"

A massive sigh left his body, my head dropping several inches with the exhale. "My darling Caitlin, why would you ever leave this place? It is *magnifico*. Space to run, views everywhere you turn. Grass, trees, mountains. Until I came here, I did not know how hard it was to walk on ground that was not flat. The sensation of walking on grass or rocks. You can feel it through your shoes. I never expected that. The people are wonderful. And the food! This is the perfect place to raise a family."

My stomach twinged, listening to the awe in his voice and knowing what he wanted. I wasn't ready to settle down and be a parent, and we had already had several heated conversations about the subject in the month we had been here. Even after everything that had happened to Sera and me in Yellowstone and then Piedmont, I knew I didn't want to spend my life here. There was an exciting world beyond the protection of the dome, and I wanted to be out there exploring it. Gio and I were expected in Canada soon to take up my role as the ambassador for the Association of Collective Communities. All my life, Mum had spoken about making a good first impression. The last thing I wanted to do was to turn up waddling and pregnant. I tried to plead my perspective once more.

"I grew up here, remember? It is as boring as hell. Nice to visit, but dull. Everyone knows your business."

"How could you ever be bored with this?" His sweeping arm took in the spectacular vista before us. Craggy cliffs, ancient archaeological sites, and raging oceans. Gio had been spellbound by the standing stones at Callanish, spending hours wandering amid them, touching each surface. He was awestruck by the tomb that formed the portal through which my parents had traveled many years before. Had it not been for that portal opening on equinoxes and solstices, we would never have met. Every time we traveled anywhere, Gio insisted we stop and explore every ancient croft we passed, bowing his head to pay his respects to the original residents, the old gray stone walls, and burned-out roof trees of old thatched roofs bearing witness to the generations of families who once lived here. He constantly touched the stones and grass and asked incessant questions about the varieties of peat and heather, wanting to climb every mountain path and gaze down at the valley below for hours. He loved the wild coastline, cliffs plunging to sandy beaches, meeting with the roaring ocean beyond.

"You forget *amore mio*, I grew up with the same view. Nothing ever changed. Here, you turn in a different direction, and there is something new to discover."

His enthusiasm was contagious, and part of me was filled with joy that he was happy here in my family home. But my stomach churned as I watched his face, turned to the sky, eyes closed against the light. We couldn't stay. I tried once more.

"Eventually, you have seen it all, and this becomes mundane too."

Gio gasped and pointed at the sky behind us. "What is that?"

Adjusting my head on his chest, I turned to observe the flock of birds flying in low formation under the dome. When I was a child, Dad had told me how they used to slam into the fabric when it was first installed, but now, like us, they had adapted, knowing when to turn and follow the curve.

"Birds," I murmured, closing my eyes again and enjoying the crisp pre-storm air on my face.

"I have never seen birds in real life." Gio sounded mesmerized. "I thought they moved their wings. These..." He struggled to find the right word in English.

"They soar," I filled in the blank. "Birds do flap sometimes, but then they glide."

"What type of bird are they?" he asked.

Squinting, I tried to focus on the tiny black specks above but couldn't see past the sun's glare. "I don't know."

I felt the disappointment as his body softened and relented, knowing each new experience was a thrill for him. "I remember seeing black cockatoos and other wild parrots when I visited Australia as a child. Galahs, Corellas, Lorikeets. They were beautiful and so brightly colored. Seeing all the different birds and animals was one of my favorite parts of being there."

"Koalas?" he asked excitedly.

I laughed. "Mum and Dad say everyone thinks of koalas when they think of Australia. Yes, koalas, but lots of others too. Wombats, possums, kangaroos, echidna. There are lots of snakes, but I didn't see any."

"What is an ee-kid-nar?"

"A kind of spiny anteater. Like a hedgehog or porcupine."

"I would love to see that."

"Well, maybe we can travel there now that the portals are reactivated. There aren't any antipodal points in Australia itself, but there are off the coast of New Zealand, which isn't so far away geographically, although the air is thin now. My cousin still lives in Australia with his family, but not in Kiewa, where..." I froze mid-sentence, not wanting to relive my past.

Gio caught the hesitation and knew the reasons behind it. He cupped my face with both hands, pulling me toward him, kissing me to dispel the awful memories.

"Come on." Pulling away, I stood and held a hand out to him, appreciating the distraction. "We need to get home. Dad is cooking."

"Your father is a wonderful cook." Gio grinned, taking my hand and letting me pull him to his feet before kissing me again, picking up the picnic basket, and tethering it to his horse.

"Well, it didn't rub off on me," I teased, running my hand up the inside of his top before turning to mount my own horse. "You had better not think I am the stay-at-home domestic type."

"You, my love, have other talents."

"Oh, what might those be?"

Daylight disappeared as he turned me around, and his mouth pressed into mine, kissing hungrily and pushing me back into the chilled wall of the ancient broch. I wanted to protest, knowing we needed to get back, but my traitorous body responded to his.

"Again?" I groaned as he gently laid me on the patch of grass where I could see the ocean, the storm closing in.

"Forever."

CHAPTER 2

WE WERE EXTREMELY LATE for dinner, and Katrin grinned maliciously at me across the table. After we tethered the horses and washed our hands, I tried my hardest to smooth my hair, but with no hairbrush, it still looked wild and windswept. Guilt wracked me as we entered the kitchen. My family was seated at the dining table waiting for us and, judging by the glares, clearly had been for some time. As soon as we entered, they pounced on the food laid out in the center of the table and began serving portions.

"Did you enjoy your ride?" Kat mocked, emphasizing the last word, making me blush. Gio, English being his second language, missed the slight inflection and the inference.

"I had never seen a horse before I came here," Gio explained earnestly. "I didn't know learning to ride would be so difficult."

"Oh yes. Riding can take some getting used to," Kat continued, grinning wickedly, unperturbed by the death stare I shot her. "Lots of banging. You often end up with a sore ass."

"Katrin!" Mum snapped as I glowered at her insinuations. Kat smirked at me, and I detected the subterranean giggle from Xanthe down the table. Gio caught the look and turned to me, confused and seeking an explanation.

"Would you like some pasta?" I asked him, ignoring my older sister.

"The pasta is *magnifico*." Carmelo beamed at my father. Since our arrival a month ago, Dad and Carmelo got along like they had been friends forever. Illy had already returned to work, scheduling meetings with the new underwater communities along the forty-fifth parallel. Dad had taken Carmelo under his wing, getting him to help with the orchards, greenhouses, and aquaponics.

"Are you still keen to help me bottle the whisky tomorrow?" Dad asked, and Carmelo nodded enthusiastically, chewing industriously.

"I promised I would help Illyria with maintenance at her office, but I will come afterward, yes?"

"Your turn to do the dishes, Caitlin," Mum directed over the table as I shoveled in the last mouthful of pesto.

Dad protested he would do it, but Mum shot him one of her famous ice queen glares, and he relented.

"It is fine, Mum; I don't expect to freeload."

"Good because you won't. I need you tomorrow at headquarters for a consult. Giovanni can also help your father bottle the whisky?"

While phrased as a question, we both knew it wasn't. Gio smiled and nodded. He would do anything asked of him, and I suspected he would like to see how it was produced. He had enjoyed drinking it as an alternative to wine. His face was priceless when he had first been introduced to the different flavors of whisky, gin, and apple and pear cider.

While here, Gio was keen to try everything he could, recognizing our visit as temporary. Mum, Sorcha, and Kat had included him in their medical procedures as much as possible, explaining the techniques and rehabilitation required. He loved learning and asked incessant questions proving his interest. I suspected Mum would have liked him had she met him professionally, but she kept him at arm's length. Her loyalties were always with me. I wondered if that would ever change. She respected him for his professional knowledge but hadn't quite thawed enough to like him. Gio told me privately he always felt that she was testing him, both professionally and personally, and he was fearful he didn't meet her exacting standards.

"That would be wonderful." Dad beamed at Gio. "You can come up with me, and Carmelo can meet us there later. It will be a big day tomorrow, so we need all the help we can get."

Trust Dad to be the welcoming one. Dad had liked Gio and Matt as soon as they arrived, making them feel welcome and including them in everything he did. Sera and Matt had made a side trip to visit the nanotechnology lab at Clava and then to Newgrange to see Tadhg, but I had stayed here, despite Gio's evident desire to visit more communities. After what happened last year, I did not want Gio running into Reilly or Finn, a collision of new and old. That could raise questions I did not want to answer.

Dad tapped on our door early, and Gio slipped out of bed.

"Don't go," I moaned, rolling into the warm space he had vacated. "It is cold." Even though it was late summer, the previous night's storm had dropped the temperature significantly, and I enjoyed the warmth of a man in my bed, especially when he slept hotter than I did.

He threw on his top and warm jacket, shivering. "I will never get used to the climate here," he agreed, sitting on the side of the bed and nuzzling my neck. "How do you not freeze to death?"

"We find hot men to keep us warm," I crooned, loving the attention and running my hands up his back. "Especially in winter when it is freezing. This isn't really cold at all. In winter, every woman finds that a passionate man sharing her bed is essential."

He pulled back and watched my face, barely awake. "How many hot men?" He choked on the words.

"Only one at a time," I responded cheekily.

His face rapidly turning purple in the pre-dawn light made me chuckle, and my arms shot out from under the blankets, pulling him atop me.

"You. It is only you," I whispered seductively, running my hands past the waistband of his pants.

"Don't," he moaned. "I need to go. Your father..."

"Will understand," I teased, pressing my fingertips into his firm butt cheeks, but I relented as I felt him resist, finally pushing him away. "Fine. Go. Bring some whisky home," I called as the door closed softly behind him.

After Gio left, I tried to sleep, but the sound of chickens clucking and scratching around outside kept me awake. Finally, I dragged myself into the kitchen and turned on the coffee machine. The whirr of beans grinding was loud, reverberating through the small kitchen, so I didn't hear Illy and Carmelo coming up the hallway. I stopped short as I turned to get the milk, watching them kiss passionately in the doorway. I had never seen her so happy and relaxed as he cupped her tiny face between his enormous hands. She was in her professional office clothes, dark hair neatly groomed, Carmelo looking casual in his t-shirt and jeans— what he had worn when he and I worked together in Piedmont. I smiled at the memory.

Illy caught sight of me watching and smirked as I turned away to froth the milk, embarrassed to have been seen watching them.

"What?" she teased. "Think you are the only one to enjoy the benefits of a new man?"

Illy had been part of my life since I was born. She was my second mother. But I had never known her in a couple, and it was strange to see her in this light. Sera and I were thrilled to see her so blissfully happy. Her elder daughters, Summer and Ally, not so much, and after meeting Carmelo and putting him through his paces, they had disappeared back to their work. Their father, Luca, had been part of their lives until they were eight, and although Carmelo was the younger half-brother Luca never knew he had, the girls weren't thrilled about a replacement. Alasdair, like us, had never known Luca and was pleased his mother had met someone who loved her and treated her like a queen. Sera and I were fond of Carmelo. He and I had grown close during our time in Piedmont. Despite only being here for a month, Carmelo had adapted to life on Lewis like he was born here, chatting to everyone he met in a mix of Italian and English. Illy was learning Italian rapidly and practiced with him every afternoon, walking around Roseglen, pointing out objects and naming them in Italian and English.

Mum appeared behind them, still wearing her emerald silk robe, and whispered, "Cradle snatcher," as she passed Illy in the hall. Illy grinned, and Mum plopped herself at the table, bleary-eyed. Mum smiled gratefully as I handed her my coffee and turned to make another.

Illy slipped out the door arm in arm with Carmelo, and as I stood at the machine, I watched her start up her electric vehicle and head up the road toward the headquarters at Garynahine. Carmelo hadn't driven in over thirty years, and although Dad had offered to teach him, he hadn't yet accepted. Gio had wanted to learn after his first trip from the airport to my home, desperate to master this new skill. Matt was more obsessed with the mechanics of the vehicles and how they functioned rather than wanting to learn to drive.

For a moment, I wondered why Dad hadn't taken Carmelo with him to the whisky still, but realized in the next instant that most of the cars we had here could only carry two people, and very few carried four. *Couldn't he have taken Carmelo and left Gio with me?* I grumbled inwardly, knowing that was likely my mother's controlling influence.

"What do we have planned?" I asked over my liquid breakfast.

"I want to see the design of this leg brace you made for the little boy on Piedmont I keep hearing about. There is a child with bowed legs on Orkney, and I was wondering if we could adapt them."

Now she was talking my language. I stood, excited. "Sure, I can fetch the designs and…"

"Breakfast first," she said firmly. "It will be a big day. Eat something. Can you make me some toast while you are at it?"

Mum asked questions all the way to the clinic and, upon arrival, steered me into her office. Mum deliberately failed to mention that she had set up a video conference call between Orkney, Piedmont, and ourselves using Sera's new satellite systems. While I had been trialing the system to meet with my new colleagues, including Riccardo, the appointed ambassador to Piedmont, and one of my former colleagues from the engineering team, I scowled, realizing I had been set up. She had never had any intention of me not participating.

As we came online, I was thrilled to see Gianni but struggled to understand much of what his family told me without Gio to interpret. After lots of gesturing and Gianni demonstrating, I worked out that the braces were working mostly as designed but needed a little tweaking. He had a slight over-extension when he walked, and it was causing him some pain in his knees. With Carmelo here and Matt due back from Newgrange today, I considered how I could achieve this.

Riccardo? No. He is busy settling into his new role. Perhaps Joseph? I thought, making a mental note to send him a message on how to adjust the straps and the pivot points so they didn't give Gianni blisters. The boy on Orkney, Charlie, came online late as the team struggled with technical issues, which was probably just as well. He looked terrified but relaxed visibly when he saw Gianni's face and was joyous at seeing me. When I asked, Gianni stood to show his braces, and I saw Mum assessing how they supported him but allowed a full range of motion.

Charlie's case differed from Gianni's; I could see that immediately. Unlike Gianni, who Mum confirmed had muscular dystrophy, Charlie's legs had grown at the wrong angle, leaving him with a strange dia-mond-shaped aspect to his legs. I wasn't sure the same style brace would work. Gianni had low muscle tone and hypermobility. This boy's legs looked like they had grown inward from the knees, most painfully.

Hip dysplasia? I wrote on a piece of paper in front of Mum so that they couldn't see.

Blount disease, she scribbled back, not taking her cool professional gaze off the screen.

? I drew beneath.

Without glancing down, she wrote in a far neater script than me, *Growth disorder tibia. Turns lower leg inward. Getting worse.*

Surgery? I scribbled, barely legible, still chatting away happily to Charlie about his favorite horse, Nessie. Gianni's eyes popped wide, hearing Charlie talking about riding a horse, making Charlie puff his chest with pride that he could do something Gianni couldn't. I glanced back at the paper on the desk.

Needs it. Parents won't let me. Convince them.

Bloody hell! Just a bit of pressure. My mother was an exceptional orthopedic surgeon known across all communities as the best in her field. She was also forthright, direct, and, like Illy, could convince people to do anything. If she needed my help, then this family must be adamant that they didn't want surgery.

Charlie's mother sat behind him in the room, looking fearful. I didn't know her. A mousey-looking woman dressed in worn but clean farming clothes, she flinched whenever Mum spoke. I thought I had seen her when I had visited Orkney for some of our joint birthdays, but I had never spoken to her. Rotating between Lewis, Ireland, and Orkney, the entire community was always invited to our birthday. If she was so scared, why on earth would she let me construct this for her child?

She heard what you did, Mum scribbled, picking up on my reticence. *Wants you. Gerry told her you were the best. Fancy a trip to Orkney?*

Thanks. I flashed a look at her. Talk about being dropped in it. *Sure,* I wrote underneath. If nothing else, I could introduce Gerry to Giovanni. Perhaps a trip to Orkney would compensate for not visiting Newgrange with his brother.

As simply as I could, I explained to Charlie and his parents what I had done for Gianni, the purpose, and how they were adjustable. The mother nodded cautiously but didn't take long to consent to my visit to meet with them. We made plans to visit Orkney in a few days so I could measure Charlie and construct some braces. Uncertainty plagued me. This child needed surgery. Why on earth wouldn't they let Mum operate?

After we disconnected the call, I rounded on my mother. "You could have warned me. He needs surgical intervention."

"I didn't want you to say no."

"When have you ever known me to refuse a challenge?"

"Well, never," she admitted. "The problem is, we could have tried bracing if he was younger than three, but Charlie is five, and while he is small, he is too far gone. Surgical intervention really is all we have."

"Describe the condition to me," I said, leaning back in my chair and stretching, trying to picture the issue. "It was hard to tell from the camera angle and the glare. Besides, I didn't want to make him feel scrutinized."

"Blount's disease is a bow-legged deformity, in Charlie's case, just below the knee joint and the top of his shin. It is caused by an abnormality of the growth plate in one or more leg bones. Without better X-rays, I can't even tell if both legs are equally affected, but I think so. From what I saw today, I am fairly sure Charlie's outer side of the tibia has grown here," she pointed to the location on my leg, "but the inner side of the bone hasn't. That is a fairly common presentation, or rather, it used to be. This is the first case we are aware of in thirty years."

"Can you show me a picture?"

Mum paused momentarily, then stood and pulled a thick medical text from the shelf above the desk. Flipping past pages, she opened it to a page with a front-on and side-on diagram of the lower leg. Squinting at the small font, I studied it, thinking about the mechanics.

"So you are trying to twist it back, but slowly?" I asked.

"Yes, but he will need a full leg brace with his knee in full extension."

"How would you treat it surgically?" I asked. "Maybe I can replicate something on the outside?"

"That is the second-best option," Mum admitted. "If they let me operate, we would do a guided-growth procedure. Basically, small metal plates are attached to the tibia on the healthy side of the growth plate to stop the growth on that side of the bone, in Charlie's case, the outer or lateral side. This allows the abnormal side of the growth plate to catch up, the medial side."

"I see what you mean. So as the medial tibia grows, it kind of straightens the leg."

"Exactly. But Charlie is getting to an age where we must do it soon."

"What happens if we do nothing?"

"There is a more severe procedure called a tibial osteotomy."

"What does that entail?"

"We cut the tibia bone just below the knee joint, realign it to the correct position, and insert a plate until the bone has healed into the straightened position."

"Ouch."

"It is far more invasive, and I would like not to get to that."

"Why won't they let you do this?" I asked curiously. "His mother was clearly scared of you."

"Honestly, I don't know. They have never met me, as far as I can recall. They are crofters, devoutly religious, and have little to do with the town residents, so it went a long time before anyone knew. When the med team on Orkney became aware, they contacted me. The mother, Bronwyn, was happy enough for Charlie to see the local doctors but clammed up when they wanted to seek my advice."

"You must have some idea. Are you sure you haven't met her?"

"I am certain we have never met. Illyria and I have discussed it, and we can only come up with two things.

I was part of the team that rescued the Orkney women all those years ago from Mousa, although I know she wasn't among them. She may have heard something about me that scared her. But I suspect it is because she was among the last forced partnerships."

"Forced partnerships?"

Mum sighed and dropped into the chair beside me. "The Collective, back before Illy took over, forcibly paired up people based on their genetic profile to ensure that all genomes were replicated. Each person was forced to have a child with their scientifically chosen mate, not their love choice."

"You are fucking shitting me?"

"Language, Caitlin! But no, I am not. It was a phase of the project that was particularly distasteful. She was one of the last, and I understand it was a highly traumatic experience. Especially had it been a few more weeks, it would never have happened. Illy abolished it as one of her first acts as Chief. But Bronwyn is likely resentful. As the mother of you and your special sisters, maybe she sees me as complicit, even though I wasn't."

"I don't doubt she was resentful, being made to sleep with someone who was not her husband. But Charlie is not that child?"

"Goodness no. Illy stopped that horrendous practice fifteen years ago. It was her second or maybe third child. He would be sixteen or so now. Charlie is a later-in-life child. A bonus baby."

"I thought she didn't look young. How many children does she have?"

"Thirteen."

My mouth dropped. "Holy shitballs. Really? Do people have that many children? Have they not heard of contraception?"

Mum laughed. "Probably. But more likely, they need help to run the farm. So they keep having children."

Bloody hell, I hope no one thinks I am having that many! I looked away from Mum so she wouldn't see my discomfort.

"Okay, so the best choice is to straighten the leg into a natural position slowly." I grabbed my sketching pad and pencils and drew. As the sketch evolved, I remembered my earlier thought of contacting Joseph to help Gianni.

"Mum, I just need to call Piedmont, okay? Gianni needs a few tweaks to his braces, and I can't do it from here. I'm unsure when I will get there again, and it needs to be done soon."

Contacting the communications team on Piedmont, I was a little taken aback when Francesca was the person on the other end of the radio. She was frosty and monosyllabic, clipped in her tone, and kept cutting me off mid-sentence. As bluntly as possible, I passed on the message to get Joseph to contact me. She terminated the line before I finished speaking, so I made plans to call back in a few hours in case she didn't follow through. If I caught the next shift, someone else might answer, and I might get a warmer reception.

"Who was that?" Mum asked, re-entering the room as I disconnected. "Surely they aren't all that rude? Illy said how lovely everyone was."

I sighed. "That was Francesca, Gio's former girl-friend. She doesn't like me much."

Mum chuckled. "Can you blame her? He is here, with you, having a wonderful time and seeing the world. She is at work in an enclosed underwater community. I'd be pissed too."

"Perhaps," I said, relenting slightly. "But I hope she passes on the message. Gianni needs his braces adjusted. I would have asked Carmelo. He helped me build them. Or even Matt. But they are both away."

"All the more reason the ex hates you." Mum smirked. "She loses her man to you, and then you take him and his friends to see these amazing places for months."

"Actually, there is a little more to it than that." I explained about walking in on Giovanni and Francesca arguing the day their name came up on the list for an apartment of their own, Francesca screeching at me, ending in me dropping Francesca on her butt.

Mum clapped a hand over her mouth to block the hysterical laughter. "Oh, I wish I had seen that! You are so my daughter, Caitlin."

I flushed, wondering if this was a good thing.

"Tell me exactly what happened. Don't leave out anything."

Mum left to see day patients, and I brainstormed ideas for leg braces for Charlie. They needed to differ from Gianni's. Gianni's were rigid and offered support as his muscles had no strength. These need to be adjusted slowly to correct the bowing of the leg. I wasn't sure such a thing was possible, but Mum insisted it could. *If someone is prepared to make the adjustments*, I thought, highlighting which parts needed to be adjustable and which were supportive. Frustrated at my lack of progress, I flicked through pages of my sketchpad, trying to generate different styles and designs.

Between patients, Mum came to look over my shoulder.

"That looks complicated."

"What you are asking me isn't simple. It will need constant monitoring and adjusting. If Charlie is in pain, his parents will just take them off and stop asking for assistance."

"They can be adjusted. You can do that. I know you can."

"You know I can't, Mum. I am supposed to be going to Canada."

"I meant you can build them to be adjustable. Regarding the ongoing management, I have spoken with Gerry. He has agreed. If you show him how, he will make the trip out to their farm once a month and make the adjustments. Or better still, if they can get him to the clinic once a month, they can satellite call you, and you can review and coach Gerry on what to do."

I sighed with relief at that. Gerry had been the father of Soli, one of my sisters, but one of the three who was murdered when I was six. He had saved my life and always treated me like a daughter. He was a kind and respectful man and would likely already have earned the trust of Charlie's family.

"That would work. Okay, when do you want to go?"

"In a few days? Why don't you bring Giovanni? He might like to see another community."

"Sera and Matt too?"

"I don't see why not. They are due back from Newgrange any time now. Are you okay to keep designing this alone? I need to get on with my day."

CHAPTER 3

THE MED CENTER WAS noisy with a steady stream of traffic, and after endless pointless interruptions, I returned home to focus on my designs. Setting myself up at the dining table, I spread the papers and medical texts across the table so I could see the presentation of the condition and tried to envisage how to manipulate Charlie's legs into the correct position slowly. The challenge would be something that would fit now, turn the bowed tibial bone and provide support, but was highly adjustable, both for height and for the corrected motion, especially as I wouldn't be there to make any amendments to the design. All without hurting him. This entire situation made me uncomfortable. These weren't adjustments to an inanimate object or machinery. This was a child, and external bracing was far from the best solution. Unlike Gianni, where there was no possible surgical intervention, I couldn't help but feel I was meddling in Charlie's treatment when I wasn't offering the ideal solution.

The sound of crunching footsteps outside the window pulled my attention from my sketches, and I glanced out the window. Dad and Gianni carried crates from the trailer attached to the back of the electric vehicle. They disappeared into the greenhouse, and I sighed. *There goes my quiet afternoon.*

Dad greeted me coolly as he entered the kitchen, placing two bottles of whisky on the bench, careful not to make eye contact. Gio closed the door behind him, crossed the room, and kissed me, as was his routine. But they were acting strangely, and the conversation was forced, stilted. It wasn't interrupting me that had caused this situation; I was reasonably sure. I watched them skirt around each other for the first time since we had arrived home. As soon as Dad had assessed Gio's motives toward his daughter as being honorable, he had liked him, or so I thought. Had they disagreed? Dad didn't fight with anyone as a general rule. He was quiet, calm, and rarely challenged anyone. Gio respected his elders and certainly wouldn't seek to offend my parents. But something had happened. It was chilled between them. No. I sat back and observed. It was a touch too formal, too polite.

Gio offered to help Dad to prepare dinner, and Dad coolly accepted. I didn't want to interrupt or be drawn into this awkward scenario. Leaving my papers scattered across the table, I slipped outside to avoid helping. Mum pulled up and stepped out of her vehicle as I closed the door and smiled.

"A word, Caitlin."

We had spent the best part of the day together, so I was perplexed about what she urgently needed to tell me. I had started designing but was nowhere near ready to show her my plans. But Mum could be so impatient. I began to tell her that, but Mum started walking briskly down the valley, tossing her long silver-highlighted blonde mane back over her shoulder, implying that I should join her. Hurriedly I laced up my boots and caught up, wondering what on earth was going on.

"About Giovanni," she started as I came up to her side, and my heart, already pounding from the brief run, tried to burst from my chest.

Here we go. Does she not like him? Did he do something wrong, and they want him to leave?

"Your father and I like him a great deal."

"Okay." That didn't stop the thoughts from churning in my mind. I was wary. I had vast experience with this type of conversation. This usually led to something I didn't like.

"We are wondering what your feelings are toward him. He isn't your first boyfriend. Far from it. How is he different?"

How did I answer that? Gio was a man, not a boy. He made me feel whole. He treasured me and challenged me. Had his own goals and dreams but supported me in mine. He didn't feel threatened by me, as many men were. But how did I explain this to my mother?

"I am waiting, Caitlin."

I sighed and tried to explain how I felt. "I love him, Mum. Yes, I have had boyfriends, but nothing like this. As soon as I met him, I knew he was different. Special."

Mum nodded slowly as she strolled down the path, and I realized she understood. She was brilliant, a born leader. Dad supported her but never challenged her. "Can you see yourself spending your life with him?"

Illy had asked me that question before we left Italy. I gave Mum the same answer. "I can," I admitted. "Every day we spend together feels like a gift. He is charming and intelligent, and I love spending time with him. He is the first man who treats me like I am valuable and challenges me to be the best version of myself. I've never felt like this, Mum. It is like I am complete somehow."

"Good."

"What brought this chat on? Not that I am not pleased that you like him," I rushed to add.

"Giovanni asked your father today if he could marry you."

I stopped dead in the path, throwing up dust, unable to process what I had just heard. "I'm sorry. What?"

"He asked your father if he would consent to him marrying you."

"Bloody freaking hell."

"So you had no knowledge of this." Mum pursed her lips. She wasn't doing a good job containing her entertainment at my reaction.

"No, I bloody well didn't! I'm a person, not a possession! He doesn't need my father's *permission*!"

"It was a sweet thing to do," Mum said gently, smiling at my tirade. "But I agree, a little outdated."

"I am not an object! A toy! He can't just ask to own me! What—does he think Dad will just sign me over?" My face flamed, and I was levitating with fury. Mum's cool hand rested on my forearm, trying to calm me down and not laugh at my reaction.

"Sweetheart, he loves you. I agree. I would not have taken kindly to someone asking my father. Between you and me, I am thrilled that you are pissed off. But the way Dad tells it, Gio desperately wants to be accepted by your family. All of us, your siblings, too. He no longer has parents of his own, so he didn't want to offend us. He was fearful we would disapprove as you have only known each other a few months, and he would never do anything to alienate you from us. That is respectful."

"Maybe," I growled, not getting over the shock of learning that he had asked my father before me. Well, that wasn't entirely true. He had told me he wanted it all before we left Italy but knew there was no rush. I wasn't expecting this. Not today.

"So, back to my original question: how do you feel about him?"

"Like I want to tear his arms off right now!" I seethed. "Followed by his balls, which I will shove down his throat and watch him choke on."

"Ah, Caitlin, you are so much like me."

"Even though you didn't want me?"

"Who told you that?"

Fuck. I hadn't meant for that to slip out. My frustration at Gio had lessened my filter. Mum stood waiting, the cool look still firmly on her face. There was no backing away from this. Finally, I whispered, "Illy told me what happened on Clava. To you. That I wasn't a planned child."

Mum inhaled deeply and turned me to face her. She held me by the shoulders, her emerald eyes staring at me intently momentarily as she composed herself. Her voice was low, and I knew her well enough to know she was holding back emotion. But her voice was calm. "I knew we would always need to have this conversation, but it never felt like the right time. I made a million excuses, but then it was too late. What Illy told you is true. I didn't plan to have you or your sisters. Of course, I knew what they had done to me, but I didn't even know of your existence until you were well on the way to being born. But that doesn't mean I don't love you with every breath I take, Caitlin. I love you exactly the same as your older brothers and sisters. It makes no difference to me that you weren't grown by me. You are mine and always will be."

"But I am not Dad's," I whispered. "How does he treat me the same?"

"Louis is not mine biologically, but he is by choice. Have you ever seen me treat him differently?"

"No, I guess not."

"Your father and I both loved Luca. He was my friend for many years, before he even met Illy. We were so close. But you are Cam's daughter through and through. The day you were placed into his arms, I saw his face melt. They call it filial imprinting. He fell in love with you in an instant, and you were his. He would lay down his life for you, Caitlin. Surely you know that."

"I do," I breathed. "It was just hard hearing it. How I came about. That's all."

"I imagine it was difficult, but Caitlin, you are my child, precisely the same as the others. I love you. I will always support you in anything you choose. So now I need to know. Do you want to marry Giovanni, or do we tell him to return to Italy? You need to leave for France soon, then Ontario, but if you can still do it, I would love to take you to Orkney first. If this isn't serious between you, it is best if you end it now. It is fairer for you both."

"No!" The thought of losing Gio felt like a knife piercing my heart.

Mum was watching for my split-second reaction. "Ah, so you love him that much. Good. I will tell your father."

"Can everyone stop sneaking around speaking about my relationships? How about someone asks me for a change!"

"Did Giovanni not ask you?"

"Kind of," I admitted begrudgingly. I relayed what Gio had said that day in the grotto about wanting it all. She smiled. "I love that he told you at the thermal baths. Your father and my first time together was at the hot springs on August."

"Ewww, Mum! I don't want to hear about you and Dad. Gross."

Mum ignored me, her eyes twinkling, and continued, "So what he is doing is ensuring your family is okay with it. That is lovely. He is one of the good ones, Catie. He loves you. That is glaringly obvious. Men like that are rare—trust me. I can read him like a book. He has made his intentions very clear. I just wasn't certain of your feelings. You are good at hiding them, you know."

"It is like he fulfills me," I told her honestly. "I feel like I take whole breaths now, knowing he is there with me."

"So why wouldn't you say yes?"

"I don't want to be owned, Mum. I want to make my own decisions, stand on my own feet."

Mum laughed heartily at my indignation. "Do you think I am owned by your father?"

"I guess not."

"I was always the tough, independent one of the two of us. But that doesn't mean I don't love him. He doesn't control me, Caitlin. But I love being part of a team, a unit. Making a formal commitment just meant we always pledged to put each other first. It doesn't change who you are, but it strengthens the bond between you. You fight harder for each other because you made that promise. Does that make sense?"

"I guess," I said, thinking about it.

"As you know, we spent a few years apart, and they nearly killed me. Every single day we were apart, I felt my heart break a little more, knowing he was in love with someone else. Don't let that happen to you. You need to be certain. This is an enormous step. But if you are, and if he is your choice of life partner, grab on with both hands and hold on tight. Ask Illy how quickly it can be ripped away. She lost her soul mate, and she spent twenty years alone."

"What was Luca like? I know he looks like me, like Carmelo. But what was he *like*?"

Mum smiled, and her eyes glazed as she stared past me over the horizon. "Luca appeared to the world to be a battle-hardened warrior. He was huge, tall, and broad. A deep, booming voice, strong and utterly fearless. He was one of those men who filled a room, no matter how big. It could have been a stadium, and he would have filled it. Everything about him was large, his size, personality, and capacity to care for those he loved. But deep down, he was a teddy bear. It only got worse when Illy had the twins. Those girls manipulated him, and he was smitten with them. I remember Ally and Summer dressing him up, putting ribbons in his hair, and he let them do anything. He was loyal to a fault. He loved to tease me, call me princess. He had the most wonderful sense of honor, commitment, and humor. I see so much of him in you. Your wit, strength, and tenacity. Your fierce loyalty to your family and friends and refusal to back down from a challenge. I can't tell you how much I love that I will always have a part of him—in you."

"Dad doesn't mind?"

"Your father loves you unconditionally, Caitlin. I admit, I worried about that for a while. But he is your father in absolutely every way that counts. He has been there for you every day of your life. That is what a parent is."

"I missed you both, Mum. Sera and I never intended to end up where we did."

"I know, sweetheart. And I know part of your reason to get away was my fault. I am so sorry if I made you feel that your genetic profile meant you were different. That was never my intention."

"It's okay. I just wasn't ready to be tied down to one man. Look how that worked out! So what did Dad say? When Gio asked, I mean."

"Your father choked, from what I understand, and took some time to recover. Then he told Gio that it wasn't his place to determine what his daughter did. He explained he would always support you in any decision you made, but you are an adult, and you make your own choices."

"How did Gio take that?"

"A little taken aback, I think. I suspect Gio thought your father would welcome him into the family with gusto. The request took your father by surprise, and he wasn't as gentle as he could have been."

"So that explains the awkwardness I saw."

"Likely. Gio is a gentleman and wanted to do the right thing, but your father, as you know, doesn't cope with surprise and reacted badly as he was caught unaware. But now that you know, what will you do?"

"Mum, I love him, truly. There is no one else, and I can't imagine life without him. But I am not sure I am ready for this."

"Well, that answers my next question."

"Which is?"

"Do you want your IUD removed before you travel to Canada? As the ambassador, it probably isn't fair to ask the med team there, and I don't think you want to ask your future husband to do it."

"Are you seriously back on the 'you are a chosen one with a responsibility' bandwagon, Mum? Don't you remember what happened after my birthday?"

"No," she hurried to say. "But if you arrive in Canada as a couple, then it just makes it harder. That's all."

"I'm not ready, Mum. That is an enormous responsibility."

"It is, but you will want this one day, possibly soon."

"Just not yet, Mum."

"What are you scared of?"

How could I tell her the truth—my childhood? Being hunted and taunted, called a freak? But Mum was as sharp as Illy in some ways.

"It will be different for you, you'll see. The world is a better place now. Illy worked hard to make it that way. People are treated fairly, with respect. Your children will be valued wherever you go. You will have people to help you. You won't be alone."

"Why do they need to know? Can't we keep it secret?"

"We are still in negotiation stages, but as the underwater habitations slowly join the Collective, it will get out eventually. As much as I want to, you can't keep that kind of information secret. You and your sisters have a responsibility to help save everyone in the future. Having children with Giovanni is wonderful as it spreads the gene pool even wider."

"My womb was booked before I was born, wasn't it?" I seethed, frustration taking over once more.

"Not quite." Mum's voice was soothing. "But you are part of a grand plan, and as much as I fought against it for years, I recognize its importance. But Caitlin, take your time. When you are ready."

"What happens if they don't join? The unhabs, I mean."

"They will. Why do you think Illy is sending you and your sister? Besides, it opens up trade and resourcing for them. They can visit other sites and free up their people to travel and learn new skills, especially the three that were never connected to the Nexus. Of course they will join."

"Even Yellowstone?"

"Some will be trickier than others. We know that. But Illy has made great in-roads with Yellowstone after the Caspians invaded there too. Give it time. Have you ever seen Illy back down from a challenge?"

"No. I still can't believe there are more, and we never knew."

"Someone knew. The same happened with us, you know. At the establishment stage, we were told there were twelve communities, but in reality, there were twelve linkages. Later we learned about even more like Shetlands and Orkney, where the antipodal point went nowhere, but they could access the Nexus. So yes, we now know of at least nine unhabs."

"It makes you wonder how many more there could be."

"It does. I traveled a lot, as you know, but even I suspect there are more out there waiting to be discovered. It makes sense that our governments would have tried to save as many people as possible from the protozoa.

Tadhg is reviewing the original Collective files, and Illy is making contact. Fundamentally, people want to be connected. It is best if we are; we can help each other and share resources. Everyone benefits."

"Even Caspian?"

"Even them. We can't leave them isolated, Caitlin. They invaded out of desperation. If we continue to isolate them, they will always be a threat. Come on. We must get back, or dinner will go cold. Your poor father is stressed enough as it is."

Dinner was stilted and awkward. Poor Dad couldn't bring himself to look at me, clearly feeling like he had betrayed me, and Mum kept shooting him reassuring looks across the table. Dad struggled socially, and Gio's question would have placed him in an uncomfortable position without realizing it. Fortunately, Katrin was working at the clinic, and Xanthe was staying at her partner's home. Thorsten had moved in with his partner, Lilian, and only dropped in occasionally. Illy and Carmelo weren't dining with us tonight. Instead, they were eating with Sera and Matt in their side of the house, welcoming them home. My mother's doing, no doubt, giving us time to talk.

As we cleared the table, Mum shooed Gio and me outside for a walk. Dad's shoulders slumped. Gio started to object, offering to wash dishes, but I dragged him out the door, reading the situation. Escaping dishes was a rare treat, and one I would not miss out on because of his desire to be accepted by my family.

"What the fuck happened?" I hissed as soon as we were three steps from the house.

"I think I offended your father," Gio said in a low voice.

"Offended?"

Gio sighed as we took the forest path. It was summer, and the daylight hours were long. Despite the late hour, it was a beautiful, clear evening. "I asked your father if he would consent to me marrying you."

"Why would you do that? He doesn't own me. I am my own woman. I make all the decisions about my life—no one else. I don't need consent from anyone to do anything. That includes you."

Ordinarily, Gio would argue with me, tell me he was in charge. Partners in life, but he was in control in the bedroom, he always said. I waited for him to disagree.

"I know that..."

"Do you? Sneaking around behind my back and asking for permission? I'm not a toy to be passed from person to person, an object. I can't be owned, Giovanni."

"I know that," he repeated in a firmer tone.

"Then *why*?" I spat, anger rising.

It was several moments before I realized Gio had stopped and was behind me. I turned, glaring at him, but refused to walk back. He saw the look of stubborn determination on my face and replicated my posture, hands folded across his chest, refusing to walk toward me. Conversing ten meters apart felt stupid, but we both refused to budge. *Take the next step.*

"My father died when I was nine," he said in a deliberately low voice, making me strain to hear him over the blanket of birdsong and insects. "My mother when I was fifteen. I had no one to talk to me about this. But Carmelo taught me about honor and the importance of showing respect to both the woman you love and her family. Matt is my only family, and he loves you. He gave his endorsement that night down at the lake, months ago. But I need to know that your family is accepting of me. I have nothing to offer you. People here have farms and houses, animals, and a life I have only dreamed of, read about in books. I have an allocated apartment barely big enough for the two of us, a monthly allowance, and we will never have anything more."

Begrudgingly, I took a single step closer, and after a pause, he did too.

"I don't want possessions and objects," I said, equally softly. "I just want you."

"I can't give you a life like this."

"Like what?"

"This place. Fresh air, sunshine, history. Oceans, mountains, and rivers. People who treat you like their own. Family. So many people who love you."

"I ran away from here, remember?"

"But it is in your blood. It is your home. You were born here."

"Actually, I wasn't. I was born to a brain-dead surrogate in a medical complex on the mainland after genetic material was stolen from both my parents. So truth be told, this is no more my home than yours."

Gio took a step forward, and after a pause, I replicated. He was still several yards away, not quite close enough to touch.

"I remember. You were a few days old when you came here. But this *is* your home. It is more than the physical land; it is the people. Your family, your siblings, your nieces and nephews. Everywhere we go, people stop to speak to us. They adore you. I can see it in their faces, all of them. You are part of this place, Caitlin. I want to be part of this, part of your world. I want to be accepted by your family. Apart from Matt and Carmelo as a godfather, I don't have a family. I don't belong anywhere."

"Yes, you do."

"Where?"

"With me."

Gio lifted his arms, and I fell into them.

"I am not happy you went behind my back," I breathed into his chest.

"I wanted to do things right," he whispered into my hair.

"Right would have been to treat me like an equal and ask me."

"Would you have said yes?"

"Ask me and find out."

Gio pulled back, and I looked up into his face, the setting sun reflecting in his eyes.

"Caitlin Mackintosh, will you marry me?"

"Yes, Giovanni Accardo, I will," I whispered.

Gio took a moment to register what I had said, then an enormous grin broke across his face.

"Really?"

"Truly. I want you. If this is what you want, we can make it official. I don't need it. I know what my heart wants. But if you want to, make it official, that is, I will do that. For you."

"I do. I really do."

I felt myself become weightless as he lifted me to his mouth, my feet swinging.

"I love you," he whispered to my lips.

"I have never loved anything or anyone as much as I do you," I admitted.

Gio carried me to a nearby tree and pushed my back against it, holding me off the ground. I sought his lips and found them in the shadowy light, bringing my hands to the back of his head and ran my fingers through his hair.

"I want you," he moaned in my ear.

"You always want me," I couldn't help but tease as I pulled his head toward me.

Holding me against the rough tree bark with his torso, his hands slipped my jeans and knickers over my hips before working on his own. I held on as he tilted me toward him, and his hands held my hips in place. Leaning back into the tree, I watched the orange glow of sunset reflect in his hair as we found our place.

"First time against a tree," I asked cheekily as he helped me dress.

"There are no trees in Piedmont except in the orchard," he admitted. "So yes."

"Well, maybe we had better try that again before we leave."

"Leave?" Gio's eyebrows furrowed in confusion.

"That was what Mum needed from me today. There is a little boy with a leg condition needing braces. Would you like to come with me to Orkney? The Orkney Islands are farther north than here. Windswept and beautiful, phenomenal archaeological sites I would love to show you. It is cooler, but has even longer daylight hours in summer."

"I would follow you to the ends of the earth," he said, thrusting me into his chest, winding me for a moment.

"Well, Orkney is pretty close," I admitted. "It was remote even before the world changed, Dad says."

"I want one thing in return," he asked.

"Name it."

"I want to marry you before we leave here."

My body went rigid. "Why so soon? You have only known me for a few months. What if you change your mind?"

"Because I want *you*, Caitlin. I keep telling you this. You are mine, and I won't let you go. I want everyone to know you chose me. When we travel to new places, I want to be introduced as your life partner, your husband, not your boyfriend. I want children, I have made no secret of that, and I want them to know their parents are committed to each other. It is important to me."

I sighed. "I choose you. Above all others, I choose you. I don't care what other people think. It makes no difference to me."

"I don't care about other people, but I want you. All of you. Forever."

"Okay," I whispered. "Let's get married."

CHAPTER 4

RETURNING HOME, WE ANNOUNCED our intention to have a commitment ceremony to my family. Mum and Dad offered their congratulations and called Illy and her family over to share our news. Amidst the raucous chatter and Carmelo yammering at Giovanni in Italian, Sera pulled me into the hallway.

"Can I ask something? I need to stress. It is completely fine to say no."

"Anything."

"Would you mind if Matt and I share your day? It is absolutely okay if you say no," she stumbled over her words. "I understand if you want it to be just for you. But, well, Matt asked me to marry him yesterday on our way home from Newgrange."

My mouth dropped, and I squealed, unable to contain my joy.

"I can't imagine anything more perfect than my sister and best friend sharing our wedding day! Yes, yes, yes!"

"Goodness, you two do everything together," Katrin teased, hearing our news when she returned home from work a short time later. The house was alive with noise. All of Roseglen was here. Isla and Fraser were empty-nesters, but all of their children lived nearby, and most of them were here with their own families. Bridget and Jorja, Sorcha and Di. Kat was my only sibling left unpartnered, although Ally and Summer were also happily single. I didn't think they would ever settle down, having a regular guy in most communities they visited.

"You don't think people will think it is strange—two sisters marrying two brothers?" I asked Sera when I could get her alone for a moment.

"Since when did you care what people thought?"

But I did care, I realized as I glanced around the merry chatter of the room. These people had known me since birth. I wanted them to like Gio. Accept him. Especially my extended family. Gio held Louis and Iona's youngest, Emma, and chatted to Iona in the corner. Louis had disappeared. Mum was speaking animatedly to Illy and Carmelo, who had barely stopped hugging Sera and me when he heard the news. Dad was subdued. He didn't cope with the noise and so many people in his home. I shot Dad a smile, and he half-smiled back. I wandered over to where he stood in the corner.

"Are you okay with this, Dad?" I asked him, surprised at how much it meant to me.

Dad's face broke into the broadest grin. "All I have ever wanted is for you to be happy, sweetheart. Giovanni is a good man, and he loves you. That is the best gift any parent could ask for."

"I love you, Dad."

"And I you, sweetheart. If he is the man you choose, your mother and I will support you to the ends of the earth."

"Do you like him, Dad?" I asked, suddenly needing the answer.

"I do," Dad admitted so quickly I knew it was the truth. "He is hardworking, honest, and understands the value of family. He loves you, and that is everything I want for you. Now, when will this event take place?"

"You had better ask Mum. She is dead keen to get me off to Orkney before we leave, and Gio wants to marry before we leave Lewis."

With a deadline of one week, Auntie Di accepted the challenge of planning the largest party Lewis had ever seen with two commitment ceremonies. Bridget offered to contact our extended family from all the other communities to invite them, most of whom would need to leave home almost immediately to get here. I had sisters and friends on Newgrange, Orkney, and here, and I knew all would accept the invitation to witness Sera and I marry the men we loved. Likely, they wouldn't believe it unless they saw it with their own eyes. I had been adamant all my life I would never settle down; I wasn't a one-guy kind of girl until him.

Quick trips between communities were now often undertaken by helicopter. Jake had taught Summer to fly in my absence, and she had found her niche. She was a natural, according to Jake, and had picked it up quickly. Being mechanically minded, she had also learned a lot about maintenance and repair from Tadhg and could often be seen grease covered and surrounded by parts at the airport. This allowed travel to be fast and contained, minimizing exposure to the thinning air outside the domes. With no plant life, oxygen production was minimal, so portal or air travel was preferable. The bonus for Ally and Summer was that it gave them another avenue to pursue their smuggling duties undetected by the Collective. Sera and I were still the only people who knew their actual line of work, but flying between sites on Collective business provided a legitimate cover. I was more than a little jealous that Jake had taught her to fly and not me, but I appreciated that with Illy's offer for Gio and me to move to Canada and act as ambassadors for the Collective, Summer was a logical choice. Illy offered to contact her and provide her with a list of people to transport here and home. I was thrilled that Summer would be here too. She and Ally were as much sisters to me as they were to Seraphine.

As the news spread to Garynahine and more people descended on our house, Illy grabbed a quiet moment and pulled me away to her half of the house. It was nearly midnight, and I was tired. It hardly felt like it was this morning that I was speaking to Gianni, unaware that within a day, my life would change.

"I have something for you."

She sat me on her bed and shuffled items around in her wardrobe. I watched her, perplexed. I stood almost a foot over Illy, having inherited both my parents' height, and she was half my size. Nothing of hers would fit me. Mum had told me the story once of how Dad had described her as the military budgie, and although I had never seen a budgie, I knew they were small agile birds, much like the tiny sparrows that lived here. She finally pulled a black clothing bag on a hanger from the cupboard and closed the door.

With my head tilted, I watched as she unzipped the bag and presented me with a pewter gray silk dress.

"Try it on," she urged. Sighing, I humored her. I wasn't a dress person and, after the important part of saying yes, hadn't thought ahead to what I would wear. Just standing up in front of everyone was stomach-churning enough without wearing something I was uncomfortable in. She beamed at me, her eyes twinkling with excitement. Realizing I wasn't getting out of this, I slipped out of my jeans, hoping she wouldn't notice the stains. I pulled the dress over my underwear, surprised that it slid over my body like warm chocolate.

Illy closed her bedroom door and steered me to stand in front of the full-length mirror that hung behind. My mouth dropped as she stood behind me, peering around my side. It was breathtaking, a slinky dress that skimmed over my curves in a most flattering way. Inch wide straps plunged into a low v-neckline. It was simple but gorgeous, and even I was surprised at how much I loved it. The pewter color highlighted my dark hair, green eyes, and pale complexion.

"Where did you find this?" I asked, staring at my reflection as she pulled my hair out of my ponytail, fluffing it around my face. I couldn't believe it was me. I looked so ... *different*.

"I found it a while ago on one of my trips, and the second I saw it, I knew it was meant to be yours. So it has been sitting in my wardrobe all this time. Waiting."

"How long ago?" I asked curiously, turning to see the side view and running my hands over my stomach and hips.

"Strangely enough, when you and Sera were missing. I went to Newgrange to help Tadhg set up surveillance, and Jake could get us moving as soon as we had news of where you were. We were terrified you had ended up on one of the uninhabited and undomed sites with no food and unable to return. Admittedly, I didn't do much, but I felt better being busy than sitting around here doing nothing and worrying myself sick about you both. Anyway, we went to Dublin one day to source some electronic parts. Tadhg wanted to amplify a signal. While waiting for Tadhg, I was pacing up and down the street. There was a dress shop, formal wear, and I stopped dead when I glimpsed that dress in the window. It called to me is the only way I can describe it. I needed to clean the dirt off the window, but I stood there, staring at it, and I knew, without question, it was *yours*. It was the strangest feeling, standing in a deserted city, seeing a dress, and knowing deep down I would see you wearing it one day. It was like a sign that we would find you happy and healthy."

"And you did," I whispered.

"We did."

"Thank you, truly," I said, running my hands down the silky fabric that caressed my curves. "I love it. I can't believe I am saying that about a dress, but it is wonderful. What about Sera?"

"I got her one too. You will get to see her in it later."

The week flew by, us madly making arrangements for guests, food, and delaying our trip to Orkney. To my delight, Gerry had agreed to come to the wedding, accompanying my Orkney sisters, and their partners and children, and would return with us by sea, giving me more time to spend with him. Callie, Tadhg, and our Newgrange family were also coming, most of whom I hadn't seen since my twenty-first birthday. Only seven months, and never could I have predicted this was where I would be.

Di was in her element, asking me to choose between colors, food and wine options, and locations, most of which I had no idea about. Gio wanted to be actively engaged in decision making, Matt and Sera too. Not that I had given it a great deal of thought. I had never thought I would marry. But I had always assumed people turned up and said some words. I didn't realize how much planning went into a big event. Thank goodness Di loved it.

Getting ready with Sera made the day magical. Kendra had insisted on doing our hair and makeup, to which I had begrudgingly agreed, but with ultimate veto rights over anything too outlandish. I won by wearing black knee-high leather boots under my dress. With a pointed toe, slight block heel, and buckles up the side, I loved them and would not be dissuaded. Sera had gone with the more traditional option of open-toed shoes.

"You can't!" Kendra looked shocked when I lifted the dress to show her.

"Why not? You can't see my feet, anyway. I want to be comfortable, and it needs to be me. I'm not a heels kind of girl. Besides, they will get stuck in the grass as I walk."

After a great deal of negotiation, I relented and permitted Kendra to curl my almost hip-length hair into loose waves, letting it cascade down my back with some tiny wildflowers woven in around the crown and secured with pins. Mum let me borrow her pendant, and I had asked Dad to make Sera and me matching bouquets. He refused at first, saying he didn't know how, but I insisted. I wanted something from him to hold. He relented, and I learned from Mum that he had scoured the valley for wildflowers to intersperse with lavender and roses he had grown himself. He had left the bouquets on the dining table for us. They were beautiful and smelled amazing. With our hair and makeup complete, Sera and I disappeared into my room to put on our dresses, the last step before our ceremony. I slipped off my robe and into my dress.

"Are you ready?" I called from behind the door that separated us.

"One, two, three!" We both stepped into the room and stared at each other, speechless. Sera was wearing a stunning ruby-colored dress, almost identical to mine. Full length, slinky, and with a light smattering of sequins around the neckline. Sera was slim, but this dress made her glow in the morning light. She was gorgeous.

"I love it!" I breathed, spellbound. "You look phenomenal." The ruby color set off her platinum hair to perfection, and she was radiant. "Matt isn't going to be able to keep it in his pants," I teased.

"You too," she said, awestruck. "I have never seen you look so breathtaking, Catie. That color suits you. Gio is an incredibly lucky man."

I reached to embrace her, careful not to crush her dress. A knock sounded at the door.

"Come in," I called, and we stood back, ready to greet them.

Our mums stood there, their mouths wide, seeing us. My mother was wearing her emerald-green dress from her second wedding to Dad and looked stunning, the brilliant green highlighting her Nordic features. Illy wore a knee-length navy slip dress with lace overlay that set off her dark hair and sapphire eyes.

"Oh, Catie." Mum sighed. "You are so beautiful. Your father is going to flip when he sees you. Did you get my gift?"

"I did, and thank you." I reached for her, and she embraced me as Illy hugged Sera before swapping.

"Thank you for the dress," I whispered to Illy. "It is perfect."

With our mothers driving us, we made our way to the clifftop near Mangersta. Being so close to the equinox, we were careful not to travel near the stones at Callanish. None of our guests wanted to accidentally get whisked away to an island off the coast of New Zealand on their way home. I had suggested getting married near the broch at Carloway, but Mum had quietly told me that was where Dad's wife Laetitia had been taken, and it could bring back terrible memories for him. So we had chosen another location farther south on a flat grassy outcrop with views over the ocean toward Italy, Gio's home. I gulped as Mum drove around the last corner, and I saw what Di had done.

Neat rows of white chairs with red and green ribbons tied to the back filled the grassy space near the cliff edge. There was a small cove just beyond the dome, a sandy beach, and steep cliffs plunging to the crystal blue water, roaring onto the beach, the muffled sound on the other side of the geodesic dome. The grass was brilliant green, interspersed with tiny purple, yellow, and white wildflowers. A flat white stone had been laid at the far edge of the clearing, large enough for the four of us to stand, with the spectacular ocean views as our backdrop. It was a glorious fall day, the sun streaming through the dome and the cloudless blue sky meeting the waves beyond. There were no celebrants here. Couples pledged their love for one another and made a commitment, witnessed by family and friends. There were no prescribed pledges. Vows were personal and heartfelt. People were everywhere, milling around. It felt like everyone I knew had come dressed up for the occasion. Dad was talking with Carmelo but turned as he saw us approach. Shaking Carmelo's hand in farewell, he walked up the aisle toward our vehicle, extending a hand to help me get out with some semblance of grace. Trying to calm my jittery stomach, I hugged him, and he whispered, "I love you so much, Caitlin. You look breathtaking."

"I love you too, Dad," I whispered back as I slipped off my jacket, revealing my dress. He held my hand for a moment, staring at me with such adoration.

We waited for Illy to pull up behind our vehicle, and I heard people rushing to find seats. As Sera emerged and straightened her dress, I reached for her hand, our three parents standing behind us. Illy handed us the bouquets my father had lovingly prepared.

"Ready?" I asked, my back to the crowd. She nodded, and I turned to stand beside her, facing our family and friends, clutching her hand with one of my own and my flowers in the other, feigning a confidence I didn't feel. My heart was racing, palms sweating, but I stiffened my spine and tried to look composed. I saw my siblings and their families in the front rows, and as Gilly's violin started, all turned to watch us approach.

Giovanni's face was a picture when he saw me, blinking in astonishment. My heart shuddered as I walked toward him, my sister by my side, nerves getting the better of me. Matteo looked similarly awe-struck, staring at Seraphine. Carmelo stood behind them, a hand on each of their shoulders, looking as proud as if he were their father.

Last week, Dad had taken Gio and Matt to the tailor to get something suitable made. "Not a suit," I had insisted. "Casual, please." Gio had smirked and ignored me. But standing with his back to the ocean, he looked breathtaking in tailored black pants and a crisp white shirt, the top two buttons undone, a tiny smattering of his dark chest hair poking through. I fought the desperate urge to play with it and run my fingers through it. Matteo and Carmelo were identically attired, the sunlight glinting off their neatly groomed dark hair.

My face ached from smiling as Sera and I walked the length of the aisle between the chairs, the gasps making me smile even more as we passed. Focusing on my new family at the end, I had no eyes for anyone else. Rarely had anyone seen Sera and me in dresses and never as dressed up as this. Likely, they never would again. I missed my jeans, but today was special, and I felt it. With everyone watching, I felt beautiful but awkward and self-conscious as I swished down the aisle, pleased I was wearing boots under my dress and not likely to trip and break my nose.

As we took the last step of the aisle and faced the smooth white stone, I let go of Sera's hand with a final smile at her. She took my flowers and stepped behind me, and I held my hands out to Gio, who grasped them both in his own, praying he wouldn't notice me sweating. He leaned in to kiss my neck and whispered, "You are the most beautiful woman I have ever seen. I am the luckiest man alive."

As Gio pulled back, Carmelo turned to me and kissed me on the cheek, then Seraphine, and went to find his place in the front row beside Illy. He took her hand, and she snuggled into his shoulder as she beamed at us, her face filled with joy.

During the planning stages, Gio and I had agreed to go first, though I was now regretting that decision. Holding both of my hands in his and gazing into his eyes, the world ceased to exist. I had no doubt that he was the man I wanted to spend my life with. The sheer bliss I felt outweighed any doubts I had once had. *Him. It is him.* Sera was behind me, supporting me, not that I needed it. Taking a deep breath, and trying hard to speak with confidence, I heard my father gasp from the front row as he listened to my words,

"Giovanni Alessandro Accardo, I love you.

You cannot possess me, for I belong to myself.

But I give you love, which is mine to give.

You cannot command me, for I am a free person.

But I choose to serve you, in order to aid you.

I pledge that yours are the eyes that I will smile into every morning,

I shall be a shield for your back, and you for mine.

I shall not slander you, nor you me,

I will honor you above all others.

When we disagree, we will do so in private,

And tell no others our grievances.

This is my pledge to you,

For this is a marriage of equals."

I flicked my eyes over at my parents as I recited my vows and watched as my mum snuggled into Dad's shoulder, and his arm slipped around her to pull her closer. Their vows. I had made Mum teach me as a surprise for my father, for he was my father. I may look like a hybrid of my mother and Luca, but he had always been there for me, supported me, and loved me. I wanted to include their vows on my special day. Show them how much they meant to me.

Gio pulled me slightly closer as he recited in a husky voice,

"Caitlin Claira Jorgensen Mackintosh, amore mio,

I am alive today because of you. You are my sunshine, my starlight.

I was living in darkness until you shone your light into my life.

You are my soul and my conscience.

> *You make me a better man just by loving me.*
>
> *I will always support you, love you, guide you.*
>
> *As you walk your path in life, I will walk beside you.*
>
> *Per sempre. Always."*

Tears sprang to my eyes as he whispered the last line, and I fought them back.

> *"I commit to you as long as love lasts,"* Gio repeated, slightly louder.

> *"I commit to you as long as love lasts."*

Then he whispered so low I barely heard him, "But for me, that will be forever."

Gio turned to look at Matt, who handed him two simple gold bands laid on a black velvet cloth. I held out my hand as he slipped his ring onto my finger, and I repeated the action, sliding mine onto his. He was mine. His hands cupped my face, and he kissed me so deeply I forgot we were in public. As the crowd cheered and applauded, the sound broke into my bubble, and I pulled back slightly and gazed up at him. He slipped his arm around me, and we turned to face our family.

With Gio's arm securely around my waist and gripping both bouquets, we stepped back to act in our capacity of support to Sera and Matt. I could barely process Sera and Matteo's vows; I was mesmerized by the man standing before me. I desperately wanted to leave and be alone with him, but I knew this day wasn't just about us. I forced myself to focus on Sera and Matt, taking their promise in both Italian and English. I was surprised to realize I knew many of the Italian words and soon cheered along with the crowd as they sealed their vows with a kiss.

Matt reached over and kissed me, then Sera flew into my arms, the smile lighting her face with joy. The four of us stood side by side as our parents came and hugged us, followed by a wave of siblings, family, and friends.

I heard the music start, and people got up to mill around the food tables; a happy buzz of chatter hung over the clifftop. Gio didn't leave my side as we weaved through the crowd, accepting well wishes, hugs, and kisses. Children ran around happily as parents chatted and caught up. My sisters from other communities made their way over to me either one by one, or in small groups, and I introduced them all to my husband. Gio was charming and kissed them all on both cheeks, treating them like he had known them forever. Many were clutching young children or were pregnant, and I felt a pang watching him greet each child, introduce himself, and tickle them, knowing that this was something he desperately wanted, but I wasn't sure I was ready for.

Finally, we found ourselves alone for a precious few seconds, and plucking the flowers from my hands and placing them on the last row of empty chairs, he pulled me behind a bush out of sight of the crowd.

"You look exquisite," he said with such feeling that I laughed.

"You need your eyes tested!" I teased. "Why? Did you think I would turn up in jeans?"

"I wasn't sure," he twinkled at me, "but this. I was not expecting this." He held me at arm's length before pulling me back against his rigid torso. "I order you to take this dress with us to Canada so I can see you wear it again."

"You order me? That didn't take long, did it? Married five minutes?"

"I want to see you wear it again," he growled in my ear.

"Wait until you see what is underneath," I teased as I played with the chest hair poking through his shirt. His breath heated my neck, and I felt his hand sliding the dress up my legs on a mission.

"You are ruining my makeup," I breathed as his mouth found mine.

"Don't care," he growled, stealing my breath. The bubble descended, and the world ceased to exist. The clear ringing of a glass being tapped, signaling speeches, broke into my consciousness.

"Come on." I pulled him back into view and shook my dress down. "We need to make an appearance. They can't have toasts about us if we are missing."

"I so desperately want to tear that dress off you," he rasped in my ear, making my stomach lurch.

"Later," I whispered as I grabbed his hand, and we made our way to the back of the crowd. "Besides, if you tear it, I can't wear it again, can I?"

Sera and Matt appeared beside us as we stood behind the back row of chairs, and Sera dropped her head on my shoulder as we watched Illy call the crowd to attention. She was radiant and looked so blissfully happy that it made my heart sing. Despite everything that had happened to us, all the torment, I was ecstatic it had ended like this.

Illy stood on the white stone, waiting for the crowd. Everyone quieted and moved closer, ready for the toasts. She looked so tiny in her navy lace dress, fine streaks of silver glinting in her dark hair, but Illyria commanded attention, nonetheless.

"Thank you all for coming today. Some of you from quite a distance to see the commitment of Seraphine and Matteo, and Caitlin and Giovanni. Before we toast the happy couples, I hope you will indulge me in one more commitment ceremony."

Gio and I turned to each other, checking we had each heard the words correctly. We had. Illy beamed as she beckoned to Carmelo, who took three steps from the crowd to stand beside her, taking both of her hands in his. The look of delight across his face was clear even from the back where we stood. Sera squealed, her hand clapped to her mouth.

In Italian and then English, Illyria and Carmelo made a formal pledge to each other. Everyone looked shocked as I scanned the crowd, especially Allison and Summer. The wide-eyed stares and gaping mouths betrayed their horror at gaining a new step-father. Mum stood off to one side, beaming, giving away that she was in on the secret. Sera and I led the cheers as they kissed, and Illy blushed, a rosy tinge coloring her gorgeous ivory complexion most attractively. We rushed forward to embrace them both. I reached Illy first.

"Congratulations!" I held her tight.

"Thank you," she said, beaming at me. "I hope you don't mind me hijacking your day."

"We would always have said yes. You know that. Why didn't you tell us?"

"I wanted it to be a surprise. He makes me so happy and loves you girls like you are his own. Besides, you get to a point in your life where you don't waste time. Embrace every day, Caitlin, and don't waste a moment. I intend to."

"Mum!" Sera squealed, turning from Carmelo to her mother. "Why didn't you say something? I am so happy for you!"

Carmelo was shaking hands with Matt and Gio, and I saw my father approaching to congratulate him. Soon, everyone had engulfed us, hugging and kissing. Even Ally and Summer were smiling, pulled into the pervading joyfulness. Just as I was starting to feel overwhelmed, Isla put her fingers into her mouth and whistled, evoking a stunned silence from the ear-piercing sound.

"How about some quick speeches, and we get this party started?" she called to thunderous applause.

My feet hurt from dancing and standing for hours. Everyone I knew wanted to congratulate us, meet Giovanni, and hear about how we met. Many toasts were proposed, and I took small sips of wine, terrified of passing out.

"That is new for you," Gio whispered, taunting, in a brief conversation lull. "I've never seen you drink so slowly."

"Do you want me passed out on our wedding night?" I hissed back.

Gio plucked the glass from my hand, teasingly placing it on the nearest table. "I want this to be a night we will never forget."

As a gift, our parents had vacated the house for two days and two nights, letting Sera and Matt stay in Illy's end of the duplex home, with Gio and me on my parent's side. The fridge was stocked with food and wine, and we had nowhere to go, and no one to see.

Driving slowly through the dark, I fought to keep my vision focused on the path ahead. We staggered out, merrily drunk. Gio swept me up and tried to carry me through the front door but couldn't reach the handle. Laughing hysterically, I opened it for him, nearly tumbling out of his arms. He pushed it closed behind him and carried me to my room. Our room. Someone had been here since I dressed this morning. The bed was freshly made, the room lit with candles, and the fresh scent of wildflowers filled the room, small vases covering every surface. A bottle of wine and two glasses sat on the cleared bedside table.

"Now, about this dress." Gio hadn't been able to keep his hands from the silky fabric all afternoon and evening, caressing my curves at every opportunity.

He stood back in the moonlight, the adoration etched into his face as I pulled the pins from my hair, letting the flowers fall to the floor. Placing his hands on the sides of my ribcage, he slowly traced his hands around my curves through the dress, babbling incoherently in Italian.

"What are you saying?" I whispered, suddenly worried.

"Every man there wanted to be with you. Every woman wanted to be you." He sighed. "Yet I am the one lucky enough to take you home. I promise you. You will not be able to walk tomorrow."

He slipped one strap from my shoulder, then the other, and the dress slipped down to my hips, where it paused, lingering on my curves. With a shimmy, it puddled around my feet, and I stood in the moonlight dressed in the new lingerie set my mother had gifted me and my knee-high black leather boots, buckles glinting in the silvery light.

I heard the sharp inhalation as he took in the sight. "*Dio mio!*"

"Do you like?" I pivoted so he could get a side view of the sheer black lace bra that accentuated my ample breasts and womanly figure and matching black lace knickers with a cheeky cut-away bottom. I leaned back so my hair fell over my shoulders, giving him a full view. His hands found my bare ass as he pulled me toward him.

"Wear this every day," he moaned in my ear. "I order it."

"Order it?" I pulled back with a wicked grin. "I don't take orders, or did you forget?"

"I forget nothing," he rasped as his hands ran over the knickers, caressing me through the sheer fabric. "But we are in the bedroom. I am in charge."

I started to unhook the bra, but he pushed my hands away.

"No. Leave it on."

"The boots too?" I asked cheekily.

"They stay."

"My turn." I untucked the shirt from his waistband and slowly unbuttoned it from the top, planting a kiss on each newly exposed spot down his chest. His head rolled back as I took my time exposing his chest, running my lips across his chest, and finally slipping it off his body.

Gio kicked off his shoes as I undid his pants and slipped them off, leaving him naked.

As his hands came around my face, the world went black with the frenzy of passion as we devoured each other. It felt familiar, yet new and exciting. My stomach jittered with butterflies as he laid me on the bed and covered me with his muscular, taut body.

"I love you," he breathed.

"I want you," I murmured, desperate to have him inside me. He took his time, tracing his fingers around my breasts, his fingers running down my stomach to my hips. His fingers slipped inside my panties, and I felt the moisture coat his fingers as he placed one finger, then two inside me. Arching my back, I encouraged him as he deftly explored me, my head rolling back on the pillow.

"Please. I can't wait."

He groaned as he slipped inside me. "I love it when you are so wet for me. I love you, Caitlin. My wife."

Unable to speak as pleasure gripped me, I cried out as we surged together.

"I love you too." I sighed as he crashed down beside me but with a glint in his eye.

"Tonight, there will be no one and done," he teased.

"Promises, promises," I shot back, unsure I could take any more. "Take my boots off, though. My feet are killing me."

"This time, we take it all off." Using his teeth, he deftly pulled the lacy knickers off me and over the boots. I sighed as he unbuckled my boots and tossed them on the floor, feeling lighter than I had in hours. His hands crept in behind my back as he unhooked my bra, using his mouth to pull the straps down my arms, finally hovering over me with the fabric hanging from his mouth.

"This will also come with us to Canada," he demanded, tracing it over my bare chest.

We finally fell asleep near dawn, exhausted, but engulfed in love.

CHAPTER 5

TWO DAYS AFTER OUR wedding, Gio and I set off for Orkney, accompanied by Illy and Carmelo, my mother, and my Orcadian family, returning home after our wedding. Sera and Matt wished us a tearful goodbye at the dock, heading off to their posting in Japan. They were leaving earlier than us to undertake an intensive program in katakana, kanji, and hiragana script, as well as spoken Japanese upon their arrival in Hokkaido. After the delay for the commitment ceremonies, they couldn't delay any longer by coming to Orkney.

"I don't know when I will see you again," Sera wailed as she clung to me on the dock, Matt appearing equally distressed to say goodbye to his brother. Summer was standing back, watching. She was keen to get moving. Like Matt and Gio, Sera and I had never lived apart.

"Soon," I promised. "The forty-fifth portals open every month, so we can visit. I would love to see Japan."

"Promise me?"

"I promise. I am so jealous of you. Remember those books we read as kids? Japan looks so beautiful. Besides, we can talk every day. As soon as I get to France and you get set up in Hokkaido, we will work out the time difference and talk. We need to do this together, Sairs. I still can't believe we let your mother talk us into this."

I knew I would miss Sera dreadfully. We had rarely been apart for more than a few days in our lives. Even in the few minutes we had been at sea, several times I had turned to tell her something, and a pain struck me in the heart, knowing she was on her way across the world. Summer was flying them to France, where they would wait for the portal to open to Hokkaido.

"I know this hurts," Illy said, watching me stare over the rail at my home in the distance. The oxygen was thin, but short stints outside were fine. Our oxygen concentrator used hydrogen peroxide to generate oxygen inside, so the doors were closed. But we were fine as long as we were mindful of the warning signs: shortness of breath, rapid breathing, and sweatiness. Gio's face when I first took him outside the dome was priceless when he felt the wind pierce his body with its icy fingers.

"Why did you separate us?" I wailed, unable to hide my sorrow, especially from her.

"I need you both, but in different places," Illy explained. "I have been doing this job for a long time, and I need a break. I am getting older, and I want to think about retiring at some point. Spend time with my husband. If anyone knows that life is to be embraced, it is me. I need people I trust, and I trust you implicitly. Strong leadership in each community is essential. Someone who advocates for their people.

Besides, you need to focus on your marriage in the early years, Caitlin. Friendships are wonderful, siblings too, but you need to build that secure base with your partner. You need to rely on him, and Sera needs to rely on Matt. You will disagree with Gio. It is only natural. It builds resentment if you turn to someone else for support, which isn't good for a marriage. Trust is everything."

"I know. It is just that we have been through so much together. I feel like I am missing my left arm. She has always been there for me, and I for her."

"Your mother and I are very much the same, you know," she twinkled. "We have been best friends since before you were born, but she knows I must focus on my marriage now. It doesn't mean I love her any less, but Carmelo and I need this time. Like you, we haven't known each other for long, but it just feels right. We need to build a foundation, and you do too."

"I am truly happy for you both," I said, turning away from the waves and looking at her. "I had no idea who Carmelo was when I met him, but I liked him instantly. He was so kind to me, respectful, and he has always acted as a father to Gio and Matt. Then to learn he was my uncle was beyond wonderful. But now that he is my stepfather is even more incredible."

"He is an amazing man." Illy smiled, her face lit with joy as it always did when she spoke of him. "He is like Luca in some ways and very different in others."

"Is that why you were attracted to him?" I dropped my volume so we couldn't be overheard.

"Initially, yes. He looks so much like your father that it blindsided me momentarily. It was like having Luca return from the dead after twenty years, and all the oxygen was sucked from the room. You were there.

But he is different. Softer perhaps, or maybe I have forgotten. He is intelligent, kind, and respectful. I accept him for the man he is, Caitlin. He is no replacement. I love him for him. He knows that."

"Have Summer and Ally accepted him yet?"

Illy sighed. "No. I hope they will in time, but they are adults and live their own lives. All I want from them is tolerance and respect. They don't need to like it. He is my choice, and that is all that matters. Enough about me. Go. Your husband wants you."

Gio was standing farther down the deck, staring at the trees growing outside the dome, the trees Sera and I had been forced to plant as punishment less than a year ago. Even from the ocean, the brilliant green glared against the landscape of dirt and rock.

"Careful," I warned him as Illy and I approached. "Don't get too close to the edge. The spray can hit you in the face unexpectedly, and I am not losing you only two days after we were married."

"Tell me again how they grow outside the dome?" he uttered, confused. "I thought nothing could survive out here."

"Many years ago, Dad discovered a species of moss immune to the protozoa. But more than just growing outside of the domes itself, the moss allowed plants to grow in the immediate vicinity. It was on a remote Scottish island, so Dad has been propagating this moss, and using it to rehabilitate the earth. Then, Sera and I planted all the trees. They were to protect the dome fabric. Like you, we have severe storms, and the dirt is pitting the fabric, weakening it."

"You planted all of them?" Even from here, it was clear there were a lot.

"Every single one."

"That would have taken you weeks."

"It did," I responded curtly, still cranky from that particular punishment. It had been learning that we would be used as labor by the Collective to perform similar tasks that had, in part, been why Sera and I had reactivated the portals.

"And you deserved it," Illy piped up merrily from behind me. "Now that you are married, perhaps you can tell your lovely husband what you did to deserve that one?"

"We came home from Newgrange unannounced," I fired back, daring her. I shouldn't have. She took the bait, gleefully.

"You came home unannounced, as *you*, Miss Caitlin, received two marriage proposals on the same day and rejected them both. There was a challenge over you, leading to a brawl, if I recall correctly?"

Don't push me. The cheeky look was crystal clear. *I can tell him everything. I will win.*

My face flushed scarlet.

"Two?" Gio turned to me, his eyes glinting dangerously. "On the same *day*?"

"Maybe," I muttered, humiliated.

"But she only said yes to you," Illy finished sweetly before sweeping past us.

Gio stared after her, Illy's hair swishing in the wind before rounding on me.

"How many men have proposed to you?" he barked.

"Four, including you," I mumbled.

"Why didn't you tell me? About the others?"

I shrugged. "It is like you and Francesca. I was single when we met, and I never considered any of the other offers."

"Why did they propose on the same day?" Gio asked suspiciously, glaring at me. I felt like an ant being scrutinized.

"Only two did."

"That is not an answer. What made two men think you were the woman they wanted to spend their life with?"

The red on my face deepened as I realized I wasn't getting out of this and needed to face the music. "I was seeing them both, okay? I wasn't serious about either of them. Then they got into a fight over me. Sera and I left to avoid further conflict, and Illy made us plant trees as punishment. That is the full story. Are you satisfied?"

"No. Did you sleep with them both?"

"Maybe."

The thunder exploding across his face made me relent, but I couldn't help but poke the bear just a little.

"Yes, but not at the same time."

The forceful exhale hit my cheek as he hissed, "Where are these men now?"

"Newgrange."

"Right. So that explains why you didn't want me to travel there."

"Maybe." I stepped to the railing to look out over the ocean, knowing I was immune to the spray, and he wasn't.

"Was it that you didn't want me to meet them, or you didn't want them to meet me?" he asked suspiciously, standing a safe distance behind me.

"Both. But it didn't seem right to come home with my hot new husband after rejecting them and rub their noses in my happiness. I'm a bitch, but I have some standards."

"Happiness?" he questioned.

"Neither of them made me feel the way you do," I confessed, turning out to sea to avoid his judgment.

"And how is that?"

Bloody hell, will he let it go already? "You know how I feel about you," I whispered. I could hear the thumping of children racing around inside the lounge, peering out the fogged-up windows. All of my sisters' children were immune, but many of the adults were not, and they were not allowed outside without an adult to supervise.

"Tell me."

I grabbed his hand and dragged him down to the engine room, the only place on the vessel where we could have some privacy. As soon as his feet hit the bottom rung, I yanked him off the ladder and maneuvered him into the small space between engine casings, the sound of our feet on the metal floor barely registering with the loud banging of the machinery echoing through the space.

Grabbing at his top, I ripped it off his torso before stripping off my own.

"I had boyfriends before you." I pushed him against the wall, unbuckling his jeans. "I wasn't innocent when we met. You knew that. But neither were you, so don't you dare try your chauvinist double standards on me."

Gio was watching me, scowling, not preventing me from tearing at his clothes, but not touching me. His lack of engagement was frustrating, and I shoved him hard in the chest.

"What?" I demanded. "What is it you need to know? How many men I have slept with? What does it matter? Two days ago, I told you how much I loved you. I married you, didn't I?"

He ignored me, remaining in the alcove, still and unmoving. He watched me with cool eyes.

"Fine," I snapped and turned to leave. As I bent to pick up my top from the floor, I felt the arms circle my waist and snap me backward, forcing me to drop it again.

"You promised me you would never lie to me," he growled in my ear.

"I didn't lie. You never asked. It wasn't important to me, so I didn't think it was worth sharing," I snapped back, fighting to escape Gio's grasp as his chin rested possessively on my shoulder. He didn't own me.

"Three different men asked you to marry them, and you didn't think that was important enough to tell me?"

"For fuck's sake! They didn't want *me*. They wanted immune children, you moron. That is all anyone ever wants, that fucking legacy. Why do you think I took so long to tell you? I thought you were different." I was thrashing now, fighting to get away.

Gio spun me around so quickly I lost my balance. He caught me as I stumbled and held my arms a fraction too tightly, his fingertips pressing into my forearms.

"Is that really what you think?"

"Of course. I am *chosen*," I sneered. "Chosen for what? To be a brood mare? Do you wonder why all of my immune sisters are married with kids, yet so many non-immune ones are not partnered? I'm not an idiot. It isn't about me, but what I can offer."

"That isn't what Callie said. She said they were brokenhearted when you left."

There was a pause as I let that sink in. "You knew!" I shoved him as hard as I could against the wall, fuming. "You knew all this time, yet you tortured me over it?"

Gio's stern face cracked, roaring at my indignant face. "She told me yesterday. I just wanted to see if you would tell me the truth."

"I don't lie," I seethed. "I didn't tell you because there was nothing to tell. It wasn't serious. They were like all the others. They wanted me for what I could offer them. Children who would form the foundation for a new society, an immune society. Who wouldn't want that? I thought *you* were different."

"*All* the others?" His eyebrows raised. I looked away, ignoring the baited comment. "Is that why you never told me?"

"Partly," I growled. "I wanted someone to love me for who I am, like Dad loves Mum. I wanted my great love, not constantly worrying that I was being manipulated for being a freak with benefits."

"You are not a freak." Gio nibbled my ear, making me moan slightly.

"But I am," I hissed, barely able to string words together.

"Would it make you feel better if I said I was happy to never have children if it is what you wanted?"

I pulled back slightly, dragging my ear from his teeth. "But it is what *you* want."

"Not at the risk of losing you."

"That isn't true. You might feel like that now, but at some point, that bone-deep desire will overtake you, and you will resent me. I've seen enough of my family and friends be consumed by that desperate urge to have children. I can't be responsible for that."

Snatching at my top, I flew up the stairs, panting. I saw Gerry sitting on the aft deck as I emerged from the engine room, hastily pulling my arms through my sleeves. He looked up and smiled as I approached, asking me to sit with him. I appreciated the distraction and his non-acknowledgment of my half-dressed state as I flew out of the hatch.

Gerry told me about the projects he was working on at home, and I slowly felt my muscles relax. He questioned me about my forthcoming deployment to Canada, and the projects I had initiated in Piedmont. The differences between the domed and underwater communities. We talked about his family, his children, and what they were all up to.

"Thank you for saving my life," I said in a lull, laying a hand over his as it rested on the deck chair. "I am alive because of you. All the places I have seen, the people I have met. These wonderful experiences are because you came with us. You saved me."

"I'm so proud of you, Caitlin," he said in his low Welsh drawl, his hand rolling over and taking mine in his larger one. "Watching you grow into the woman you have become. So many people would carry a chip on their shoulder after what happened to you, but you brushed yourself off, took that trauma, and turned it into drive and passion. You have become a remarkable woman. A leader. You help people. That is the best thanks you could give me."

"I'm so sorry about Soli. I loved her too."

It was true. It had been fifteen years since we had lost Soli, but I still remembered her. Her sweet smile and gentle manner. I felt the shadow fall over me and looked up to see Gio watching.

"Thank you," he said hoarsely, choked with emotion, "for giving me my wife. You saved her, and she saved me. Your actions that day saved most of my community."

"I am just glad to see her happy. It was a beautiful wedding, and I am thankful to have been part of it." Gerry beamed as he stood, clapped Gio on the shoulder, and disappeared back inside.

"I told you that his daughter Soli was one of my sisters that was killed," I said softly to Gio as I stared out over the waves, and he sat beside me, taking Gerry's vacated seat. "She was six, her skull shattered with a rock and drowned by someone she knew and trusted. I often wondered how he could love me so much when his child was brutally taken from him. I wondered why he accompanied us to Australia when his daughter wasn't among us."

"That was not your fault." Gio matched my tone, speaking equally softly. "He doesn't blame you. There are evil people in the world and good people. You are one of the good ones."

"But there are so many evil people. That is what scares me. What if I can't protect my own child?"

"I meant it. If you don't want to, I understand. I chose you, not what you can offer."

"Did you mean what you said in your vows?" I asked suddenly, turning to him. "The part about me saving your life?"

"I meant every word. You are mine, Caitlin, and I am yours. Forever." He lifted me onto his lap and kissed me until time stopped.

With the waves roaring in my ears, and my heart full, I didn't hear the footsteps on the deck approaching. Throat clearing caught my attention, and I looked up to see my mother smirking at me. I blushed, wondering how long she had been standing there and how much she had seen.

"As much as I don't want to break up the honeymoon, I need you, Caitlin."

Giving Gio one last dreamy kiss, he removed his hands from where they were cupping my breasts inside my top, smirking and not looking at all remorseful about being caught. I stood and followed my mother into her cabin where Illy sat, looking grim.

"What is it?" I asked as Mum closed the door firmly.

"We need to tell you something."

CHAPTER 6

WHEN I RETURNED, GIO was lying on the bed in our cabin, propped up against pillows. He lifted his eyes over his book and saw the dark look instantly. He placed the book with the printed pages down across his legs. "What is it?"

"Tadhg intercepted a communication."

"About?"

"Me."

Gio swung his legs off the bed, the book falling to the floor with a thud. "What about you?"

"That's the problem. We don't know. It was just my name."

Gio tilted his head to the side. "Who is communicating about you?"

"They have no idea. It was encrypted, but it was my full name, even my middle names, so it was very specific. Tadhg reviews messages occasionally and noticed that one had no sender or recipient. So he worked on it, worked out the symmetric key to decrypt it, and called Mum. But it was anonymous, so they didn't know where it originated and where it was being sent."

"It could be nothing," he said. "You are helping Charlie on Orkney. Maybe someone asked who you were, the person who helped Gianni. Or any of the other projects you have worked on. We share expertise all the time. I do it myself with medical consultations."

"Perhaps."

Gio didn't need words. He sensed my discomfort. "You aren't convinced?"

"Very few people know all of my names. Besides, why encrypt it? Why hide the sender and recipient?"

"Why is any message encrypted?"

"To ensure that the data being sent is secure."

"Well, that could be all it is. Keeping it confidential. It is likely nothing."

"True," I agreed, not wanting to scare him. It probably was nothing, just paranoia after being stalked as a child making me jumpy.

"Why didn't they tell me?" he asked. "Or both of us together?"

"They didn't want to scare us," I admitted. "But Illy convinced Mum that they should at least tell me."

"They thought I would be overprotective of my beautiful wife?" His eyes twinkled at me.

"They thought I should be the one to make the decision about whether to tell you or not. As you said, it is likely nothing."

"I am pleased there are no secrets between us. Now that I know about all these other men."

I grimaced at the taunt and glanced out the window. "Come on. We are nearly there. Orkney is beautiful as the vessel comes in to dock. You can see the brilliant green for miles. You'll love it."

CHAPTER 7

CHARLIE'S CONDITION WAS FAR more shocking in real life, and I found it hard to keep my face neutral when he shuffled into the consulting room at the medical clinic. Following my mother's lead, I didn't react. I just smiled warmly and greeted him and his parents. The Orkney clinic was almost identical in layout to the one on Lewis, and I realized that it would have been established at settlement, all the communities getting the same resources. Over the years, doctors had specialized and undertaken additional training at Clava near Inverness or Auckland Island off the coast of New Zealand. I knew from Mum that Lewis had produced more capable doctors, including several specialists such as herself and Jorja, who specialized in women's and reproductive health. Aunt Sorcha worked mainly in pediatric medicine after her time with the Punan people of Borneo. Kat and the rest were generalists, enjoying the diverse aspects of medicine. Gerry introduced us, and I watched Mum's calculating eye assess his movement and gait.

Charlie's parents had accompanied him, both quiet types, flanking him as they entered. His mother clutched his hand, looking terrified, and it was immediately apparent that it was Mum she feared. Unless we got her on our side, we would achieve nothing. That was plain. After introducing myself to Charlie, who hid his face in his mother's lap, I addressed her directly, talking about Gianni and what I had done for him on Piedmont.

"Can you do that for Charlie?" she whispered.

"I will try," I admitted, not wanting to lie to her but equally not wanting to scare her with medical labels and descriptions. "But Charlie's presentation is different from Gianni's. Gianni has poor muscle tone. His legs are floppy and must be restricted so he doesn't overextend. We are trying to strengthen his legs. Charlie's legs are different in that they need to be straightened. I will do everything I can to help, I promise. But surgery would be faster."

"No!" Bronwyn's reaction was immediate and savage. "No surgery."

"Okay." I smiled at her in what I hoped was a reassuring manner. "Let me take some measurements, and I will consider what I can do. Can we meet again tomorrow?"

The following days were filled with meetings with Charlie's family, trying to convince them that surgery was the best option, but offering external braces as an alternative. Ultimately, Gio convinced the parents that while I could build braces, the best chance of long-term success was surgical. They hadn't known he was coming, and he had initially not understood much of what they said, their Orcadian accent being difficult for him to understand. But once he became used to the inflection, he introduced himself as the physician on Piedmont. He talked about his diagnosis of Gianni over a long period, the pain the little boy suffered, his continuing deterioration, and the medical team's inability to do anything to help. He spoke passionately about wanting to assist the child but being unable to until I arrived and offered an alternative they hadn't considered.

"Would Gianni's parents have permitted surgery?" Bronwyn asked him, boring into his eyes after sending Charlie outside to play.

"Not immediately, but yes," he replied gently, holding her gaze. "Watching their child in pain and suffering every day is something no parent should bear. Surgery is short-term pain but worth it. They would do it in a heartbeat compared to watching their son struggle day after day. But we can't fix Gianni's issues with surgery. Every day he will suffer, and all we are doing is helping him remain mobile and in as little pain as possible. This is your best chance for Charlie to live a normal life. A pain-free life."

Bronwyn looked over at Nick, a blank look remaining on his face.

"What is your concern?" Gio asked, returning her attention to him.

Bronwyn clammed up and wouldn't answer that, making me ask, "Is it pain you are worried about?"

"Partly," she admitted. "He isn't in much pain now, so why would I do that?"

"We brought good pain relief with us," I assured her. "Pain from surgery is very short term, and we can manage that. As my husband says, surgery is his best chance of living a normal life. As he grows, the pain will increase, and we can't fix it later."

"Is this what you would do? For your child?" She looked at Gio and then at me.

"It is," Gio responded without hesitation, making my stomach flutter. "I would do anything for my child to live pain-free."

Bronwyn looked over at her husband, then back at Gio and me. "I agree, but I have one condition."

"Anything," Gio said.

"*You* perform the surgery."

Gio looked at Bronwyn kindly. "I'm a general surgeon. Freyja is an orthopedic specialist. She is exceptional at what she does. I would want her to treat my child."

"No." Bronwyn was resolute. "You do it, or it doesn't happen."

Gio nodded slowly, glancing at my mother. Mum was doing well to maintain her cool poise, her face not showing the hurt I was certain she must feel. "How would you feel if we did it together? I will be there every step of the way. I will treat him like my own son. I promise."

Bronwyn glanced at Nick, and he nodded in agreement. I had barely heard Nick utter five words in the days we had been here. Gio was right to get Bronwyn to agree. She was the decision maker.

"When can you do it?" she asked.

"Tomorrow," Gio said. "He will need to fast from bedtime tonight. Nothing to eat or drink. Not even water, please. It is important. We will do it first thing tomorrow. Do you want me to explain the procedure to him?"

Mum sat beside me silently, watching this scene play out. I kept waiting for her to interrupt, to take charge, but to my astonishment, she let Gio take control. At one point, I left the room to ask Charlie to return from the waiting room outside. He looked terrified when he was told he was having an operation tomorrow. But Gio was wonderful, sat beside him and drew pictures. He showed him on Charlie's legs what he would do, pointing to the places where adjustments needed to be made and demonstrating on his own legs the full range of motion that could be achieved. Finally, when Charlie had agreed, he told them where to come and at what time, what to expect and what they could do to support them.

The family stood to go, and Bronwyn threw her arms around Gio.

"Thank you," she sobbed. "Thank you for helping my son."

"Why didn't they accept the offer from you?" I asked Mum when I could see them outside, walking down the path supporting Charlie. His movement was jerky and awkward, and walking was slow and ungainly.

"I have no idea. As I said to you back home, I have faced resistance from them from the beginning. The only thing I can think of is that I am the mother of the chosen children, the modified ones, and they fear me."

"Well, being scared of you, I understand," I joked to thaw the chill, "but it has been twenty years. Surely people have forgotten. Besides, I am one of the chosen ones, and they aren't scared of me."

"Fear is such a powerful force." Illy spoke from the corner of the room. I had forgotten she was sitting out of the way, observing. "Bronwyn had a forced partnership child, and from what I understand, he forced himself on her. I don't think she ever got over it. Likely she sees Freyja and me as the face of the Collective, authority figures, even though we weren't responsible. She blames us. Seeing us brings back those memories."

"Did this happen everywhere?" Gio asked.

"Not everywhere. Orkney agreed to the forced matings. Lewis did not."

"Why did they agree?"

Illy sighed but recognized that Gio had a right to know. "The spread of resources was not equitable then. Clava and Auckland Island centrally controlled all supplies and medicine. By signing up for the Collective's policies, Orkney opened up trade and access to equipment and technology. The trade-off was reproductive pairs, and a child from each pair was the price they paid."

"Illy stopped that horrendous practice long ago," my mother interjected firmly. "Now. About Charlie."

"I am sorry if I stepped on any toes," Gio apologized to my mother. "But I could see she wanted me to do it. I have little knowledge of orthopedic surgery, but I would love to learn, to assist."

"I would love to teach you," Mum said so gently I was surprised it was my mother. "I thought we would get nowhere with them, and then she took to you. I am grateful, Giovanni. You will make such a difference to that little boy's life."

"Helping people is why I chose medicine," Gio said, smiling at Mum. "I lost my father when I was young but knew I wanted to heal."

Mum thawed and flashed him an engaging smile. "I knew I liked you. But don't test that. I warn you. My daughter will always come first."

"As she does with me."

"I am here, you know," I cut in. "Talk to me, not about me."

"Caitlin," Mum snapped into surgeon mode, "I need you to build something different, support braces for after the surgery. By tomorrow?"

I sighed. "Guess who is getting no sleep tonight?"

"Do you want some help?" Gio asked.

"No, you need sleep if you are operating in the morning. I won't be responsible for that." Gio nodded, accepting this truth. I turned to Illy. "Can Carmelo help me?"

"Sure. I'll find him and send him to you. Where will you be?"

"Gerry's workshop."

CHAPTER 8

"I CAN SEE WHERE you get it from," Gio enthused, bursting into the room. "Your mother is brilliant. She knew exactly what to do, explained the procedure to me step by step, and even let me do parts of it. I was in awe of her. She is so meticulous, so cool. I wish we could stay on Lewis for longer. I could learn so much from her."

I cracked open an eye from my nap. After pulling an all-nighter with Carmelo and Illy, designing and building modified braces, I was exhausted, but Gio's enthusiasm was contagious.

"Mum is pretty good at what she does," I admitted. "Did you know she was a vet for a long time before she moved into medicine and orthopedics?"

"I think you told me once. But she is amazing, Caitlin. Like you."

I grinned sleepily. "How is Charlie?"

"He will be fine. Your mum was so gentle and showed me ways to minimize the pain for the patient during the procedure. She focuses so much on what is best for the patient. She is so knowledgeable."

"I get it. Mum good." I sighed. "So, when can we go?"

I enjoyed visiting Orkney, but Gio and I staying in a single room within a shared house with my mother, Illy, and Carmelo was getting a bit much, especially when we needed to share a bathroom, and we were newlyweds. Not precisely the honeymoon of dreams, although I suppose Illy was also on her honeymoon.

"A few days. Your mum wants to monitor Charlie overnight, but he can start moving tomorrow. She wants to teach him the rehabilitation exercises and check that everything went according to plan."

"It always goes to plan with Mum." I grinned. "She is a perfectionist, and rehab is more about teaching the med team here than Charlie. You watch. Mum strongly believes in teaching others—capacity building, she calls it. Then she won't get called back again to do the same job."

Three days later, and we were back on the *Eurydice* heading to Lewis, only this time, it was much quieter without the Orkney residents and children. Carmelo, Illy, Mum, Gio, and I sat up drinking and talking, telling Mum about life in Piedmont. Illy had been fascinated with the governance model and how they had adapted to a democratic society so quickly. After many interviews, she appointed Riccardo as the ambassador, and I was thrilled. He was calm and considered all viewpoints. He and I had worked together building the biogas units, and he accepted everything I suggested. Riccardo's ability to get the best from a team would be an asset to the Collective, and I could see his respect for Illy from the first time they met. He was a brilliant choice.

"How are you going to handle Yellowstone?" I asked as Illy poured more whisky, and I took another piece of cheese from the basket gifted to us by Charlie's parents. Gio had taken to whisky like he was born drinking it, insisting we take a few bottles to Canada.

"I might revert to my military training for that one," she admitted. "They won't understand a community approach."

"No, they won't," I agreed, recalling Sera's and my miserable month there. "They are brutal, although not as bad as Caspian, I guess. Jake said life in the Caspian community was pretty grim."

"At least Yellowstone is receptive to conversations. Caspian won't even engage with other communities after we ousted them. They have with us, knowing we can help with their desalination issue. But even then, everything is on their terms."

"What happened in the other communities they invaded?" I asked. The events of those few days still haunted me, and Illy caught the look.

"Yellowstone was prepared. After you escaped, they monitored the portal. So there were casualties on both sides, but the few remaining attacking Caspians got back through the portal before it closed."

"What? The portal runs both ways?" I asked. "I didn't know that."

"Nor did we. But clearly, it does. We also didn't know that the wormhole could jump from site to site within the window. They have developed technology that allows them to jump to one location, then cut it off and link to another within minutes. That was how they managed to attack three locations on the same day. They sent an attack party to Yellowstone and returned within minutes. But they were successful in attacking Canada."

"You never told me that! And you plan to send me there?"

"The Canadians were overrun. They had no idea the portal was even active again. But Yellowstone was quite willing to help after we told them what happened, so they assisted us in ousting the attackers from their neighbors."

"How? Surely the Caspians killed off the locals and sent their own people through at the next full moon?"

"They would have. But because of your intel, we approached Yellowstone and asked them for assistance. They were still less than happy about what happened to them and their own casualties and were quite willing to assist. So Jake took a few helicopter loads of men. We got them in through the access hatch in the roof of one of the pods and wrested back control."

"Wow. So are the Caspians pissed?"

"That is the biggest mistake of victors throughout history. Never underestimate the desire for revenge by the fallen. You don't ever rub their nose in their defeat. So, following Sera's advice, we offered them help to fix their desalination plant."

"Did they accept?"

"They did. They wouldn't let us land, but we dropped the components and instructions. Jake was allowed in, just to help connect it up, but that was all. It is repaired, working better than ever, and we don't expect any more problems. They are happy where they are and don't need to expand now that their own community is safe."

"That is a relief. Have you been there?"

"Not yet. I intend to, but I have other matters requiring my attention." She beamed at Carmelo, who was holding her close. "But Jake says they are happy enough."

"How much did he see about repairing it?" I asked thoughtfully as I sipped my whisky. "I'd love to know more about how that process works. Perhaps..."

"No." Illy cut me off but with a smile. "You will be far too busy in your new role to think about desalination technologies."

I grimaced, realizing that Illy would dictate what I worked on for the next few years. Surely I could still have a few passion projects?

"Carmelo and I will come with you to France, though. They are an important strategic partner, being so close to Scotland. We need to use their portal on the full moons if we are to make travel easier for us, so it makes sense to keep them happy. It is a short hop with Summer from Lewis to France. I am even thinking of building a permanent helipad on the coast near their community, to make things easier."

"Come on." Mum stood and drained her glass. "We need some sleep." She grinned at Illy and me, knowing that wasn't what we had planned.

"Are you sure you are okay with going to France?" I asked Gio as we prepared for bed. We would only be on Lewis for a night, and then Summer would drop us in the French unhab community to meet up with Magali and Nasir. Magali was planning to teach us both French and Gio about oncology, her specialty. Nasir was teaching him about pediatrics. Unlike Sorcha, who had just graduated from university, Nasir was also one of the original settlers. But he had worked as a pediatrician in Canada and Australia before joining the Collective. Gio was beside himself at the thought of all this specialist training, and I smiled, listening to him so excited about the opportunities he had been afforded.

"Everything is wonderful, and it is all thanks to you, my love." He sighed as he wrapped his arms around me.

"Me?"

"If you hadn't come to my home, chosen me, and brought me to meet your family, none of this would have happened."

While in theory, that was true, the reality was a little different.

"Honey, that is true, but they gave you those opportunities as they see your potential. You are a wonderful doctor, and Mum and her friends just want to help you succeed."

"I had no idea all of these specialties still existed."

"I don't think I have ever seen you so excited about something." I grinned.

"Except you." His chocolate eyes glinted at me. "I am always excited about you."

"Even now that we are married and boring?"

"Boring? Who is boring? Shall we try something different tonight?"

"Always." I grinned wickedly.

CHAPTER 9

GIOVANNI AND I WERE scheduled to spend three months in France, undertaking a challenging French immersion program and building relationships with our French counterparts. Nasir had been appointed as ambassador to the ACC, the Association of Collective Communities. While I had known him all my life—he and Magali had adopted one of my sisters Mariette—I was now seeing him in a different role, that of a leader. Initially, I thought Illy and her colleagues had made a strange choice and couldn't determine why she hadn't appointed a local like she had with Riccardo. But as I watched, I realized his strengths. Nasir was quiet and thoughtful, but when he spoke, you knew he had listened and considered your comments, and his responses were always insightful, moving the proposal or conversation forward. Nasir had an extraordinary ability to bring people together and treat them as equals, making every perspective heard and valued, and I learned a lot from him. After some weeks, I realized Illy was highly strategic in her appointments. Sera and I were loyal to her, as was Nasir. But strangely, so was Riccardo. Sera's and my marriages, plus her own to Carmelo, had cemented the relationship between the Italian underwater habitation and our own communities. Sera's and my work in Piedmont meant we were already trusted. Yellowstone had refused an ambassador, as had Caspian, but that hadn't come as a surprise. At least we were on positive terms with Yellowstone, despite their caution.

While within our apartment Gio and I spoke English, as soon as we stepped foot outside, Gio and I were only permitted to speak French. While the Canadian community spoke both English and French, Illy recognized that we needed to speak both languages well enough to understand all perspectives and make decisions for the entire community's benefit. Illy also noted quietly that she didn't want us to hear people speaking in French and not understand what they were saying, especially if it contradicted an order I had given. Sometimes I wondered about Sera and how she would go learning Japanese, but that allocation had been made as she and Matt were more technical than Gio and me, and Hokkaido possessed technology that Illy was keen to learn more about.

Magali was an excellent teacher, patient and calm, especially when I struggled with gendered nouns. Mum said she was already a lovely, mellow woman, but she was even gentler now as she had raised three children with Nasir. All of them were married and had their own children now, and Magali had welcomed living here for a time and helping us.

"Argh! Why are fish male and mice female?" I groaned, trying to finish my homework one evening as Gio prepared dinner. "It isn't like I am a vet. Why does it matter?"

"Genders, I understand. It is the same in Italian. Try learning diagnostic techniques in French!" Gio called from the kitchen. "I keep getting confused between English, Italian, and French, although at least some words are similar."

"I'm worried I will never learn," I confessed. "At least you speak two languages already."

"I like Magali. Tell me her story."

"Over a glass of wine," I insisted.

"You know you won't be able to drink when you are pregnant."

"Good reason not to be pregnant, then!" I shot back. "Happy to practice, though."

"When do you want to think about a family of our own?" Gio asked, opening the bottle.

"We have known each other for less than a year," I pointed out. "That is an enormous step. What if you wake up one day and decide you hate me? We can't divide a child in two."

"That will never happen," he promised, pulling me into his lap, carefully balancing his glass. "We are married, remember?"

"Yes, but marriages don't always work out."

"Ours will," he pronounced confidently.

But what if it doesn't? I thought, too scared to say the words aloud. "You said you wouldn't push it if I decided I didn't want to."

"Do you not love me, Caitlin? Is that it?"

"I love you more than breathing," I admitted. Sometimes it hurt my heart when I saw him, especially when one of the charming French girls here openly flirted with him. But I was scared that he wouldn't always want *me*.

"What is it then? I see you with children—you like them, and they adore you. Why does this scare you so much?"

"Do you remember when I told you of my childhood? Children taunting me, calling me a freak?"

Gio exhaled forcefully, his breath warming my neck. "I do."

"What if that happens to our child?" I whispered. "I don't think I could deal with that. Seeing them terrified, knowing that I am responsible for that. My mum wasn't given a choice. These babies turned up on her doorstep. But I never want a child to experience what I did. It wasn't just verbal. Kids hurt me. Threw rocks and punched me. Groups of them surrounded me on my way home from school, taking turns to hit me."

"You are forgetting something."

"What?"

"You have me now. What if I promise to always protect you and our child?"

"But you can't. My parents couldn't protect me. Gerry couldn't protect Solstice."

"It still haunts you, doesn't it?"

"Sometimes," I admitted.

Gio plucked the glass from my grasp, lifted me atop him, and paused, his face a few centimeters from my own. "I promise I will protect you. I will protect our children. All of them."

"Bloody hell. How many do you want?" I asked, fear striking my heart.

"All of them," he murmured as he kissed my neck, distracting me from my homework.

CHAPTER 10

"I HAVE NEVER HELD a leadership role," I confided in Illy one afternoon as she sat down to teach me more about my role and tasks as ambassador. She was only staying with us in France for the second month before moving on to Japan to meet with Sera and Matteo, who had been there since we left for Orkney. "What if they hate me? What if I mess it up, they kick me out, and I make things worse?"

"You won't," she assured me. "Rule number one: remember that you are not there to be liked. You are not there to be everyone's friend. You are there to be respected. There is a difference, Caitlin. Everything you do will be judged. People will watch, so always act with integrity. People respect someone who models good values, and you do. How you go about it is up to you. You will need to find your own style, but you have seen enough outstanding leaders to know what one looks like."

"Fair, ethical, always willing to help," I surmised, immediately thinking of Illy, Mum, Sorcha, Bridget, even Callie. They were all wonderful women, amazing leaders, but with different styles. "People you trust. Honest, maybe?"

"That is a good start. One tip I can give is to get to know your team as people. One of my earliest bosses in the Army used to 'do the rounds' every morning. He would walk around the offices and greet everyone, spending a minute or two catching up with every person, no matter how junior. The cleaners, the catering staff, everyone. He treated everyone like an equal, like they were valued. It gave him a jumpstart on any problems that might be brewing before they became insurmountable issues. People who were having a minor dispute, something that was going wrong. With that small gesture, he showed he was approachable. He cared and valued his team. He knew everyone. Their partner's name, their kids or pets. Even what sports teams they supported. People felt they could talk to him, and that meant they came to him when something was wrong. They didn't sweep problems under the rug. That is something to watch out for. People not trusting you enough to tell you when something is going wrong, hiding mistakes. Then there is what you do when something goes wrong. It always needs to be a balance of reward and consequence."

"Oh, I've had enough consequence from you to last me a lifetime!"

Illy grinned. "Sometimes it was about being perceived to be fair. I couldn't treat you differently than anyone else. People would have noticed and questioned my judgment. Sometimes it was not allowing a precedent to be set. If I allowed someone to always slack off from work, and others saw it, then it would encourage them to do the same. Remember that the level of behavior you tolerate is the level of behavior you will get. Don't allow people to disrespect you, Caitlin. You might be young, but you need to set the boundaries early. Treat people with kindness and respect, but set a clear expectation that you expect the same in return and don't tolerate any less. Remember that you are a guest, but you also control all the Collective's resources. They know it. You know it. They want what we can offer, all the resources from all the Collective communities. Tropical fruit, rice, alcohol, technology, training, access to experts, and even livestock. You wield a great deal of power, but don't let it go to your head. Use inclusive terms like 'we' and 'colleagues' whenever you speak or write something. People notice and feel part of the team. They then want to be a valued part of the team, and they work harder. Lead by example. Never expect anyone to do anything you wouldn't. It helps that you have a technical background. So sometimes make sure you go and help them out if there is a problem. It makes you approachable and not distant. People will trust you more."

"What does an ambassador actually do?" I asked.

"Well, as of last week, Canada is a full signatory to the Association of Collective Communities. We will start by going over the charter and reviewing the set of rules we use to govern and establish procedures. We have an agreed mission and set of values that we swear to adhere to that you, as ambassador, must strive to embody at all times. Much of your time will be spent preparing and representing your community on committees for various functions, such as law, technology, and trade."

"Joy."

Illy grinned. "They aren't that bad. Some meetings are a little dull, but the people are all lovely. Besides, Seraphine will be at the full council meeting and some committees too. You know Tadhg, Riccardo, and Nasir. I am on most of them and can guide you. They had a committee to make decisions before, but they are happy to advise you until you are ready to take over. This is a mixed blessing. They can guide you, but they are also assessing you. Remember, you are in charge. Do you recall what I taught you about a win/win outcome?"

"I do." I smirked, remembering having this conversation with Gio.

"It is critical that you approach all negotiations with that mindset. You want the best outcome for your community but also for others. This isn't about making others lose. So, in a trade deal, all parties must get most of what they want. It isn't always easy, but there is nearly always a way if minor concessions are made. Does that make sense?"

"It does." I had seen Illy negotiate enough times to know what she meant. "Wait, what do you mean by my community? I thought I was there to act as your representative."

"You are. Did you miss the part where I am Chief of the ACC? I delegate my authority to you at a local level through an instrument called a Delegation of Authority. You have the power to enforce the ACC's policies and procedures, but you will be the most senior person in that community. You represent them at all negotiations with the ACC, and you should strive to support them the best you can."

"What were you thinking? I'm twenty-one! I can't be the most senior person!"

"You can, and you will. It was a condition of their acceptance into the Collective. Seraphine is precisely the same age. Yes, you will need to prove your worth, but you have been officially appointed. I nominated you, but the full council voted, and it was unanimous. You are the ambassador to the Ontario, Canada community of the ACC, Ms. Caitlin Mackintosh, or are you using Accardo now?"

"Mackintosh is fine."

"Thought so. Your Dad will be thrilled. Makes it easier since Seraphine wants to be known as Ambassador Accardo."

"Bloody hell, now I am completely freaked out."

"Which part? Seraphine changing her name?"

"No, that so many people are relying on me."

"Trust your instincts, Caitlin. Your instincts are usually spot on. Treat people with respect, and follow the rules. If in doubt, reflect on the values, and ensure that your decision aligns with the ACC's values. You will be fine."

"What about Gio? What does he do?"

"He also needs to sit on some committees and steering groups, but his role will be mainly medical in scope. There are a few of them, ensuring that we spread skills and resources across all communities equally, that specialists are available and on call. After all his training with your mother, he will be an asset. He takes charge if you are absent for any reason, and he becomes acting ambassador. But the title and responsibilities are yours. There is an excellent team there. I have met them several times. You will get an EA, and all the support you need."

"What is an EA?"

"An executive assistant. Her name is Mandy, and she is a gem. Super organized and efficient. She will manage your diary, basically telling you where to be and when. She will help prepare meeting agendas and minutes and ensure they are distributed before and after each meeting."

"So, be nice to her, is what you are telling me?"

"Exactly. If she respects you, she will work her ass off for you."

"Noted. But I feel like a fraud. I have no experience, and no idea what I am doing. What if they work out I am clueless? They will send me packing within a month!"

"Worrying is normal and just means you want to do a good job. I would be concerned if you came strutting in like you knew it all. Yes, you have things to learn, but you are a fast learner, Caitlin. Seraphine too. You will do fine."

"I'm not getting out of this, am I?"

"No. You will be presented as Ambassador Mackintosh of the ACC. Now let's see about getting you some professional clothes. You can't turn up to meetings in jeans."

CHAPTER 11

ILLY DRILLED ME UP to sixteen hours a day, every day, for a month, training me on policies, procedures, governance processes, and even how to read financial statements. Where possible, she even made me try to learn them in French.

"I don't understand the difference between current and non-current assets!" I moaned, letting my forehead hit the timber table with a thunk. "And then you want me to explain the concept in French?"

"Take a break. Go for a walk. We can resume in an hour."

Slipping out the door, I slunk down the hallway, my head spinning, knowing I had bitten off far more than I could chew. Most of this stuff made no sense. I was an engineer, for fuck's sake. What did I know about balance sheets, trade margins, and consolidated revenue?

People greeted me as I passed, but everyone was busy with somewhere to go. Suddenly I missed Sera terribly. Because of the time difference and workload, Illy forbade us from speaking during our training.

The only support I had was my husband. Unlike me, Gio loved his time here, learning from Nasir, who explained techniques slowly in English and French, but much of his learning was hands-on, not academic like mine. Gio had realized treating children was also his calling and had already spoken with Illy about specializing in pediatric medicine at some point. I was envious. He had always known that medicine was for him, much like Katrin. She had known from the time she was a child that medicine was her calling. It had taken me a lot longer to find my niche, but as the days passed and Illy tried to cram more management speak into me, the lonelier I felt. Gio came home bursting with excitement about what he had learned each day, and I didn't want to bring him down by telling him I was desperately unhappy. This wasn't what I wanted to do. Help people—yes. But by building things. I thought of Gianni and Charlie and the difference we had made in their lives. Maybe I could specialize in medical equipment and devices? They needed someone to look after the technical equipment: CT scanners, MRI machines, x-rays, even ultrasounds. I loved combining my interest in helping people live better lives with my skill in engineering. But I was committed. I stopped short, trying to catch my breath. I had made a mistake. I should never have said yes to this.

I slipped into the central tunnel and climbed down the slippery metal stairs to the moon pool. I hadn't been to this one. I hadn't been into any since the Caspians had invaded Piedmont. Despite being invited, I had been in no fit state to attend the funerals, grief gripping me that I hadn't been able to save them.

Sitting on the edge, I let my feet dangle into the pool, staring at the water below. I wasn't cut out for this. I wished Sera was here. She was my support, my rock. We had lived our lives together; she had my back. She had never let me down. She knew what I was thinking the minute I was thinking it. Now here I was, less than a year after that fateful day, married, my husband desperately wanting children, Illy putting the pressure on me to learn stuff I couldn't give two shits about, and my best friend halfway across the world. I couldn't even contact her, knowing the communications were monitored. I couldn't understand most of what people said to me. French at native speed sounded like a pretty lyrical backing track, and I felt like an intruder. My brain was overflowing. I couldn't take it all in. It was just all too much. My head in my hands, the solid mass of stress of the past month pushed up into my chest. Curling into a ball on the steel floor, I let the tsunami burst.

Clattering footsteps on metal woke me as Gio pounced on me.

"What are you doing?" he bellowed, fear and the metal surrounds making him louder than he intended. "Are you alright? Are you sick?"

As my thoughts returned to some coherent process, I realized he thought I was planning to drop through the moon pool. Take the ultimate step.

"I'm just so tired," I sobbed. "I can't do this. Any of this."

Gio lifted me from the floor, studied my face as he held me by my armpits, and tossed me over his shoulder. As he carried me down the underground hallway, he asked, "When was the last time you slept for more than a few hours? Every time I wake in the night, you are reading."

"I can't remember," I sobbed. "There is so much to learn. I can't take it all in."

"Right."

I bounced like a rag doll on his shoulder as he marched down the hallway, striding past people walking in the opposite direction. The door was open, and despite hanging upside down facing Gio's back, I sensed Illy standing in the living room.

"Oh, you found her." The relief in her tone transitioned to concern when he didn't lower me immediately. "Is she alright?"

"No, she is not!" I could feel the anger echo in his bones as he kicked the door closed. The slam reverberated through the room. "You are working her to exhaustion! How long do you think she can keep this up? Because if this is what you have planned for her, I forbid it. We will return to Italy and live a normal life."

As Gio gently laid me on the couch, he stood and glared at Illy, his back to me, acting as a shield. He towered over her, not threateningly, but I knew without a doubt that he would protect me with his life. At that moment, I felt the love well up inside me.

As I slumped on the couch, barely able to lift my head, I waited for Illy to fire back. She was the Chief, and he had just bellowed at her. Instead, she stepped to the side, looked down at me, and spoke softly.

"I wondered when you would hit the wall. You are exhausted, Caitlin. I am so sorry to be the one who pushed you."

"You *knew*?" Gio boomed at her. "You pushed her deliberately? She doesn't eat. Rarely sleeps! All she does is fucking work. Look at her! I'm done. She is done." He was shaking with fury, something I had rarely seen.

Illy ignored his passionate tirade and sat beside me, her tiny form taking up so little space that the sofa barely shifted while I felt like a giant useless lump making the cushion sag. "I'm so sorry, Catie. I didn't mean to break you. I was trying to prepare you so that it wasn't so difficult when you got to France. I wanted you to feel confident in your ability to lead."

"It's okay," I whispered.

"No, it isn't. I should know better. When I was your age and training in the military, that was standard practice: work people until you broke them. Drill them, not let them sleep, exhaust them physically and mentally, then build them up. Mold them in the image of a leader. It is archaic and unfair. I didn't mean to do that to you. I am sorry, truly."

Gio was still bristling with rage, his face glowering.

I held a hand out to him. He stepped forward and took it, still glaring at Illy seated beside my legs.

"Tell her," he snarled. "Tell your mother what you told me at the pool."

"Mum, I can't do this. This isn't for me. I hate it. I have no interest in financial statements, policies, and trade protocols. I want to build things, to help people. That is my purpose. Not this."

"You will help people," she soothed. "Do you remember what you did in Piedmont? All those people you saved? You are a leader, Catie. All the good ones struggle at first. But people trust you, believe in you. We need you."

"She is right." Gio gripped my hand tighter, and I looked at him, confused. Ten seconds ago, he was ranting about taking me home. "You are a leader. The people at home are thrilled that you are an ambassador. Many wanted you to represent them, not Riccardo."

"Really?"

Gio shrugged.

"What do you need, Catie?" Illy asked. "Sleep?"

"I don't know," I whimpered. "I'm so bone-deep tired, I don't know what I want. I don't understand anyone. In English or French. I feel like I can't learn."

Illy stood and faced Gio. "Give her something to sleep. A good solid night's rest." She looked back at me. "When was the last time you slept ten hours?"

I slunk further into the couch, considering. "Weeks. Longer. Probably at home, before the wedding."

"That was ten weeks ago, Caitlin! Are you telling me that you have not had one decent night's sleep between the wedding, the trip to Orkney, and now two months here?"

I shrugged, and Gio looked at me accusingly. He often asked me how I slept, and I never told the truth.

"You are running on vapor. No wonder you have crashed. Right, I am ordering some food. Shower. Then eat. Then sleep. Get her something, please." Illy barked the last order at Gio. He glanced at me, but left, leaving Illy and me alone.

Illy softened as the door closed behind him. "I'm so sorry, Catie. I didn't mean to break you, really. Is there anything else going on?"

My eyes filled with tears, and she held me as I sobbed.

"Let me guess. It is a combination of everything. Being away from your sister and best friend for the first time in your life. You two are so bonded, so I knew that would be hard. Being away from home, in a strange place, where you don't speak the language. Being newly married and navigating all that means. Then being pushed into a new job that you aren't sure about, where I am expecting more and more of you. Working sixteen-hour days for weeks on end, not sleeping, and trying to study during the night. The bar keeps getting higher, and you feel you will never live up to the unattainable standards I set. Is that it?"

"Pretty much." I sniffed into her shoulder.

"So you are trying to do it all. You aren't sleeping, and now you are shattered?"

I nodded.

"So here is what we are going to do. Tomorrow, after a full night's sleep, you are taking a day off."

"But I have so much to learn," I protested feebly.

"That is true, but I can prioritize. You learn the essentials now, and after you arrive, I will come and help you settle into your role."

My face broke. I was going to disappoint her. I knew it.

"Caitlin, I want a commitment from you. Six months. Six months as Ambassador, and if you still hate it, I will remove you and replace you. You can return to engineering anywhere you like. Every community would love to have you. But you need to give me enough time to find someone else. Deal?"

"Deal." Guilt wracked me for letting her down. "I'm..."

"Don't you dare apologize. I should have started training you sooner, but I didn't want to intrude on your time with Giovanni meeting your family. Especially after everything you went through in Piedmont. Besides, I was a little distracted by Carmelo. It is my fault. I shouldn't have left this until the last minute. Tried to cram it all in you."

"I feel like I can't fit anything in my brain. Please do it differently for Sera."

"I will. I can rearrange my schedule and spend two months there. Then when you travel to Canada, I will meet you there. You won't do this alone."

"I wish I could come to Japan," I said wistfully.

"I know you miss her, Caitlin. She misses you, too. But the time would always come when you met someone and needed to focus on your own life. Surely you see that."

Truthfully, I didn't. Sera and I had always joked that we would live in a joined house, much like my parents and Illy. Fortunately, I was saved from answering as Gio returned.

"Slow acting or fast?" she asked.

"Relatively quickly," he responded, still eyeing her suspiciously.

"Right. Well, you two shower. I will get you some dinner, and then Caitlin is to take that medicine and sleep. Do you understand?"

Gio nodded.

"I will be back in twenty minutes. Is that enough?" Illy was barely holding back the smirk.

"It is."

"Good." Illy slipped out the door, closing it firmly behind her.

"I see what you mean about her being a bossy boots," Gio said in a lowered tone. I grinned at his use of my expression.

"Will you wash my hair?" I asked, feeling dirty but unable to summon the strength to do it myself.

Having someone lead me to the bathroom and lock the door felt decadent. He slowly removed my clothes as I stood there, zombified. "I wasn't going to go through the moon pool," I whispered, remembering how he found me. "I just needed to be alone. Away from people. I didn't know where else to go."

Gio turned on the shower as he quickly shed his own clothes. "Why didn't you say something? Why did you let me wake you every night when you weren't getting enough sleep?"

I slumped into his arms, and he steered me into the shower cubicle. "Because I wanted you too."

"*Amore mio*, we have our entire lives together. I can go a few nights without having you."

"I don't want you to," I whispered, finding his lips as his hands massaged the shampoo into my scalp. My hands dropped lower and I stroked him, feeling him harden under my hands.

"Now? Surely you are too tired."

"I want you, but you need to do all the work."

By the time Illy returned, I was dressed in a soft navy robe gifted to me by Xanthe, a towel wrapped around my damp hair, and lying on the couch. Gio was buzzing around, hanging wet towels, dressed in gray sweatpants and a fitted t-shirt. It was the outfit he had worn the morning he kissed me for the first time, I realized through my haze of exhaustion.

Illy placed the tray on the table, lifted the silver lid, and carried my plate over to me. I tried to pull myself up to a seated position but failed, slumping in a highly inelegant manner. Gio lifted me as Illy arranged the cushions, and he lay me back down. Illy left Gio's plate on the table and returned with the tray.

"Eat, then sleep," she commanded. "That is an order." I caught the wicked glance she flashed at Gio. *Leave her alone,* it said.

"What is this?" I asked, staring at the molten pile of cheese with an array of meats, bread, and pickles.

"Raclette," Illy said proudly. "Usually, it is eaten with the cheese melting on an iron at the table. You dip your items in the cheese. But today, I thought you would prefer to eat in the privacy of your home. Now, take those tablets, please, so I know you will sleep."

"Yes, Mum," I droned, dutifully swallowing the tablet before I dipped a piece of the delicious bread in the melted cheese. My eyes sprang wide. "This is amazing!"

"I know. I love fondue and raclette too. It is a special type of cheese. They make it here. It has a divine nutty flavor, don't you think?"

I dipped a piece of cooked meat into the cheese and closed my eyes. "This is heavenly."

"I will leave you to it. Return the dishes in the morning, will you, after a sleep-in? I have also arranged for you to take a day off, Giovanni. Sleep well."

With that, she swept out the door for the second time, closing it with a click.

"This is so good," I raved. "Try it."

Gio carried his plate over to the sofa and sat beside me, grinning at my ecstasy. "Should I feel jealous that it is cheese that made you this happy and not me?"

"It is you *and* cheese." I sighed, my mouth filled with melted goodness.

"As long as I rate in the top two."

"Always. What shall we do with our day off tomorrow?"

"I order a sleep-in, then breakfast in bed."

"You order?" I yawned.

"I prescribe," he amended. "Then I shall see what I can do to keep you relaxed. Finish your plate, and I will get you to bed."

"What do you want to do today?" Gio asked me as I stretched beside him. I curled into his side and sighed.

"Sleep, nap, rest, maybe read a book. Then sleep some more."

"Do you want coffee?"

"Does a bird have feathers?"

Gio pulled back, startled. "I think so. I have never seen one up close. But what does that have to do with coffee?"

I giggled. "Sorry, maybe that is an Australian thing. As kids, when someone would ask something really obvious, we would make up answers that were also obvious. Dad taught us. Things like 'Do you want breakfast?' and Thorsten would answer, 'Does a bear shit in the woods?' Dad said when he was a kid, the answer used to be, 'Is the Pope a Catholic?' Does that make sense?"

"I will never understand English." Gio shook his head. "But at least I could have answered the Pope one. Of course, he is Catholic. We all are."

"Um, not all of us. I'm not."

"What do you mean? You are Christian?"

"Ah, no. When our parents were sent to their original community, August Island, off the coast of New Zealand, there was a deliberate practice not to choose devoutly religious people. They felt that the community would get along better if they were multicultural;

that is, lots of different cultures were represented but not religions. They thought that religious conflict was something they could do without."

"Everyone in Piedmont is Catholic." Gio gaped at me. "We were all baptized. Aren't you?"

"Not as far as I am aware. Unless you count nearly being drowned as a seven-year-old. I'm not saying some people didn't continue their faith. Tadhg and most of the Irish in Newgrange certainly did. Callie was raised Catholic, Illy was Presbyterian, but they weren't religious when they were chosen. My parents were nothing, so we aren't either. Why? Is this a problem? You certainly didn't say anything when we were getting married."

"I think it is not as important to the generation born there. But to the older ones, like Carmelo, faith is important. It is part of the end-of-life ceremony. We say a prayer for them."

"I've never seen you go to church or even pray."

"Because I don't. People did—in the early years. There is still a small chapel on Piedmont. But it is a solo path now. People meditate and seek answers. It is one of the reasons we meditate each day, to ask God to guide us. We have a ceremony for the birth of a child, asking for them to be blessed. We say a prayer of thanks and farewell at the end of life. In between, I guess we try to do our best to be good to others and live with the values of honor and goodwill."

"How did I not know this? I've never even seen the chapel."

"There is one here, too. Most of the people here are also Catholic. As a doctor, we ask all our patients, so we know what their wishes are when the time comes."

"When were you planning to tell me?" I sat up in bed, feeling like I was sleeping beside a stranger.

"I just assumed you knew."

"How would I know? You said nothing. You didn't ask me when I was your patient. Not even when we got married." I was getting quite worked up now.

"Caitlin," his hand lay firmly on my arm, "I did not deceive you. I just assumed you knew. That everyone knew. Before you, I had never met anyone outside of Piedmont, so I assumed the entire world was the same. Then, it never crossed my mind. I did not lie to you."

"I thought Catholics didn't believe in sex before marriage?"

"In the old ways, yes. But since our parents moved to the new communities, that all changed. We were encouraged not to place false expectations on a relationship. What if you married someone and realized you weren't compatible?"

"So you were encouraged to shag everyone? Try before you buy?"

Gio laughed. "Not exactly but it wasn't an expectation anymore. My mother told me that when she was a child, it was. A woman was expected to be pure when she was married."

"Pure," I spat. "What is she, a fucking tablecloth? Pure, my ass."

"I agree. I am glad those practices were left behind. But when we choose to marry, it is forever."

The penny dropped, and I finally understood why he was so adamant that I was his, forever.

"Does this mean you don't believe in divorce? Separation?" I whispered, unsure I wanted the answer.

"Some people do separate, but it is rare. Mostly, we are certain before we choose a partner. Why do you think I was single when I met you?"

My heart began to race, and I sat up, trying to catch my breath.

"Are you unwell?"

"No, I am fine."

"Did you think this was temporary?"

"No." I breathed through my tightening chest. "I promised to be yours as long as love lasts."

"You are worried that it won't last?"

"Something like that."

Closing my eyes, I waited for the tirade. His anger or disappointment. Instead, he laughed. "Caitlin, marriage is a lifelong commitment. You choose someone you love, and you work at it every day. You find things you enjoy doing together. The little things. You start with a solid base, and you build on that. Raising children, supporting each other in their careers, and helping each other achieve their goals. It doesn't mean you need to sacrifice anything. You are a partnership, a team. Some days you disagree, and things aren't perfect. But you go to bed together and try again tomorrow."

That was very much what my mother had said to me the day she told me that Gio wanted to marry me. What I had seen my parents embody.

"Are you sure I am that person?"

"I am positive. My mother used to say that 'love is a verb.' It took me a while to work out what she meant."

I wracked my brain trying to remember grammar at school. "Surely love is a noun," I spoke slowly, thinking. "If it is an intense feeling, then it is a noun."

"No, Mum was right. She was a teacher, after all. It is a verb. Love is an action. It is the feeling, the desire. But more than that, it is something you work at every single day. It is an active choice. Now, let me get you coffee and croissants. That seems a good thing to build a marriage on."

As I lay in bed after Gio had left, I tried to pinpoint what I was apprehensive about. He would never leave me. That was clear. But shit happened. Look at my parents, separated for years after my mother went missing and Dad was lied to. Illy, losing Luca tragically. But was that a good enough reason not to try?

Lying on my side, I pushed my hair back and stared out the window. Gio had raised the blind before he left, and I could see across to the Pyrenees in the far distance. Mountains I could visit, but he couldn't. Why me? I wasn't special, except I could do this. I could swim from this pod, climb that mountain, and dance in the rain. But I would need to do it alone. My lungs deflated as my breath left me. Suddenly, I wanted nothing more than to hold the hand of my own child and splash in puddles like my father had done with me on Lewis. Safe puddles under the dome, but I had loved playing in the muddy masses of water. Dad had laughed as I would find the deepest puddle I could, jumping in it just to see the water fly everywhere. I could hear my childish giggle as the mud spattered all over me. Dad would let me jump, kick, and play until I was done. Then he would take me home to bathe me, change my clothes, and let me drink hot milk. I would never be able to do this living in an underwater habitation. I walked to the window to stare at the mountains. But I could never do this if I didn't have children. It would be different for my children. They wouldn't be hunted as I was. Tortured. Illy had made the world a different place, a better place. And now, it was my turn to help. An epiphany bubbled within me and sparkled to the surface. I knew. I needed to accept this role as ambassador, wife, and mother.

CHAPTER 12

"MAGALI," I ASKED DURING a break in my tutorial a few days later, "can I ask something?"

"*En Francais,*" she replied instantly.

"I can't," I admitted. "It is too technical."

"*Essayer, s'il vous plaît.*"

"You were a doctor before you specialized?" I stammered in French.

"*Oui.*"

"Can you remove an IUD?"

Magali's eyes raised. "*Oui, je peux. Qu-en est-il de Giovanni?*"

"It is him who wants this."

"*Et toi?*"

"Me? Oh Maggie, I don't know what I want."

She relented and switched to English, recognizing the sensitivity, lowering her voice. "It is a big step, Caitlin, becoming a parent. You need to be positive. There are other alternatives, you know."

"I know. My aunt Sorcha taught me about natural options, but I can't have it removed in Canada if I am the ambassador, can I? It is best I do it now."

"Do you want children, *mon cherie*? When we spoke about this last, when you were at Newgrange, you did not want children. You told me many times."

I exhaled, unsure of what to say. Finally, I told the truth. She had known me my entire life.

"I do, and I want them with him, but I am so scared. What if someone hurts my children like they tried to hurt me?" I whispered.

Magali embraced me. "What happened to you was horrible. But it was a long time ago, Caitlin, *mon cherie*. Mariette, Fairlie, Oriane, all your sisters have children. It is only you and Seraphine who do not. I think there is no need to worry. So, if you want this, I can do this for you."

"When?"

"Any time. It is not difficult. It only takes a few minutes."

"Can you do it now?" *Before I change my mind.*

"*Oui.* Come."

I felt strange returning to our apartment after the procedure, like I was unsafe. It was uncomfortable more than painful, but my unease stemmed from feeling unprotected. Something inside me had shifted, and I was uncomfortable in a way I couldn't put into words. I was grateful for the time alone with my thoughts. Gio had left a message that he was performing a procedure with one of the med team on a child with a complicated arm fracture. I felt exposed, scared. What if I was a terrible mother? What if I had a child like me, challenging and determined? What if our marriage failed? We had only been together less than a year, and here we were—married and considering children. He had been with Francesca for years. Was I the rebound? Would we make it? My own parents had spent years apart and had separated for a brief period during my childhood. They were so madly in love, but what made me think I could if they couldn't make it work? Then there was Illy, who finally met her soul mate in her thirties, but was left alone to raise four children when he was wrenched from her with one single gunshot. Could I raise a child alone? But worse, what if my child was a target? I knew what Magali had said was true; it had been more than fifteen years, and the nutcase who had led the attacks on my sisters and me was seeking revenge against my mother. But people always feared what they didn't understand. Like it or not, I was different. My child would be too, and that would never change.

Gio had made it blatantly clear he wanted children. Lots of them. He had been in a perpetual state of joy staying with my family, meeting all my siblings, nieces, and nephews, especially Louis and Iona's four children who lived nearby. In his rare free time, he assisted Xanthe at the school, teaching the children, and they adored him. I had often smiled watching him outside playing with the little ones, seeing him in the role of a father.

I gazed out the window to the beautiful snow-capped mountains beyond, the spectacular view over the Pyrenees. The crisp snow was brilliant against the clear blue sky. I felt the sudden urge to speak with my mother. She had lived this. A strong, independent woman who had several children, including me. Then she was given the responsibility of finding homes for the special children. How had she reconciled the fear of something happening to us with the desire to have a child?

As I hugged my knees to my chest, I realized I wanted a child with him. I was just scared. Scared of what happened to me, scared of being unable to protect them, like Gerry. He had never forgiven himself for Soli's death. He had trusted the boy who had murdered her, and that trust had killed her. A friend of the family, a neighbor they had seen regularly. Then he used that trust to destroy Gerry and Saba.

I puttered around, unable to eat, and finally took myself off to bed, lying awake, fearful of what I had just done. My thoughts flip-flopped between believing I had done the right thing and wanting it put back. I heard the door close softly but lay still, keeping my breath light so Gio wouldn't realize I was awake. I wasn't ready to discuss this. Straining my ears, I heard him undress and felt the shift in temperature as he lifted the quilts and then slipped in beside me. I felt him pause, not wanting to wake me, and roll over to his pillow. Guilt plagued me. *Why can't I tell him what I am feeling?*

My heart was pounding, and I gasped, bolting upright. Sweat beaded on my brow as I tried to slow my breathing, dispelling the memories that plagued me. Silently, I slipped out of bed and padded into the kitchen for a glass of water. I stood at the window watching the moonlight glow over the fresh snow in the distance, a beautiful blue echo reflected in the white. I had seen snow on Lewis but nothing like this—sharp, jagged peaks with white points pointing to the sky twinkling with stars. I pulled my jacket off the back of the dining chair and curled up on the couch, staring into the night. How could these people live here, trapped, with such stunning beauty on their doorstep? Did the view destroy them, knowing they could never touch it? The children who had never felt fresh air on their faces? But mine would. That single thought struck me like a bullet. My children could go out there, play in that snow, and not be affected. *What makes me special?*

I sensed the movement behind me and tilted my head in the darkness.

"Why are you out here all alone, *angelo mio*?"

"Couldn't sleep."

"Nightmare again?"

"What do you mean—again?" I asked, confused.

The sofa sank beside me as his warm body wrapped around mine. "Do you not remember?"

The truth was, I had been plagued by nightmares most of my life. It was unusual for me not to wake with a jolt, my heart pounding out of my chest.

"What is it that keeps you awake?"

"I don't know." I sighed.

His arms tightened. "We promised never to lie to each other. Do you remember?"

I did. I tried a gentle version of the truth. "I'm a little scared," I admitted, not wanting him to see me as weak.

"What are you scared of?"

He wasn't going to make this easy. "What if we have a child, and that child becomes a target? What if I am a terrible mother and don't know how to relate to a child?"

Instead of reassuring me, Gio murmured, "I understand."

I wanted to blurt, "How could you possibly understand!" when he continued speaking in a low strangled tone, the pain breaking through.

"I lost my father when I was barely nine. My mother when I was fifteen. We were lucky to have them for so long, but I have lived more years without a father than I did with one. What if I don't know how to parent a child? What if I make mistakes?"

I leaned back into him. "So, we learn together."

I felt his breath catch before he spoke again. "Does that mean...?"

"Let's have a baby," I whispered, barely audible.

WE BID MAGALI, NASIR, and our friends in France goodbye and endured the portal to Canada. Fortunately, we had heat suits to minimize the worst of the swirling. There was no way I wanted to arrive covered in my own vomit. While it was torturous, it was improved knowing Gio was with me and where I would end up. The last time I did this, I was running from Yellowstone and praying it would take me somewhere better.

We were met with a formal ceremony led by Max, the most senior official here. We were welcomed, given gifts, and escorted to a brief morning tea, allowing us to mingle. People came and introduced themselves, and I smiled, shaking hands, knowing I wouldn't remember any of the names tomorrow. Tomorrow, a full day of meetings had been scheduled. I sensed courtesy but reticence, that sense of being kept at arm's length. It made sense. We weren't known or trusted. While Gio was from Piedmont, I was the ambassador from the above-ground communities, ones they hadn't known about until less than a year ago. We were strangers and would need to prove ourselves, me especially, as I could sense the surprise at my youth. Likely they were concerned, as I was now tasked with ensuring this community was fairly represented at Collective meetings. Illy was here too, but after greeting us, she lingered near the officials, mainly speaking with Max. She had been here several times over the past few months and was well known. But Illy instilled confidence, something I doubted I could ever do. As the room emptied, signaling the end of the soiree, I contemplated staying to be polite, but Illy encouraged me to see our apartment and settle in, so I scampered.

Gio and I sighed with relief as we closed the door to our private apartment. It was exhausting constantly being polite and professional. Our bags had been left inside the door for us to unpack. Stepping around them, I walked over to the window with a lovely view over the lake and the Bruce Peninsula to our left. We weren't far from land, a spectacular rugged coastline with sheer rocky cliffs. I could see that the clifftops had once been covered in trees, pine trees by the look of it, possibly conifers, but they had all died, and the remaining stumps were tilted at precarious angles, many of the rotting timber lying in swaths across the dead earth.

The apartment was tiny, a single bedroom barely wide enough for the double bed and wardrobe, although it also had a view over Georgian Bay and into Lake Huron. The main living space was a combination kitchen, dining, and living room, with a bathroom/laundry off to one side.

"Goodness, it is tiny! You would want to really be in love to live here!" I laughed, and Gio swept me off my feet.

"We are, aren't we?"

"You don't even need to ask. I love you more than anything in the world."

"Even chocolate?"

"Even that, although chocolate runs a close second. Maybe cheese too."

We had heard from Illy that this community had been quite successful in making chocolate, and their primary trade products had been maple syrup and chocolate, prior to the Nexus being deactivated. Dad had occasionally made hot chocolate for us as children on special occasions, usually on Christmas Eve, melting a block of chocolate into a saucepan of milk. But it wasn't plentiful enough to drink every day. Mum had a weakness for chocolate, and she still told the story of how Luca had once raided a chocolate factory to keep her supplied for years until the community on Lewis had finally perfected the art of growing cacao, fermenting, drying, and roasting the cacao beans between coffee bean batches.

I pondered Illy's advice and considered the elements that made her an excellent leader. She was firm but always fair, I begrudgingly needed to admit. She treated everyone equally and always acted with integrity. But she had an underpinning sense of humor and was always approachable. Everyone knew they could approach her with any problem, and she would listen and seek to assist. I aimed to replicate Illy's style of leadership, starting my days by meeting people and getting to know them.

"Do you want to rest or explore?" Gio asked, scanning the tiny space. "We can unpack later."

"Let me hang up my suits," I said. "I couldn't bear Illy scowling at me if they were creased, and I couldn't be bothered ironing them."

"I never thought I would see you in a skirt and jacket," Gio taunted.

"And you rarely will," I shot back. "Most are pants and tops. I only let her make me one full suit for really formal meetings. Pants are the closest I could get to jeans. Give me time. I'll make jeans acceptable for meetings."

The pods here were all silver on the outside with white interiors, in contrast to the Italian pods which were color coded. But there was signage everywhere in English and French, making navigation easy. Some of the signage looked new, making me wonder if this was for my benefit.

We found our way to the main deck, a lovely well-lit space, not dissimilar to Piedmont, making me relax slightly. The walls were all white but displayed enlarged photographs of what I assumed were parts of the old Canada. They were beautiful vistas of snow-capped mountains, brilliant blue lakes, and brightly lit cities, all clearly pre-dating the pod's construction. I stopped to study them as we passed. Plants grew everywhere, much like Piedmont, and I smiled, thinking of Dad. I couldn't wait to get him here. Now that we were posted on a three-year secondment, he would have plenty of time to visit, although I wondered where they would stay. Illy had already visited Seraphine and Matteo in Japan and reported that despite finding the language challenging, they loved the technology in the Hokkaido community. They had been welcomed and included almost immediately.

We wandered around, feeling like strangers in this familiar but unfamiliar place. It was like Piedmont and France in layout, but the people were strangers. People smiled, but no one stopped to speak to us, and I felt a touch like an intruder. What if they didn't want me? What if Illy had forced my posting on them, and I was resented?

Gio sensed my discomfort, and he steered me back to our accommodation. As we turned into our corridor, we saw Illy approach. She beamed as she saw me.

"Just who I wanted. Are you free to come and meet your new assistant?"

"Sure."

Illy smiled at Gio. "Okay if I steal your lovely wife?"

"She is your ambassador, so of course." Gio gave a slight bow. Illy still intimidated him in her official capacity.

Mandy was everything Illy had said. Forthright, intelligent, but crazy organized, so much so that I felt like a shambling mess before her. Her desk was a color-coded system of neatly arranged files and papers, carefully placed so that she could place her hand on anything at a second's notice. Just looking at the intensity of her organization made my messy engineering brain spin. I secretly hoped she wouldn't try to organize me. I worked better when surrounded by sketches and diagrams.

Mandy was mid-fifties at a guess with black glossy hair cut into a no-nonsense bob with a thick blunt fringe. Her dark eyes sparkled with wit, and I sensed she had a wicked sense of humor, but she was highly respectful and professional in front of Illy. She was the Chief, and everyone appeared to be on their best behavior when she was around, an attitude I tried hard to replicate. Mandy was engaging and made me feel welcome immediately. Illy and Mandy discussed the appointments they had scheduled for my first week: many video conferences with the other communities collectively and individual meetings with my counterparts in other above-ground and under-water communities. I sighed when I saw the list of names. I knew at least some of them, which made me feel slightly more comfortable. I kept waiting for someone to tap me on the shoulder and say, "Excuse me. We have just worked out that we made a mistake. You clearly have no clue and don't belong here at all. Can you pack your bags, and we will take you home?"

"Have you prepared the briefing papers I requested?" Illy asked, and Mandy produced them instantly, making me groan inwardly when I saw the stack of papers I was expected to not only read but digest and intelligently assess. Illy sensed my turmoil and grinned at me. "You will have some time, and there is more information there than you need at this point. We included it in case you were interested in the negotiations that have led to this point, some of the research and qualitative and quantitative studies, so you can take a deep dive if you want to."

Deep dive, I thought. *I might take a deep dive into the fucking ocean and swim away.* Illy never said the role would entail a lot of tedious reading and attending painful meetings. But maybe that is what she did? I tried to rearrange my expression to something suitably interested.

"Thanks, Mandy. Which do you suggest I read first?"

"I have ordered them for you," she said with a smile. "The first folder relates to your first meeting tomorrow, so you might want to read that one tonight. The rest can wait."

The top folder, colored with blue tabs, was roughly two centimeters thick. My shoulders slumped. There went my relaxing evening of settling in and snuggling with my man.

"How do you feel about having dinner with me?" Illy suggested, evidently reading my mind. "I can tell you most of it and save you some reading. Then you will still have time to rest and settle in to your new home."

"Thank you. That would be wonderful. Do you want to eat here?"

"How about you come over to my place? I'll send Carmelo over to eat with Giovanni. Then we can talk uninterrupted."

While I desperately wanted to have my first meal with my husband in this place, I knew we would have many more. I was here on a three-year assignment. We would have many dinners together, even if I bailed after the six-month commitment. Illy had just returned from Hokkaido as we finished up in France. I was envious that she had seen Sera, and I hadn't. So many times in the months we had been separated, I had turned to tell her something, and my heart hurt realizing she wasn't there. I knew we were on some of the same committees and reference groups, but it wasn't the same. I wanted to talk to her about juggling marriage, careers, and at some point, babies. If she was here, I knew she would have my back. She would tell me what I was doing well, what I wasn't, and what people said about me. We had always said we didn't want children, but we would raise them together if we did. In all our years of adventure, I never would have thought that we would end up as the most senior officials in our communities and physically separated. I loved Giovanni more each day, but I missed my sister so much it physically hurt.

Settling in on the couch in Illy's assigned apartment, I tried to listen to Illy talk about reference groups and shared resources, but the sinking feeling that I had made an enormous mistake by coming here kept pulling me down. I tried to ask intelligent questions, proving I had listened, but the sickening feeling weighed on me.

"What is it, Caitlin?" Illy asked in one pause. "You look like I have just murdered your favorite pet."

"I'm sorry. I am trying to pay attention, really. But it is a lot to take in. I'm terrified I will mess this up and make you ashamed of me."

"Look, I am going to give you some free advice. Listening makes you appear more intelligent than speaking. Try not to push your perspective too hard. Too many people say the same thing but in different words. That might prove they listened, but that doesn't move things forward. Look at Nasir. He listens, then when he speaks, it is well considered and thoughtful. People know he paid attention. That is a wonderful skill for a leader. Talking doesn't make people listen. Be the one that takes it in and makes a suggestion to take the conversation or the project forward. That is the leader. That is a person who is respected."

I nodded.

"Go to bed. You'll do fine. I have faith in you."

I wonder if you will still feel that way in six months, I thought as I padded down the hall to our apartment, confident I would let her down.

CHAPTER 14

MY HEAD SPUN FROM the constant stream of meetings and conferences, the information that kept being stuffed in on top of an already full brain. My face hurt from the fake smiling, acting pleased to meet everyone. I would never remember everyone's names.

Two days after we arrived, Mandy dragged me away from my desk in the late afternoon for Friday night drinks. The way she delivered it, oh so casually, I was expecting a few people at an apartment, much like Sera's colleagues in Piedmont. Here, it was a whole community affair. I froze, standing in the doorway to the central pod heaving with people. The last time I had seen so many people was when the Caspians invaded Piedmont and congregated everyone together. My heart skipped a beat, and Mandy sensed my hesitation.

"Not used to so many people?" She smiled at me.

I covered my discomfort. "You got me. There are nowhere near as many people as this on Lewis, my home. Goodness, I don't think I know this many people!"

"You soon will," she soothed. "Everyone is dying to meet you. We have all heard about the amazing things you did in Italy. The engineering team and tech teams are busting to schedule meetings with you."

I glanced at her hopefully, and she laughed. "Illyria said I was to keep you on the business of leading for the first few weeks. Your passion projects can come later."

"Bloody Illyria," I muttered, making Mandy gape at me at my disrespect of the Chief.

"I have known her since birth," I admitted, realizing she thought I was horribly disrespectful to my boss but also recognizing that they didn't want to suspect Illyria of appointing me as favoritism. "She and my mother are best friends, and she lived next door. She is also my best friend's mother, so we were raised together after Illy's husband passed. I love her like a mother and respect her. But she has doled out more punishments to me than I care to admit. Very creative punishments."

Mandy guffawed, making me like her even more. Any woman that could laugh so heartily and not care what people thought of her was my kind of woman. "I understand." She smirked. "I was raised in a small community, and it was the village's role to raise the children. So all the adults dealt out punishment if it was warranted."

"Was it often warranted?" I asked cheekily as a glass of red was simultaneously thrust into my hand and hers, and I was forced to step into the central pod. There didn't appear to be servers. Random people just picked up a bottle from the long tables under the windows and did the rounds, topping up glasses until the bottle was empty.

"Every single time," she cackled, copying me and taking a healthy mouthful. "It felt like I was always in trouble."

"Me too. Sera and I were always in trouble for something."

Mandy and I found a quiet spot and shared stories of our misspent youth. Well into our third glass, we had relaxed significantly. We were laughing raucously as she told me a story involving her graduating class carrying her school principal's car into the school cafeteria. The principal had found it, not appreciated the joke, and couldn't get it out again. I felt an arm slip down my front and a warm kiss on my neck. I leaned back in my chair to receive a kiss on my lips, then tilted forward to introduce Mandy to Giovanni.

"Ah, the new husband." She grinned, draining her glass. "I remember being in that phase."

"What phase?" I asked.

"The 'only have eyes for each other' phase." She grinned at me. "When you would rather be with each other than with anyone else in the world."

"How much have you ladies had to drink?" Gio eyed us suspiciously.

"What is it, two glasses?" I said, flashing a look at Mandy to ensure her silence.

"Three," she responded firmly, glinting back.

"Fine. Maybe three."

"Then I need to catch up. Excuse me while I track down some of the local vintage."

Mandy watched after Gio, her head tilted slightly.

"Are you right there?" I teased, drawing her attention back to me.

"That is a fine specimen you have," she drawled. "You are lucky he has that shiny gold ring on his finger. That should keep the single ladies away."

My eyebrows hit my hairline, and she cackled madly at my horror, clutching at her chest. "Honestly, no one would dare go near the new boss' man. You are safe. But he might not be. A few of the men have been giving you the eye, too. You fill out your own clothes rather nicely."

I spun around in my chair but saw no one even remotely looking in our direction. "I think you are full of it."

"Maybe." Mandy stood, lifted her empty glass, and sauntered away.

A full glass was placed on the table before me, and I gazed up, slightly glassy-eyed.

"That is your last one."

"I think you are dreaming," I slurred. "The wine is excellent, but it is French. I hear the local product is nothing to write home about. It is the end of a busy week, and I am going to enjoy a sleep-in tomorrow."

"Oh, are you now? What if I have plans for us?"

"They can wait. I am exhausted." After a sigh, I relented. "What did you have in mind?"

"We have been invited to lunch with some of my colleagues."

"Oh, lunch is eminently doable. Breakfast … maybe not."

"What if I have plans for us for breakfast?" His voice dropped into a growl, and I blinked at him innocently.

"Breakfast in bed?"

"Something like that. I have barely seen you since we arrived. You fall into bed and snore before I even turn the lights out."

"I don't snore!"

"You do, and it is kind of cute. But I have missed you."

Knocking back the glass in one swallow, I stood, wobbled, and held my hand out to him. "Let's do the rounds and get home. I might need some rest."

CHAPTER 15

ALL WAKING HOURS IN my first few weeks were crammed with back-to-back meetings on site and via teleconference with other communities. I regularly needed to excuse myself to dash off to the nearest bathroom as I exited one meeting before commencing the next. Lunch was almost always wolfing down a sandwich at my desk while reading papers for my afternoon appointments. Everyone wanted to know about me and my background, asking about Lewis, Newgrange, France, and Piedmont. The similarities and the differences. What resources and specialist skills were available, and how my new community could access them.

Each morning started with a meeting with Max and the leadership team, where they raised issues, and we discussed how we could solve them collectively. Often, my role wasn't to assist in a practical capacity as much as it was to act as a sounding board, but I realized I desperately wanted to help. Each Tuesday, I attended a meeting with all the other ambassadors, discussing issues common across all communities. I was thrilled to see Sera, although we found time to speak most days, if only for a few minutes. It was surreal to see her dressed formally, much like me, seated at a board table, halfway across the world. She sat before a window, and I could see snow-capped mountains behind her, a spectacular vista of ice and snow.

Mandy was a godsend. Highly competent and organized, she knew who, where, or what I needed at the precise moment I needed it. Her record-keeping was impeccable, and I felt prepared for all my meetings after she briefed me. If I was to be honest, I thought she could do this job better than I could. Every morning, she greeted me at the office with a coffee and pastry. On the third day, when I realized she would do this for me daily, I could have kissed her. I knew what Illy meant by keeping her on-side.

Despite initially planning to stay longer, Illy departed after a month, assuring me I was doing fine and stating firmly that I could cope without her. Summer collected her, staying one wild night and consuming copious amounts of food and wine, and by the time I left, my ears were buzzing from all the laughter. But as I watched them depart, I felt a pang of envy, wishing I could fling myself into the helicopter and go with them. Return home, where I knew everyone. Here I was treated with respect. People were polite, but I had no friends. No one I could talk to or describe how I was feeling.

Gio had been welcomed onto the medical team immediately and found integration into the community much easier, working alongside other doctors and treating patients. In some ways, I was jealous and felt he had it easier. He could bond over common topics of medicine and treatment plans. *Maybe I should visit the engineering team,* I thought, but I wondered how I would fit engineering projects into my hectic schedule. I missed getting my hands dirty, feeling like I was helping. It hadn't been until I had helped Antonio with the aquaponics and Joseph with biogas units in Italy that I made friends and been accepted. I made a snap decision.

"Mandy, can you tell me who oversees engineering?"

"Jean-Gabriel," she answered immediately.

"Can I meet him?"

"Would you like me to arrange a meeting here or in his office?"

"No, I was thinking you could take me down to meet him if that is okay with you."

"Whatever you wish. Now?"

"Give me five to finish my coffee, and yes, that would be wonderful. We must be back for the leadership meeting, so it will just be a quick visit."

I could hear the colorful swearing and clanging of tools being hurled against the concrete wall that radiated out into the hallway as we approached. Mandy flushed and halted several meters from the open doorway.

"Perhaps another time is best," she whispered, turning to walk away.

"It is fine!" I laughed and moved to stand in the doorway.

A rugged, bearded man was lying on the floor underneath a pump, cursing and swearing. His pants were streaked with grease, his face obscured by the clearly faulty equipment. Minor components were lying around him, a puddle of oil beside him, and tools were scattered about haphazardly.

"Fuck me! Why does nothing ever work..." he seethed, and Mandy cleared her throat politely.

He snapped his head up and cracked it on the casing.

"Fuck!" he ranted, clutching his graying head. "What do you want?"

"Um, can I help at all?"

Jean-Gabriel looked up at me, and his brow furrowed. "Who are you?"

Mandy took two steps into the room. "Jean-Gabriel, allow me to introduce our new ambassador, Ms. Caitlin Mackintosh."

The look of horror that replaced the cranky look on his face as Mandy uttered the word "ambassador" made me force back the laugh bubbling into my throat, and I extended a hand.

"Hello, Mister..."

"Lennox," he stumbled, trying to get the words out. "Please call me Gabriel." He took my hand and shook it, then looked at the grease all over it.

"I am so sorry..." The redness deepened.

"It is fine," I assured him as he handed me a cloth. "Despite my appearance, I am actually an engineer. Please call me Caitlin. We haven't met yet."

Relief flooded his face. "I am so sorry for the language. I..."

"Please don't apologize," I assured him. "You should have heard me trying to set up a photobioreactor on Piedmont. I am fairly sure I said far worse."

He glanced up and down at my work attire like he didn't believe this. Illy insisted that I dress for the role and had requested the tailoring team in France make me tailored pants. I missed my jeans terribly and wondered how soon I could change the dress code. Most of my meetings were via videoconference. As long as I wore a neat top, no one could see what I wore on the bottom half.

"What is the problem?"

He sighed, realizing that I wasn't leaving and not wanting to insult the new ambassador further. "I don't know. We have an oil leak, intermittent at first, then a steady drip. I thought it was the piston rings, but it doesn't look like it."

"Do you have some overalls I could borrow?"

"Behind the door."

I closed the door and pulled the navy coveralls off the hook, kicking off my shoes and stepping into the enormous overalls. Using the hair elastic I usually kept around my wrist, I pulled my hair back into a messy bun, rolled up the overlong pants, and sat beside him, avoiding the oil spill.

"Can you run the meeting without me?" I asked Mandy. "Please offer my sincere apologies and let them know that something unexpected cropped up." Returning my attention to Gabriel, I said, "Explain the problem to me."

Several hours later, Gabriel and I had refurbished the pump, worked out the issue, and we had commenced diagnosing faults in several other pieces of equipment. He stared at me the first time he heard me swear, then laughed.

"For goodness' sake, don't tell anyone!" I flushed, realizing it wasn't a good look for the ambassador to be swearing with the head of engineering.

"If it is any consolation, it makes me like you even more." He grinned. "Now, do you have plans for Friday night? I'd love to have you and your family over for dinner."

"Just my husband Giovanni and I. No children," I informed him.

"Good. We won't need to mind our language then."

"You don't go to the drinks?" I asked.

"Normally, no. I need my peace after hours. Now I wish I had. May not have made such a fool of myself."

"What do you mean?"

"Swearing and not knowing who you were. I'm sorry about that, by the way."

"It is fine. I am sorry I didn't come and visit sooner."

Jean-Gabriel and his partner Deb hosted us for Friday night dinner, although with all the drinking and laughing, it was early Saturday morning before we left. Deb worked in the agricultural team. Initially, I found her standoffish, but I soon realized she was shy. Another reason why they didn't attend community events. "Slow to warm up," as Dad called it. She reminded me a lot of Dad. Once she realized I knew a reasonable amount about greenhouses, orchards, and all types of growing, she was easy to talk to. As we chatted about all the projects here, on Lewis, and in Italy, I realized my glass had been filled several times as I made frequent trips to their bathroom.

Jean-Gabriel had a wicked sense of humor once well-lubricated, and he swore to murder me if I ever called him by his full name. "Only my mother called me Jean-Gabriel," he laughed, "and only when I was in trouble. Gabriel will do just fine."

"It isn't a good look if anyone sees us rolling drunk up the hallways!" I whispered in a loudly exaggerated fashion to Gio.

"No one will see us. They are all asleep!" he hissed back, far louder than necessary. "Besides, you are the big cheese. You can delete the footage."

"Big cheese. Where did you hear that expression?"

"One of the doctors said it about you. I liked it. You like cheese."

Stumbling into the wall, I giggled softly. Gio tried to steady me but stumbled himself, making us both laugh.

He fumbled with the key as I stood, hopping around, busting for the bathroom. Not even bothering to do up my jeans, we flopped onto the bed.

"Do you like it here?" he asked unexpectedly as the window weaved in and out of focus pleasantly.

"I do," I yawned. "I am still unsure about the job, but meeting people makes life so much better, doesn't it?'

Gio pulled back the covers and rolled me under. "It does."

CHAPTER 16

"ANGELO MIO, **DO YOU** know what today is?"

"Friday?" I groaned, cracking an eye open, wondering why I was being woken in the dark.

"Yes, but it is more than that. Today is a very important day."

Do I have an early meeting I forgot? Did Mandy not remind me? I relied on her so much. *Shit.* I wobbled to a semi-upright position, trying to remember.

"Wha...?"

"Today, *amore mio,* is one year since you crashed into my life."

It took me a moment to process that. Between being in Yellowstone and then a concussion and fractured skull, I hadn't paid any attention to the date we had arrived in Piedmont.

"You should have told me. I would have done something." I tried to push the hair out of my face and roll over to look at him. He was sitting on the side of the bed, dressed casually. Not what he usually wore to work.

"I wanted to surprise you. Come with me."

"It is the middle of the night," I whispered as we staggered down the hallways. "Don't you want to wait until morning?"

"But this is when we met."

Gio led me into one of the lower-level rooms, the thermal springs, and I smiled, knowing what he had planned. We hadn't had time to visit yet, but I knew they had some, the same as Piedmont. This city was also located over a geothermic vent that powered the city. But when I opened the door, I gasped. The room was filled with lights scattered across the room and looked like a fairy wonderland. Every surface had tiny lights in small glass jars. They covered shelves, flat rocks, and even the far side of the pool. To one side of the flat area was a small table covered in a white tablecloth and two chairs. Gio locked the door behind us and led me to the table.

"Do you recall when we met? I promised to take you out for dinner?"

"I do. But you lied. You couldn't keep your hands off me. Are you telling me you are making me dinner a year late?"

"I am."

"When did you do this?"

"I got some help. You are not expected at work today." Gio fed me a grape as I looked at him in astonishment. "Swim first?"

After a long blissful soak, he pulled me toward the edge, draping a towel around me. I shivered with the temperature change as I wrapped the towel around myself, trying to warm up. Gio steered me toward the table and guided me into one of the chairs. He handed me a small box. My face dropped.

"I didn't even know it was our anniversary. I didn't get you anything."

"I do not get you gifts because I want one in return. Why do you think everything must be reciprocated? I do it because it gives me pleasure to make you happy."

"*You* make me happy. I don't need gifts."

"Open."

Inside was a silver bracelet, solid chain links with a heart at the closure. There was a single object hanging from one link. I peered at it closely in the shadowed light. "It's a tiny bottle!" I laughed as the fairy lights twinkled around us and reflected off the shiny surface.

"It is a memory bracelet." Gio took it from me and did up the clasp over my wrist. "Each year on our anniversary, I will get you a new item for the bracelet, something that reminds us of the year that has passed. Then when we are old, we can look back on a lifetime of wonderful memories."

"This is beautiful." I was lost for words and stared at the silver glinting in the twinkling candlelight. "Kind of like your gratitude journal?" I asked finally, knowing I needed to say something.

"Exactly. The heart is because you have mine, always and forever. The bottle reminds me of our first conversation when you told me you wanted wine instead of water."

"I am fairly sure that isn't what I said."

"It is what I remember. Then ordering you not to drink with a concussion and you disobeyed me. Which you have done consistently ever since."

"You love me for it. I'm never boring."

"Boring is not a word that could ever be used to describe you, my love."

"I love it." I lifted my wrist and watched the bottle dangle. "How did I ever get so lucky to get sucked into that portal and for you to be the one who found me?"

"I like to think a higher power took a hand in that. Do you know—I never went there. I hadn't been down to that lake for years. But that night, Matteo was in such a bad way, and I was desperate to do something to save him from taking the final step. I wanted him to remember our father and the impact that had on us, losing him. Then he met Seraphine. I wouldn't have thought it possible for someone to have such an instant impact on another's life. But then I met you, and I knew. You were the one."

"Matt still has bad days," I said softly. "Sera told me. But he can see the good times now, and they mostly outweigh the bad."

"That is all any of us can ask for, isn't it? That we have more good days than bad."

"Thank you for all of this. I love you so much." I threw my arms around his neck.

"Are you hungry?"

"I am always hungry," I teased.

Gio cut some cheese and held it to me on the end of the knife. I took it and ate it, a delicious blue, as he cut a piece for himself.

"What is under there?" I asked, noticing the white cloth-covered lump against the far wall.

"Meals for later."

"Later? How long do you expect to be here?"

"All day."

Gio fed me another piece of cheese, goat cheese this time, and held his hand out to me. I took it and stood, unsure of what to expect. He gently lifted me to my feet and held me at arm's length.

"I love you so much that sometimes my heart will burst. I still can't believe I get to have you all to myself."

"Greedy," I teased. "Other people need me too."

"You are mine, *angelo mio*. Only mine." His arms jerked unexpectedly, pulling me toward him, and I crashed into his chest. "Promise me."

"I am yours," I whispered into his ear, suddenly needing him more than words could express. "But you are mine. Say it."

"I am yours. *Per sempre.* Always."

His lips crashed into mine in a frenzy, making my stomach lurch and my breath come quicker. He dropped my towel and ran his hands down my back, pushing me closer toward him. I wanted to crawl inside him and stay there, safe and hidden away from the world. My hands snaked around his taut back and ran up to his shoulder blades, pushing him into me. His hands scooped me up under my bottom, and I wrapped my legs around his waist, not breaking lip contract. We were both gasping, desperate to be closer. Laying me on the white towel he had spread earlier, he lowered onto me, his weight making me feel safe.

"I love you," I murmured, finally able to take a breath. "Happy anniversary, my love."

CHAPTER 17

"**GOODNESS, THERE IS GOING** to be a population explosion," Mandy muttered as she closed the door, expertly juggling two cups of coffee and a plate of scones. "We will struggle with schools, teachers, and hospital beds soon. Not to mention apartments in a few years."

"You can't stop that." I smiled at her. Mandy had two children of her own, and despite moaning about how difficult they were, she adored them. I also suspected she ruled them with an iron fist, but I had heard stories of her teen boys getting into mischief when she wasn't around.

"It feels like the entire team is expecting at the moment," she grumbled. "How will we get anything done?"

"How does it work? Do they take time off?"

"We encourage all new parents to take the first three months off, both men and women, and then we provide places in one of our early childhood facilities. But we let parents take a mix if they like, so one parent can take three months, followed by the other, or one parent can take six months off."

"That is very equitable. Does it work?"

"Usually. Even if the father stays home with the baby, we allow feeding breaks, so he can bring the baby in to work so Mum can feed and then get back to her job. Or one of the educators will call the mother when the baby needs feeding."

"I like that idea," I admitted.

"When are you contributing to the population?" she teased.

"Not anytime soon," I fired back. "Too busy here."

"You don't want children?"

That was a complicated question and one I wasn't prepared to give the complete answer to. Mandy and I got along well, but she was older than I was, closer to my parents' age. Her children were older teenagers. She also didn't know my history.

"I do," I admitted, "but perhaps not just yet. Giovanni is dying to have kids, but I need to be ready. I'm not quite there."

Mandy nodded knowingly. Since we met, I had suspected she could see right through me. Mandy was sharp and perceptive. Not quite as perceptive as Illy, but she still reminded me of Mum in so many ways: anticipating needs, reading motives, and super organized.

Despite no longer using contraception, as each month passed, I was equally thrilled and saddened that I wasn't pregnant. It was a strange sensation, relief that my life wasn't about to change forever, yet disappointment that we weren't taking this next step together. I had heard from Summer after her last trip to see Jake in Newgrange that Reilly was now married and expecting his first child. I was pleased for him but strangely sad for me. He had proposed what felt like a long time ago, and I had run away. If I had accepted, would I already be a parent? But how different my life would be. An image of me living in Newgrange formed in my mind. Pregnant, living in a small white cottage with a garden and a view. Then again, after my beating as a child, there was no guarantee I could even have children.

"So, what can we do to manage the population?" I asked to dispel the images.

"Well, expansion is out of the question, and no one has the stomach for restricting the birth rate, so we just need to condense apartments again."

"What do you mean, again?"

Mandy sighed. "This has been an issue for decades. Every leader has faced the issue, but none have found a satisfactory solution, so we continue to make housing smaller, but we are limited. There used to be larger apartments, family-sized ones with three bedrooms, and we moved families with older children into those. Couples had a single bedroom, and families with one child or two children of the same gender had a two-bedroom. But there was a lot of pushback from families, not wanting to be constantly shuffled from apartment to apartment. It caused a lot of disgruntlement. People like their home and neighbors and didn't like being forced to move."

"I get that." I did. Gio and I were housed in a tiny single-bedroom place, which was fine for now. If we had children, I hadn't thought that someone else would be moved out to accommodate us.

"So, what did you do?"

"We kept moving the walls to make them the most compact space possible. There are no more three-bedroom apartments, just ones and twos. We did away with larger places years ago. So no matter how many children you have, they are all crammed in one room."

"How do they do that?" I had visited a few apartments, and the bedrooms were tiny.

"Bunks mostly. Some families use their sofas as beds for younger children. But two to a bed, and bunks and trundles is how most families accommodate."

"It is a shame we can't expand," I said, more to myself.

"We can't. No room. Although no materials, we could probably overcome. But we can't work outside. So, we shuffle. Again. I'm glad I'm not the one to break the news. More than once, we have talked about limiting children to one or two per couple, but no one wants to enforce it."

"It is rather distasteful," I admitted, thinking of Yellowstone and its forced sterilization policies. No one should be involved in my reproduction other than me and my partner, but I couldn't fathom why people would want more than two children in such a tiny place.

As Mandy headed to her desk, I replayed the conversation and wondered why we couldn't expand. I could go outside the dome, although no one here knew that besides Gio, and he would never betray my secret. The Collective tightly controlled communications, and Illy had ordered the existing communities not to disclose the previous projects of the Collective, including the forced partnerships to ensure all genomes were replicated or the genetic modification of selected zygotes, producing my sisters and myself.

Materials were accessible in nearby cities. I knew from Illy and satellite footage that we were located in Georgian Bay off Lake Huron, close to Toronto. That had been a large city, I was fairly sure, and likely had building materials. Some would have disintegrated over the years or be damaged beyond use. But some would still be useable, plus we could freight materials in from the land biosphere sites like Newgrange and Lewis. If we built more extensions to the main pod, allowing for population growth, we would need more food pods and accommodation.

I gazed out the window at the land beyond. Illy knew how to manufacture the fabric used to construct the domes in the above-ground communities. Gerry had told me about his role in helping to replace damaged panels. It was a task Sera and I had been allocated. Would it be possible to build a new pod on land and rehabilitate the earth with Dad's moss? Then perhaps we could expand on land? Or even build pods where we grew crops in pots above the ground, not needing to rehabilitate the infected earth. Then we could repurpose the agricultural spaces to become living spaces. My mind whirred at the possibilities. But connecting this pod with a land-based one—how could I achieve that? A boat would work in the short term, especially an enclosed vessel like some of our yachts. Getting on and off would be the problem. We simply couldn't keep people safe.

The concept wouldn't budge, and I couldn't focus on my work. We had a significant problem—overpopulation. As the ambassador, it was my role to address the issue and find solutions. I logged into the satellite footage and tried to assess how far we were from land. Less than a kilometer at the nearest point, I guessed.

The pods here moved up and down to access sunlight and to avoid storms, but they were fixed in location. Linking a bridge to the mainland would be challenging but not impossible, and certainly a better long-term plan than a yacht. I sent Tadhg a message asking for confirmation of my measurements. He knew an awful lot more about calculating the distance from satellite footage.

Sighing, I turned my attention to the orders for the next full moon. If I didn't get my work done, other people could not complete theirs. Summer and Ally were doing a roaring trade in legitimately transporting excess whisky and cider from Lewis and Newgrange to France, and then from there, it could be dispatched to all the underwater habitations. Tadhg and Callie had worked out how the Caspians had accessed all portals within the same window, bi-directionally, and had taught all communities on the forty-fifth parallel how to control the destination and ensure each passage operated in both directions. Illy had proposed making the controls centrally operated from Clava to the ambassadorial group, but it had been a contentious issue. So, for now, we each managed our own. It was only a problem when someone jumped the gun and programmed into a different location, as had happened to us in our first month here. We were supposed to trade with France. I was really looking forward to the wine and cheese we had ordered, then Italy connected to France first, booting us off. I was fuming, and Riccardo was most apologetic that it was one of his team who had misjudged the timing. Fortunately, they disconnected quickly, and we managed to get most of our supply through before the wormhole closed. After that, we had agreed to time the connections so we could maximize the opportunities. But it also meant that Summer and Ally's illegal side business was booming. All Jake had done was give them a more straightforward method of transporting goods between communities without paying tax and being detected.

I couldn't focus on prioritizing the orders. *What if...* I flicked over to a blank page in my notebook and sketched.

A shadow looming over me startled me, and I jerked up to see Gio grinning down.

"How long have you been working on that?" he asked, the grin reaching his eyes.

I glanced out the window that ran along the side of my office, surprised to realize it was nearly night.

"Ah, um. Well, all day, I guess."

"I've seen this look. The day you designed braces for Gianni, and again when you made a set for Charlie. What are you up to this time?"

"Close the door," I whispered. "Mandy told me that when the population gets too big here, they reduce the size of apartments."

"You are safe. She has gone. She passed me in the hall. That is true. We did it at home too. It was that or limit births, and no one really wanted that. They tried that once in Italy, but it didn't work. People just refused to stop at one child."

"She also said there has been a population boom or was about to be."

"She is correct. It feels like every second case I see at the moment is an obstetrics one. On the upside, I will have a lot of pediatric work soon. Catharina says it is because people feel safe again, which took some time after what happened with the invasion here.

Several hundred people died, but those who lived now want to have children."

"She is probably right. There is nothing like having your life threatened to reassess your priorities. So I was thinking, what if we extended the pods? I am waiting for a reply from Tadhg, but I am fairly sure we are less than a kilometer from the shore. What if we built an enclosed bridge and a domed pod on land? Then we could move growing to the landside pod and reuse one of the greenhouse pods as housing. Over time, we could house animals, aquaponics, and even the crop pods like corn and wheat out there and expand more here. We would always need to live here to access many of the resources, including fresh water, but could come and go each day."

Gio smiled broadly at my excited speech. "Can bridges be built over that kind of distance?"

I forgot Gio had no experience with bridges and grinned. "Oh, most definitely. The skills were there in the old world, so it can be done. I would need some help, though. That is more civil engineering, but I am sure Callie could help. Technically, she is an electrical engineer, but she has done a lot of construction projects too."

"You know who could assist? Joseph. His father was one of the original construction team in Piedmont. He was apprenticed to him, and his father taught him everything. He told me about it once."

"He is brilliant. I wish I could bring him here."

"Why can't you? It is only two weeks until the full moon."

I considered that. "I was planning to ask my father to come at some point to help with the aquaponics. I don't have time to keep advising Deb and her team, but Antonio knows as much as I do now. We could ask them both."

"How will you explain you can go outside?"

I sighed. "I have no idea. Short of arranging fully enclosed suits for everyone, I don't know that I can. That tiny piece of gossip would spread around the world in five seconds flat. Illy has kept the communications fairly tightly controlled. We all know that you can't control everything, but the communities don't know yet, other than you and your brother." While not entirely safe, Nasir, Sera, and I would certainly say nothing, nor Illy herself. Riccardo didn't know, and Yellowstone and Caspian hadn't yet joined the ACC. Illy had demanded assurance that none of the above-ground communities betrayed the confidence of the ACC. The leaders she had in place were all loyal to her. We were safe, for a time.

"What will you do when everyone knows?"

"Accept it, I guess. It is no different from my life before I came here. Everyone on Lewis knew. It wasn't a secret. The exception is that I am the only one here. At home, there were a few of us."

"Talk to me about this design of yours."

Pulling some strings, I managed to get Joseph and Angelo seconded here for a month. Riccardo wasn't pleased to lose them but also accepted my offer that any improvements we made here would next be replicated in Piedmont. He knew me well and respected me. He recognized my ideas would benefit the majority, so he didn't take too much convincing. Joseph and

Antonio were thrilled to be invited and accepted readily, promising to bring Gio's favorite wines. After his anniversary gift, I desperately wanted to give him something.

The portal team watched with astonishment as Joseph and Antonio took turns hugging and kissing me. Antonio lifted me and swung me around at one point.

"You are married!" they gushed, offering profuse congratulations, kissing me on both cheeks.

"I'm the ambassador," I whispered as they muttered to me in Italian about the stunned looks they received over this highly familiar greeting. "I think many of them are scared of me, anyway. They will gossip about my three boyfriends for weeks! Come on. I'll show you to your apartment."

It had taken some negotiation to get access to an apartment for a month while they were here. Fortunately, a couple had requested a nanotechnology placement in Japan, and I had sent them with a care package for Sera, wishing I could go myself. Speaking every day was wonderful, but I missed having her here, working together. Our conversations were likely monitored, so we couldn't speak about what was really happening, our opinions of our colleagues in other communities and such. Videoconferences were the best. I could tell so much more by seeing her face than I could from words.

"Thank you so much for helping adjust Gianni's braces," I said to Joseph as we walked up the corridor. "How is he doing?"

"He is well. He said to send his love to you both, and he wants to see you soon. Where is your new husband?" Antonio asked as we climbed the stairwell to the upper level, where the lift would take us to the main pod.

"He wanted to be here to meet you, but a woman is having a baby," I explained. "That is the main reason I asked you here."

"To help with babies?" Antonio looked shocked.

I laughed. "No. We have a lot of young families having children, and we urgently need to expand. I have some ideas. I need Joseph's help designing some plans, and I am desperate for you to help the team here with aquaponics and the vineyard. Don't tell them I said so, but the wine here is not much better than grape juice."

"Ugh." Antonio screwed up his face. "That is urgent. I will see what I can do. But only for you. We brought your gift."

"Thank you. I mean it. Thank you so much."

"We are so excited to visit. We have never left Piedmont. This is a wonderful opportunity. Everyone is so jealous," Antonio explained.

"You should have heard the women in communications complaining that only your friends got these opportunities. Perhaps we can stay longer?" Joseph added, his familiar cheeky twinkle lighting his face.

"If it is as bad as you say, it will take me a while to get your growing to a standard," Antonio said thoughtfully.

"You have a month to improve things here," I advised. "Riccardo wants you back, and he made it clear he can't let you stay away longer than that."

"Since we lost you, Matteo, and Seraphine, everyone needs to work harder," Joseph teased.

"Sorry." I smiled at them. "But if what we have planned works, then we will all benefit."

"I believe you." Joseph grinned at me. "I have never seen you not succeed in a project. While Antonio is bringing your wine up to an acceptable standard, I will help you. Tell me your ideas."

CHAPTER 18

"THIS IS YOU." I showed them to their tiny one-bed-room apartment with views of the rugged cliffs beyond. "I assume one bed is enough?" Ever since I had walked in on them both that day in the storeroom, they had never hidden their relationship from me. Even when it wasn't common knowledge, not even by their families, they had trusted me enough to keep their secret. After the day Gio had suspected Antonio and I were having an affair and punched him, giving him a decent black eye, I had apologized profusely to them both for betraying their secret. They had forgiven me and Gio. It had only been a few days later that the Caspians had invaded, and Joseph and Antonio had realized that life really was too short to keep secrets.

Joseph flashed me a cheeky look as he dropped his bags and scanned the room. "Why do you think we accepted? We still do not have a place together in Piedmont. We stay over at each other's apartments like teenagers."

"Well, why don't you get married?" I fired back. "Then they have to, don't they?"

"We cannot," Antonio explained.

"Why?"

"Men do not marry men."

"Yes, they do. How many times have I told you that love is love? On Lewis, Newgrange, even here. Men marry men, and women marry women. Why should it matter?"

"But we cannot at home."

"So, get married while you are here." Shocked silence filled the tiny apartment, and the air thickened. "Um, that is, if you want to," I muttered, feeling like I had overstepped the mark. My cheeks flushed with embarrassment. Who was I to assume that they even wanted that? When I looked up from my feet, I saw them gazing at each other, fireworks shooting between them.

Joseph turned to me. "You are the ambassador. You will marry us."

My instinct was to protest, to tell them I couldn't. But I was the ambassador. I knew how much they loved each other. Why couldn't I marry them?

"Sure. Tell me when," I said quickly to cover the discomfort of my blunder.

That took the wind out of their sails quite visibly.

"Uhh..." Antonio and Joseph looked at each other in confusion.

"Well, today is Thursday," I thought aloud. "How about Saturday? That gives you a day to prepare. Write your vows and such. Then we can have a day off to recover before starting work on Monday. Who do you want to attend as your witness?"

"Just you and Giovanni. We do not know anyone else here."

"Here, they require two witnesses. I can't if I am officiating. Leave it with me. I will find someone."

"Married..." Antonio gazed at Joseph with such adoration that I nearly swooned.

"I'll let you get settled in. I'll be back in a bit." I slipped out the door unnoticed.

After leaving our visitors, I made my way to the kitchen. They liked me after I had overseen the construction and implementation of several kitchen improvements.

"Can I ask an enormous favor?"

"How enormous?" Jodi beamed at me. She made spectacular cakes, and I had meant to thank her for the anniversary cake she had made for Gio and me.

"Two wonderful friends of mine are getting married in two days. Would it be possible..."

Jodi's eyes lit in delight. "A wedding? You need catering? Cake?"

"All of it. But only for five people, if that is okay."

Her face fell. "It is not a celebration with only five people."

"I know, but they have just arrived from Italy, and they don't know anyone."

"Well, what better way to meet people? Leave it with me. I'll arrange something. Just bring them to the function room at 5 p.m. on Saturday."

"You are a goddess among women." I beamed at her, knowing we were in for a feast.

"I know. Tell my husband!" She laughed, returning to her meal preparation.

"Oh, and Jodi? Thank you so much for the delicious cake you made for my anniversary."

"Did you like it?"

"I think we have both gained several kilos after eating that! It was divine. Best cake I have ever tasted. Can you make another one?"

Jodi pondered that for a moment. "I have a better idea for so many people."

"I am sure anything you make will be superb."

"5 p.m. Saturday."

"We will be there."

Returning to check the guys had settled in, I took them off for a whirlwind tour of the pods. We made our way to the agricultural pods first, finding Deb working on tying tomatoes to a trellis. Deb was apprehensive at first, looking at me like I was setting her up, even though I had warned her over dinner the previous week that they were coming.

Deb, Gabriel, Gio, and I ate dinner together every Friday, and they had become some of our best friends in the months we had lived here. Gabriel and I often chatted about projects we had worked on. He told me about some of the training he had undertaken before they had moved here, his time at university, industry placements, and holiday work. *He must be a similar age to my own parents,* I realized one evening, although he treated me as a colleague and peer and not a daughter. Their children were grown, and their son was partnered, his wife expecting her first child, but Gabriel and Deb were entertaining and full of information. We lost hours over dinner and drinks, chatting about places we had been or projects he was working on. When the time was right, I was dying to tell him what I had brought Joseph here for—my idea to spread to the mainland.

"My dad would love to meet you," I must have told Deb a thousand times. "You would get along fabulously!"

"Maybe one day, now that you have re-opened the portals, we can."

Antonio, quieter than Joseph, watched Deb respectfully and allowed her to show him the projects they were working on. I was desperate to show him the upgrades I had introduced but bit my tongue, allowing her to walk him through, slowly pointing out varieties and upgrades, things she was proud of. Antonio asked questions showing his interest, and slowly she warmed to him. By the time I left, they were chatting away like old friends.

After leaving Antonio with Deb and the agricultural team and seeing his eyebrows raise as he was shown the limited aquaponics tanks and pitiful excuse for a vineyard, I smirked and left him to his work. Antonio was a genius at growing things, much like my father, and I wished I could introduce all of them. Dad often said that back in the old world, people went to shops to buy food and never really thought about the work that had gone into growing or raising it. Growing up on Lewis, with a greenhouse almost at our front door, and regularly being asked to collect eggs, collect milk, choose a fish, or assist Aidan with grain milling, I knew exactly where all my food had come from. It was a bizarre concept that people were so far removed from their roots. Many times I had been asked to repair equipment or improve tools required to plow, mill, or even process the mash at the whisky still. After Luca's death, Louis had taken over the coffee roasting, and that too required a degree of precision, so every time I drank a cup of coffee, I knew

Dad painstakingly grew and harvested the beans, Louis dry processed them, removing the parchment layer, and roasted them before we ground them to drink. But even here, people rarely stepped foot out of their own roles, their own pods. Gio had little idea how food was grown until I arrived in Italy and talked to him about the process, the skill, and technique.

Perhaps I should encourage people to mentor each other, I considered, watching Antonio run his fingers along the grapevines, assessing as Joseph and I headed toward my office.

"So, tell me what we have planned."

I took Joseph's hand and pulled him to the window on the far side of the pod.

"Do you see that land mass?"

"Sure."

"That is the Bruce Peninsula. We will build a bridge from here to there, and then construct an above-ground dome to establish a new greenhouse over there. Several, eventually. I have plans to start with one, then using internally connected passageways, we can expand and grow more."

"How?" Joseph looked at me, perplexed. "Do you want to grow everything above ground in planter boxes?"

"Some," I admitted. "It is easier to work slightly elevated. But my father grows a special type of moss that rehabilitates the earth. It neutralizes the protozoa, allowing us to regrow in that space. I think I told you about it."

"I remember you and your sister telling me about planting trees outside your home biosphere."

"Exactly. Dad and my aunt spread the moss first and kept it damp. Then, they made Sera and I plant trees."

"How did you do that outside the dome?"

"Oh, we were protected," I said dismissively, not wanting to engage in that line of questioning. "We have suits, much like the heat suits we use for travel. We used to travel outside the domes quite a lot. I think I told you as long as you don't ingest the water, you are fine. There is an additional issue now: the oxygen outside is thinning, making it difficult to work outside for long. But there are ways you and I can overcome that, too."

Joseph's eyes glittered with ideas.

I laughed. "Hold those thoughts. Let's head back to my office, and we can start brainstorming ideas."

"Brain … storm?" he asked, confused.

"Coming up with lots of ridiculous ideas, and we choose the least ridiculous one to build! Come on."

"How can you be sure it is safe?" Joseph asked as we walked. "Our elders were told it would be hundreds of years before the protozoa died off."

"That isn't quite true. I read a paper about the protozoa and modeling on the likely long-term effects years ago. There are two stages of protozoa, and from what I read, this one spread so quickly that scientists didn't have time to study this one over a long time span."

"What are the stages?"

"There is an active stage, where they feed and reproduce, and a cyst stage. As cysts, the protozoa can survive harsh conditions, such as exposure to extreme temperatures or harmful chemicals, or long periods without access to nutrients, water, or oxygen. Being a cyst enables parasitic species to survive outside of a host and allows their transmission from one host to another."

"But once they are cysts, they are safe?"

"Sadly, no. When protozoa are in active form, they actively feed. But the way I understand it, they can convert both ways."

"How long until they are extinct?"

"We don't know. But I am fairly certain they are still active. Some of our trees died when we planted them outside the domes, those we planted slightly too far from the moss. I'm no scientist, so I am unsure, but the cysts are likely still active and cover the globe now. The part we don't know is how long they survive without a host."

Joseph nodded. "My father taught me a lot about construction principles. But what makes you think it is safe for us to build out there?"

I smiled at him. "Because there are a lot of above-ground communities under biospheres, of course. I just want to build one for each of the underwater communities, partly to expand but also so that people, children, can experience life outside. Dirt, fresh air, sunshine."

"We can build the bridge, but will plants grow? We have never done it for two reasons. We couldn't get back to land safely, and plants will die as soon as they get wet."

"I don't see why not. We can water them initially with safe water from here, then the water evaporates and falls again. Dad taught me when he built more greenhouses. We grade the earth into a slightly convex shape and build gutters around the outside to catch the condensed water and re-use it. The plants then produce oxygen through photosynthesis. It is just a smaller version of what we have at home. I know you haven't seen it, but we have enormous geodesic domes with breathable fabric that spans hundreds of square kilometers."

"Tell me about this fabric you use."

"What we used originally was thinner, but over the past few years, we have developed a slightly thicker fabric. It is still breathable and waterproof, so air molecules pass through, but not water."

"Why did you need to replace it?"

"It was designed to last hundreds of years. It is robust and can withstand heat, rain, and storms. What the original designers didn't consider was that when all the earth's vegetation died, significant erosion would occur, resulting in dust storms where dirt is constantly battering the domes, pitting the fabric. So it has slowly degraded over the thirty years it has been in place. When we replaced panels, we just reused them to build greenhouses. Nothing was wasted."

"The dust storms are why we need to spend more time underwater," Joseph said, sadness creeping into his voice.

"I know. But if we can slowly rehabilitate the earth and plant vegetation, it does a few things. Plants produce oxygen, which helps us to breathe outside. We can expand our growing and potentially even living spaces. Our children can spend time on the land, learning about growing food and where they came from. The ultimate goal I am hopeful of achieving is that you lose fewer people to *il buio,* the darkness. We don't have the problem you do in the above-ground communities, and the only difference I can see is exposure to the outside world."

Joseph nodded, taking it all in. "I understand. If we can achieve this, it will be..." He trailed off, lost for words.

"I know. It is quite ambitious. But I think we can do it. The technology is there. We just need to link the underwater and above-ground pods."

"This would be life-changing for so many people."

"Can you start sketching?" I asked. "I have one quick errand to run."

The following day, Joseph met me early at my office. Mandy dropped in at various points during the day, leaving glasses of water, sandwiches, and other snacks on the side of my desk. She didn't interrupt, for which I was eminently grateful. Joseph had extensive knowledge of old civil engineering projects, and I suggested that we ask his father and Callie to review them once he and I finalized a design. I also planned to ask Jean-Gabriel, knowing he had labored on building projects in his college days. Joseph and I used pages and pages of paper, sketching enclosed bridges, tunnels, and even a ferry. But I desperately wanted an enclosed bridge, allowing anyone to cross to land regardless of the weather. Winters here were wet and cold, and Mandy said they had more cases of the darkness, depression as they called it here, during the dark winter months. Many people would be required to plan, build, and maintain the space. But if it was successful, we could replicate this everywhere.

"I love this, Caitlin," Joseph said in one pause. "Thank you so much for asking me. I have never set foot on land, and I can't believe I might do that in my lifetime."

"Giovanni's face was a picture when he stepped foot on Lewis, my home." I laughed at the memory. "He didn't realize that land is uneven, unlike your pods, where the flooring is perfectly flat. It took him some time to adapt to the inclines, rocks, and just uneven surfaces. He stumbled and tripped so many times in the first few days."

"I can't wait."

"I can't wait to be the one to show you."

Mandy popped her head in the door, waiting until I looked up before speaking.

"I'm headed home. It is late. You might want to do the same, especially with tomorrow's special event. I am looking forward to it."

Joseph looked up, confused.

"I asked Mandy to be the second witness," I explained. "I can't. Gio will be one witness, but with your consent, Mandy will be the other."

"You would do that? For me?" he asked, perplexed, like he couldn't believe a stranger would do this.

"Of course. Why wouldn't I want to be part of a loving couple committing to each other?"

"Because we are two men." His voice dropped to a whisper, clearly embarrassed.

"So? Are you marrying a goat? Because I have a problem with that. Two men, meh, that is fine." She waved her hand dismissively.

Joseph looked at me to translate.

"*Capra*," I explained. "Are you marrying a goat?"

Joseph's eyes sprang wide, and I realized what he thought I meant. Trying not to laugh, I explained, "She is not calling Antonio a goat!"

Mandy cackled in the doorway at the look of horror on his face. Finally, Joseph understood and smiled at her. "Marry husband. Not goat," he explained.

"Then I would love to be your witness. I will see you in the morning, and may I be the first to congratulate you on your marriage."

I wondered if now was a good time to let him know Jodi had likely invited the entire community or at least everyone who wasn't working. A quick assessment of his tense posture showed that information could freak him out, so I said nothing. He needed a good night's sleep, and it wasn't likely he would run screaming from the venue, not if this was his only chance of marrying his beloved.

"It is time to go home. You must be exhausted. I am sorry for keeping you out for so long."

"The time flew by," he admitted. "I love working with you again."

"And I, you. But please don't tell Riccardo. He might call you home early. I'm not ready for you to leave, not until we have completed a design."

"We have four weeks. We will get it done."

CHAPTER 19

WHEN LEARNING OF THE wedding, Gio offered to take Saturday off work and help the couple prepare. After a relaxing morning and a shared lunch with lots of laughter, Antonio asked for advice on how married life was different.

Gio and I looked at each other, unsure of what to say. Finally, he spoke, more emotional than his usual amiable self. "I fell in love with Caitlin quickly. I knew she was the one. The woman I would spend my life with, grow old with. But marriage, for me, is a commitment. We swore we would always put each other first and never go to bed angry. We don't always agree, but we know we will work it out. Together. We work toward common goals. I feel more secure in knowing that we both made that promise."

"What he said." I grinned. But the three of them looked at me, and I relented, knowing they wanted more. I sighed, trying to explain. "I always knew he was the one. A formal commitment was less important to me. I knew we would wake up together and go to sleep together. My heart was his and his alone. But I didn't realize the sense of peace that came with saying those words in front of other people. I know he has my back, and I have his. I always knew we would grow old together, but now, after saying those words in front of other people, we have a sense of harmony. We are a pair, a unit. I promised to look after him, knowing he will look after me. Does that make sense?"

"It does," Antonio admitted, gazing at Joseph.

"Can you tell us your vows?" Joseph asked.

"It is probably easier if Gio explains them in Italian," I admitted. "The detail might be lost in English."

Once he had finished, and I saw the tears well up in Antonio's eyes, I knew it was time to leave.

"You need to get ready. I will leave you." I kissed all three of them and slipped off home to dress, collect my parcel, and head to the venue alone, knowing Gio would safely escort them there.

Everything was perfect, and standing just inside the doorway, I took a moment to scan the beautifully decorated room and the long tables laden with food. Another table was laid out with wine, beer, and soft drinks. Most guests already had a glass in hand, milling around wearing their finest outfits. Most people only had one formal occasion outfit, so they wore them with pride. People were steadily drifting in, some with children in tow, being forced to behave. Everyone passing greeted me, and I made sure I thanked everyone involved in organizing this event so quickly. I was offered a glass of wine. The red liquid swirled before me, and I was sorely tempted to take the edge off my nerves. I hated public speaking. But the last thing I wanted was to slur with the entire community watching. Politely, I declined but noted what was on offer.

The guests of honor arrived right on time. Gio showed them in, and Joseph's and Antonio's mouths hung wide in astonishment as they entered the function room. The space was enormous, almost as large as the Soggiorno deck in Italy. Plants grew on every available upright surface, tiny fairy lights entwined around them, twinkling in the late afternoon light. White tablecloth-covered tables filled the far windows overlooking the bay. Jodi's team had outdone themselves, and I was desperate to sample the enormous array of delectable-looking food. My stomach rumbled in anticipation.

Catching my eye, Gio ushered them toward the small stage near the entrance. As we had agreed, we would ensure the ceremony took place first. In part so they wouldn't lose their nerve in front of all these people, but also so that the day would be about celebration. The crowd surged forward to form a semicircle around the stage. I took the two steps to stand on the stage before Joseph, Antonio, and Gio, discretely slipping Gio the small package.

True to her convivial nature, Jodi had invited the entire Canadian community to their commitment ceremony. While not everyone could make it, the space was crammed with people. No one passed up the opportunity for a party. Joseph made eye contact as he stepped up before me, and I looked down. I thought they would kill me as they moved to stand beside me.

"Is everyone here?" Joseph whispered into my ear as he bent to kiss me.

"Nearly," I whispered back. The Canadians loved to party, and when Jodi told me yesterday how many people were attending, I released as much wine as possible from the stores without leaving us short. I had already placed an order for more next month, although I hoped that we might soon produce more of our own with Antonio here.

When we were in France, Gio also had several outfits of formal attire made for when he needed to act in an official capacity. He had happily loaned a shirt and pants to Antonio and Joseph. They weren't dissimilar in size or coloring, and with a few minor adjustments, the three of them looked handsome and blissfully happy. Gio was wearing his wedding outfit, I noted, and for a moment, I wished I had worn my wedding dress.

A sense of joy pervaded the room. After our conversation earlier, Joseph and Antonio had written their own vows, and Gio helped me to translate my official part into Italian so I could use both languages. He had also interpreted their vows, so he could repeat it for the benefit of the audience. I stood behind them, facing the room. They stood face to face and couldn't take their eyes from each other, making me smile. I read each line in Italian, then English. As they made their promise, they paused, waiting for Gio to repeat it in English, though I doubt anyone couldn't feel the love between them.

I nodded at Gio, and he slipped the small wooden box from his pocket, cracking it open to display the two identical rings. Antonio's hand flew to his mouth, and Joseph stared, speechless. Finally, Joseph chose one of the matching rings, slipping it onto his husband's outstretched finger. Antonio hurriedly followed suit. The room filled with applause as they kissed, and I glanced at Gio, remembering our wedding not so many months ago. I recalled that feeling of bliss as he kissed me, knowing that people were watching and cheering but only having eyes for him.

When they came up for air, I congratulated them both.

"This!" Antonio waved his hand at me, the silver ring glistening in the light. "You did this?"

"You need proof when you go home, don't you?" I teased. Vacating my position on the stage, I left them to enjoy the crowd of well-wishers surging forward wanting to congratulate them and toast to their marriage. I slipped off to find Gio, who greeted me with a glass of wine.

"You did a wonderful job," he said, kissing my cheek and surreptitiously cupping my bottom in my emerald-green fitted dress. "I like this. I will enjoy removing it later."

I rolled my eyes, not wanting to encourage him in public. "They look so happy, don't they?" I smiled at him. "Do you remember our wedding?"

"If I had forgotten this quickly, you should probably get me checked for dementia," he teased. "I will never forget how you looked as you stood there in the sunlight, wearing that beautiful dress. The sun hit your beautiful green eyes, and my heart stopped beating, unable to believe you were there for me." His voice dropped an octave. "When will I get to see you in it again?"

"Soon," I whispered, taunting. "We have a formal dinner in a few months when the leadership team from the above-ground communities visit. I will wear it then. Assuming it still fits."

"You have barely changed in size since I have known you. It will look stunning, and I will be proud to be the man with you on my arm."

"So you are not proud of my achievements but of my appearance?"

"Both." Gio kissed me into silence as the room ceased to exist, and I heard nothing but my own breath.

"Come on," he whispered as he pulled away reluctantly. "We need to speak with people."

The event proved beneficial in many ways. People I had met briefly, I now had time to speak with in a relaxed setting, over a drink and delicious canapes. The engineering team were huddled in a corner, enjoying the drinks, and toasted the happy couple several times as I spoke with them. Gio's colleagues came to speak with us, as did the catering and administrative teams. Mandy looked gorgeous in a sunset orange dress, highlighting her lustrous black hair, her husband Jacques not leaving her side. I thanked him for letting me have her during business hours and explained how much I relied on her, raving about her skill. Jacques was a quiet man, one of the technical team. I knew from Mandy that he specialized in computers, and he had been responsible for many of the technical upgrades to the systems the team here enjoyed. He looked so proud as he stood beside her, beaming at her accomplishments.

As the hours ticked by, I found myself relaxing and enjoying the company, not even wondering where Gio had disappeared to as I chatted with Jacques about technologies Sera had mentioned they had in Japan. Just as I was introducing Joseph to Gabriel and the engineering team, I heard the tinkle of a spoon being tapped against a wine glass, and we all turned to see who was calling our attention. It should be me, I realized with a jolt of guilt as I pulled my attention from Gabriel. I should be the one toasting the happy couple.

Relief filled me when I saw it was Gio at the front of the room, waiting for the crowd to settle. The room was enormous, and a microphone had been set up for the service and speeches.

"Thank you all for coming." He smiled. "For those of you who have not met me yet, I am Giovanni Accardo. While you have welcomed me here, where I enjoy working alongside your talented and dedicated medical team, I was born and raised in Piedmont, the Italian underwater community. Like many of you, I had never been outside. My entire life was lived in the only world I knew—the pods. I have known Angelo and Joseph since we were children. We grew up and went to school together. We have been friends, colleagues, and part of the same extended family, much like you are all an extended family. I am thrilled to be the first to officially toast to their marriage. To my good friends, Joseph and Antonio, may each day you fall more deeply in love. May your lives be filled with moments of joy, that when you look back, you realize stitching them together forms a tapestry of wonderful memories. I wish you a lifetime of happiness together. Please, raise your glasses. To a lifetime of happiness."

The crowd dutifully repeated the line and drank to Joseph and Angelo, who had made their way to the stage, and now stood beside Gio, beaming. Just as I thought they would speak, Gio continued.

"Our Italian community is very much like this one, a group of people who form a large family. We care for each other, and look after each other, especially when we face challenges. Over the years, we have faced many, and they are not so different to your own. Overpopulation, illness, and loss of key members of our community. Many suffered from the darkness and took the ultimate step. My mother was among them. When you live in such proximity, it is especially diffi-cult to deal with such tragedy and loss."

Murmurs of understanding followed this. I looked around. Clearly, the darkness was an issue here too. I must remember to ask Mandy about it on Monday.

"Last year, two strange young women arrived in Piedmont, in the middle of the night, after they reac-tivated the portals that had kept us isolated for four-teen long years. I was a child when the portals were deactivated, so I barely recalled a life where we were connected. I was most fortunate in that I was the one who found these women. Had I not, I may not be standing before you today, and these wonderful friends of mine may not be married. Now, I am proud to say one of those strange women is my lovely wife Caitlin, a talented engineer and your ambassador."

Cheers responded to this, and I blushed fiercely, hoping he was done. Many people had turned to look at me. I tried to maintain my poise, secretly wanting the floor to open up and swallow me.

Gio continued, "In the time that she was in Piedmont, Caitlin helped many people, including Joseph and Angelo." He looked at them, and they both beamed at me. I knew where this was heading. My eyebrows raised. *Please don't tell them.* I tried to beam the message to him via telepathy.

As I shrank down the wall, Gio told the commu-nity what happened the day the Caspians invaded and what I had done. How he and his brother had been dragged out of bed in the middle of the night. How he had watched helplessly as his friends were shot. Murdered. What I did to save them, overpowering one guard, then another. Joseph and Antonio nodded in agreement as I tried to wedge myself into the smallest space I could in the corner. The room hushed as Gio continued, painting a detailed picture of what happened that day, the feelings of those being held hostage and those who lost loved ones.

When Gio had finished, Joseph took the microphone and spoke, nerves making his Italian accent more pronounced.

"Caitlin was the first person who knew about the love between my husband and me." He beamed at Antonio as he used the word husband. "We were worried about what people would think, but she did not treat us any differently. She told us we would be accepted, even as two men. She taught us that love is love, no matter who those people are. That was a year ago, and we have learned so much from her. She saved our lives and the lives of thousands of our family and friends. We are so proud to call her our friend. It means everything to us that Caitlin was the person to marry us."

Antonio took the microphone next and talked in a mixture of English and Italian about how we had met, the projects he and I had worked on, and the benefits I had added to Piedmont. There was laughter and red faces when he regaled the crowd with the story of the day Gio had punched him, thinking he was having an affair with me. But it was when he described in detail how he felt on that day, being held captive, fearing for not only his own life, but that of his love and his family, that I sensed the atmosphere change, softening slightly. Tears rolled down his face as he spoke. People looked over at me, assessing, seeing me through a different prism. It was uncomfortable, and I felt exposed. Antonio clutched Joseph's hand as he described how that was the turning point for them both, realizing how close they came to losing each other that day, and knowing that they needed to be honest with themselves, regardless of what others thought. Life was too short to hide their true feelings. A quiet hush fell over the crowd as he spoke, dredging up memories of the invasion here, no doubt, the people they had lost and how close they too had come to losing their lives.

Finally, Gio resumed his master of ceremony duties and turned his attention back to the happy couple, and amid loud cheers, Gio asked Joseph and Antonio to cut the cake, a magnificent tower of croquembouche that stood well over six feet tall. It must have taken the team days to make, yet I had only given them two days' notice. Cutting was challenging, and they laughed as they shared the knife to slice the thin web of caramel glazing the surface of the pastry puffs, and several tumbled onto the table. Jodi bustled to the front, kissed them both on the cheek, and shooed them away, handing them a plate with two of the delicious-looking choux pastry balls filled with custard. Several of her team moved forward to assist, and within minutes, a white ceramic plate was thrust into my hand. I bit into the gooey, delectable goodness and closed my eyes as the chocolate, caramel, and custard filled my mouth. Gio appeared beside me, a plate in his hand.

"Why did you do that?" I hissed, swallowing my mouthful of pastry, trying to keep a smile plastered on my face for the people lingering nearby.

"I will tell you later," he whispered, kissing my cheek as people approached to speak with me.

Music filled the room, making conversation difficult. People drifted off to dance, sit in corners with a drink, or left to take children home. It was late, and I knew everyone was on their best behavior as I was here. No one would let their hair down while the ambassador watched. It was time to go.

"Please stay," I said to Gio as he chatted with some colleagues. "I'm tired and heading home to bed."

"No, I'll come too." We wished his workmates a wonderful evening, and he steered me on a lap around the room, farewelling people as we passed. Antonio and Joseph were slow dancing together, their heads resting on each other's shoulders, arms around each other. People watched, basking in the glow of the love that radiated from them.

As the song finished, we caught their attention and were showered with kisses as we wished them goodnight. The music came back on, an up-tempo number, and I could see they were dying to get back out there.

"Have a wonderful night," I wished them both, kissing them both in turn.

"Thank you. For everything," Antonio said, looking so earnest I laughed.

"It is my pleasure. I'll see you on Monday."

Gio fired off something rapid in Italian that I didn't quite catch, and the happy couple flushed furiously.

"What did you say?"

"Best you don't know."

The corridors were filled with people streaming in and out, tag-teaming over the care of children. Some carried dessert home to partners.

"What was that all about?" I snapped as soon as the door closed to our apartment. "You hijacked their day. This is their wedding. It wasn't about me. No one needed to hear what you said in your speech. It wasn't fair to them. Besides, I don't want to be reminded about what happened. Likely the people here don't want to either."

"It was important. I spoke with Joseph and Antonio first. It was with their full agreement."

A low growl from my throat warned Gio I still wasn't happy. "Why?"

"Yesterday, I overheard some of the medical team talking."

"So?"

"They were talking about you."

"What did they say?" I eyed him suspiciously.

"They were, how do you call it, bitching, that you were too young to lead them, to take this role. One said she had no idea why you had been chosen. Another said Illyria had placed her children in these roles only because she wanted to control all the communities for her own ends. Not because she wanted the best for the people here but as a dictatorship."

"But they all knew about what happened in Piedmont."

"They did. They were attacked here, too. It wasn't until after you freed us and Illyria arrived that the Collective overthrew the Caspians in Canada and sent them home. But not before several hundred people were killed. They needed to hear firsthand from people that you saved that it was you that freed us, and by association, them. They had no idea of your role in all of this."

"You still shouldn't have done it. It was embarrassing," I snapped, now even more humiliated. "It wasn't the right forum."

"It needed to be done, and there are no other full community gatherings where there was the potential to give a speech. Even those who knew *about* you, what you did, it is abstract. It is different to have someone describe a situation that happened thousands of miles away, to have that person in front of you suddenly. It was months ago, and people forget quickly. Sometimes, you need to be reminded that ordinary people do extraordinary things, although you, my love, are far from ordinary. You have nothing to be embarrassed about. You should be proud."

"I was humiliated. You could have warned me. I would have left."

"You would have said no."

"With good reason. You know that time still haunts me. I don't want to think about it, let alone have everyone here told about my actions. Why can't we forget about it?"

"I know it pains you. But your legacy is that so many people live because of you. It was the perfect opportunity to have everyone together for a social occasion for three of us to stand up and describe what you had done and not just on that day. I might be accused of bias, but Joseph and Antonio cannot. Then there are the friendships you made, the projects you worked on, substantially improving our lives, and all in a short time. A place that wasn't yours then. Maybe now they will give you a chance."

I relented, recognizing what he had done. For both of us. "I hope so. I like it here."

"As do I. These are good people, *angelo mio*. They need to know you are, too. I want to give us the best start here, raise a family perhaps."

"And here I thought you just enjoyed practicing," I teased, ever so slightly tipsy.

"That is one of the best parts. Now, how do I remove this dress?"

CHAPTER 20

JOSEPH MET ME IN my office early Monday morning, looking so radiant I was compelled to comment.

"You look the happiest I have ever seen you," I told him. "Marriage suits you."

"Even a week ago, I didn't dare to dream this would be possible. Married! People were happy for us. I can't tell you how happy this makes me, Caitlin. And it is all because of you."

"It has very little to do with me," I teased. "You were a couple long before I crashed into your lives. I just said a few words to make it official."

"You did a lot more than that. When we return home, we hope we will be accepted like all other married couples. We will be eternally grateful."

Mandy arrived, saving me from further embarrassment by handing us both a coffee and presenting us with a plate of pastries.

"Wait until you try the Danish," I told Joseph. "The pastry chefs here are phenomenal."

"That cake was amazing," he agreed.

"Was there any left over?" I asked, wondering if there was a chance of another one of those delicious custard-filled pastry balls.

"They were all gone by the end of the night," Mandy teased. "You left before Jodi and her team offered seconds."

I sighed mournfully. "I should have stayed. So what did you get up to after I left?"

Joseph began to speak, and Mandy cut him off. "Wouldn't you like to know? Maybe next time you will stay and find out." She sauntered out into the front office, leaving us alone to work on our design.

Joseph laughed. "You have met your match, my friend."

"Oh, I know," I groaned.

"She admires you."

"Huh? No, she doesn't."

"Are you blind? Every single person in that room Saturday night was talking about you and what you have done in the time you have been here."

"Bullshit. They were not."

Joseph shrugged. "If you say so."

Lowering my eyebrows, I asked, "You mean after Gio's speech? I am still not impressed about that."

"No, that was so that people could understand your motivation. I mean before that. People were talking about what you had achieved here: engineering projects, trade, and helping the kitchen staff be more productive. They couldn't work out your motivation; some wondered why an outsider would help them this way. One said you had achieved more in a few months than the previous leaders had in years, so what did you get out of it. Others commented on what long hours you work."

"But I am here to help." My tone bordered on incredulous, and I tried hard to lower it. "That is my job."

"No, that is your personality. Some here saw you as an outside appointment, something that was forced upon them, and suspected you were here for the interest of the ACC and not the locals. It is rare, Caitlin, that someone helps others and gets nothing in return. It didn't take long for them to revise that opinion, but that is why we spoke on Saturday. So we could explain how you had done the same thing in Piedmont."

"I don't know what to say," I mumbled, equally mortified and proud.

"I will treasure this day," Joseph teased. "It may never happen again."

Catching an hour here and there between my commitments, by the end of the third week, we had finalized a design, complete with a project plan, materials list, and a full set of scaled architectural diagrams.

"What are the next steps?" Joseph asked. "I have never worked on a construction project."

I pondered that. "I would like to send it off to Callie and a few other people for input. I will need the support of the Collective to gather resources, especially for the geodesic dome fabric. We will need to collect materials to build, and I will definitely need Summer's help to drop concrete pylons in place. I know Jake has been teaching her to fly a heavy-lifting craft. Securing them to the lake bed will be one of the most difficult jobs, especially as we can't dive and excavate. I'm not even sure how to do that."

Joseph nodded. "What about steel pillars instead?"

"Certainly possible. Let me talk to Gabriel about that. He might have some ideas."

"Are you two eating dinner here tonight?" Mandy called from the front office. "Want me to arrange some dinner?"

"Do you mind? Or do you want to get home to your husband?" I taunted Joseph.

Joseph rolled his eyes at me and called back to Mandy, "Dinner, please." Turning his attention back to me, he said, "I can't believe we will go home in three days. I feel like we could stay another month and still have work to do."

"It would be wonderful if you could stay," I admitted. "Perhaps you could return for the building phase?"

"Does that mean you are staying?" He lowered his voice, although I could see Mandy had left.

My six months were up, and I needed to give Illy an answer about my future here. She had offered me any assignment I wanted. Anywhere I wanted to go.

"I'm happy, for now," I whispered. "We like it here."

"This is your place, Caitlin. You fit."

"Do you think so?"

"I know so. Not that you wouldn't be welcome everywhere, but you are part of this place. I can't wait to tell everyone back home what an amazing leader you are."

"Thank you." Overcome with emotion, I leaned across the desk to hug him. "I'll work on Riccardo to get you both back here, soon."

"We would love that. Antonio is desperate to check in on his projects, too. You should see what he has done."

"I get regular updates—don't you worry," I twinkled at him. "I know. He has done the most wonderful job. The vineyard is refreshed and on track. The gardening pods and orchards are thriving, and the aquaponics are flourishing. I can't believe he did all this in a month."

"You know he learned a lot from you. You could have done this."

"I don't have any time," I moaned. "The last day off I had was after your wedding."

It was true. The last months had been frantic, learning the role and starting new projects. Apart from the first few days when I felt out of my depth, I loved it. I had been accepted and welcomed. My ideas were implemented, and people stopped to speak to me as I passed.

"You know, I really do like it here," I said, surprised to hear myself speak the words.

"I am pleased to hear it," Mandy announced as she juggled a tray through the door. "Now, there was a choice: potato dumplings or moussaka. I brought one of each. I figured you could battle it out." Mandy placed the tray on the desk between us, lifting the white cloth and releasing a cloud of steam. "Enjoy. I'm off home. See you tomorrow."

"See you in the morning," I said. "Have a lovely evening." Turning to Joseph, I asked, "Which would you prefer? I'm not terribly hungry."

Joseph opened his eyes wider. "You? Not hungry?" It was a joke in Italy that I was always hungry, but tonight I wasn't. I shrugged. "Maybe I ate too much at lunch."

Joseph squinted at me. "You ate what I ate."

"Well, it is your lucky day. Kartoffelkloesse or moussaka?"

"Do you mind if I have the gnocchi?"

"It isn't gnocchi," I advised. "This is slightly different but similar. I've had them before." I pushed the plate of dumplings toward him. "Try them. They are so good!"

Joseph forked one into his mouth and closed his eyes. "*Delizioso!*" he exclaimed, forking another.

I smiled at his enthusiasm as I took a bite of moussaka. "Now. About these materials..."

CHAPTER 21

"GOODNESS, LAST NIGHT'S DINNER didn't agree with me," I muttered, tumbling back into bed after my third vomit for the morning. I felt washed out, sweaty, and gross.

Gio yawned. "What did you have?"

"Moussaka," I groaned. "I thought it tasted a little odd at the time. I should have chosen the dumplings, but Mandy brought us one of each, and I let Joseph choose."

"I also had moussaka." Gio stretched languorously beside me. "Mine tasted fine. Did you drink too much?"

I scowled at him. "I drank nothing. I was working. Joseph and I need to get as much done before he heads home. They leave in two days."

"You have been working long hours. Likely you are exhausted. I order a day off."

"I can't," I groaned. "It is two days from the full moon, and I have so much to do. I'll take it easy and not eat anything. My stomach is empty now, anyway. After a shower, I'll be fine."

"Let me get you something for the nausea, then. Do you like ginger?"

"I love ginger."

"Good. I will make you some tea. Sip it during the day and eat light meals when you can."

"Yes, Doc."

I dragged myself out of bed and rolled into the shower, wishing I had time to install a pressure showerhead here. I was so used to the forceful spray at home or the one I had installed in our apartment in Piedmont, and I detested the slow, methodical drip of shower water here. It took forever for me to get my thick dark hair wet enough to lather and rinse clean. On my next day off, I promised myself, I would ask Gabriel if I could have a spare pump.

I nibbled at some toast, but refused coffee, the smell making me gag. Gio looked at me appraisingly, but I assured him I was fine. After my shower, I was feeling brighter and headed off to work. Mandy greeted me with coffee and an almond croissant, which I did my best to nibble at throughout the morning, but I tipped the coffee into a plant when she wasn't watching. The last thing I wanted to do was offend her. Mandy worked harder than anyone, anticipated my needs, and prepared papers, research, and anything I needed as soon as I needed it.

Mandy had cleared my afternoon schedule, allowing me to spend a block of time with Joseph, finalizing diagrams for outside pods. He hadn't asked how I intended to build them, and I hadn't volunteered. But the architectural designs we had come up with were superb. Detailed cross sections of the enormous structure and the enclosed bridge-tunnel to connect this community with the land one. After a great deal of discussion, we realized that rehabilitating the earth with Dad's moss before using it as an enormous greenhouse was probably best. Wild storms still raged across the continent and would batter the dome's shell. It snowed here in winter, and that would make working there uncomfortable, even with the thin copper threads I had planned to run through the frames, heating them so that the greenhouse could be heated in the cooler months. I planned to ask Sera about sensors for heat and water when I got the chance so that we could operate controls from the safety of the pods, but for now, this project was between the three of us only. Antonio had given many suggestions to improve the vineyard growing here and on land. Freeing up one of the greenhouse pods would enable more accommodation to be constructed using that space.

"Goodness, I will miss you," I told Joseph during one break. "I wish you could stay."

"We would love to," he admitted. "Everyone here accepts us for who we are. But we wonder if that is because we came here as a couple. People didn't know us as children, didn't know our families. We feel welcome here."

"Perhaps that is true," I admitted. "People see you as you are when you arrive somewhere new. You can reinvent yourself. I felt like that in both Piedmont and here. They don't know the child I was. They see me for who I am now."

I waited for Joseph to tease me, as was his habit.

"You are a wonderful leader. I have heard many people talk about you. How nothing is beneath you. They have seen you help in the kitchen or with mechanical problems. They like that. They see you are a leader but also see you as one of them. Am I explaining that right?"

"I like to help," I admitted. "I feel like I am under-qualified for this job. I would be much happier helping with the engineering team, truth be told. I know you need to leave the day after tomorrow, but I wish we could find a way for you to stay."

"If they do not accept our marriage at home, may we return?"

"I can't believe you are even asking that. Of course, you can, but why wouldn't they accept your marriage?"

"No same-sex couple has ever married in Piedmont. There are such couples naturally, and most live together, but none have married."

"Well, you will be the first, and I am sure they will welcome you home and recognize your union. But if they don't, I would have you back in a heartbeat. Everyone here would welcome you. You are such a valuable addition to the team."

Joseph threw his arms around me and squeezed me tightly. "I would love to work with you again. They only need to look at us wrong and we will, how do you call it, hop the next portal express out of there."

I laughed at his use of my expression in his Italian accent.

"I will really miss you."

"Caitlin, this isn't right," Gio said, watching me wipe my face after vomiting for the third time. "You are never sick. We need to get you to the med center and assess you. This could be any number of things. Does your stomach hurt? Could it be appendicitis?"

"A little," I admitted. "I just feel tired, and I can't stop vomiting."

His eyes lit, and he wiped the sweaty hair from my forehead. "*Angelo mio*, do you think you might be pregnant?"

I closed my eyes and thought. Maybe. I was so regular, but I had been busy. My eyes sprang wide in alarm. Maybe. I hadn't thought about it. It had been so many months and... I closed my eyes to keep the waves of nausea at bay. When I opened them again, Gio was staring at me intently.

"I am scared," I admitted. "I was beaten badly that time as a child. Mum and Aunt Sorcha always thought I had internal bleeding. The bruising was so bad. But after he attacked me, we were running again. They had no access to medical equipment, and they couldn't do much about it. I read the medical notes once. Mum wrote them up when we got home. Once a doctor, always a doctor, I guess."

"And?"

"Mum was fearful that my ovaries or fallopian tubes had been damaged and I couldn't have children. When we met, you and I, it wasn't an issue."

"So what changed?"

"You."

"Me?"

"I knew you wanted children, so I asked Magali to remove my contraception when we were in France."

"That was months ago."

"It was. Each month that passes, I thought maybe it was true, and I couldn't have children."

"Why didn't you tell me you thought you were infertile?"

I closed my eyes and rolled my face into the pillow. A long pause froze the air between us. "I didn't want you to leave me," I finally whispered.

"Leave you?"

I rolled back and stared over at him. "When you knew I couldn't give you what you wanted. It was easier to tell you I didn't want children. I saw you with Louis' children—how much you adored them. I see you play with every child in the clinic. I know how desperately you want to be a father. What if I couldn't give you that?"

"When were you planning to tell me?"

"I don't know," I whispered. "I was hoping I wouldn't need to."

Gio rolled out of bed and strolled out of the room, the door clicking closed behind him. So there it was. He knew. I was likely barren and couldn't fulfill my wifely duty. The nausea rose again, but it was nothing compared to the pain piercing my chest. I felt like I was splitting in two. Closing my eyes, I tried to sleep after the closing of the door echoed around the room, but images tortured me. The shadows under the water reached for me once more, returning to take me now that I was facing life alone.

A strange squeaking sound woke me, and I cracked open my eyes to see Gio plugging in a portable monitor beside the bed.

"What...?" I croaked as he pulled back the sheets.

"Let us test this theory of yours."

Tears filled my eyes. "I can't," I protested. "I don't think I can stand knowing."

"Caitlin," Gio spoke gruffly. "Let me make something perfectly clear. I will never leave you. You are mine. Now and forever. If you cannot have children because of something that is not your fault, then we will find another way. Do you hear me?"

"Another way? What other way?"

"You were born by surrogate. Your aunts, Jorja and Bridget, they all had children, didn't they?"

"They did." I saw where he was going with this.

"So, we find another way."

Gio dripped some clear aloe gel on my stomach, and I giggled at the cool sensation making goosebumps pop up on my skin.

"Lie still. Now watch," Gio said, gesturing toward the screen with his free hand as he ran the wand over my stomach, studying the screen. I vaguely remembered this as a child on Kiewa, the ultrasound Mum and Sorcha had done on me as the others packed to leave, but this was far more detailed. I watched as he clicked and took photographs, not taking his gaze off the screen.

"Do you see that?" he said, pointing at a tiny black shadow the size of a grain of rice.

"Is there something wrong?" I started to sit up, and he pushed me down firmly, looking more intently at the screen. "A tumor?"

"A tumor ... of sorts. But it is only wrong if you call becoming a mother wrong. But I don't think I would use that word." He wiped the gel off my stomach and replaced the wand into the holster beside the machine.

I gaped at him. "Mother?"

"About eight weeks, at a guess."

"Really?" I blinked, unable to take this in.

"I think we have found the cause of your illness."

My arms trembled as I held them out to him. "A mother? I can't. I don't know how."

"And you think I do? You have parents. I lost mine long ago."

"And you are alright with this?"

Gio kicked off his shoes and slipped back into bed, fully clothed. I felt his arms pull me toward him and opened my eyes to look into his face.

"This is the best news of my life after you agreed to marry me. You will always come first for me, Caitlin. Know that. But being a father is a dream come true. I am thrilled beyond words to be a father, but knowing that we will do this together means everything to me."

"A baby," I breathed. "I can't believe it. We are having a baby."

"All that practice was put to good use," Gio whispered as he brushed my hair from my face and kissed my jaw. His hands cupped my breasts, and his warm lips worshipped them. "I had better get my fill now," he mumbled, "because they won't be mine for a time."

I lay back against the pillow, shell-shocked. I was going to be a parent. I had been around Louis and Iona's children enough to know this was a messy, noisy reality.

"Gio," I whispered, drawing his attention back to my face from somewhere near my stomach. "I'm not ready to tell anyone. I need some time. Please."

He returned to kissing my stomach, whispering in Italian.

"What did you say?" I caught some of the words but not all.

"I was greeting my son or daughter." He grinned up at me. "But yes, it can be for us only. At least until we can't hide it anymore."

"I need to go to work. The guys are traveling tonight, and we need to complete a few things. Will you meet us at the portal before they go?"

"Absolutely. They are our family too."

Wishing Antonio and Joseph goodbye was more challenging than I could have imagined.

"It must be hormones," I told myself as I fought back the tears. After a month of spending hours each day together, and dinners and laughter every evening, I would miss them. It was like saying goodbye to Sera and Matt all over again. I hated leaving people I loved. Part of me desperately wanted to tell them our news, but it was too soon. I had only known for a day myself, and this news was for Gio and me alone at this point.

Standing back, I watched them hold hands as they entered the portal, dressed in silver heat suits. A pang of longing filled me, wishing it was me heading to Italy or home. The overwhelming urge to tell my parents consumed me. This was news to be broken in person, not via radio or messaging.

CHAPTER 22

HIDING MY MORNING SICKNESS proved challenging, especially when I needed to stop drinking coffee, which my team knew I was addicted to. Gio brewed me ginger tea each morning, which I sipped throughout the day. Mandy gave me a curious look but said nothing, although I suspected she knew something was afoot. In the nearly seven months since we had been here, not once had I not moaned for coffee every morning.

"Are you sure the immunity will be passed on to this child?" Gio asked me one day after work as he rubbed my aching feet. "How can we be sure?"

"It can be determined with a blood test now. Every birthday as a child, they would take some blood from each of us and test it. The testing has also been done on all of my sisters' children. They are all immune. There is no reason this child won't be."

"Will it be a girl?" Gio asked, screwing up his face. "Didn't you say all the chosen ones were girls?"

"No, our generation was all girls, and that was deliberate. But we were created in a laboratory so they could choose the chromosomes. We are all half-sisters except Sera and I, who are full sisters. They did it deliberately to ensure the babies wouldn't accidentally pair up. By being all girls, they minimized that risk. I also read somewhere that the X chromosome was easier to modify."

"Read somewhere?"

"Sera and I knew we were different from a very young age." *Freaks*, I wanted to say, but didn't. "As soon as we were old enough, we went looking. We always knew we had four parents, Freyja and Luca, biologically, Illy and Cam, by choice. All the girls had four, only most didn't know who their biological father was. Sera always knew. Illy knew, but I'm not sure how. I was ten when they told us we were full siblings. We were sisters anyway, and best friends, so it only made that bond stronger. It was partly because Mum didn't want me to see my father differently. But what we read was that the genome we carry, the immunity, is dominant and always will be. So all of our descendants will be immune."

"That is quite a legacy. But why are there so few of you? You would think if they could make children immune, they would produce hundreds."

"I don't really know. For a long time, I thought my mum had donated her eggs, and that was all she donated. Apart from three others, Ruby and Scarlett, whom you met at the wedding, and one other, those three were my aunt's, that is, my mother's sister's children. All the others were my mum's daughters. It wasn't until we were on Piedmont, after the ... incident, that Illy told me the truth. Clava kidnapped my mother when she and Illy were seeking help and forced this upon her. But what I know is that my mother and my aunt were the only two genomes they could modify to be immune, so that is why there are so few. As for why they let Mum go, I don't know. But it must have been traumatic. She has never spoken about it. If it weren't for Illy, I wouldn't know."

"You told me." He spoke in a low, gentle voice, knowing this still pained me. "But our children will be immune? All of them?"

"They will."

"So why didn't they keep looking for other genomes so that they could produce more?"

"Illy says it was to control the gene pool. They didn't want too many in the first generation. Only my mother's genome could be altered to produce us, so we are all related. If they produced too many, we would all be inbred within a few generations."

"That is true." Gio nodded thoughtfully. "But they never found a vaccine to inoculate people against the virus using this technology?"

"Not as far as I know," I admitted. "Illy took over from the scientists when I was seven, after the Nexus was deactivated. Their leader was killed, and I suspect there is a story there, but Mum would never tell me. Anyway, they asked Illy to take over, and she agreed, but she set the rules."

"Was it so different before?"

"I was a child. I don't remember," I admitted. "But to listen to people, yes. Both Jorja's and Bridget's children are not theirs, although they were never told. The Collective interfered a lot in people's relationships before Illy. We both saw it on Orkney with Bronwyn. Mum says she was one of the last forced partnerships, where they forced a mating between chosen genomes to ensure all genes were reproduced. Mum thinks that was why Bronwyn feared her. She saw her as part of the authority. Illy too. But Bronwyn saw you and me differently."

"Your mother told me," he said softly. "It hurt her."

"She said that?" My mother was a stone-cold bitch, according to most people. She would never show vulnerability.

"You could see the pain in her eyes. She desperately wanted to help Charlie, but the parents didn't trust her and for no logical reason."

"They trusted you," I said gently. "I have seen you with children. You are a natural father. This little one is so lucky to have you."

"You will be a wonderful mother." He smiled. "Although I am worried about what I will do if it is a girl, and I am outnumbered."

"What do you mean?"

"From the day we met, you have not done a single thing I have asked. What happens if this little one is as defiant, obstinate, and intelligent as her mother?"

"You always said you love a challenge."

Gio sighed. "I do. I love trying to tame you. But I think this little one will keep both of us on our toes."

"I wish I could tell you that isn't true, but Sera and I were hard work as kids. Mum always said it would be karma when we had children of our own."

"Karma?"

"The way she tells it, karma means that people's actions in this life will affect their future existence. I think it is a bit more spiritual than that, reincarnation and future lives and such, but that is the gist of it."

"I know what karma means. Although we pronounce it slightly differently, it is the same word in Italian. What I meant was, what have I done? Your misspent childhood will now come back and haunt me in my parenting!"

"Hey!" I gave him a gentle shove.

"This child could be the devil, and I would still love them."

"I want to tell my family in person," I told Gio over dinner a few nights later. "I have been thinking about it, and I would like to take some leave, head home for a few weeks, and tell them all together. But I want to see their faces. I don't want this to be news delivered over a radio."

"I understand. This is special, our first child. I know it isn't your parent's first grandchild, but I can't wait to tell Carmelo. He is the closest thing I have to family. We should invite Matteo and Seraphine, too."

"I've been thinking about that. I would love to have all the family there, but I can't think of a way of getting them all to gather without announcing it or at least making them all suspicious. So any ideas, I'm all ears."

"All ears? How can you be all ears?"

"It is an expression." I grinned. "It just means I am listening."

"I don't know why you couldn't say that."

"But I thought it would be easiest if we used the forty-fifth parallel to France and then got Summer to collect us from there. Jake isn't flying as much anymore now that she is so proficient."

"But the next opening is in a few days."

"I know. But I thought if I announced some leave for next month, it wouldn't look suspicious. We will have been here well past our original commitment of six months, so it doesn't look like we are abandoning our roles. Plus, by that point, I will be twelve or thirteen weeks, and that is a safe time to make an announcement to our family, isn't it?"

"Usually anything after twelve is safe."

"So, I make plans to take leave, and tell Sera I would love to see her. We can ask if they can take time off too. I can't push it, or she will get suspicious, but with four weeks' notice, I am hopeful they can plan to head home. Meet us in France. Maybe we can meet with Riccardo and Nasir, and then we can travel back to Lewis together. Summer can collect all four of us if there isn't too much baggage, and we only need a bag of clothes each."

"I would love to catch up with Nasir. I have some procedures I would like to learn more about."

My face fell. I desperately wanted to spend the time on Lewis with my family. Thirty days would fly by. I didn't really want to be hanging around France, where I would be asked to consult on projects. That wasn't a holiday.

Gio caught the look. "But not this time. I will let the team know I will be away for a month."

"What will you tell them?"

"That I am taking my beloved wife home to see her family. It is the truth."

"I can't wait to see them and see their faces. Mum especially. I don't think she ever thought we would take this step."

"This is everything to me," Gio choked up unexpectedly. "You, and now this. I never dreamed I could be this lucky, so blessed."

"You could have had any woman you wanted in Piedmont," I asked suspiciously. "Why were you single when I arrived?"

Gio sighed. "As you know, Francesca and I were together for many years. She always believed we would reconcile, and she intimidated every other woman who looked at me. Bullied is probably a more accurate word. She is quite a forceful woman. They were all scared of her until you came alone."

"Is that why you kept me secret for those early weeks? I just thought you were ashamed of me, and you didn't want people to know about us. It wasn't until after the Caspians came that you were seen with me in public. Everyone knew about Matt and Sera but not about us."

"I was never ashamed of you, my love. It was two things. One, I didn't want Francesca and her friends to scare you off, although now that I know you so well, I didn't really need to be fearful of that. The second was that I wanted you. From the moment I saw you, lying there, your long dark hair fanned out across the sand. That spectacular body..." Gio's arm caressed my breast and waist. "I picked you up, and my heart lurched. I knew I wanted you, and I was fearful that you wouldn't want me. Then we spoke in the hospital, and you acted like you found me attractive. I wanted to see if you treated every other man the same. If they didn't know you were with me, would other men try to get in your pants? Besides, it was fun, keeping it secret."

"I slept with you on the third night there. For how long were you planning to test me?" I was starting to feel indignant. *He had doubted my loyalty?*

"Before I took you to the *le terme,* the thermal hot baths, I saw you wandering drunk through the hallways. I touched you, and you span around like you would break my nose. When I saw your face relax, that was when I knew. You liked me. I just needed to show you I wanted you. Other men had noticed you already, especially after you went to work with Matt. I heard men speaking about you. Only you didn't speak any Italian, so they thought they were safe. Several were planning to ask you for dinner."

"So why keep it secret?"

"Because, my darling, I wanted to keep you all to myself."

I crinkled my nose and eyed him suspiciously. "Really?"

"Truly."

"Who was planning to ask me on a date?" I asked, suspicion turning to curiosity.

"I will never tell you."

"Why?"

"What if you had regrets? Would you have chosen them over me?"

"I was yours that night," I admitted. "I have not as much as looked at another man since. You are enough for me."

"You? She who had two boyfriends before me?"

I blushed and looked away. "You are enough. You will always be enough."

CHAPTER 23

I SIGHED DRAMATICALLY. "I NEED a break."

Mandy looked up from the papers she was preparing on my desk. "Do you want a day off?"

"Honestly, I would like to take a few weeks off. See my family. Go home, I mean. Just for a month," I hastened to add, realizing she thought I was planning to leave. "I thought I might see if Sera can come too. We could pop over to France and travel home from there. We can meet with Nasir and anyone else who is free. I need to walk on the grass again," I said wistfully.

"I barely remember grass," Mandy whispered. "There are trees here, plants of all kinds. But the scent of pine forests, rolling down grassy hillsides, lying in the sunshine gazing at clouds, the fresh blast of wind in your face. I miss all of those things."

She smiled, so did I. But it hadn't been so long for me.

"I'm so jealous of people who live landside," she admitted. "I miss nature."

"How long has it been?" I asked. Mandy and I had worked together for months and had become very close. She was supportive, and we regularly teased each other. I thought I could ask her anything.

"I was nineteen when I came here." She stared out the window, a faraway look in her eye. "Things were bad then. My mother had passed, and my grandmother too. I had nothing left. I was studying politics at university. But I was offered the place to come here. I thought I could make a difference, so I did."

"Politics?" I asked softly. "Is working as a diplomat close enough?"

"You are the diplomat." She turned to look at me. "I am the assistant."

"No. We are a team, Mandy. We do this together."

"Thank you. I appreciate that. Truly."

"Illy once told me that a team will often achieve what an individual cannot. I didn't appreciate it at the time, but she was right. Look at what we have accomplished in a relatively short time. But no one of us did it alone. We share the load, the challenges, and the successes. I can't wait to build this bridge and let you walk on the earth again. Not grass perhaps but solid earth."

All the air rushed out of her with an enormous sigh. "I can't tell you how many nights I have dreamed of walking on the earth again, the land of my ancestors."

"I will do this for you. I promise. Now, will you act as ambassador in my absence?"

"You don't want Max?"

"I want you."

The month flew by. Mandy crammed meetings into my schedule to allow me to take a month off, although I knew she would be fine to take over. I promised I would still be contactable if I were needed. Sera and Matt also arranged to take a holiday, and she squealed at me over the videoconference, overjoyed that we would see each other again after nearly a year apart. The last time we had been together had been just after our wedding, the day we had set sail for Orkney, and she had flown to France and off to her new life in Japan. It was hard to talk openly on radio or video-conference, knowing that people could listen. But her look of pure joy when she told me she would see me in a month kept me going through the long nights of reading, writing briefing papers, chairing meet-ings, and writing file notes. I would happily do three months' work in the space of a month to see my family and spend time with my sister.

When no one was looking, I rubbed my slightly swollen stomach, overjoyed that I would share this with them soon. I had finally accepted that this little person would join us, and sooner than I realized, and I was surprised at how much I was looking forward to it. I had never been one to obsess over babies as some of my sisters had done, gushing and cooing over each new arrival. I enjoyed slightly older children, those I could talk to, read with, or play games with. I couldn't engage with babies in the same way, so it was an odd sensation knowing that I was entirely responsible for this new life. A person. I was growing a person. Sometimes I found myself wondering about this child. Would they look like me? When I was in the shower, I spoke to them and tried to explain about their family, our lives and how much we loved them. Gio had told me we could tell from an ultrasound if it was a girl or boy any time from now, but I knew he was desperate for a surprise. Personally, I would have preferred to know. It made it more real somehow, but it was our first child. I could give him this.

Gio rarely left me alone when I was home, bringing me water and talking to my stomach. He insisted on cataloging all the changes to my body as the weeks progressed. My stomach had started to swell, a hard, rounded mass barely visible under clothes, but more prominent when I was naked. He would rest his cheek on my belly when I lay down and speak to our baby in Italian.

"Do you want him or her to be multi-lingual?" I asked one day. "How did your parents do it?"

"Mum spoke English with us, and Dad spoke Italian. Of course, they both spoke both languages, so we always spoke both. We used to mix them up as children, but it was fine. Mum was a teacher, as you know. She used to say that communication was the most important thing, not language."

"How are they different?"

Gio paused, thinking. "Mum used to speak in simple language with us when we were children, start with a noun, then build on it. So things like chair. Then, blue chair. That would progress to, sit on the blue chair. Dad would do the same in Italian, so we learned to say it both ways."

"I like that, but I need to brush up on my Italian. Otherwise, you and our child will speak about me!"

"Our child." Gio sighed. "I can't believe I am going to be a father."

"Do you care if it is a girl or boy?"

"Not at all. Over time, we will have both."

"Bloody hell. How many children are you planning?"

"All of them," he whispered in my ear. "I plan to keep you pregnant. You look *beautiful.* Your skin glows, and your hair gleams in the light. You look so radiant."

Now that the first weeks of sickness had passed, I felt well too. My breasts felt full and round, even more so than before, and I had always had ample. Gio must have been in mind-reading mode as he cupped them, weighing them before plunging his mouth to my nipple. "They get bigger each day," he murmured appreciatively. "They are so beautiful. Can you stand?"

"Of course. Why?"

He beckoned me to the window. I stood to stare at the night sky but was startled when he engulfed me from behind, suddenly naked.

"Goodness, you are lucky no one can see us!" I teased as I felt my robe slip off my shoulders and land on the floor. "You can't do this against windows on Lewis. Anyone could walk past."

"I plan to use trees on Lewis," he rumbled in my ear as I felt the hardness press into my lower back. "They offer an equally beautiful view of the night sky."

I cried out as he pushed into me from behind, and I rested my forehead against the glass. His arms slipped around and held onto my belly as he pounded into me. My eyes closed, unable to focus on the night sky beyond as I felt the connection between us. I felt the tingling start, and my breath come quicker. Before I could enjoy the moment, I was empty, and he spun me around to face him.

"I want to see your eyes," he told me, resuming his place. "I want you to see me. Only me."

"Oh God, I love you," I moaned as he thrust into me. My head rolled back and hit the glass, but I didn't care. My knees were trembling, barely able to hold my body upright. As he reached his own climax, his head dropped onto my shoulder, exhausted. I held him there for a moment until he recovered his breath, then he scooped me up and laid me gently on the bed.

"You used to throw me on the bed, remember?" I teased. "Am I too fat now to toss?"

"You are beautiful. I just don't want to hurt the little one."

I gaped at him. "So you are happy to pound me senseless against a window but not happy to drop me on a bed?"

Gio flushed. "Maybe."

"I need to sleep. I have an early morning meeting with Auckland. Bloody time differences."

"I can't guarantee I won't wake you in the night." His breath warmed up my neck.

"You can wake me anytime," I crooned, slipping into sleep.

I slipped out of bed early, sighing at needing to leave my warm cocoon. As he had done nearly every night since we had met, Gio had rolled me to face him in the dark hours of night, leaving me with no doubt that he loved me.

As I stood in the shower, the water dripping from my long hair down my body, I tried to rouse myself. *Soon, Caitlin,* I told myself. *Work now. Holiday soon.* I would do almost anything to see my family, my sister, again. Even get up before dawn. I quickly washed my hair, taking a moment to caress my belly. I could get by a few more weeks before I needed larger sizes. By then, everyone would know. I gave my stomach one last stroke before turning off the shower.

As I dried off, I heard Gio call out. "Come and kiss me goodbye."

I wrapped the towel around myself and padded off to the bedroom, leaning over to kiss his sleepy face. "Go back to sleep," I ordered. "We don't both need to be awake this early."

Gio pulled me down to lie across him, and I berated him. "I can't. I am clean and need to go to work."

"But I want you."

"You always want me," I teased. "Tonight. We have one more night before we leave. Can you arrange dinner? I will be home late."

"Don't I always? I need to keep you both supplied with nutrients. I won't take any risks with my son."

"What if it is a daughter?" I teased. "Does she not get your nutritional diet?"

"I will love them regardless," he whispered, returning to his pillow. "Have a good day."

"You too."

I tiptoed around the room, getting dressed and closing the door quietly behind me.

CHAPTER 24

"AH, CRAP! I'VE LEFT my ring on the bedside table!" I looked at Gio in panic as we entered the lower level of the community. Our bags had already been taken as I had been caught at work and was now rushing to make the opening. "I meant to pack it, but I was in such a rush to make the portal I forgot."

Gio smiled. "We should have it adjusted so you can still wear it."

"That wasn't what I meant. I don't want to be without it for a month. But I don't think we have time to go back up to the apartment and get it."

Gio saw the look on my face. "It is only a ring. A symbol of the love I have for you. But it is just that—a symbol. I am here. I won't leave your side. You will only be without it for a few weeks. We will be back soon. It isn't important, Caitlin. Focus on our trip. Our wonderful news."

I calmed slightly and smiled. "You are right. It is only temporary. My fingers, like everything else, have swollen thanks to…" I broke off, hearing other people nearby, but lowered my voice to a whisper. "I am so excited. I can't wait to tell my parents. Come on. We are late. The portal will open any minute now, and we will barely have time to get into our suits."

"It is only temporary." I smiled at Mandy, who stood near the outer wall enclosing the lake, as I hurriedly clambered into the bulky heat suit we used for portal travel. Her face was drawn, and I sought to reassure her as I pulled my arms through the sleeves. Gio and I were traveling first, so we didn't miss our window. The freight would go second.

"We will be back in a month, I promise. You will do a wonderful job, but I have far too much to do. We need to get building on the landside pod and..." The rest of my words were drowned out by the vortex opening, the roaring as the water swirled.

As I leaned down to pick up my bag, my hood fell forward, obscuring my peripheral vision. I didn't see the movement until it was right before me. Three men, dressed entirely in black, appeared under my nose. Gasping, I dropped the bag. Gio cried out beside me, and as I was jerked upright, I watched him fall to the sandy bank, his cry echoing in my ears over the roar of the vortex. As I watched, a red stain appeared, staining the silver fabric of the now cut-open suit, the knife handle barely visible, still embedded to the hilt in his stomach. Instinctively, I reached to help him, but my unsecured hood was thrust back, and a cloth was slapped onto my face. My arms were grabbed, one man gripping each arm, dragging me backward toward the swirling water. Twisting to get away, to get to Gio, I saw my colleagues running toward me, and I fought desperately to get free. Mandy's mouth was open in shock as she registered what was happening. It felt like the world was encased in mud as I watched their faces in slow motion as I was pulled backward into the water, my head spinning from the metallic-smelling rag pressed against my face. The last thing I saw as I was sucked into the whirlpool was Gio lying dead on the sandy bank, his silver heat suit soaked in the spreading pool of blood.

CHAPTER 25

A LOW VOICE ECHOED AROUND the room, and I fought against the waves of nausea threatening to drown me. The metallic scent of the cloth that had been held to my face still seared my nostrils, making me wince.

"Ahh, I see you are awake." The thick, rumbling accent with an odd intonation roused me from my stupor. This was not someone I knew.

"Not … really…" I grumbled, cranky at being woken.

"Good. You understand me then."

I understand you fine, fuckwit. I seethed internally as the memory of my love lying lifeless on the sandy bank came flooding back. My last sight of Giovanni, bleeding out with a knife embedded in his stomach, clearly imprinted on my mind. The red stain spread as I watched.

"It is time."

Time for what? Before I had time to consider that, huge meaty hands yanked me from my lying position to an upright seated pose. I swayed, the room spinning unpleasantly and taking on a cloudy tinge at the edge of my vision. I closed my eyes, willing it to stop. I swayed and flopped back into a lying position, pausing for a moment before rolling onto my side, trying to get my bearings. I felt my stomach convulse. Even in my woozy state, I knew full well where I was. The accent. Caspian. They had come for me. Killed my husband as I watched. The waves didn't cease, and I wondered if I could projectile vomit off the bed and manage not to lie in it.

"Come. They are waiting," he boomed, pulling me up again, forcing me to maintain the seated position.

"Who?" I hissed through gritted teeth, fighting the brutal waves of nausea. Traveling through that horrendous portal and being anesthetized wasn't doing great things for my mood.

"The Committee." He sounded out the word like it pained him. Clearly, he had never said the word aloud in English. His accent was thick, and his English was difficult to understand. With my eyes closed, I had to fight to interpret each word he was saying.

"The Committee?" I asked, trying to buy a little time. If only I could get my thoughts straight.

"The Committee," he confirmed gruffly. "They want to speak with you. Now."

That sounded ominous. This wasn't a happy committee of sewing or growing herbs, clearly, nor a wine and book club like my aunt Di had started on Lewis. The reverence he used in the title, combined with his being more fearful of being late to meet with them than of me, evidently meant they were the key decision-making body, and he was a worker. Fuck. Why would they want me? My brain was racing. Being an ambassador? Possibly. Nothing to do with their new salination. They would have taken Jake for that. The only logical answer was they wanted to confirm that

I killed the people who invaded Piedmont. Evidently they knew that already, though goodness knows how they knew it was me. There were no survivors from the invading party. Carmelo, Leonardo, and I had seen to that. Did that mean they were after all of us? I resolved not to name my friends if that was why they had brought me here. Mum had instilled integrity into us as children. You never rat on your mates.

Fighting back the blurred vision and the desperate need to lie back down, I glanced at my captor through lowered lids. Like all the others, he was dressed entirely in black, from the black leather boots, identical to the footwear I had stripped from my first kill on Piedmont to the utilitarian black pants and shirt. His greasy dark hair was clipped short, day-old stubble tinged with gray, and I could smell the bracing, pungent body odor from beside him. He stood and reached for me, and I ignored his hand, pulling myself to a standing position using the spartan metal framed bed for support. Despite standing several inches shorter than him, I stared him in the eye.

"Show me the way," I commanded.

My captor clicked his fingers, and two guards appeared from outside the room. Lunging at me, they forced a black cloth bag over my head, and I felt my hands being tied with coarse rope behind my back. I was dragged for what felt like kilometers, up stairs, into lifts, and down passageways. My body was still numb from the drug they had used, but as it wore off, the sensation of pins and needles wracked my arms.

"For fuck's sake. This is fucking overkill," I seethed, the darkness exacerbating the nausea. My head was swirling, and my ears buzzed unpleasantly. I had been in enough unhab communities to know they were all built to a standard template, a central pod with smaller pods at regular intervals. Secure water storage below and a central pillar with a lift. While I couldn't find my way back to any one room specifically, it wasn't like I could run. Where would I go? It was twenty-eight days until the next portal opened, and they would watch me every second. After what I had done to their invading party on Piedmont, there was no way they would trust me.

Fighting the waves of nausea, I was pushed down more passages, shoved through doorways, and dragged into rooms. The guards finally stopped, and gripped mercilessly by the shoulders and my hair yanked back, I was forced to stand upright, still fighting the overwhelming urge to vomit.

CHAPTER 26

"MACKINTOSH," THE HEAVILY ACCENTED voice rumbled at the other side of the room. The cloth bag was yanked from my head, and I turned my face into my shoulder, squinting, and forcing my eyes closed against the brutal light. My hands were still tied behind my back, and I fought against the restraints.

"Who is asking?" I snapped when I could control the river pouring from my eyes, fighting against the light after so long in darkness.

"Are you Caitlin Mackintosh?" the voice boomed more forcefully, spacing out the words with a strange intonation on the syllables. It was like he was mispronouncing a strange word he had never heard spoken.

"Yes." I stared at him as defiantly as I could with my blurred vision. Five of them, all in black, were seated behind a long table before me. I had flashbacks of the interrogation committee in Yellowstone. "Why are you asking? You know my name. Who are you?"

"I am Viktor. Are you responsible for the death of our comrades?"

Well, at least they weren't planning to waste time. "Which comrades?" I fired back, annoyance getting the upper hand at their directness.

"I think you know. The ones you *murdered*." His accent was thick, almost unintelligible, forcing me to strain past my ear buzzing to understand what he was saying.

"The ones who invaded the Piedmont community?" I fired back, angered by his accusation. "The comrades who murdered innocent men, women, and children? In their own home? Yes. I am responsible." There was nothing to be achieved by lying. They knew who I was and what I had done. They would kill me anyway. Why prolong the inevitable? Now that I had confirmed where I was, I knew beyond doubt I would never make it out alive. Killing Gio. Taking me. This was payback. I may as well tell them all of it. Confess. But there was no way I was selling out anyone else.

The man across the room nodded, like I had passed a test.

"We have an offer for you, Mackintosh."

My mouth dropped, and I rapidly closed it. "An offer?"

"You will join us. "

"I will... *what*?"

"You took down twenty-five trained soldiers. You will join us."

I shook my head to remove the confusion and the certainty with which he spoke. Surely I had misheard. "You are offering me a *job*?"

"*Da*. We want you to train our teams."

I slowed my speech. I must have misheard in my post-anesthetic state. "I killed your people, and you want to offer me a job?"

"You sound surprised, Mackintosh."

"Because I am. I thought you were bringing me here to kill me."

"That remains to be seen. Had that been our only goal, we would have done that already, would we not?"

I tried not to picture my last sight of my husband, a knife firmly embedded in his gut, rammed up to the hilt, as he lay beside the lake. The black cloth thrust over my nose and mouth as I saw him reach for me, falling to the sand. The last time I saw him alive. Distress welled in me.

"My husband," I croaked. "What happened to my husband?"

"He was a hindrance. Of no consequence."

"He was my husband!" I hissed, anger surpassing the grief as I pictured the agony on his face as he bled out into the sand. Seeing me taken but unable to come after me.

The man shrugged, nonchalance crossing his face.

"What happens if I refuse?"

"We will kill your mother. Maybe that will make you ... reconsider."

"My mother?"

"She is Chief of the Collective Communities, no?"

Actually no. My brain whirred through the drug haze. My mother Freyja was Illyria's second in command but now didn't seem the time to correct him. They clearly thought Illy was my mother, and I wasn't about to correct them.

"My mother is here?"

"*Da.*"

"Show me."

"I think not. We took her from Yellowstone. She was alone. They were more … fortunate. She knows you are here."

Fuck. So they do have her. I knew she had been in Yellowstone but was planning to meet us in France, so we could all travel home together. Before we enjoyed our holiday, Sera and I would spend the first day with her debriefing. Carmelo was at home on Lewis, helping Dad. While he often traveled with Illy, she had insisted she go alone this time. Yellowstone was still not part of the ACC, unprepared to relinquish its archaic policies. The relationship was cordial but mostly arm's-length. They wanted to trade but refused to accept the charter and equality agreements that the ACC insisted on. It was a work visit, not a social one. Illy thought it would be too distracting to have Carmelo attend, although I knew he wasn't happy about letting her go into a hostile environment alone. Despite his size, Carmelo was a teddy bear. Illyria was his world, and he would do anything to protect her. Now that decision had likely saved his life. But not hers.

My interrogator read my reluctance. "It is a simple request. If you agree, we will let her go. If you refuse, we will kill you both. You know we can harm more of your friends. We know much about you, Mackintosh."

"What do you want from me?"

"Simple. Join us."

"What if I agree? What will you do with my mother?"

"We must question her. We need to learn what she knows."

That made sense. But I pushed it. "Then you will let her go?"

"That depends entirely on you, Mackintosh."

My head was spinning, and I refused to answer any more questions, desperate to buy more time. My brain was still fogged, and I wasn't thinking at my higher levels. I knew that. Best to delay and come back when I was functioning better.

Frustrated with their lack of progress, and my lack of willingness to defect, I was dragged forcefully from the room, the black cloth sack thrust once again over my head. For the second time today, I was dragged down cold passageways until finally the blindfold was lifted, and I was hurled into a cell. I stumbled across the room, crashing into the bed. I didn't need long to take it all in. I was alone. It clearly wasn't part of their plan to let me confer with Illy.

"It would be best if you comply." It was the man who had woken me.

"Best? Or what?"

"These men do not accept no."

Seething internally, I was unable to respond.

"You are upset."

Turning to glare at him, I bore into him. He was unperturbed.

"Get past the emotion, Mackintosh. Make a decision. Quickly."

The door slammed, the iron hitting concrete reverberating around the space. This was smaller than the cell Seraphine and I had been jailed in on Yellowstone. This space was tiny, barely long enough to accommodate the single bed, which was wedged tight between the walls at either end. Barely a meter of free space ran between the long side of the bed and the black iron bars that ran parallel. A filthy metal bucket, presumably to be used as a toilet, lay on its side on the floor. Disrespect to me or left by the cell's previous occupant—I couldn't tell. The bare single mattress was stained in so many shades of yellow and brown that I was fearful of sitting on it. That thought made me snort. It wasn't like I was getting out alive. A skin parasite was probably the least of my worries. I paced, taking two steps before needing to turn and pace back. It felt like a short dance, avoiding the rusty bucket as I reached the wall. My mind turned to Giovanni. My heart physically pained me. Upset? I was past being upset. I was fuming. How dare they wrench me away from him and slaughter him in cold blood? I placed my hands on my stomach and forced air between my teeth. I wasn't alone. But I could never let my captors know. If their policies were anything like Yellowstone, my child may not make it, not valued as a contributing member of the team. Or they would allow me to give birth, removing the child from me, possibly so they could use him or her as collateral. But how did I survive this? Accepting their offer was repugnant on so many levels. After what they had done to people I knew and cared about in Piedmont, not to mention the damage they had done in their week-long rampage in Canada, it was a flat-out no, not negotiable. But would I need to accept to keep my child safe?

As I paced, my head began to clear. I tried to plan. They had Illy too, allegedly, but I hadn't actually seen her. I called out, projecting my voice down the concrete passageway outside, but no one responded. My voice echoed around the cold, hard surfaces. I had been abandoned in this tiny cave. Exhaustion forced me to reassess my options, and finally, I lay on the feral mattress, praying I wouldn't catch anything from it. Wafts of stale sweat and urine from previous occupants made me feel sick, and I closed my eyes, bracing myself against the onslaught. To distract myself, I tried conjuring Gio's face as we had seen the image of our baby. Not how he looked as he died. I needed to remember him as he lived, not how he was taken from me. His face when he saw me in my wedding dress. The dress that still hung on a wooden hanger in our wardrobe in Canada.

CHAPTER 27

FOR DAYS, I LAY on that stench-ridden mattress, dry retching from the smell of stale urine, pondering what to do. The hunger pangs clenched my stomach, but finally subsided as no food came. A single jug of water was all I was provided, no cup. Weakening my resolve was clearly their strategy.

I knew enough from what Sera and I had read in the files in Yellowstone that children were not valued in these communities. They were consumers of valuable resources, air, water, and food until they were old enough to become assets. The concept of living in a loving family was alien, and each woman was permitted one child before being permanently sterilized.

If I told them I was pregnant, they could force me to have an abortion or take my child as soon as he or she was born. They owed no loyalty to Gio and would likely consider the child a distraction for me. They had no way of knowing the child was immune, and as long as I drew breath, I would never tell them. I had no faith that my child would be cared for or loved. The more I thought about it, the more unlikely it was

I would even be permitted to keep the child. Would that be worse? Knowing that my child, Gio's child, was alive but not being permitted to raise them? Allowing them to live but to be raised in this hellhole? They would likely use the child as a bargaining chip to ensure I complied. Escape was my only option, but there was little chance of that. My only weapon was my immunity, and that did me no good sitting here in a concrete cell alone. Remembering our escape from Yellowstone, I checked the door for the key, but they had removed it. Of course, they had. No windows and no other exit route. I was trapped. Worse, they had Illy. Gio was dead. I had to keep reminding myself. I couldn't believe it. Only a few days ago, we were packing to see our family. But now he was dead, and I was as good as. Another knife plunged through my heart, and I curled up into a ball, praying for the pain to stop.

As I lay there, I visualized Sera and Matt arriving in France just moments after we were due. I wondered how long it would take them to learn what had happened. Likely, not long. They would be confused upon arrival to see we weren't there. But the Canadian team had seen what had happened. The freight team. Mandy saw me as they grabbed me. She would radio everyone. The Yellowstone team would do the same. But to what end? No one was coming after me. Even if they wanted to, they couldn't. It would be another month until the moon portals opened again. A lot could happen in that time.

Trying to be rational, I considered the offer, but the overwhelming sense of grief consumed me. Then the tears started again. No. I fought them back. There was time to cry later. Right now, I couldn't lose my head. If I let emotions rule me, then I was as good as dead. *Fight, Caitlin*, I told myself viciously. These people had killed my friends on Piedmont. Even more in Canada. Slaughtered my husband for no reason other than he was there, standing beside me. If they were to be believed, they had also kidnapped Illy, so they had no boundaries. I no longer cared what happened to me. Gio was dead. Tears filled my eyes as the image of him flashed into my mind, knife firmly embedded in his gut, lying on the sand bleeding out. I choked them back again. *No.* Clenching my hand into a fist, I punched myself in the thigh, focusing on the physical pain. Emotion could take over later. Right now, I needed to focus. Formulate a strategy. The problem was, this time, I had Illy and a baby to think about. It wasn't just about me.

Exhaling, I closed my eyes and tried to relax as Illy had taught me in France. Focusing on my breath—inhale and exhale. Relaxing my muscles, I let my mind go blank. As I felt my body getting heavy, I could see my mother's face standing beside Illy. They were watching me, waiting to see what I would do. A wave of disappointment flooded me, and I knew what I needed to do. It would kill them both to think I would accept an offer like this. To leave my family, my friends. As an ambassador, it would be devastating to the ACC to have me defect to the Caspians, the enemy. Every person in Piedmont would hate me, be ashamed of me. I knew I couldn't do it, no matter what the personal cost.

My father's face flickered into view, pale and distraught. His distress at losing me was palpable and made it hard to breathe. Maybe I should agree and try to find a way to escape later? My mother appeared beside him in my vision, and his head dropped to his chest, beaten. She was right. If I lived, it wouldn't take long for them to learn I was pregnant. Then I would never get away.

"I'm so sorry," I whispered to my unborn child. "But it is better if you and I do not survive this day than for you to grow up in a place like this. I want you to live, to thrive, but not like this. I couldn't live knowing I had sacrificed you to them."

With both hands gently on my stomach, I visualized my child, Gio's child, and tears fell that neither of us would make it. It was too early to feel movement, but the slight swell of my stomach was enough. Would this child look like him or me? A girl or a boy? It didn't really matter now, anyway. "I'm so sorry," I whispered again.

I'm sorry, Mum, I sent the thought out into the universe. I was sacrificing Illy by refusing to join them. Not that I had any faith that they would let her go unharmed. Likely, I would never know the truth. I doubted they would allow me access to communications equipment to contact my parents. My poor father. It would kill him, knowing I had defected. But would it kill him more if I were dead? I knew they would parade my corpse in front of the ACC, evidence of what happened to people who crossed them.

As I dropped into the fog, crowds of people surrounded me. I was standing in the middle of the Soggiorno deck, and they completely encircled me. People I knew. My parents, Gio, Sera and Matt. Carmelo and Illy. They were all watching, waiting for my decision. I glanced to my left and saw Viktor, the interrogator, holding his hand out. I turned back to my family and friends and watched their faces. Sad and ashamed, some turned away from me. Mandy was looking at her feet, refusing to make eye contact. Sera was pleading with me. To save her mother? Or to not give in? I couldn't tell. My heart started to pound, and my breath came faster as I tried to read their faces. Turning around the circle, I looked for guidance. Some held their hand out to me, others refused to acknowledge me, and I felt the waves of panic take over. I didn't know what to do. I closed my eyes and clenched my fists, unable to decide.

A small hand slipped into mine. I looked down to see Gianni looking earnestly at me.

"Gianni?" I asked.

"They would have killed me," he whispered, shame filling his voice. "You can't join them. Take the high road, Catie."

My heart burst out of my chest, and I bolted upright, gasping for air and instantly awake. But the dream lingered, and I knew I had made my choice.

CHAPTER 28

VIKTOR GLARED AT ME as I defiantly gave him my answer. I was dragged back to the cell to reconsider. A one-time-only deal, I was told. I nodded, resolute. Gianni's face hovered behind my closed lids, not permitting me to change my mind. Even if it meant sacrificing Illy's life, my own, and that of my child, refusing was the right thing to do.

I tried to sleep but spent most of the time apologizing to my unborn child, telling them little things about their father, knowing that they would never meet. I suddenly knew how Illy had felt, being pregnant and alone with Alasdair. "I'm so sorry." I sent the prayer out to her. I hoped it would be quick for both of us.

It took several days for me to be hauled in front of the Committee again, although Tribunal was probably more accurate. Judge, jury, and executioner. Cocking my head to one side, I couldn't recall where I knew that expression.

"What is your answer?" Viktor barked as soon as the black hood was removed, and I blinked madly, trying to adjust to the onslaught of light. Good, so there would be no courtesies.

"I would rather die than join you," I responded calmly, although my stomach was churning.

"As you wish."

Viktor nodded as he strode toward me, and my captors held my arms back as he drew back his arm and punched me in the stomach. Caught off guard, I doubled over with the impact, but he yanked my hair back and crashed his fist into my nose before I could focus. The sound registered next. I heard the sickening crunch and was temporarily blinded by the white light of pain that burst behind my eyes. He didn't stop. His fist connected with my jaw, my eye. My cheekbone. Once the barrage of blows commenced, I could barely catch my breath.

"Coward!" I hissed, spitting blood from my mouth when he paused for a second to roll up his sleeves. "Need to hold back a woman before you beat her?"

"Let her go," he commanded and grabbed my left arm as it was let go, forcing it unnaturally behind me. Even as it snapped and the pain made me faint, I refused to let him hear me scream, biting my tongue instead. He kneed me in the back, and I curled into a ball as the kicks kept coming. My shoulders, my head. *Not my stomach*, I thought, wrapping my arms around my legs, trying to protect myself the best I could. Some unintelligible words followed, and then it really began. For an eternity, they took turns. Four men against me, Viktor being the most brutal. He dragged me upright by my hair, his face only centimeters from my own.

"Have you reconsidered yet?" he taunted. His breath was foul, and I turned involuntarily from the stench of unbrushed teeth.

"Never," I hissed with as much venom as I could muster through my smashed ribs and face. I refused to wipe the blood. I would not give him the satisfaction.

He nodded calmly and punched me in the stomach once more. Initially, I fought and tried to block the blows. But after a kick took out my knee, I stumbled to the concrete floor and knew I would never get up. Solid kicks landed on my back, hips, the back of my head. Each blow shuddered through me until finally, I was numb. *How much can I bear before I die? Please. Stop.* An eternity ensued, and despite the pain, I felt myself drift and remove myself from my body. It was like I was there, but it wasn't me. When every breath is agony, each landing blow has no impact. Blissful oblivion took hold, and I drew my final breath.

CHAPTER 29

"CATIE." THE VOICE SOUNDED familiar, but I couldn't pry my eyes open. The pain was excruciating. Surely being dead shouldn't hurt?

"Caitlin! Come back!" the female voice demanded, the desperation piercing the fog in my head.

Let me go. I can't. It hurts to breathe.

The hand grazed my hair softly, then laid along my cheek. After a moment, it was removed, and I could feel the stickiness where the hand had been and tried again to open my eyes. Forcing them open, I realized one was glued shut, and I turned away from the sudden onslaught of light. It was Summer. She was there, talking to me.

"Caitlin, stay with us. I need you. Please."

"What … happened?" I grunted, every syllable tearing another hole in my throat.

"They dropped you and Mum out of the pod into the contaminated water."

"Where … are … we?"

"Caspian Sea. Kazakhstan."

With no effort, my eyes closed as I waited for death to overtake me.

Summer spoke again, more forcefully. "We need you, Catie. Mum is dying. She insists she talks to you."

"Mum?" I croaked, unable to focus on what she was saying. The words were familiar, but my brain couldn't process them.

"She swallowed water when they dropped her into the sea. She saved you, dragged you to shore."

I lay there with my eyes closed, unable to process what Summer had said. Illy was dying? No, Illy was invincible. Cracking an eye slightly ajar, I saw Ally hovering over me with a filthy cloth. She was cleaning my face, and I winced as she touched every wound. She half smiled, half grimaced at me.

"Bloody hell, they did a number on you. What did you do?"

"Wouldn't join them," I mumbled. "They killed me."

The sound of Illy moaning in agony and thrashing around in the bed beside me pulled me from my head-splitting fog. Cracking my single eye that was not swollen shut, I tried to roll my head and looked at her, squinting through the pain.

"Move … closer," I whispered, struggling to get the words past my swollen throat. Summer looked at me, confused, but obeyed, rolling the trolley out of the way and lowering my bed beside Illy.

Illy's cramping lessened temporarily, and she looked at me with glassy eyes as she straightened slightly. She croaked breathlessly through the griping pain, but the words were audible enough.

"Oh, Caitlin. I am so sorry this happened to you. But you will be okay, darling. You are a survivor. Both of your parents are survivors. You are tough. You will make it through this. But before I go, I need to tell you…" Another spasm of agony gripped her, and she cried out, her tiny body contorting in pain. She convulsed on the bed beside me, and all my pain was forgotten as I focused on hers.

"Allison, do it. I want to go on my terms, not like this. Please. I beg you," Illy cried as spasms wracked her again.

"Fuck! What do we do? I'm not losing my mother too." Ally was pale and hyperventilating, pacing up and down, Summer trying to placate her. Illy was doubled up in pain, trying to muffle the screams as the protozoa infected her, dehydrated her, and her organs shut down.

"How long has it been?" I whispered to Summer.

"About twelve hours."

"I've been out for that long?"

"We tried to rouse you but didn't want to hurt you. Then Mum begged us to wake you so she could say goodbye. We were fearful of brain damage."

"No risk there," I started to say when another groan from Illy filled the room.

"What are you doing for her?" I grunted, trying to roll closer so I could hold her hand.

"There is no cure," Ally mumbled. "We know that. All we can do is make her comfortable."

"You are a doctor," Summer turned on Ally, emotion getting the better of her. "You spent years working with Freyja and Katrin. Think of something!"

Ally blanched, the thought of losing her mother stressing her to the eyeballs.

"Okay, think Al," she muttered. "Caitlin is immune. Why?"

"Genome," I groaned, my shattered body causing me to weave in and out of consciousness.

"Agreed. But how do I replicate that? Here? With no equipment except a first aid kit?"

"How do you become immune to something?" I whispered, the words breaking from pain as the conversation with Gio replayed in my mind.

"Vaccination. Or, in your case, DNA. I think what I read about you girls is that you can be infected, but your body fights off the infected protozoa before it can affect you. It neutralizes the threat, much like the moss does."

"What fights infection?" I groaned, the act of speech hurting as air pushed through my lungs and swollen throat.

"White blood cells are the key players in your immune system."

"Okay, how do they work?" I squeezed Illy's hand as she writhed beside me, trying to keep my mind off my own pain. Her attacks were becoming more frequent. She could barely catch her breath in between. It hurt like hell as she squeezed my hand, crunching the already mangled bones. Not like I cared. Everything hurt already. What was one more injury?

"White blood cells are made in bone marrow and are part of the lymphatic system," Ally recited, as if reading from a textbook. "White blood cells move through blood and tissue throughout your body, looking for foreign bodies such as bacteria, viruses, and parasites."

"Do you think that is what happens to us?" I groaned, my own pain rivalling Illy's. In my teens, before I moved to engineering, I had read enough of Mum's medical texts to have a decent understanding of basic biology. Not to mention all the medical records relating to myself and the other immune children I could get my hands on.

"It must be. If you are infected, something must fight it off. With any virus, it is the white blood cells that fight infection. The problem is, I don't have a centrifuge."

"So we give her a blood transfusion. Could she become immune?" I asked, the speech making me exhausted. I looked up at Ally with my single, functioning eye. The movement of my eyeball made my head throb.

"Possibly. I don't see any other alternatives."

"Could it cause harm?"

Ally considered for a moment. "I don't see how. She is dying anyway." A low moan from Illy writhing in the next bed drowned out her next words.

Grimacing with the movement, I tried to expose my arm. "So do it. How much do you need?"

"To fight off the protozoa? I have no idea. I don't think it has ever been tested."

"How much can you take safely from me?" I asked, trying not to let her hear the pain rapidly killing me.

"I can't," Ally protested. "You have lost a lot of blood already, likely internal bleeding too. It is too dangerous."

"Mine is immune. Take it." *I'm dying anyway*, I thought. *Gio is dead. I have nothing to live for.*

"I think in a normal donation, they took half a liter."

"How much do we have?" I grunted as my stomach began to squeeze, making all my other injuries echo in sympathy.

Ally grimaced, thinking. "I was never great at the theory. But five liters, I think. And it will take a few days for your body to replace that blood it has lost."

"What if you took a liter from me?" I forced air through my lips to minimize the pain. "Then that is a liter of immune blood to her five liters of contaminated blood. But I am bigger, so maybe more than 20%."

"Or we could withdraw her blood and replace it with Caitlin's?" Summer suggested. "That is what you do with dirty fuel."

"This is well past my knowledge level," Ally admitted. "But that makes sense. Then 20% of her total blood would be new. But I can't. 20% is the point where the patient goes into hemorrhagic shock. Caitlin has already lost a lot of blood. We can see that." Even I could. My clothes were soaked in blood. My blood.

"What other choice do we have?" Summer asked, her face whiter than I had ever seen.

"None that I can see. I refuse to let her die. But we could kill Caitlin in the process."

"It is my choice. I don't care. Do it. Now." I looked over at Illy writhing in pain. "She is my mother, too. I won't let her die without a fight. Hook me up. Now."

"Argh," I grimaced, doubled over from the sudden onslaught of cramps. Summer looked at me, concerned. "Are you okay? You can't be infected."

"I ... know..." I forced the words through gritted teeth. The pain griping at my lower belly was agonizing, like a vice squeezing my insides. I prayed I had no serious internal injuries, but I knew I likely did. They hadn't held back with the beating. They had plainly intended to beat me to death. The kicks and punches had landed on every inch of my body. Every movement was agony.

"I'm fine. Help her," I moaned, lying beside Illy and holding out my arm for the needle to be inserted.

"Are you sure?" Ally said, watching my face contorted in pain.

"She will die," I panted. "Do it. Now."

"Catie, you are bleeding!" Summer pointed to my jeans. Several blood stains had dried, but the fresh blood was visible. A dark patch grew as I watched.

"Losing … baby," I groaned again. "Get the line in."

"You are pregnant?" Ally's mouth dropped open.

"Was. Get it done."

"I can't, Cait. I can't take blood from you when you are this badly injured. It could kill you."

"Look," I roared with more intensity than should have been possible under the circumstances, "nothing is going to save my child or my husband. You can save my mother. Fucking well do it, or I will do it myself!"

Illy's eyes fluttered open beside me, grimacing in pain. I lay beside her, and I gripped her hand. The pain in her eyes wasn't just from the protozoa. She knew. She could hear. And she was with me. I might be losing one life. I refused to lose two. I could grieve later. Not today. I would not lose her.

Slowly, Ally withdrew a little less than a liter of my blood, monitoring me carefully, ensuring she stopped before the symptoms started. Cold, clammy skin, drifting in and out of consciousness.

"More," I urged, not caring if I lived or died. I could see Gio smiling at me near the light-filled cloud lingering near my head. We would be together soon.

"No." I felt Allison withdrawing the needle from my vein. "It is enough."

I watched, dazed, as she hooked the line up to Illy and watched her transfuse her.

We watched Illy closely, but nothing changed as the time ticked by. She was dying as we watched. I no longer cared about myself. I would not let her go.

"Ally," I croaked as an idea floated into my mind. "Stem cells. Try my stem cells."

Ally exhaled. "There is a way to do that from blood, but I don't have the equipment. This is a very basic clinic that was ransacked years ago. The only way I can do that is to take them from your bone marrow, Catie, which is hideously painful. The pelvic bone is the best place, and I am almost certain yours is broken, possibly in multiple places. I have no anesthetic to give you or I would."

"I can't be in any more pain than I already am," I groaned as Illy writhed in the bed beside me, her tiny hand still in mine. "Do it. Now."

"You won't be able to stay still. Intraosseous needles are awful. I need to push it into the bone. That takes a lot of force."

"Do you even have one of those needles?" Summer asked.

Ally nodded, her face looking green at the thought.

I flicked my eyes open at Summer and dropped Illy's hand. "Roll me over. Hold me down," I ordered as forcefully as I could.

"Do it," I snapped. "Now."

With Summer's weight bracing me on my side, Ally inserted a large needle into several places of my rear pelvic bone, extracting marrow. I tried not to move, to scream, but it was excruciating. I closed my eyes and focused on my breath, trying to minimize the lung expansion, positive my ribs were broken.

"Enough!" I heard Summer snap as the edges of my vision began to flicker in and out, and my body slumped. "You are killing her!"

Over the next six hours, Illy's condition steadily improved. The excruciating spasms that wracked her body lessened, and after an eternity, she reached the point where she could sit up and talk to us.

"How do you feel?" Ally asked as I watched weakly from where I lay beside her. I no longer had the energy to speak. Just opening my single functioning eye was a challenge.

"Weak," she admitted. "Like I fell from a roof and broke every bone in my body. But no more pain. Do you have a plan?" she asked Summer.

"Jake is on his way. I got a message to Tadhg, and he and Jake are coming. Ally needed to stabilize you both, and we can't move you easily. We were in the small chopper. We don't have space for both of you, not lying down."

Holding Illy's hand, blackness swallowed me once again.

When I regained consciousness, I felt Ally's hand squeezing mine. "Welcome back. Try to stay with me this time, will you?"

"Why were you even here?" I asked her in a strangled tone, praying the pain would kill me quickly or knock me out again.

Summer answered, "The radio was buzzing with news that you had been kidnapped. The Canadians were sure it was the Caspians again. We were in France anyway, so it wasn't far. We came to do a recce. We had been here for a few days, lurking on the coast, watching the community through binoculars."

"Feeling stupid is what we were feeling," Ally piped up.

"True. We had been cooling our jets for ages and were nearly out of supplies."

Ally picked up the story. "We were about to leave when we saw something drop. We thought it was a bag of rubbish being thrown out the bottom hatch, the moon pool. Some of the communities still do that. A minute or so later, we saw another bag dumped; only that time, we had the binoculars trained on that spot and clearly saw an arm. Mum's arm, as it turned out. That was when we knew they had you."

Despite the pain at facial movement, I couldn't help but smile at the word recce. Reconnaissance. A word Luca had used with the girls, and they used themselves when scoping new smuggling markets.

"Then?"

"We did nothing. You would have drowned being unconscious in the water. But it was less than a minute before they tossed Mum out, and tossed is the right word. Mum was conscious, so once she saw you, she cupped your chin and towed you to shore. We didn't want to draw attention to ourselves, but using Dad's watch, we caught the setting sun and caught the glass face on it, catching Mum's attention. It took ages, but finally, she saw and headed toward us."

"Why were you in France early?" I asked, more to remain conscious than because I cared. Past her, I could see their mother, her eyes closed. *Please be okay,* I prayed. *There has been enough loss today.*

"The usual. The Toulouse community has produced a new variety of white wine fetching an outrageous price. We have quite a few people looking for some."

"Shhh!" Summer hissed, realizing the incriminating nature of Ally's words.

Illy smirked. "Do you seriously think I don't know what you do?" Illy spoke without opening her eyes.

Ally and Summer's faces blanched.

"How stupid do you think I am?" Illy's eyes popped open, still glazed, but amusement lingered.

"Uhhh..." Summer slurred.

"I have always known." Illy closed her eyes again, and even through my own distorted mental processing, I could hear the humor. "Your father would be so proud. He had a rebellious streak a mile wide. How many times do you think a radio message was intercepted and ignored or a satellite moved slightly? Your sisters aren't the only ones with skills."

Ally gaped, horrified that they had been busted. Illy looked at her directly this time.

"Just be a bit more discreet, will you? The tax we apply to trade goods pays for our resources. While we don't seek to make a profit, the Collective provides all shared services and tax pays for that. You are lucky that Tadhg and I are the only ones who know. If anyone else finds out, I will need to make an example of you."

I grimaced and only partly from the pain. "Why did you punish Sera and me then? Planting those awful trees?" I croaked.

"Well, because other people knew, of course. I couldn't be seen to be going easy on you. But after all the times you have enabled your sisters' activities, you deserved it."

"Sorry," Summer muttered to me. "I never meant to get you in trouble."

"It doesn't matter now," I mumbled, feeling the darkness reach for me once more.

"Rest," I heard Illy's voice this time as she squeezed my hand. "Jake will be here soon. I won't let you go, Catie. We will take care of you."

CHAPTER 30

TRUE TO HER WORD, Illy was still lying beside me as we heard the noisy helicopter land outside, her tiny hand still clutching my larger one. Ally went out to greet them, and I could hear her mumbled voice as she gave Jake and Tadhg a quick briefing on their way into the room. An audible gasp reached my ears, and I saw the shock paralyze Tadhg's face for a moment as he entered the room and saw me, despite Ally's evident warning about my appearance. As I watched, he dry-retched and needed to turn away to get in control of his emotions. Well, that answered that question. Clearly, I looked as bad as I felt. The twins had refused to let me see myself in a mirror, unable to clean me up enough with the limited water we had, Ally grumbling that she didn't have enough sutures to even start patching me up. What clean water they carried was needed for drinking, and while I was immune, they were not. The last thing I wanted to do was expose them.

Tadhg helped Summer to carry Illy, who was looking brighter as time passed. Jake and Tadhg would transport us, and Ally and Summer would fly their craft home, meeting us there. Both needed to refuel, but Summer knew the locations.

Jake was a solid man, ex-military, and nuggety in build. The last time I saw him was at my wedding. He lifted me effortlessly from the bed, making me close my eyes and remember how Gio had carried me like this.

"We will have you back with your man soon," Jake promised as he carried me to the open door of the helicopter, every movement making me wish I was dead so the pain would stop.

"He is dead," I squeaked as he lay me on the mattress on the floor in the back, and a lone tear leaked against my will. I had promised myself I would hold it together until I was alone. But I couldn't let Jake talk about him. Not yet.

"No, he is alive. The team in Canada moved quickly and stabilized him. He was lucky. Abdominal wounds bleed quickly, and the knife perforated his liver. The liver can heal, or so they tell me. He will be okay, Catie. We will have you back with him soon. He is still recovering, but he can travel soon. I'll travel there myself to get him for you, I promise."

Alive. I lay back on the small pillow and closed my eyes as the door slammed closed, exhaling deeply. He was alive. But our baby wasn't, and I would need to tell him. I heard the door open again, then close, but I couldn't open my eyes as I processed the news. *He is alive.* The helicopter whirred into action, making it impossible to hear what Tadhg and Jake were saying up front. Probably just as well. Before he turned away, I had seen the look in Tadhg's eyes, just for a moment.

Wondering how on earth I was still alive, the shattered sack of bones all that remained.

"You know you can't tell anyone about this. What you did today."

I cracked open my eye and saw Illy seated beside me. She would have insisted. The back of the helicopter only had space for one stretcher. I lay on it as Illy sat beside me and held my hand, her sapphire-blue eyes boring into mine. She was looking healthier all the time. I just wanted this pain to stop. I wasn't sure I could deal with hours of this shaking and the noise that echoed through my shattered skull.

"If people knew you could pass on immunity to others, you would be hunted again. I can't live through that a second time. The first time nearly killed us. Your parents and me. But you were little then, and we could protect you. Your sisters are scattered everywhere now. Many have partners and children. Their own children are immune and would be a target. We can't keep them all safe. You would be like the golden egg, everyone wanting a piece."

"I ... know..." I croaked, the shuddering of the helicopter reverberating through my bones, making speaking a challenge. *Can I donate my bone marrow if I die? Should I tell her now, in case I don't make it?*

"I won't let you die," she hissed, gripping my hand. "You saved me, Caitlin. You need to hold on, my girl. I won't let you go."

I weaved in and out of consciousness, feeling the craft soaring, stopping, then soaring again. The low roar of the rotors spinning overhead engulfed me like a blanket. Finally landing, and voices, familiar voices, drifted into my zone. I fought to hear them, listen, but couldn't as I fell downward again. Bright lights roused me as I was being laid flat on a smooth, icy surface. Cracking open my single unswollen eye, I saw it was Jake lifting me. I cried out as the piercing pain crippled me, and I prayed for it to end.

Steady bleeps of machines broke through the haze, and a low soothing voice spoke to me, Mum's voice. She kissed my forehead as she and Sorcha strapped me into the MRI machine, and I felt the bed slide into the tube. *It is like a coffin*, I thought. I heard the angry exclamations in the lulls of the pounding and thumping of the machine. I closed my eyes, blocking it out.

"What?" I asked when they finally pulled me out. Mum's face was white. Sorcha's brilliant red.

"Tell me," I ordered as forcefully as possible when every breath was agony. "The truth."

Mum turned away so I couldn't see her face. Staring at my aunt, she relented. Sorcha started cataloging my injuries. "Every rib is broken, some in multiple places. Your left arm, collarbone, nose, jaw, right eye socket, and several metacarpals in your right hand. Right patella cracked and dislocated, fractured pelvis in three places. Fortunately, that last one isn't severe, as that could have been life-threatening. All of those can be fixed, although we are worried about the vision in your right eye. But it is the abdominal swelling that concerns us most. You took some beating, Caitlin, and we can't see past the swelling. We will need to operate to clean up and assess the internal damage."

Blinking away tears, I turned away. Was it not enough that these assholes had stolen my child? Would they prevent me from having more?

"Call Jorja and Katrin," Mum said to Sorcha as I closed my eyes. "We will need their help. We can't do this alone."

"Mum," I whispered as she placed the mask over my face.

"What, honey?" She removed the mask just as the edges of my vision blurred.

"Is Illy okay?"

"She is sweetheart, thanks to you. She will make a full recovery."

Mum went to place the mask on again, and I stopped her. "Mum, this wasn't random. They knew where I would be."

"What do you mean?"

"As they were … beating me, they said things that made me realize they knew more. About me. My family. That I was headed home. Things they couldn't have known. I need to tell you, now, in case."

"I'll tell Illyria. Sleep now. I'll see you on the other side. I won't leave you, Catie."

CHAPTER 31

SORCHA WHEELED ME TO the front entrance of the med center. The seated position was agonizing, even loaded up with painkillers. Dad lifted me into the vehicle, one of the few with a bench seat in the back. With Mum cradling me, he drove as slowly and carefully as he could down the bumpy dirt roads.

"Fuck, Campbell, take it easy," Mum hissed as I cried out for the eighth time. I couldn't do it. Every jolt and shudder was agony, reverberating through my bones. I could feel every break, every incision, even after a week in the hospital. "Stop for a minute, will you?"

I lay in Mum's arms, shaking from the assault of the rutted roads.

"I'll get them fixed," she promised. "I'm so sorry. We thought you were better off recuperating at home. Some privacy."

"It's…okay," I whispered as the shuddering lessened.

"Are you okay to keep moving? We will go as slowly as we can."

I nodded and braced myself, closing my eyes and trying to block the torment.

I breathed more easily when the car stopped in front of our house, and Dad's powerful arms lifted me, curling me into him. Other people's voices broke through, welcoming me home, but I couldn't deal enough to check. I buried my face in his chest, unable to look at my home, my family. He smelled so familiar, but I felt hollow. This wasn't my place. I was an imposter. Alien. Mum gently shooed everyone away as she cleared a path into the house, into their room, the only one with a private bathroom. Mum pulled back the covers as Dad deposited me into bed, stroking my hair off my face.

"Sweetheart, is there anything you need?" He spoke so softly I barely heard him. As if speaking harshly would hurt me more.

How did I say I wanted to die? I had caught a glimpse in a mirror as they wheeled me from the hospital to a vehicle to rehabilitate at home. My body was so colored I had forgotten what my normal skin tone was like. Every shade of black, blue, purple, and yellow, some bruises almost green. What skin wasn't bruised was gray from lack of oxygenated blood. Stitches in my face, hand, knee, stomach, and pins in my legs and hip where Mum had tried to repair the breaks. They had broken me and not just physically. The pain crippled Dad's face every time he saw me. He had no game face, and the guilt and despair that wracked him made me feel so much worse.

"I'm fine, Dad," I whispered, trying to force the words through my narrowed throat. "I feel terrible throwing you out of your room."

"We wanted you to have privacy." Dad smiled wanly at me. "Your own bathroom, and there is more space here for you to move around."

"You need to sleep," Mum soothed. "You need rest to heal, Catie. Giovanni will be here soon. Summer went to get him."

How could I tell her that every time I closed my eyes, I saw the dark figures spring out of the lake, grab me and pull me through the portal? Even though I knew he was alive, and was on his way here, I couldn't bear thinking about how I had seen him last. Blood pooling on his stomach, collapsing on the sand as I was dragged away. The look on his face haunted me. I didn't dare think of what he would think if he saw me now.

"Here." Mum opened her hand and held out tablets to me. "Sorry, I know they are hard to swallow." I took the large brown irregular-shaped tablets the pharmaceutical team manufactured here. I didn't care. Nothing could hurt me more than the wounds I had already suffered. The swelling around my eye had lessened slightly, and I could see better now that the headaches were under control with pain relief. My vision was blurred, but I wasn't blinded in my eye as they had initially feared, the swelling to the optic nerve being only temporary. Kat had made me wear an eye patch for nearly a week until she could assess the damage. While my vision wasn't what it was previously, she still hoped it would be temporary. Running my finger along my face, I could still feel the breaks along my cheekbone, jaw, and nose. Mum had reset them, but the ache of broken bone pierced through the dulling of the pain relief she continued to feed me.

Each day, I could hear voices in the house. Family and friends. Sera and Matt weren't yet here, but all of my siblings dropped by. Louis and his family. Xanthe, Thorsten, and Katrin. Aunt Sorcha and Di, Kendra, and Mei. Even our neighbors dropped by with meals and to visit. Finally, I asked Mum not to let anyone see me. I was embarrassed by how I looked. Each time I caught a glimpse of myself in the mirror, it was like I had been transplanted into a stranger's body. I didn't look like me anymore. My eye black, my face so colored I looked like a child's drawing.

"People care," Mum said when I begged her to keep people away.

"I can't do it, Mum. I see the pity in their faces, and I replay it over and over. I'm not ready."

"I understand."

I woke to the chatter of voices outside the window, several women and a deep male voice. Gio's voice. Mum had kept me informed of his surgery and recovery. The team acted quickly, saved him while I was still being held in the cells in Caspian. All the time I thought he was dead and wanting to join him, he was fighting to live. A few days ago, Mum told me he had recovered enough and would be here soon. Jake, as he had promised, was going to collect him from Canada, traveling in short hops to get him here to me. He couldn't travel through the vortex with a fresh abdominal wound. I told her to tell him no, stay there. But it was too late. He was on his way. The front door creaked, and I heard footsteps padding up the hallway. I couldn't face him, not like this.

The bedroom door was open, so I could call if I needed anything. The mattress dipped as he sat tentatively at the edge of the bed, gingerly to not jar his own wounds. I couldn't look at him. How could he look at me the way I was? Broken. Irreparable. I couldn't stop the tears cascading down my cheeks. I felt the soft kiss on my cheek and his warm breath, so familiar, but now so distant. I closed my eyes and froze, unable to respond. I could hear the rumble of his voice speaking to me, but I couldn't absorb the words. But I could hear the tone. Anger. Concern. Then Mum's voice. I could hear Kat too, shooing him away.

"Give her time," she was saying. "She has suffered more than any of us realize. She can't speak about it yet. Be patient with her." I closed my eyes. *Just go*, I prayed. *Leave me.* This would be so much easier if he had never come for me. I could let go of everything. If only he had left me alone.

I woke to the warm body lying beside me and instinctively thought it was Gio. But as the sweet scent of vanilla wafted over me, I knew it wasn't him. I rolled my head to check, every bone grating with the foreign movement. I had refused painkillers except to sleep, hoping they would block the horrors that haunted me. It was Illy. She felt me move and rearranged herself to not impede me. She said nothing; she was just there. We lay like that for an eternity, staring at the ceiling. A single tear rolled down my cheek. I didn't have the strength to wipe it away, so I just let it roll. Another followed, then another, until they were all falling. I felt Illy's tiny arms wrap around me as the tsunami broke, and I remembered the feeling of utter helplessness as they punched, kicked, and beat me, interspersed with memories of the beating I had endured on my seventh birthday. But this time, the overwhelming urge to protect my child had overcome every other thought. That sense of futility, but doing it anyway. Feeling him or her slip away, never having taken a breath. My mother needing to clean up what was left of her grandchild. No wonder she had called Jorja for help. Illy held me until I had nothing left, and I slept.

When I woke, she was still there.

"I'm fine," I whispered. "Go and be with Carmelo."

"Carmelo is fine. He understands and wants this. I won't leave you, Caitlin. Not until you are ready."

"What if I am never ready?" I whispered.

"Healing takes time, darling. But I am not going anywhere. We are all here for you. When you are ready."

Illy and Mum took turns staying with me so I wasn't alone. Not speaking, not asking questions, just the comfort of knowing I was safe. Nurtured. They held me as I cried, brought me water, helped me to the bathroom, cleaned my wounds, and brushed my hair. They didn't ask questions other than how I was feeling physically, Mum checking my wounds. I was glad Illy didn't ask how I was emotionally. There weren't words for that. One minute I was stone-cold and numb, the next, all the pain of what I had experienced hit me in a torrent, and I couldn't breathe.

By the eighth day at home, I could tell Illy snippets of what happened. The interrogation. The demand to join them. But I couldn't tell her what happened when I refused. The threats, holding a knife to my throat. Cutting me. Not empty threats as it turned out. I lifted my fingers and ran my fingertips across the rough stitches where they had sliced me as a warning. That time. They meant to kill me, and they had enjoyed it.

"They knew things. About me, about you. Where I was and where I was going. The timings. Someone betrayed me."

"I know. Your mother told me."

"Who?" I whispered, unsure I wanted to know. I had played all the options through my mind. Someone here? In Canada? But so few people knew Illy was my second mother, and I called her Mum. I always called her Illyria in formal meetings, never anything else.

Illy inhaled, and I sensed she knew more.

"Tell me."

"When you are strong enough."

"Now."

"Tadhg and I have spent days trawling messages and communications, both verbal and written. We found several, very simple written messages, all from the same source. All with information about you."

"Who?" I squeaked. "Who sent them?"

Illy paused before responding. "They were sent from Gio's messaging system."

In all of my suspicions, my fears, never once had I considered that my husband could have betrayed me. I turned away and stared out the window. Was it all a lie? Our marriage, our baby? But why? What would he possibly gain from sacrificing me? They had stabbed him and killed our baby. Or was it all a ruse? His wounds weren't that severe if he was here, now. Less than three weeks since they had taken me. Was he here to try again?

"Why?" I whispered.

"I said, sent from his system. I've been around long enough to know that matters aren't always black and white. I don't automatically assume anything. We will investigate. Don't jump to any conclusions."

"But it is pretty damning, isn't it?"

"On the surface of it, yes. But the messages were encrypted. Does Gio know how?"

"Likely not," I admitted, "but Matt does."

"I had thought of that. They are coming here, too, so I don't need to alarm Sera unnecessarily. They were supposed to be picked up in France with you, but with Summer deviated to collect us in Kazakhstan, and then she went with Jake to collect Giovanni, waiting for him to be well enough to travel, they have been cooling their jets in France. Sera calls several times a day and is desperate to see you. But keep this to yourself, Caitlin. No one needs to know."

"Who knows?"

"Only Tadhg and I."

"Mum?"

"No. She is too close to you. She can't be objective. Even if I can prove it isn't him, she will always harbor doubts. I can't do that."

"What about Carmelo?" I asked softly. He had been best friends with Gio and Matt's father.

"Again, no. This is not my first investigation, Caitlin. The fewer people that know, the better. Leave it with me. I will handle it."

"Are you alright?" I whispered, remembering what had happened. The pain she had endured.

"I am, and I am immune. Your mother ran all the tests, but it seems to be permanent. Thanks to you. I will be forever in your debt," she said softly beside me. "My children still have me because of you. I owe you my life, Caitlin, and I know it came at an immense personal cost."

"Ally did it," I whispered. "Not me."

"It was your idea; I heard you. So don't try to deflect Caitlin. I won't let you. You saved me, even when you were critically wounded yourself. Now that I know you have a fractured pelvis, and you allowed her to draw marrow without an anesthetic, I am blown away. If what you did was not the most selfless act I have ever known, then I don't know what is."

"You saved me too," I whispered. "I don't remember, but Ally told me you towed me through the water to the beach. Tell me what happened."

"They dropped you out of the pod first, unconscious. You were face down, and I thought you had drowned. I had no way of knowing how long you had been there, floating, when I splashed down on top of you. At first, I thought you were dead, but as I rolled you over, I realized you were unconscious, but breathing. Barely. I couldn't see your body, but I could feel the slightest movement. The water was so dark and muddy, but your face was such a mess that I wasn't sure you would make it. But you never leave a man or woman behind. I worked out the nearest shoreline and started swimming, towing you by your chin. I hoped like hell you didn't have a spinal injury, but I figured making any injuries worse was still better than being dead. Then a light kept flicking me in the eye."

"Luca's watch?"

"You remember that part. Well, I see that as his small role in saving you. As you know, Ally and Summer were in France waiting for us when they heard the message from Canada. They repositioned a satellite with Tadhg's help and were watching, but rather than wait around, flew to the coastline nearest the community and waited for days. They were watching with binoculars and saw me get dropped. After they attracted my attention, I knew where to head. They met me on the shore and carried you to that tiny medical center in town. It had been ransacked, but they carry a well-equipped first aid kit that your mother assembled for them. Bearing in mind, Ally did partly train as a doctor. I blessed your mother for that foresight."

"When did your symptoms start?"

"Not for hours. I walked with them as they carried you. We tried to clean you up but knew you would need surgery, so there was no point in doing anything but keep you comfortable and minimize possible infection as we had no antibiotics or pain relief. We called Jake, and he brought Tadhg to find us. It wasn't until later that my pain started."

"It was agony, wasn't it?"

"It was, but probably no worse than yours."

"So many people died that way."

"They did."

"I can help them. We know how."

"I said this to you before, but I doubt you remember with the state you were in. You can't tell anyone, Caitlin. No one. Not until we know who betrayed you and why."

"I just can't believe it was Giovanni," I croaked, remembering how much I thought he loved me.

"Truthfully, nor can I. But didn't you say that when your mother and I deactivated the Nexus all those years ago that his father was killed?"

"I did. The shaking caused a pump to break free of its housing and crushed him. He drowned. Gio was nine. Matteo ten."

"And the Caspians tried to drown us?"

Fuck, she was right. I turned away, unable to respond.

"I promise you. I will get to the bottom of it. I will never let this rest. But for now, it needs to remain secret, okay?"

Sera and Matteo arrived in a whirlwind of chatter. The joy, laughter, and snippets of conversations filtered up the hall, the happiness of them being home. Everyone was pleased to see them, and my stomach clenched, knowing that we had scheduled this family reunion to share our news. The front door slammed, and I heard Gio and Matt speaking rapidly in Italian as they walked past my window and caught enough words to know they were talking about me. *Perhaps it would have been easier if I had died?* I mused. They could all have attended my funeral, grieved, and then moved on with their lives. This way, I was here, under their noses, impacting everyone else's pleasure.

Despite my protestations, most days Sera sat with me, read to me. She had blatantly ignored my mother and visited me as soon as she arrived, but I could hear the pain choking her as she breathed, just being near me. Seeing me.

"You didn't need to come," I breathed when I could finally form words on the third day of her visits.

She put the book down. "I would always have come. We were planning to be here anyway, remember? Family gathering?"

"I wanted to tell you about my baby," I whispered, choking on the words I knew I would never speak again. *My baby.*

"I know." She paused, and I felt her body go rigid. "And I wanted to tell you about mine."

"Oh, Sairs, that is wonderful news," I sobbed, unable to hold back the tears. "How many weeks?"

"About thirteen."

Me too, I wanted to say but couldn't. "We would have had our bubbas together," I finally managed to say, my constricted throat strangling the words.

"Catie, I am so sorry," she sobbed into my hair. "This isn't fair. I was there too that day in Piedmont. I was equally responsible. It isn't right that you bore the brunt of it and not me."

"I am happy for you, Sairs. Truly. How is Matt taking the news?"

"Beside himself." I felt the storm cloud lift from her now that I knew. "He is ecstatic, over the moon, and won't let me do anything! You'd think I was the first woman to ever be pregnant the way he carries on."

"They are more alike than you think," I breathed, thinking of Gio talking to my stomach, not letting me drink, and getting cranky hearing I was helping the engineering team.

"They are. He is a wonderful man. They both are."

I knew what she was asking. But I couldn't let him near me. Not now.

"I need to go soon. I've already been away for three weeks. We are in the middle of so many projects. But I wanted to make sure you are okay before I go."

"I'll be fine, Sairs, really. I just need a little time."

"Why did you keep me?" I whispered to Mum as she lay beside me in the dark. She wasn't asleep. I could tell by her breathing.

"You didn't choose this life, Caitlin." She spoke so softly I had to strain to listen. "But I wanted you, all of you. When Clava offered me the babies, I wanted to keep you all. But there were so many of you. Your dad found homes with people we love and trust, our extended family. Our Caim. But you were mine the instant we laid eyes on you. Dad too. Our hearts just expanded to include you, too."

"But I am different."

"No, you are special. I knew from the beginning that you wouldn't live a conventional life. You were a trailblazer from the time you were a toddler, willful and determined as you were. Goodness, you were a handful. Your father could never control you and eventually gave up trying. Once, when you were three, you led a coup at the kindergarten because you didn't want to do music class. You told all the other kids how boring playing instruments was and forced them to boycott music too, so you could play outside."

She had told me the story before, and I forced a smile.

"I am so proud of the woman you have become, Caitlin. We both are."

"I am still a freak, Mum. What would people do if they knew what I could do? The immunity, I mean."

Mum forced out a breath. "Illy and I have been talking about that. We can't keep your immunity secret forever. Too many people know. But we can keep that part secret. That you can help others."

"Who knows? About Illy?"

"Summer and Allison, but they are sworn to secrecy. They are indebted to you for saving their mother. They won't say a word. Sorcha, your father, and me. That's it. Even Katrin doesn't know."

"Why didn't you tell Kat?"

"It isn't personal. But where do you draw the line? If you tell Kat, do we tell Louis? What if he tells Iona, and she tells Isla? I trust them all, Catie, but this is enormous. Life changing. If the wrong person hears of this, it could change everything."

"I guess."

"We won't do anything to risk your safety. Ever."

"I love you, Mum."

After ten days at home, I could sit up without feeling like I would die all over again. My ribs ached as I moved, but at least I could breathe without the pain stabbing me on every inhalation.

"Tell me," I croaked when Mum came in for her shift of sitting with me, suddenly needing to know. "What lasting damage is there? Will I be able to have children?"

Mum sighed. "We don't know, Catie. When your swelling subsides, Jorja will check. She worked half the night to save your right ovary. The left was damaged beyond repair. But we are hopeful your right is still functioning. I hope you don't mind us asking her to assist."

"No," I whispered. "I don't mind." After all that had happened to me, what was one more procedure? One more invasion. "Can she tell me now?"

"I'll call her and get her to come this afternoon. It has been two weeks, and you are healing well. She might be able to tell, but there are no promises."

"I know."

"Catie, I know I don't speak of this, but did you know I suffered from post-traumatic stress disorder after what happened to me?"

Rolling on the pillow, I turned my head to look at her. "No. I didn't know."

"Ordinarily, I wouldn't talk about it. It is in the past, and honestly, I don't like to think about it. But I thought maybe you might like to hear that you aren't alone. I've been there, and if it is any consolation, I do understand."

"How did you get through it? The dark times?"

Mum sighed so deeply I thought she had no breath left. "It took me a very long time," she finally admitted. "Years. You know some of it, but I can fill in the blanks if you need me to. Someone we knew took Louis, shot your father, and Luca. Then Illy and I were kidnapped when we went looking for Louis. They held us prisoner, injected us with all sorts of drugs, and operated on me without my consent. Twice. Stole eggs from me. A lot of eggs, as it turns out, although I didn't know that at the time. Then we were let go. I made it back home with Louis, and Illy learned she was pregnant with Alasdair."

"Did they harm her? Illy I mean."

"No. She was collateral damage. It was me they wanted."

"She was collateral damage for me too," I mumbled. "So was Gio. I can't believe she has been harmed twice, and neither time was her fault."

"Nothing that happened was your fault, Catie, not one thing. It took me a long time to accept that what happened to me wasn't my fault either. I blamed myself for years. There is more to it. While we were being held prisoner, a man there molested me, assaulted me, and I screamed. He broke my nose and my cheekbone. That action saw him expelled from Clava and us released. But that was ultimately why he sought revenge against me, and the form that took was hunting you and your sisters. Because of him, Ceri, Soli, and Beth were murdered. For many years, I blamed myself."

"You screamed because a man attacked you? How could you possibly have known he would come after us?"

"I didn't. But like you and Kat, I have a sharp tongue. I said some cutting things. Nasty things. I should have shut up and said nothing. But I have always wondered if I had kept my mouth closed if your sisters would still be alive."

"Oh Mum. You are not to blame for what happened."

"But guilt isn't logical, Caitlin. Then when you were six, I went back to Clava to train as an orthopedic surgeon. Things were different by then. It had been years, and I thought I would be over it. But that was when the nightmares started, the flashbacks. I hadn't really dealt with it, you see. I came home, and your father was healing after being shot. Illy was struggling after Luca was murdered and learning she was pregnant. The next thing we know, we have all of you to raise. So I didn't work through it. So when I was there, even though it had been six years, it all came back in a rush. A sound could trigger memories of the clang of handcuffs against the metal bars of the bed. A whiff of anesthetic gas could torture me with the memories of being operated on, restrained."

"What did you do?"

"I was alone when I was there. I left you with your father so I could study and train. I tried hard to bottle it up. Then I came home."

"Was it better being here?"

"Well, I turned into a stone-cold bitch, according to Illy. I was horrible to your father and blamed him for marrying Laetitia, even though logically I knew that wasn't his fault. I couldn't deal with the numbness that had paralyzed me. Then I left him."

"I remember that," I said, thinking. "People said you had a new boyfriend. I remember getting into a fight with a boy from Garynahine over it. I said you would never leave my dad, and he said he had seen you kissing another man."

"You never told me that!"

"Was it true?"

"Kind of. It wasn't serious, I mean. I started seeing someone else, a surgeon from Clava. Yes, we kissed, but that is all. I never cheated on your father."

"I have a memory of you and Dad getting back on the yacht when we were headed to Australia, happy. Was that it?"

"Your aunt and Illy decided that your father and I needed some time alone, to … reconnect." Mum smirked. "They said that they would not travel across the world with us scowling at each other. Well, it worked. We spent a week alone on that deserted island and worked out why we loved each other. We have never been apart after that."

"Did Dad know? About the other man?"

"He did. I told him everything, Catie. We keep no secrets. How I felt hollow, like an egg, brittle but empty inside. I built a wall around myself, kept myself safe from shattering the shell. If I didn't let anyone in, then they couldn't hurt me. I blamed your father when he did nothing wrong. It took me a very long time to work through the pain, the betrayal, and the feelings of helplessness. Feeling like I didn't fight hard enough. But eventually, I worked through it, and you will too. You will come out the other side stronger. But you need to share your feelings with Giovanni. Don't do what I did and shut him out. He is a survivor in this too."

"Survivor?" I asked blankly.

"You need to see yourselves as survivors, not victims. It is an important distinction. A victim is passive, someone who had something done to them. A survivor is an active choice, someone who experienced great pain and loss, as we have, but rises above it. Thrives. You can choose to be a victim or a survivor, Catie. It is your choice."

I nodded, understanding. "How long does it take?"

Mum looked me deep in the eyes. "There is no set timeframe, but I am going to tell you something that someone wise told me, and it helped a great deal. Healing isn't linear. You have good days, then awful days. You think you are fine, and then out of the blue, something turns you into a mouse scurrying into a hole to hide. But you will rise, Catie, and you will conquer. You are a powerful woman. I know you will overcome this. Rise from the flames."

"Like a phoenix?"

"You used to love that story when you were a child." Mum grinned. "Especially after what happened to you in Australia. You made me read that book to you every night."

"Do you still have it?"

"I think so. I will look for it. Why? Do you want it?"

"I do. I want to read it again."

Jorja arrived mid-afternoon with a small ultrasound machine.

"It isn't as good as the one in the clinic," she warned me. "But I can get an idea if that is what you want."

"I need to know," I whispered. If I knew I was barren, I would need to let Gio know. Let him choose what he wanted with all the options in front of him.

Mum held my hand as Jorja set up the equipment, lifted my nightdress, and ran the cold gel on my now flat stomach. I closed my eyes, not wanting to see their faces, to hear the inevitable. They were silent for the longest time, and I could feel the wand move, then stop and push down slightly as Jorja sought a clearer image. I could feel Mum's breathing stop and start again. Finally, Jorja lifted the wand, replaced it in the holster, and wiped my stomach.

"Well?" I asked, opening my eyes.

Jorja looked me in the eye. She had always been forthright, and I appreciated it. I didn't want half-truths. "There are no guarantees for any of us, Caitlin. I need to start with that. The healthiest of women can struggle to conceive, sometimes for no logical reason. There are so many factors at play. But as you have conceived once, the odds are good for conceiving again. Your left fallopian tube is damaged, likely permanently blocked. But your right appears sound. The surrounding swelling has gone down, and it appears intact. The good news is you only need one. You will be fertile every second month, but that is enough. Some women with only one functioning ovary produce eggs every month anyway, sometimes more. The body is wonderful at adapting."

I nodded and closed my eyes.

"Is that what you needed to hear?" Mum whispered in my ear.

"It is. Thank you."

"Where is Giovanni?" I asked Illy when she took over her shift with me.

"With Carmelo and Matt. Do you want to see him?"

I ignored that question, still not knowing the answer. "Is he okay?"

"He is doing well. He is strong, and your mother says the med team in Canada did a great job. He is still in some pain, but he will make a full recovery."

Exhaling, I accepted this. He would be fine.

Illy cut into my silent thoughts. "I have questioned him, and Caitlin, I think he is in the clear. It broke him seeing you. You can't fake that kind of grief and rage. Gio wanted to go there and kill them all with his bare hands. Carmelo would have helped. He is more like Luca than I realized in that way, defending his kin. Gio is a mess. He hasn't eaten or slept in days, which isn't good for his healing. He keeps asking to see you. But you need to be ready."

"Does he know the messages were sent from his account?"

"No, but he knows something is up. I grilled him for three hours, Catie. He knows someone is behind this. I would bet my life it wasn't him though."

"Does he know? About the baby?"

"He does, and that is one of the other reasons I genuinely believe it wasn't him. He is truly heartbroken. I hope you don't mind me telling him. I thought it better that he heard it from me. Your mum couldn't do it, or your dad, so I did."

Bile rose into my mouth as I thought of the joy on his face when I had told him he was to be a father, and now? We had nothing and likely never would again. I turned my face to stare out the window. I could see Louis' children playing on the grass with a skipping rope.

"Tell him to go home, back to Piedmont. I am broken. He can do better."

"I will not."

"Please. How can he possibly want me now?"

"He loves you, Caitlin. He is here, despite not being recovered himself. He wants to help you. You will get through this, I promise. It will take time, but you will recover. You are strong. So many people love you and are supporting you. You need to let them. You will overcome this."

The following day, Sera came to say goodbye. Matteo lurked awkwardly in the doorway.

"I will stay if you want me to," she whispered, and I could hear the grief making her voice raspy. This was torture for her, wanting to stay with me, but knowing that her being here caused me pain. I remembered Illy's words about putting my husband first. I didn't know what would become of Gio and me, whether we would make it or not. But I didn't want her to also feel guilty about the demise of my marriage. Bracing myself, I spoke as bravely as I could.

"You need to go. They need you there. But I want news, reports, please. Regular updates on you and the baby. Ultrasound pictures. I am happy for you, truly."

"I know, Catie," she sobbed. "I just wish it was both of us."

I looked up at Matt and beckoned him into the room. He lingered awkwardly beside my bed, and I forced a smile. Usually, he would have hugged me, kissed me, but he kept his distance, knowing I was broken, and not just physically. I sensed he was bursting to say something about Gio and my refusal to see him, so I got in first.

"Take care of my sister and my niece or nephew," I spoke as clearly as I could. "I can't wait to meet them."

"I will," he promised. "Take care of yourself, okay?"

I nodded, but every movement caused me pain, so I wasn't really sure how to do that.

"Safe travels."

Sera knew me well. She cradled me to her, and I just felt the slight hard bump under her top. I tried not to grimace, remembering how my stomach had felt just a few weeks ago. Now it was black with bruising and riddled with stitches like a badly stitched blanket.

"Stay safe," I whispered in her ear. "Both of you."

"Call me, Catie. Please," Sera pleaded.

"I will. Just let me get out of bed, okay?"

CHAPTER 32

MUM FORCED ME TO start rehabilitation, which was initially taking slow walks around the house with crutches, Dad, Mum, or Illy supporting me. Soon I progressed to the garden, struggling with the uneven ground. I glimpsed Gio watching from a distance as I focused on not falling but just wished he would leave me. Move on. Meet someone else. Go back to Piedmont and start afresh, even Canada. Rehabilitation was excruciating. Every tiny movement hurt, and I spent much of my time angry and swearing at my inability to perform regular movements, but I enjoyed the fresh air and sunshine, and enjoyed sitting outside for longer periods. The smell of pine trees and the heather on the hills in the distance. Home. Being alone, away from people, was soothing, but unexpected sounds made me jump.

You fucking idiot, Caitlin, I berated myself as I rested on a bench Dad had made years ago and stared down the valley. *There is no one here. No one will hurt you.* But I had thought that before, on Kiewa, when Aunt Di's nephew had tried to murder me. Maybe

I was a freak. A monstrosity. Perhaps when all was said and done, I shouldn't have been born. A genetic aberration.

A lone tear escaped, and I wiped it away angrily. Victim or survivor. I pondered those words. I was both, in truth. Right now, I felt like a victim. Would I ever be able to look back and feel like a survivor? But was it worth it if I was alone?

"For fuck's sake, can I have real food?" I grumbled as Dad appeared with a tray of soup and pureed apple.

Dad glanced at me, his eyebrows raised, but said nothing about my language. I had earned a free pass, at least for a little while.

"I suppose you are using up all the manky apples on me, keeping me *regular*," I sniped, mimicking my mother's words.

Dad sat on the side of the bed. "You can have solid food when Mum says your jaw can chew," he said softly. Before I could respond, he gazed out the window. "Did you know, before we came here, when I was young, nearly everyone bought fruit and vegetables at shops?"

I grimaced and nodded, recognizing that Dad was about to start a long-winded and likely boring story of "life before." But I had nowhere to go, so I humored him.

"You did. You said people bought everything."

"Did I tell you that shops only sold perfect food? You know, apples with no marks or blemishes, perfectly shaped carrots."

Now I was interested. "Seriously? Every third carrot is oddly shaped!" As children, we had made a game of identifying what carrots looked like—a person hugging a book, conjoined twins, or other weird creation.

"The level of waste was extreme. Most foods were categorized as first quality and second quality. First was sold as fresh food. People wanted perfect apples, tomatoes, that sort of thing. The seconds were often used to make frozen food or cooked into dishes. But so much was wasted. Crops were designed to all ripen at the same time to minimize picking labor. Many species were picked unripe so they could ripen on the way to the shops. Tomatoes, for instance, were picked green and then gassed to turn red. It could take weeks for food to make it from the farm to the distribution center and to a shop. Then people would want green bananas, so they didn't overripen within a day or so of buying them. That meant the entire process took weeks."

Now he was speaking my language. "Why did people want perfect food? How ridiculous! You can pick twenty apples. They all look different, but taste the same."

"It does, but I guess people wanted perfection."

"I'm pleased you didn't throw imperfect people away then," I muttered, thinking of how I looked. Every day, new bruising came to the surface, adding to the mottled layered effect.

"We did, in a way."

That shocked me, so I turned to Dad and awaited his next comment. He saw me waiting for further explanation.

"The world wasn't set up for people who weren't mainstream," he explained. "Anyone who was slightly different found life challenging. Disabilities, either physical or hidden, were particularly challenging. People in wheelchairs or with low mobility found uneven ground challenging. There were laws, rules in some places that meant buildings had to have a ramp instead of stairs, or use braille on money so blind people could read the notes, but it wasn't universal. Most people didn't think of how basic functions affected people. I had a lovely friend at university who was studying journalism. She was super smart, but she was albino, and legally blind. Legally blind differs slightly from totally blind. I'm not sure about other countries, but in Australia, it meant that the person could not see at six meters what a normal-sighted person could see at sixty meters. Julia could see but needed a large font on a computer screen. People treated her like she was different, but she wasn't, other than her physical appearance. But people with hidden issues were equally isolated. People didn't understand depression, anxiety, autism. Mental health was not something we understood. It wasn't talked about." Dad stared off out the window.

Dad had a form of autism called Asperger's Syndrome, and while he never discussed it, I knew he struggled with change, noise, and large groups of people. Over the years, we had all made small modifications without even noticing. Not bringing someone home without notice. Not changing plans at the last minute. Mum had often thought Louis also had Asperger's, but with no one here to assess it, no one bothered. We just accommodated his quirks.

"Was it so hard?"

"It really was. I am so pleased we came here and people accept everyone for who they are. Like the food we grow where nothing is wasted, now everyone is valued. We accept people for who they are, not what they look like or who they love."

Except me. The thought popped into my head unexpectedly, and I pushed it away. Dad felt bad enough about what had happened. I didn't need him to know that I felt persecuted because I was different. A freak.

Dad looked at me. "You need to let him in, Catie," he said in a voice so low I had to strain to hear him. "He is struggling, badly. He wants to help you, but he doesn't know how. It is killing him. Each day, he dies a little more. I felt like that when your mother was taken and held captive in Clava. She used to have terrible nightmares, flashbacks. I wanted to fix it for her but couldn't. I felt so helpless, not knowing what she needed. Just let him be there for you. Please."

"Give me time."

"Catie, sometimes time is taken away from us."

CHAPTER 33

FLASHBACKS CONTINUED TO PLAGUE me. Shadows and random noises made me jump, forcing me to constantly berate myself for being a fool. I was safe. This was my home. Nothing could happen to me here. Logically, I knew that. Although I couldn't shake the feeling of unease. My sisters had been targeted in their homes once before. Still, I found myself avoiding dark corners, and my heart raced when I strayed out of earshot of home. Night was the worst. The eerie silence, the wind buffeting the dome, and muffled scratching sounds outside jerked me awake, sweating, remembering the hood being thrown over my head, being thrown into the portal, not knowing where I was being taken. Skeletal fingers clutched at my clothes and dragged me under the dark, murky water. Recent events blended with the beating and near drowning I had sustained as a child. The nightmares intermingled, and once again, I was running, screaming, trying to escape the blows raining down on my body, helpless to stop it. Strong arms reached for me, plucked me from the melee, and held me tight, blocking the fists and booted feet that continued to strike at me. I curled into a ball, making myself as small as I could, but I felt warm, safe. When the terror stopped, it was Gio holding me, his face ashen and distraught.

"What did they do to you?" He gasped as he held me against him as I wept, agony etched into his handsome face. I wanted to comfort him but couldn't. The shadows were still there, lurking in the corners, reaching for me. Pulling me down. I clung to him as they threatened to drown me once more.

"Leave me," I sobbed. "Go. I am lost. You need to leave."

"Never," he hissed in my ear, his arms tightening. "You are mine, and I am yours. I won't let them take you."

"Why would you want me?" I whispered, so softly I wasn't sure he heard. "I am broken. I can never again be that woman you loved."

"I love you with every heartbeat. I will walk beside you every step of the way. Is that not enough?"

Honestly, I wasn't sure. With every breath, I was conflicted; I clung to him but was equally desperate to push him away, wanting to be alone where no one could hurt me. I was irrevocably changed. *Is love enough?*

Gio refused to leave me, and over the following days and weeks, I could describe snippets of what had happened. What Caspian was like or the little I had seen. The demand to join them, to help them achieve their goals of conquering other communities. My refusal and the threat that unless I joined them, I would die, and Illy too. Knowing that I could never betray his people by defecting. Seeing Gianni in my dreams. Remaining conscious as they stole a life from me, asking me one last time to reconsider my choice as I lost consciousness. Spitting the blood and loose teeth from my mouth and snapping my reply. Then waking in the abandoned clinic beside Illy, knowing I was alone.

"Did they touch her?" Gio choked as I paused during one particularly difficult part of the story.

"Not really. They slapped her around a little, left some bruising as they threw her out the pod, but she suffered no broken bones or serious injury. The main interrogator, the one who spoke some English, Viktor, sneered at me that she was an old woman, and it was beneath them," I croaked, struggling to form the words. "She was collateral damage. So were you. It was me they wanted. They wanted to parade me in front of her, taunt her, proving I had chosen them. She was taken just to prove they could. That we aren't safe anywhere and their powers reach beyond their own community. She was only there as they wanted to flaunt my defection to her, to the Collective."

"But you didn't."

"I did not. But Gio, your wounds, hers. They are all because of me and what I did."

"I would endure that pain again to know my people are alive, and so would she. Caitlin, you did nothing wrong. They are animals, and they will pay."

"What does Illy have planned?"

"I don't know, but Carmelo and I will make sure they are punished for this."

"You can't. That is revenge. Revenge will cause more retribution against others. Let it go."

"How can you say that? They kidnapped my wife and murdered my child. I can't forgive this."

"I didn't say I had forgiven them. I don't think I ever will. But you can't go after them. That would endanger others, and I can't be responsible for that."

"You are an amazing woman," he breathed into my ear.

No, I am a broken one. I don't think I will ever be the same as I once was. But Mum's words echoed in my head. *Healing isn't linear.*

"Will you take me home?" I whispered, surprising even myself. I couldn't deal with the looks of sympathy every time I hobbled out the door. I still couldn't look at myself in the mirror, the yellows and purples of the deep bruising still staining my face. Dad meant well, and I loved him dearly. But I could see him swallow the lump in his throat every time he saw me. Guilt that he couldn't protect me. Again. It was torturing him. I could heal in Italy, away from the daily visitors. Maybe in time, Gio and I could find each other like Mum and Dad did.

"Piedmont?" Gio looked at me, surprised.

"Yes. But before we go, there is something I need to ask you."

"Anything."

"I have the capacity to make you immune," I whispered. Gio stared at me, perplexed.

"Immune?" he choked.

"When Illy and I were dropped from the moon pool under the Caspian community, we were both exposed to the protozoa. It didn't affect me, although they didn't know that. I was unconscious, and Illy towed me to shore. She saved my life, but she was infected by the lake and swallowed cysts of the protozoa most likely. Ally, who trained as a doctor, gave her some of my blood. A lot of my blood."

"You were badly wounded. Why would they take your blood?"

"I insisted. She was dying."

"So were you. She told me about your wounds. Your mother showed me the records. It is a miracle you are alive."

"I had it in my power to save her. I thought you were dead, the baby too. I didn't care what happened to me."

Gio snuggled closer, and I knew the loss of our child hurt him. "What did they do?"

"Ally took nearly a liter of my blood and gave it to Illy. But that didn't work."

"It is too much!" he declared. I ignored him.

"So I insisted they took some of my bone marrow, to access my stem cells. It was all I could think of."

"Bone marrow?" Gio could barely force the words through his constricted throat.

"Maybe it was the marrow, maybe both combined. We still aren't sure. But now Illy is immune. The virus doesn't affect her. Like me, she can drink the water, swim in it, and she will be fine. I want to do this for you."

"Why?"

"Because if we have any chance of a future together, I need a goal. I need to look forward to something that isn't lying in this bed and hobbling around the garden. I want to take you swimming in the ocean. Dance in the rain. Stand in a snowstorm and catch snowflakes on our tongues. But most of all, I need to know that no matter what happens to me, you will be safe. If anything ever happens to us again, I know you will survive." I choked, struggling with the next words. "If we have children, they will be immune. I want that to be my gift to all of you."

Gio's face was ashen. "I can't. I can't let you go through pain again. The extraction of bone marrow is painful. I'm horrified they did that to you."

"I asked Mum. She said stem cells can be taken from several places, but she thinks only cord blood and bone marrow will work. She has studied Illy's blood and thinks it is a combination of the blood transfusion and the stem cells, so Illy likely can't be a donor, but I can. I think she called it hematopoietic stem cells."

"*Angelo mio*, no. I can't. I will not let them take more marrow from you. Not so soon. But it is more than that. You can't ever let people know you can do this. You will be a target, forever."

"I know. It is a blessing and a curse. But I trust you, and I want this. Being immune saved me and Illyria. We will now collect the stem cells from the umbilical cord from immune children when they are born, so we can inoculate more widely. It needs to be secret, for now. But Gio, I need to do this. For you."

"I would love nothing more than to dance in the rain with you, *amore mio*. But it can wait until you have healed. You can't even walk without crutches; you are in pain all the time. I watch you. I hear you cry out as you move at night. I will not put you through any more procedures."

"If we are to return to Italy, it can't wait. Other than you, I only trust my parents, my aunt, and Illy with this knowledge. They have always known about me, but I can't let anyone else know. None of the other med staff know, even here. Not even my siblings know. It needs to be done before we leave here. Tomorrow."

Gio smirked at me. "You have already made this decision, haven't you?"

"I have. They will bring the equipment here, so no one will know. It takes a few hours."

"Are you sure this is what you want?"

"It is. You stayed when I pushed you away. You could have left, gone with Matt and Sera, and you didn't. This is my thank you."

"Mum, how much do you think it will take to make Gio immune?" I asked as she withdrew my marrow. She had injected me with a local anesthetic this time, and while I could feel the needle being inserted, at least it didn't hurt. It was a strange sensation, feeling the needle pushing into my bone, sensing the pressure, but no pain.

"I don't know. We need to experiment. Why?"

"I want this for you. Dad, my family. I'm just wondering."

Mum didn't look up from my hip. "That is very noble, but I can't use you as a guinea pig, Caitlin."

"What is a guinea pig?"

Mum stifled a laugh, trying to stay focused. "I forgot you wouldn't know. In our life before, companies used to test medications, cosmetics, and a range of products on animals. Rabbits and guinea pigs were common. They kind of look like a large rat with small ears, but people used to keep them as pets."

"Why would they test on animals? What an awful thing to do!"

"It was. But there were strict rules about allowing people to use medicines and products, and companies needed to prove they were safe. So they did testing regimes on animals. But the expression, 'to be used as a guinea pig' means being used to experiment on. I don't want to use you for that, Caitlin. Your body has suffered immense trauma and is still healing."

"I just meant, if you could take the same volume from me and make three of you immune, isn't that better?"

Mum withdrew the needle and placed a pad of cotton on my hip. "Hold that firmly," she instructed as she turned to deal with the contents of the syringe. "If Giovanni was willing, we could inject him with a smaller quantity, then test his blood for immunity. The testing isn't hard. We just don't know how long it takes for the stem cells to reprogram and for his body to become immune."

"Not long, I would think. Illy recovered quickly."

"That was from the infection, not full immunity."

"True. I'll talk to him, but I think he would be okay with a smaller dose and regular testing. He is a doctor, so he could do it himself if you taught him how. What is your best guess?"

"Somewhere between two weeks and twelve is typical. Illy recovered quickly from the infection, as you know, but she was immune after two weeks, so I think it won't take long. The quantity required is the tricky part. Ally took a lot from you, so we don't know if that made a difference. Regardless, we can send the test strips with Giovanni to Piedmont. He can test himself each week and keep me informed. It is simple enough.

He can also inject himself in increments, so we can work out what is the tipping point. Illy is coming with you, so she can keep me apprised."

"I wish you could come, Mum. Dad too."

"We will visit, I promise. But when you are well enough to show us around. Deal?"

"Done."

CHAPTER 34

"ARE YOU WELL ENOUGH for an outing?" I asked Gio that evening.

"I am. Are you?"

"I am in pain all the time," I admitted. "It makes little difference where I am. But before we leave, I want to show you something. Mum says tonight is a good time, but we need to move away from the lights of the houses."

"In the dark? Are you sure?"

"We will drive if you can manage it. My hip and knee won't let me just yet. We will need to take one of the larger ones with the back seat so I can lie down a bit."

Gio's eyes lit at the thought of driving. Unlike me, who had grown up with the golf carts and electric vehicles, they were still novel for him. "Tell me where."

"The stones at Callanish."

"At night? We won't be able to see them."

"That isn't what we are going to see."

"What then?"

"Trust me."

"I trust you with my life. Let's go."

Dad insisted we pack some blankets, a picnic, and a thermos of tea. He handed the bag to Gio as we hobbled out to the vehicle; me using a crutch on one side, and Dad supporting me on the other. Gio was moving awkwardly himself, I noted, but refused to discuss his own wounds. In fact, I realized with a shock, I hadn't even seen his stab wound yet.

"Park here," I directed, pointing toward the small carpark at the back of the stones, up a steep track. Gio carried the bag and helped me hobble along slowly on my crutches over the uneven grassed ground. It was slow going in the dark, but we were in no rush.

"There." I pointed with my chin toward the small clearing, needing both crutches for support.

Gio spread the blanket where I showed him, facing the loch, the stones before us.

"What…"

"Wait," I said, slowly maneuvering myself into a position where I could lower myself onto the ground.

Gio sat behind me, his back against a flat rock, and lowered me slowly. As I sat on the blanket, he wrapped his legs around me. I felt his arms embrace me, supporting me to sit upright against his chest. It was painful, but I wanted to share this with him before we left. I had no idea when we would return. If we ever would be here again, together. He lowered himself backward slowly, resting against the rock, his own wounds not yet healed.

"Watch." I gestured toward the sky, seeing the colors start to change.

I felt the gasp as the sky changed color, the brilliant greens, blues, and purples of the northern lights putting on their show. It grew brighter and more luminous as we watched.

"What is this?" he breathed incredulously in my ear.

"Aurora Borealis. The northern lights," I spoke softly, not wanting to overshadow the magnificent show they were putting on.

"Why have I never seen this before?" he whispered, mesmerized.

"Italy is too far south," I whispered back, not wanting to overshadow the show. "It is a northern hemisphere thing, although there is one in the southern hemisphere too. It happens when electrons and protons, charged particles, alter trajectory in the magnetosphere plasma."

"No," Gio whispered. "This is *la magia*. Magic."

As we watched, I unscrewed the lid to the thermos and sipped. I gasped. I thought Dad had sent tea but realized it was hot chocolate. I closed my eyes as the velvety liquid oozed down my sore throat and took another sip before handing the thermos to Gio.

I glanced up to see his face in the colored light as he tasted the rich, silky liquid. His face was priceless.

"Is this?"

"Hot chocolate. Dad's doing, to make this special. He knows I can't drink alcohol yet. Mum refuses to let me."

"So why is it you listen to your mother about not drinking wine, yet ignore me?"

"Have you met my mother?"

Gio laughed softly and took another sip before offering the thermos back to me.

"It's fine. Have some more. It isn't my first time."

Even in the dark, I sensed he was desperate to savor more of this luscious liquid, but equally wanted to share it with me.

We watched the aurora for hours, eating cheese and drinking hot chocolate, the brilliant light show constantly changing colors. Swirls and curves filled the night sky. I felt Gio's lips touch my crown, and I closed my eyes, enjoying the sense of closeness. Away from the noise and constant interruption of the house. Just as we thought it was ending, another intense display of color would burst into the night sky, illuminating the standing stones.

"Thank you, *amore mio,*" he breathed. "Thank you for sharing this with me. I will never forget it."

"I have seen it a few times," I admitted. "But every time, it captivates me again. It is like I am seeing it for the first time. It isn't common here, but you can see it when the conditions are right. This is my favorite place, with the stones and the lights dancing behind them."

"I love it. Truly."

"When I was a child, I saw the Aurora Australis, the southern lights. They were equally magical, although not quite as vibrant. I only ever saw them once as we headed south near Antarctica. But we stood on the deck of the yacht, and it was like I could reach out and touch them, the lights dancing around me."

My stomach twinged, and I tensed, rearranging my position to conceal the pain.

"Do you want to go?"

"No. I wanted you to experience this. We can stay as long as you want."

"But you are in pain?"

"I am always in pain," I admitted. "At least here I am distracted. We can stay until you have had enough."

"I will never tire of this," Gio sighed, his arms holding me firmly against his chest. I lifted my face up to be kissed. He was warm and gentle, his lips brushing over my damaged eye, nose, and jaw. I relaxed, just slightly, wondering if we would make it.

CHAPTER 35

AS WE STEPPED OUT of the lift onto the Soggiorno deck, people stopped and stared. Not only that we had been gone for a year, and our return had not been announced to anyone, but at my appearance. Kendra had offered to put on some makeup before I left, hide the worst of it, but I refused. In our twice-weekly therapy sessions, Illy had spoken to me at length about the five stages of grief, and I recognized I was finally in the acceptance phase. I didn't need to hide. I had done nothing wrong.

But standing just out of the way, balancing on my crutches, I watched fearfully as the others carried the bags out of the lift, though I wasn't sure what I was scared of. Friends and colleagues shook Gio's hand, greeting me warmly.

We started to make our way through the main deck toward the accommodation pods, Gio hovering close in case I stumbled. Carmelo brought up the rear with Illy, chatting away merrily with everyone he saw. As we plodded through the room, a gleeful child's voice called, "Caitlin!"

I slowed and leaned on my crutches. Gianni walked toward me using his leg braces.

"No crutches!" I said, smiling widely.

Gianni beamed and practiced his English. "I help you."

"That is very kind. Gio, can you give Gianni a bag to carry for us, please?"

Gio grinned and handed him a backpack, which he proudly strapped on his back. As he walked alongside, chattering away, I assessed his movement. *I need to make some adjustments,* I thought, watching the slight hyperextension of his knees. Even with my discussion with Joseph about monitoring and adjusting them regularly, they still weren't quite right.

It was slow going across the enormous open space, and I was tiring rapidly. Gio sensed it and hovered ever nearer, but the doorway to the accommodation was only a few meters away. A gasp reached my ears, and I glanced up from watching Gianni to see Francesca, who had entered the Soggiorno deck from the doorway directly in front of us. She had been looking down at a tablet, her long dark hair obscuring her face, and she hadn't seen me until she was almost on top of us. I flicked my hair back, ignored her, and kept walking, as gracefully as I could under the circumstances. Behind me, a sentence was fired in angry, rapid Italian that I couldn't follow. But the voice. I knew the voice well.

Pivoting on my crutches, I saw Illy, standing roughly at Francesca's chin, booming at her in Italian, shaking with wrath. Francesca was red-faced, shaking her head, trembling, denying something, and unable to make eye contact with the warrior rising before her. From where I stood, slightly off to the side, I could see them both clearly. Francesca was terrified, and I had seen that look on Illy's face far too many times. She was on the warpath. I was pleased for a moment that it wasn't me she was fuming at. A small crowd was gathering, watching intently, gasps of shock rumbling through the crowd.

"What is it?" I whispered to Gio, who had stopped and was watching, his face rapidly turning purple. "What is she saying?"

"It was her," he breathed between gritted teeth. "She did it."

"Did what?" I was feeling a little cranky and only partly from pain and exhaustion. Everyone could follow the conversation except me. I had no idea Illy's Italian had become so good so quickly.

Illy had a hand to Francesca's throat, but no one was defending Francesca. I looked around at the increasing group of spectators, and they were all standing there, agape. Illy was bellowing, pointing at me, and then returning her attention to Francesca.

"What is she saying?" I urged, feeling like I was the only person who couldn't understand. Even Gianni looked horrified. Gio snapped his attention back to me and gently encouraged me toward the accommodation pods.

"No." I stood my ground, refusing to budge. "I want to know what is going on, and I want to know *now*!" I growled, letting my frustration show. "Tell me what the fuck is going on!"

Gio assumed a neutral expression as he plucked the crutches from under my arms, taking me by surprise as he deliberately dropped them on the floor, knowing I couldn't bend down to reach them. I scowled at him as I teetered on my shattered hip.

Grinning, he purposefully dropped the bags he was carrying, scooped me up against his chest, and carried me through the final steps of the Soggiorno deck amidst cheers and whoops of encouragement. My face flushed, although I had no doubt the redness couldn't be seen past the deep blues and purples still staining my face. I beat angrily on his chest, but he ignored me. Men started calling after him in Italian, and Gio held me tighter, now encouraged by the audience we had attracted.

"Asshole," I snapped against his throat. "What do you think you are doing?"

"Taking you home."

"Tell me what the fuck is going on!" I was seething at being treated like a child.

"When we are inside."

Gio strode purposefully along the corridor toward our old apartment, which had been kept for us under Illy's orders. He rolled me to face his chest so I couldn't see who he was greeting as we passed, but he didn't slow. Reaching our old apartment, Gio tossed me over his shoulder, and I cried out as my broken ribs were crushed against his bones as he fumbled with the key.

"Sorry! I am so sorry," he said, slipping me down his front and balancing me with one arm as he opened the door with the other. My feet had barely touched the ground before I was whisked up again and carried into the apartment. The door closed as he purposefully deposited me on the sofa.

"You don't need to carry me," I snapped. "I can take a few steps. I'm not completely helpless."

"No one has ever accused you of being helpless, my love."

"I can walk." I tried to stand and prove my point but was firmly pushed back onto the couch.

"For goodness' sake, when will you let me take care of you?"

But you didn't take care of me. The thought crossed my mind before I could block it, and I was shocked as soon as it popped in there. He had promised me he would always take care of me. I didn't blame him for what happened.

He saw the conflict cross my face and tilted his head to the side. "What?"

"You tell me. What the bloody hell is going on? What was Mum saying?"

Gio assessed my likely reaction but spoke after a long pause, "Illyria accused Francesca of betraying you to the Caspians."

"She *what*? That makes no sense."

"When I arrived at your home, before Illy would even let me see you, she told me that someone knew where we were; they knew too much. She asked me if I had told anyone of our plans, and I said no. She grilled me, asked me if anyone had threatened me. But it was a shock to me too, what happened to us. She questioned me for ages, asking what I remembered, who I had spoken to, but she seemed happy with my answers. I thought she had let it go, but..."

"Illy lets nothing go," I said firmly. "Ever. Trust me, I know from experience."

"I can see that. Well, she believes Francesca is behind it."

"Why would she think that? How would Francesca even communicate with the Caspians?"

"Her role is in communications. She speaks a few languages, not fluently, but well enough. She could

298

easily have accessed the communique that we were headed home to Lewis that day. Then there was the message with your name on it a few months ago. Did they ever work out who sent that?"

"It was sent from your account," I admitted. "Illy told me."

"Mine?" Gio's face went blank. "I didn't send it."

"Illy worked out it couldn't have been you. We were on Lewis at the time, remember? Preparing for the wedding and then to go to Orkney? Tadhg pulled a time and date stamp, and it was a time you were helping Mum with a surgical procedure. Mum vouched for you. There was no way you could have sent it. So they knew someone was accessing your messages. They just had no idea who it was."

"Is that why you wouldn't let me near you?"

"In part." I admitted, not wanting to discuss the other reasons. "I couldn't bring myself to believe it, but it was clear the messages had been sent from your account. But when Illy cleared you, we knew someone else was behind it. How would Francesca even know how to access it?"

Gio flushed. "She probably just worked out my password."

"That simple, was it?"

"Probably," he muttered, flushed. "I changed it after we met. But it probably didn't take a genius to work it out. I never had the need to worry about it. I only ever used the messaging system to share notes with my colleagues about cases. Then later, when Tadhg and Sera boosted the capacity, I used the system to communicate with colleagues in other communities, seeking advice about treatment options, research and such. Like we did with Charlie."

I nodded. We all used the same system for work purposes, although some personal messages too.

"Did you see her face, Francesca, I mean?" he asked gruffly.

"I did. I don't know her well, of course, but she looked … guilty. Like she wasn't expecting to see us."

"She did. She was horrified when she saw you."

"I look pretty horrible," I admitted. "Besides, few people knew we were arriving today."

"You look beautiful." I felt the kisses on the top of my head, and he brushed the hair from my face, gently cupping my cheek. "This is temporary. A few colors can't mask your beauty, Caitlin."

"Why would Francesca sell me out? I don't get it. What does she stand to gain?"

Gio pulled back and raised his eyebrows. "Seriously? You don't think she is a little jealous? Angry? You flattened her that day. She used to cry over a broken nail, get stressed about split ends in her hair, and you dropped her on her ass. She wanted an apartment and marriage with me, and she ended up humiliated."

"I guess," I smirked, remembering that day. "Likely she wasn't thrilled I took her man, and then we traveled to exciting new places."

"You forget I wasn't her man when you arrived," Gio corrected. "But yes. She was always a jealous woman."

"They tried to kill me," I whispered as shame washed over me anew. "Illy and you. We are all lucky to be alive. They murdered our child. Does she really want me dead? Over that? Surely she is not that evil."

"That is what your mother will find out. And if she doesn't, then I will."

CHAPTER 36

EACH DAY GIANNI CAME to visit, and we would take slow walks together. He was far more mobile than I, and he loved chatting with me, practicing his English and my Italian. He gave me tips on using the crutches so that they didn't hurt, and I realized how many years he had used them, painfully, until I had seen him that day, shuffling through the pods. Each morning, I eagerly awaited spending this time with him, learning more about his life. He was easy to talk to. I didn't need to explain what had happened to me other than the basics. The men who had hurt his community had hurt me too for what I did to save them. He didn't grill me, and he didn't look at me with pity. Several times I recalled my vision of him in the cell, and how I had known that not accepting was the right choice. But neither his English nor my Italian was proficient enough to tell him he was the reason I was here today. Besides, that might have been too much of a burden for a child.

For the first few days after I tried to walk unaided, Gianni and I stayed in the accommodation pod, the narrow corridor walls catching me if I stumbled and fell. But soon he encouraged me to venture into the Soggiorno deck where people stopped to chat, or we could rest at one of the many tables and talk before continuing on our way. Most days we sat and drank coffee for me and milkshakes for him, the kitchen staff waiting on us, making me feel guilty.

"I will adjust those braces for you," I promised. "Tomorrow?"

"Only if you can walk that far." He grinned cheekily.

"Ooh, a challenge. I like those. I will do my best."

Since returning, Gio was asked immediately to assist the medical team, and I had insisted he go. They were keen for him to pass on the knowledge he had gained from his time on Lewis, France, and in Canada. Like Canada, there was a population explosion here, further supporting the opinion that it was linked to the trauma of invasion. Each morning, after checking I would be okay alone, he left for the medical pod. Regardless, I was rarely alone. Between Gio, Gianni, Illy, and Carmelo, plus Antonio, Fabrizio, Joseph, and all of our other friends here, I was constantly sur-rounded by people. I barely had time to sit with my thoughts before Gio was home. Secretly, I suspected a schedule had been put in place to stay with me, much like Mum and Illy sleeping with me at home.

Antonio and Joseph took it upon themselves to stay with me most days. Initially I felt guilty, keeping one of them away from work, but I came to enjoy the company. They never looked at me with sympathy. They didn't ask about my wounds or stare at the lin-gering bruises from my bone injuries and multiple surgeries. They treated me like they always had, as a valued friend. They walked with me, took me to the gym and swimming pool. Many times, one of them picked me up after stumbling, my hip or knee giving way after standing too suddenly. Even if I fell in the shower or bathroom, they wrapped me in a towel and picked me up and allowed me to maintain my dignity. But not once did they say anything that made me think they pitied me. Joseph especially took every opportunity to tease me, call me drunk, and make me laugh. If Gio was late home, one of them would stay with me, often both, knowing without being told that after everything that had happened, I was still fearful of the dark.

Riccardo called in to visit me several times, although I knew it was to keep me in the loop, to ensure I didn't withdraw completely. Illy had briefed him, I was certain, ensuring that I didn't get too far behind in my work. Mandy had left messages, but I didn't feel up to responding. The last time I had seen her was when I was being abducted, her mouth open with shock as I was pulled into the swirling vortex to Caspian. Riccardo was lovely, and we got along well. He asked me if I would take part in some project groups, steering committees, but I politely refused. I was constantly on edge, jumping at the slightest noise, being woken constantly by nightmares, leaving me exhausted. Gio wanted to help, but I couldn't let him in. I wasn't ready to tell him what they had done.

"I blame him," I whispered to Illy as she came to sit with me one afternoon after I had been for a slow swim as part of my rehabilitation. She had sent Antonio away, telling him she would stay with me until Gio came home. "It struck me out of the blue. I didn't realize that was what I was feeling. I've tried to dismiss it, but I can't help it. When I replay that scene over and over, them grabbing me, I am overwhelmed by this irrational sense that he didn't stop it. He told me he would always protect me, but he didn't. The stupid thing is, logically, I know he stood no chance. They stabbed him, and he was lying on the sand bleeding out. It all happened in the blink of an eye. But I can't get over the feeling of betrayal. Does that make sense?"

"Of course it does. Feelings aren't always logical, Caitlin. You know he couldn't have stopped it; it had been planned for months. It was always going to happen, and he had no control. But he made you a promise, and he couldn't help you."

"Planned for months?"

"Yes, but now is not the time. I will tell you all of it when it is validated. But I have a fairly good understanding of what happened. Right now, your healing is the most important thing. Tell me what you are feeling."

"I feel anger toward him, which is stupid. I saw him get stabbed. There was nothing he could have done to save me. So what do I do?"

"Nothing. Over time, you accept he had no power to change the outcome."

"Is it normal to feel this way?"

"Caitlin, I am going to tell you something that I have told no one else, including your mother. I blamed Luca for leaving me, pregnant, and for what happened to your mother and me in Clava. He swore to always protect me, to be there for me. Then, in a single day, he was gone. He kissed the girls and me goodbye at breakfast, and I never saw him again. The thoughts plagued me like they are haunting you now. Why didn't he fight harder? Wait for me? He was shot in the heart. Logically, I know he could never have predicted that. He didn't know someone would be on the docks that day. He couldn't have survived the wound. The damage was instant and fatal. But I felt anger toward him for leaving me alone. Then I felt guilt for being angry at a murder victim."

"You understand."

"I do, Catie, and from personal experience. The difference is you are here, and he is alive. So you have that reminder every day. He got off lightly, and you bore the worst of it. I think that is why we try to push people away. But you need to forgive him. He played no part in this. It is an active process, forgiveness. You need to work at it. If you don't, it will consume you."

"How do I forgive him for something he didn't even do? I can't even tell him. I can't cause him pain over something he can't fix."

"Only you can answer that, but I would suggest taking some time, somewhere private, where you won't be interrupted. Bring forth all the feelings within you, sit with them, and let them go."

"Is that what you did with Luca?"

"It is. I took long walks and talked to him. Conjured his face and told him my feelings, all of them, until they were out there in the open. When I could accept them, I could take the next step. Forgiveness."

"I can't walk. Besides, where do I go, here? There is nowhere private. Not even down at the lake anymore. I barely get ten minutes alone."

"No, but you can sit at the thermal springs. That was a special place for you both, wasn't it? I can block one room off for a day. Take food, lots of water, even your medicine if you need to. Spend the day there. I will make sure no one interrupts you."

"Will it help?"

"It will, if you use that time to drill down and identify how you really feel. Speak to him as if he were there. Speak aloud. It isn't the same to think the words. The power is in speaking them. No one can hear you there. Yell, scream, swear at him if you need to. But don't leave there until you pour out your emotions and feel calm. You can't keep pushing him away, Caitlin. He is a victim in all of this, too. He senses you blame him, but he doesn't know why. He didn't do this. I guarantee it. You risk losing him if you can't get past this."

"Can you book it for me?"

"Consider it done."

CHAPTER 37

THE FOLLOWING MORNING, AFTER Gio left for work, I took my morning walk with Gianni.

"Just a short one today," I told him. "I am tired."

"You are still in pain?" he asked in a mix of Italian and English.

"A bit," I admitted. It was true. Different things hurt on different days, and there were only so many times you could answer "Yes" to the question, "Are you in pain?" I had finally accepted I would likely always be in pain. Healing was slow and incredibly frustrating. I desperately wanted to return to normal, to get back to work and use my brain, which was rotting through lack of use, but I couldn't stand or sit for long without pain. Lying flat was the only position I wasn't in pain, but that made me feel like a patient, helpless, and that was a feeling I never wanted to experience again.

After Gianni left, I hastily packed a bag with towels, a pillow, and enough food and water for the day. Illy knocked on the door.

"Come in," I called.

"Ready?"

I nodded. "Will you stay with me for a bit?"

"I will stay for a short time. But this is a journey you need to take alone, Caitlin."

"I know."

As we walked with Illy supporting me, she asked, "Have you ever done a guided meditation?"

"I don't even know what that is. They do daily meditation here, as you know, but it is in Italian, and I don't understand most of it, so I just use the time to rest."

"Do you trust me enough to try something? It isn't quite meditation but not hypnosis either."

"Mum, I trust you implicitly. Tell me what you are thinking."

"It could be challenging but potentially cathartic. Healing, if it works. But I will ask you to bring up painful memories, so you can deal with them."

"I'll try anything," I whispered. "I don't want to lose him."

We slipped into the farthest room and locked the door.

"How are you the most comfortable?" Illy asked.

"Lying down," I admitted. "My hips hurt if I sit for too long. My knee hurts when I stand."

"Okay, let's get you comfortable."

Illy spread the towels across the sandy-sloped bank and helped me to lie down. My feet pointed toward the water, and she covered me with a light blanket, even though it was warm here. She had brought a weighted eye pillow for my eyes that smelled like lavender. As I settled, the scent was soothing and reminded me of my wedding bouquet. Dad had included lavender especially, as he grew it near his beehives, and all my childhood I had picked it, loving the scent as I crushed the small buds with my fingers. The memory of my wedding flickered in my mind, making me smile. I needed to resolve this, I knew. I couldn't keep blaming him or myself.

"Close your eyes and relax. Focus on your in breath, feel your lungs expand, and focus on your out breath, feeling your lungs contract. Inhale, exhale. I want you to see your breath as it comes in and out of your body. Clean breath in, old air out. See the process as cleansing. You breathe in the new and let go of the old as you exhale."

Following her instructions, I felt myself relaxing as she guided me to inhale and exhale. My muscles grew soft, and my body felt heavy, sinking into the earth.

"You are in complete control. Remember that you can walk away at any time. You have the power. When you are ready, I want you to remember that day in Canada. See yourself walking down the hallway, through the door and into the room." Illy's voice was low and calm and blended into the background as I saw myself walking down the underground hallway to the portal with Gio, laughing and happy that we were about to see my family.

"Feel the warmth, the steam rising off the lake. Breathe deeply. Remember the scents of the room. Hear the voices of people speaking to you, see the workers shuffling cargo. You are standing beside the lake, waiting. It is calm and still. The water is dark but safe. Can you see it?"

"Yes," I whispered.

"Good. Now the water is starting to move, slowly. It is starting to swirl. Now it is moving faster and faster. Can you see it?"

"Yes."

"I want you to slow down the vision of what happened, Caitlin. You are in complete control. You have the power to stop the vision at any point. You can step away if you need to. I want you to see what happened. Focus on the details, the sights, sounds, smells. Really look. Pay attention to the small details. Watch the steps as they happened. Nothing can hurt you now. You are standing back, watching. See it play out in front of you."

Behind my closed eyes, I saw it with crystal clarity. I was speaking with Mandy, and as the whirlpool started, she stepped back. Gio and I were holding hands, desperately happy about going home to tell our family about our news. I looked up from my bag and looked at him as the portal started, seeing if he was ready. We were looking at each other, not directly at the lake. We were in heat suits. I had just pulled the hood over my head but hadn't yet zipped it up. They were right in front of me before I even realized. Three figures completely dressed in black burst out of the swirling water, armed with knives. I could smell their breath, they were so close. The silver glinted in the artificial light. One lunged at Gio, plunging the knife into his stomach. Gio fell forward slightly as he tried to bellow, but he was winded, silenced, as he dropped my hand, clutching his stomach as he fell. He didn't even have time to raise his hands to the attacker. The other two grabbed me, one gripping each arm, still holding their knives. I could feel the knives pressing into my forearms, cutting me. With my arms outstretched under their control, I tried to pull back, turn, to run, and saw Mandy behind me, her mouth open in shock as she started down the bank toward me, Gabriel close behind. But the invaders had already turned and jumped, hauling me along with them. I screamed as I was sucked into the black hole and felt Illy's hand on my arm, her voice warm and calm in my ear.

"You are safe, Caitlin. I am here. Turn around and take another look at what you left behind. See what they did, see it clearly in your mind. Can you see it?"

I could. The last thing I saw as the cloth was pressed to my face was Gio lying on the sand, reaching for me, blood pooling through the silver suit, running down the outside. Mandy's face, blank with shock. Gabriel running.

"When you are ready, slowly wriggle your toes. Move your fingers and feel the energy return to your body. Your arms and legs are waking up as if from a deep sleep. There is no rush. You have all the time in the world. Only when you are ready, open your eyes."

Following her instructions, I slowly reinvigorated my body, surprised at how relaxed I felt. Finally, I opened my eyes and saw her sitting beside me, watching.

"Can you talk about it?"

"It happened so fast," I said, looking up at her. "We were holding hands, happy about coming home to tell you about the baby. Three of them burst through, and I wasn't looking at the lake, and with the hood on the heat suit, my peripheral vision was obscured, and I didn't see them until they were on top of us. One stabbed Gio as two grabbed me. They came through with their knives, ready to attack. It was maybe ten seconds. They knew we would be there. They were ready for us."

"They were. It was the same for me. Two of them came through, and I was grabbed and pulled in before anyone had a chance to react. How do you feel?"

"Calm," I was surprised to admit. "It would have happened no matter what I had done. It was me they were after. Only me. I am lucky Gio wasn't killed, Mandy too. I saw her come after me, but she was too far away. We were gone before she reached the edge."

"Could Giovanni have done anything to stop it?"

"Nothing at all," I admitted.

"I am going to leave you. But you need to deal with this now. Talk to him as if he were here. Tell him everything you feel, about that day, about the baby, about him. Even Francesca. Say it all aloud as many times as you need to. You are safe here. Nothing can happen to you. Use the pillow to hit, scream, cry, kick. You do whatever you need, Caitlin. Get the emotions out. You need to release them. Bottling them up is not the answer. Blow the cork off but don't leave here until the bottle is empty. Promise me?"

"I promise."

"Lock the door behind me. This is a journey you need to take alone."

With Illy's help, I pulled myself up. She held me close and turned to leave.

After locking the door, I wasn't sure what to do. Soak maybe? The images replayed in slow motion of that day, and I needed to dispel them. I stripped off and entered the water, remembering the first time Gio had brought me here. Our first time together. I had known he was special from that first night. He had made me feel alive, but now I felt dead inside.

Closing my eyes and inhaling the steam, I floated, feeling peaceful and pain-free. I felt his arms around me, pulling me toward him. That desire I felt hadn't waned until now.

"I feel broken," I told him. "I worry I will never be able to please you again." I gasped as the words escaped my mouth. It was true. We hadn't been together in weeks, since I was taken, and I was fearful that he wasn't attracted to me anymore, didn't desire me. Or was I not desirable? My visible injuries had mostly healed, the bruising nearly faded. The incisions from the surgeries were all that was left as a reminder. Now it was the internal wounds that hurt and my heart.

"I blame you for not stopping them. For letting them take me," I whispered, feeling foolish, then with no response, repeated it louder. "I blame you." Tears rolled down my cheeks, and I swam to the edge, wrapped a towel around myself, and sat on a ledge overlooking the pool.

"Why didn't you stop them?" I implored the steam filling the room. "We would still have our child." I placed my hands on my empty stomach, feeling hollow. Speaking the words was soothing, so I spoke again. "How could you let them do this to me? They killed our baby. I knew I was dying, and you weren't there to stop it. To save either of us." The tears turned to rage. But it wasn't directed at him but at them—those anonymous, faceless men and women who had done this to me.

I raged and fought, screamed, and cried, and finally, exhausted, I lay in silence, staring up at the artificial roof across the cave, the humidity dripping down in a steady patter. "I forgive you," I whispered. "I forgive me. I blamed myself. I thought I hadn't fought hard enough. But they were larger. There were more of them. They had weapons. Nothing we could have done would have stopped this."

I curled up into a ball and pictured my baby, a little girl. Instinctively, I knew it was a girl. Her sweet face ripped away as I fought to hold her, a baby head with a light covering of dark hair. "I'm sorry," I whispered to her. "I am so sorry I couldn't keep you safe, protect you, give you life and show you the world. I let you down. I will never forget you."

I lay on the sand for an eternity, stewing over everything I had lost. My child, my spark. But as I saw them in my mind, the picture shifted, and I saw everything I still had. My husband, my family. My mother and father. Sera. Illy was alive. I breathed a little deeper, knowing they were all there for me. Anger filled me once more but not at Gio—at *them*. The Caspians. They had done this. No one else. I was angry at them and what they had taken from me. But I would not let them take me. No. I would survive— thrive—despite what they had done. I would never let them win.

Slowly, I pulled myself up, sitting on the sand. The pain in my hips was nothing compared to the overwhelming urge not to let them win. I would not be a victim anymore. I would face them, and I would conquer.

Feeling calmer than I had in months, I packed my belongings, slipped out of the room, and slowly made my way back to our apartment. It was dark when I arrived, and the lights were off. I thought the living room was empty and turned to head into the bedroom. My crutch clipped the doorframe as I closed the door behind me, and I stumbled slightly from exhaustion. As I turned back to the room, I saw Gio sitting on the couch, staring out over the moonlit lake, the silvery blue reflecting off the dark surface.

"I was worried about you," he said in a low voice, turning to look at me. I dropped the bag, scared to bridge the chasm. Even after my day, filled with emotion, he was distant. He felt so far away. He stood and approached me slowly.

"I love you," I whispered. "Forever."

His arms came around me, and he kissed me, and I felt weightless, pain-free.

"Take me to bed," I whispered in his ear. "I want you. All of you."

He continued kissing me for a moment and pulled back to look at my face.

"Are you sure?"

"Positive."

"I don't want to hurt you."

"I hurt anyway," I admitted. "But I need this. I want you."

He lifted me gently, letting the crutches fall, an arm securely around my back and under my knees, and carried me to the bedroom, depositing me carefully on the bed. Slowly, he undressed me, and himself, not breaking eye contact.

"Come here," I beckoned as he stood at the side of the bed, studying me. Assessing my injuries. Reaching up, I pulled him down on top of me, carefully avoiding his weight on my ribs.

"Oh God, I have missed you," he sighed in my ear as I kissed his chest. "I want you so much."

He let me set the pace, and I pulled him into me, cautiously at first, but firmer as the familiar feelings rose within me.

"It's okay," I whispered, sensing he was holding back, fearful of hurting me. "I'm okay."

"I feel like I have my love back," Gio whispered as I lay in his arms, not sleeping. "You were here physically, but they stole your spirit that day. I was fearful I would never have you again."

"I was lost," I admitted, running my fingers through the hairs on his chest as I lay in his arms. "I blamed you for not saving me. For losing our child. But it wasn't your fault or mine. They would have done this anyway, and I am so grateful you are okay. I am alive. You are alive. We will be okay."

"But our child…"

"I think it was a girl," I said, a single tear springing to my eye. "I saw her today, spoke to her. I told her how sorry I was that I couldn't save her."

I felt him shudder beside me and knew this was hard for him. "You don't need to apologize. This was never your fault."

"Then why do I feel so guilty? I felt like I should have fought harder to save her."

"Would it help if we named her?" Gio asked after a long pause. "Then we can talk about her, keep her alive in our hearts? No one else need know, but we would. So we never forget."

"It would," I admitted, snuggling closer. "I would like that. I never want to forget our first child."

"Stella means star," he whispered in my ear. "Every time I see the night sky, I think of her watching us."

"Stella," I repeated. "I love that. Our Stella." We lay in silence until I threw back the quilt and held a hand out to him.

"Come with me."

Gio supported me as we took the few steps to the end of the bed. Standing at our window, his arms keeping me upright, we stared out at the night sky and said a prayer for Stella. Gone but never forgotten.

"Next anniversary, can I have a star for my bracelet?" I whispered as we stared out into the night sky.

"I would love nothing more."

"Do you know," I said, after a long period of silence, "when I was a child, and we traveled to Australia, I saw many different stars. My mother knew a lot about constellations and the southern skies. Her parents enjoyed sailing, and her father taught her about navigating by the stars."

"Are they so different?" Gio asked softly.

"Completely different. You can see a different part of space. It is fascinating to watch the different constellations, ones I had never seen before. My favorite was the Southern Cross. It was a diamond with pointer stars. Mum said it used to be on the Australian flag. But I loved standing on the deck with her at night as she showed me Orion, Pegasus, and Andromeda. One night, we even saw Aurora Australis, the southern lights. We see the northern lights, as you know, on Lewis. But these were different, more yellow-green. I loved it so much."

Feeling me wilting, Gio carried me back to bed and started kissing me once more. My body responded to his, warmed by his touch.

"We need to be careful. I'm not ready to be pregnant again just yet."

Gio draped his arm across my naked breasts and grinned.

"We do. Your pelvis isn't healed, and you can't take another pregnancy so soon."

"How long?" I asked. "Medically, I mean." Emotionally, it would take me a lot longer to be ready, but now was not the time for that conversation.

"Twelve weeks is usually safe, but there is a greater chance of you needing a cesarean delivery now."

"I can handle that. So what do we do for the next few weeks? I don't think I can keep you away from me now."

"Try to keep me away from you," he growled in my ear. "It killed me, having you sleep beside me, crying out, and not being able to make you forget. I was scared you would never find your way back from the dark place you were in."

"Mum described it to me once as building a well around you, a solid brick wall, to keep yourself safe from the world. That is exactly how it feels."

"Your mother?"

"Freyja, not Illy. She suffered from PTSD after everything that happened to her. She still had flashbacks years later."

"Your poor family. You have all been through so much."

"That is true, but we have done a lot of living too," I admitted. "If I had stayed safe at home, I likely would be married with children by now. But I think of all the wonderful places I have been and people I have met, and I am not upset that my life has played out the way it has."

"I would never have permitted you to marry someone else." Gio's hands gripped my buttocks protectively and rolled me toward him. "It is bad enough knowing that you slept with other men before me. None after. Promise."

"But what if you leave me?" I teased. "That isn't fair."

Gio rumbled deep in his chest. "I will never leave you *angelo mio*. But if I die first, then, and only then, do I permit you to find another."

"You are better than me," I hummed in his ear as I nibbled it, making him moan with pleasure. "I forbid you from ever sleeping with another woman. Ever. I will haunt you from beyond the grave."

"You would. I know."

"Tomorrow, I will speak to one of the med team. You have IUDs here after Sorcha gave that lecture on birth control. I will ask."

"No, you will not."

"Why? I thought you just said it wasn't safe for me to fall pregnant soon."

"Do you think I will allow one of my colleagues to see that part of you? Not a chance."

I giggled. "One of the female doctors, then?"

Gio relented. "Fine. You may speak to Catharina. But only her."

"Why not Angelina?"

"Because she likes women." He sighed in my ear.

"Don't want any competition?"

"No. You are mine."

CHAPTER 38

"WHAT HAPPENED TO FRANCESCA?" I asked one evening as we lay on the couch staring out at the stars. We had identified one, named it for Stella, and each night lay and watched for her. We had moved our couch to face the window, Gio lying behind me, holding me before him. Keeping me safe. Some nights it was cloudy, and I felt an inexplicable sadness that she wasn't with me. Other nights, we sat and stared for hours, watching her twinkle in the night sky, reflected in the lake, feeling a slight thrill when we saw a shooting star blaze across the field of darkness.

"Illy confirmed it was her. They reviewed all the messages sent from her computer and found a lot of them, including the one from months ago with your name. She had accessed my messages, worked out my password. She denied it, of course, but when presented with the evidence, she finally admitted that she had been in contact with her counterpart in the Caspian community. Francesca made the first approach, and the messages confirmed she volunteered everything. They were interested and receptive, but she initiated contact. She told them you were planning to travel that day, that Illy was your mother. They knew. All of it."

I exhaled forcefully, unsure of what to say. "Where is she now?"

"On the last full moon, Illy deployed her to Yellowstone, permanently. They are working her hard, I understand."

My mouth dropped, and I leaned back into him as we lay on the couch, not breaking my gaze across the night sky. I loved Illy and her creative punishments, many of which had been doled out to me. The Players when I was a child, those who had hunted us and killed my siblings, Illy had redeployed to struggling communities, often desert ones. Francesca deserved it, but I couldn't say this to Gio. He had loved her once. Part of him would likely still be fond of her as I was of my former boyfriends. I wasn't sure what to say, and an uncomfortable silence hung between us.

I felt his arms tighten around me, pulling me closer to his chest. "I would have done far worse after what she did, selling you out," he whispered in a husky voice.

"Illy would never have harmed her," I replied. "It isn't her way. She believes in thought reform through labor, basically hard work. But she wouldn't physically harm her."

"They thought they killed you and didn't give you a second thought. You would have died if it hadn't been for Illy, Summer, and Allison. Francesca didn't care, and she knew what they likely wanted to do to you. She knew they wanted retribution for you defending us. She gave them all the information they asked for. The part I will never understand is that she was one of those you saved. She was on the list to be killed."

"Why did she do it?" I asked, rolling my head back to look at him. "Does Illy know?"

"Jealousy. Nothing more." Gio kissed my forehead.

"I understand being jealous over you," I admitted, thinking of my mother and Dad marrying someone else. "I know I would also be horribly jealous if you left me for someone else, and I was still in love with you. Maybe Illy's punishment is too harsh? Perhaps I should talk to her?"

"No. I forbid it."

"Why? We are all better than the worse thing we have ever done. She made one mistake. I've made plenty. I can forgive one mistake."

"It wasn't a mistake. She didn't accidentally give out that information. What she did was evil, calculated, and resulted in the death of our child. She fed them information about you over months, not one time. What she did could have resulted in the death of you, me, and Illyria. Potentially others in Canada if they had gotten in the way. I can't forgive that."

"That is all true, but honey, I have been to Yellowstone. It is an awful place. Not as bad as Caspian but close. I can't be responsible for her spending her life there. Maybe she didn't know what they would do? Surely she can serve her sentence and come home?"

"You are an amazing woman." Gio gently rolled me over and laid my head on his chest. "I would happily see her burn. Every time I think of how you looked when I saw you on Lewis, I would kill her with my bare hands."

"I looked far worse when Summer and Ally found us," I admitted. "I saw their faces, and Tadhg's expression when they first walked into the room. He was so horrified he needed to look away. I saw the terror on his face. I was a mess. Jake is ex-military, like Illy, and has a game face. He has seen some pretty awful stuff and managed to keep it together and treat me as he always has. But Tadhg? He was like a father to me for years when Sera and I lived in Newgrange, undertaking our training. I thought he was going to vomit when he saw me. I will never forget the look on his face. That was when I knew how bad my injuries were."

"So, why would you defend her?"

"Because I won. I lived, I got the guy, and we will have more children," I whispered.

"Promise?"

"We will. And one day, we will all dance in the rain."

CHAPTER 39

"CAITLIN, IT'S TIME. I need you to return to Canada. If you don't want to use the portal, I understand. Either Jake or Summer are at your disposal. Just say the word, and I will dispatch them."

I smiled at Illy through the teleconference monitor. She had been gone for weeks, and I missed our daily chats. Despite my now daily assistance on projects with the tech and engineering teams, I felt lazy and unproductive. She was right. I needed to use my brain before I died of boredom. I would never admit it to her, but I missed my job, speaking to people. But it was the land-bridge project I was desperate to see come to fruition. If we could make that a success, so many people would benefit.

"I know. I need to get back. I am bored doing nothing."

"We will increase the security around you. You don't need to be scared."

"I'll be fine," I assured her. "I assume you took care of Caspian."

"That is a matter to discuss in person."

"You are coming? Here?"

"No, I thought your parents and I could visit you in Canada when you have settled back in."

"I would love that! Dad will be beside himself, seeing all the greenhouses and orchards."

"Yes. He is quite excited. But he wants to see you more."

"When is Summer free to take us?"

"Any time you like. Perhaps clear it with Giovanni, and let me know?"

"I will," I promised.

With nothing to keep us here, we made plans to leave Piedmont. A dinner was held in our honor on our last night, and I was sad to say goodbye to so many friends. The Soggiorno deck was filled with tables pushed together to form long rows, and I was mobile enough to hobble around and speak to everyone, people kindly vacating chairs so I could sit periodically. No one had been in the mood to celebrate when we left last time, so soon after the memorial services for hundreds of residents. But now, people were pleased to celebrate our marriage and our appointments to Canada, if somewhat belatedly.

At various points in the evening, I saw Summer holding conversations in quiet corners and knew what she was up to. Even now that they knew Illy was aware of their side hustle, she and Ally had made no attempt to slow down. I stifled the laugh, knowing that anything was available to anyone, for a price.

Riccardo was disappointed to hear we were leaving, and while we had spoken regularly on videoconference during my months in Canada, it had been wonderful to spend time together again, strengthening the professional relationship on a more personal level, as former engineering colleagues but now peers. Our processes were similar, and we often found ourselves in agreement during robust debates. Several weeks ago, Joseph and I had shown him the diagrams of the planned linkages to the mainland, and I laughed, seeing his engineering brain ticking away.

"I promise, if it works, we will build you one next."

His eyes sparkled with excitement. "You need to come and help."

"We would love that."

It was Antonio, Joseph, and Gianni who made me cry, saying goodbye. Each of them had helped me through the most difficult period of my life, just by being a friend, being there, and not judging.

"I will miss you!" I said, hugging them each in turn. "Thank you so much for everything you have done for me."

Gianni was doing his best to hold back his emotions, and I knew if I cried, he would as well.

"I will miss you too, Caitlin. Please, can you come back soon?"

We had discussed Gianni and his family visiting us in Canada. I desperately wanted to expand his horizons and show him new places, but I knew that the portal travel could injure him if he landed in a strange position. I vowed to speak with Summer about bringing him over once I was settled.

"I will see you soon," I promised. "You haven't seen the last of me."

Joseph and Antonio stood back slightly as Gianni moved aside. "I cannot tell you how much your friendship and companionship means to me," I said, choking back the tears. "I don't think I would have made it through this without you."

"Caitlin," Antonio said in his lilting, gentle voice, "you did far more for us. We would do anything for you. You know that?"

"My ring!" I pounced on it as soon as I dropped my bags on the floor. The apartment was spotless and had been cleaned and dusted in preparation for our arrival, but my ring was still on the bedside table where I had left it. As I went to put it on, Gio asked from behind me, "Did you ever read the inscription?"

"Inscription?" I hobbled over to the window and held it up to the sunlight. On the inside, in tiny, beautiful cursive script, were the words, "*Per sempre*. Forever."

I stared at him as he came over to join me. "Why did you not tell me?"

"You didn't need to know, before. I never saw you take it off, and it warmed my heart knowing that it was close to yours. But now, I want you to know. No matter what happens, Caitlin, what challenges we may face, it is always forever, for me."

"It is for me, too."

Gio swept me up in his arms, and I gazed around at our tiny home.

"I am so happy to be back here. It is strange, but I feel closer to Stella."

"We made her here." Gio kissed my cheek. "It is where we will make her siblings."

Summer had dropped Gio and me and was planning a trip back to Lewis to collect my parents, Carmelo and Illy. Ally had remained on Lewis, allegedly taking a well-deserved break. Summer had confessed during the long journey here that Ally was planning their next transactions, which was difficult when her mother was around. Knowing Illy would be here for a period, distracted, made their smuggling operations far easier.

The helicopter Summer preferred to fly for long trips was sizeable but wasn't large enough for all of us, plus our baggage and supplies for Canada. I had insisted we carry as much of the breathable dome fabric as possible so we could start building my proposed domed greenhouse on the Bruce Peninsula, close to the community. The land pod design was complete, including heating rods to keep the greenhouse warm amid a wild Canadian winter. All I needed to do was start building it. On her next trip, bringing my parents, Summer would bring the remaining materials, so I could get started.

Mandy came to visit soon after our arrival, bringing my schedule for the week.

"Coffee and pastry in the morning?" she asked, a twinkle in her eye.

"That would be wonderful."

"We have missed you. People didn't realize how much you did until suddenly you weren't there to act as our representative. Even the engineering team keeps asking when you are back so they can get your advice."

"Ooh," I said and pulled myself to the edge of my chair. "Perhaps I could…"

"No!" Mandy and Gio chorused. "It has been a long trip. You need to rest," Gio commanded.

I grimaced but relented. I was shattered. We had needed to stop frequently to refuel the twin-engine gas turbine craft, which could only travel 700 kilometers on one tank. But it allowed us to stop every two to three hours in locations Summer knew we could refuel and take breaks, stretching our legs. Sitting in one position was painful, so I appreciated the breaks. Each time we refueled, and she ran pre-flight checks, I watched in fascination, and yet again privately resented Jake teaching Summer to fly and not me.

"I'll see you in the morning," Mandy confirmed. "Your first meeting isn't until after lunch, so I can spend the morning briefing you. Catch you up on what you missed, which isn't much. I know Riccardo has kept you in the loop."

Mandy excused herself, and I wondered how much of my job she had taken on in my absence. She would make an outstanding leader but insisted it wasn't her calling. More than once, when she had contacted me in Italy, I had suggested that she take over in a more permanent capacity, my absence already being longer than the originally planned month. She had refused, claiming she was happy to hand the reins back to me. The problem was, I wasn't certain I wanted them back. Working with the engineering team in Piedmont, I had remembered how much I loved working as part of a team. Joseph and I found our groove, anticipating need and spending much of our day teasing each other and laughing. He would encourage me to get up and move every hour, so I didn't get stiff and end up in pain.

I sighed, thinking of what I had left behind.

"What is it, my love?" Gio asked as I stood at the window and gazed over the now unfamiliar view.

"I'm not sure this is what I want," I confessed. "Ambassador, I mean. You know how much I loved working with the engineering team in Italy, and what I desperately want to do is build the land-bridge. You saw the difference between living in the pods and our lives on Lewis, even Orkney. Life at home is filled with fresh air and sunshine. People have space to move. The darkness doesn't drag people down."

"It is a different world. Your project has the potential to improve so many lives. We can still live here, as a community, but that joyous feeling of walking on land... I can't quite describe it."

"Now you know why Sera and I said we couldn't live our lives in the unhabs."

"I do. And I understand why so many of my parents' generation struggled too. They knew what they had lost."

"I want to give that back to them, all of them."

"I have the utmost faith in you. You always achieve your goals."

CHAPTER 40

I KISSED GIO GOODBYE AND slowly made my way to the office, using my single walking stick. *At least I can crack someone with it if they piss me off*, I thought, wondering who would be first in line. Doubts plagued me, and I felt heavy as I made my way through the corridors. I wasn't ready for this.

Friends stopped to say hello and express how happy they were to see me back. Judging by the looks of surprise, I got the distinct impression that many people thought I would never return after what had happened. Clearly, everyone knew what they had done to me. I held my head high, made eye contact, and greeted people as I passed. *Am I foolish for coming back here?* But when Gabriel passed me raving about the materials that had been delivered, I remembered. That was why I was here. I had started something, a project I believed in, something that would benefit so many, and I was determined to finish.

Mandy was already in the office as I arrived, her demeanor more subdued now that we were alone, different from the friendly greeting when she had visited yesterday. She stood back apprehensively as she watched me hobble into the office. I held my arms out to her, and her face cracked as she felt forward to hug me.

"I am so sorry for what happened to you," she whispered. "I should have done something. It all came flooding back when I saw you yesterday, how much pain you are in, and I felt so guilty all night. I should have come after you, stopped them."

"There was nothing you could have done," I soothed. "I am alright. I am so grateful for everything you did for Giovanni, getting him help. Saving his life."

Mandy slumped, pleased I didn't bear a grudge. "We would always have done that. He was carried straight to the clinic and operated on. It was you we were worried about. How is your recovery?"

"Slow," I admitted. "My knee was dislocated, the patella smashed, my pelvis broken, and they are the injuries causing me lasting pain. Most of the other injuries have healed. But walking is good for me, and I am getting there."

"I feel so guilty for what happened." I could hear the pain in her voice.

I lowered myself into my chair behind the desk with a sigh and looked up at her. "Stop there. You were not responsible in any way for what happened. It had been carefully planned, and it was me they were after. There was nothing you could have done. If you had gotten in the way, you would likely be dead or injured. They would have gotten me at some point. It has taken me a long time to process what happened and deal with it. But I am okay. Giovanni is okay."

"You were pregnant," Mandy said sadly.

"I thought you suspected. I was twelve weeks. That was why we were traveling. We were heading home to tell my family before we made an announcement. I lost the child, and yes, that is the hardest part. My wounds will heal, but my baby was taken from me, and I will never forgive them for that. That is the part that haunts me. Honestly, I worry that it always will. It sounds silly, but I see her in my dreams, my daughter. But I will never get to hold her."

Mandy nodded as she pulled up a chair opposite me. "Dreams are often messages."

"What do you mean?"

"You know I am native Canadian, of the First Nations. My mother is Cree, but my grandmother was Iroquois."

I had assumed but never explicitly asked. "I didn't, but please go on."

"There is a concept that my grandmother used when I was younger and struggling with school and life in general."

I looked across at her. "A word? What word?"

"Orenda."

I repeated the word, but it was unfamiliar to me. "What does it mean?"

Mandy paused, trying to collect her thoughts. "It means an invisible mystical power or energy that is present in all natural objects and people. It is the force that allows us to affect the world and manifest changes in our own lives. While we all have it, powerful hunters, leaders, and shamans all have a higher degree of orenda. You are a powerful woman, Caitlin. People listen to you. They follow you. You have saved so many people, changed so many things for the better. Without you, we would still be sitting out here, isolated. You reinvigorated our community. You have taught us so much. You saved those people in Italy. They are alive because of your actions. I know this was revenge, and it was brutal. But your instincts are spot on, so your dreams likely are too. You understand people, you guide them, and they follow you. You are a natural leader. So while you have suffered a terrible tragedy, you have the power within you to overcome this. You will have children. I feel it, deep in my bones. This act of violence does not define you. You have the power to overcome your loss and move forward. Your destiny is great. Embrace the orenda within you. Continue to use it to influence others, and make great and positive change."

"What if I have lost my power?" I whispered as she stood and closed the door, hearing people talking as they passed by in the hallway.

"You haven't. It is still there, deep down. You need to find it, and let it rise to the surface once more."

"How do I do that?"

Mandy sighed and looked at me. "I can't answer that for you, Caitlin. The journey is unique for each person. But when the time is right, your spirit will rise, and you will conquer."

"Thank you, Mandy. For everything. Mandy, what is your name, in Cree?"

"nîpiy."

"What does it mean?"

"Leaf. My mother says I was born in the fall, and as she labored, she could see the beautiful colored leaves falling from the trees. She performed the ceremony and asked for guidance. This was the name that was presented to her."

"So why do you use Mandy?"

"I was given both, a traditional name and an Anglicized name. I used Mandy at school and on my paperwork to come here. I guess I thought it was easier for other people if I used my English name."

"May I use your Cree name?"

"No one has ever asked me that." Mandy's voice dropped to a whisper. "I would love that."

"Can you spell it for me?"

"It is probably easier if I write it."

I considered the unusual spelling on the page in front of me. "Lowercase first letter?" I asked, confused. It wasn't a mistake Mandy would make. She was highly literate.

"There are no capital letters in Cree language. Even for proper nouns, like names."

"Why?"

"It is a complex language, and it has been many years. All I can recall is that nouns are animate or inanimate."

"I love it, nîpiy."

CHAPTER 41

"MUM! DAD!" I HURLED myself at them as they entered the main pod. I was running late from a meeting that had been plagued with technical issues. I had wanted to greet them at the floating helipad we had now built beside the main pod, making short hops between communities easier.

"Look at you! You barely need your crutches." Mum's face lit with pleasure.

"Short distances I can manage with just a single stick now. I get tired, but I am doing well, Mum. I am feeling much stronger."

"I can see that. Let me settle in, and I will check you over. Or has your husband been doing that?"

I flushed. "Mum! People can hear you! I am the ambassador!"

"And I am your mother. It is my job to embarrass you."

I looked to Dad for support. "Give it up, darling," he advised. "She has been embarrassing me now for thirty years. I just ignore her."

Mum jabbed him in the ribs with her elbow, but the smile didn't leave her face.

Leading the way across the main pod, I pointed out to Dad the plants that grew everywhere and told him about the greenhouse pods and aquaponics tanks Antonio and I had set up. Dad stopped to touch everything as he passed, making Mum roll her eyes at me in exasperation. Mum did everything quickly, walking, and making assessments of people and places. Dad approached life slowly and enjoyed taking in his surroundings.

Illy appeared before us as we reached the entrance to our accommodation pod and greeted me warmly before turning her attention back to my parents. "Do you like it, Campbell?"

Dad's face was priceless, opening and closing his mouth like a goldfish.

"Look at him," Illy giggled to Mum. "He looks like a kid in a candy shop, not knowing what to sample first."

"Mum, can you take Dad's bags? I want to show him some stuff. I would rather not walk all the way to your apartment and then back here again."

Mum smirked but agreed, knowing how much it meant to both of us. Illy held her arms out to accept Dad's bags, with Mum taking one extra. Mum turned and followed Illy into the accommodation pods as Dad and I watched them go. They were being hosted in a small apartment, sharing with Illy and Carmelo. As much as I loved them, secretly, I was pleased it wasn't with me. After many weeks apart, Gio and I finally found our groove, and I didn't want my parents in the next room.

"Come on, Dad." I dragged him back through the main pod and hobbled into another hallway leading into the tech pod.

"Slow down!" He laughed at my enthusiasm. "We have time, don't we?"

Dad stood back and took it all in as I showed him the climate controls, the sensors, and the automated systems. His astonishment made me laugh.

"I haven't seen anything like this in thirty years," he admitted, spellbound by the remote watering systems. "I thought much of this knowledge was lost. I am so pleased it has been retained."

"Come on. I have so much more to show you."

Over the next few hours, I showed Dad the vineyards that were thriving thanks to Antonio's help, complete with the grape skin leather production. Dad caressed the fabric between his fingers, much like I had done the first time Antonio had shown me. We moved to the aquaponics tanks, the enormous hall filled with waist-height rows of tanks. Dad stopped to check on the fish, the plants growing abundantly in the effluent-rich water above. He gasped at the greenhouse pods, and I could see him noting plants he didn't grow and from which he could take cuttings when he left. I showed him the enormous orchard pods and algal tanks that provided our oxygen. I pointed out improvements I had added based on his knowledge, but in some cases, we had tweaked, using engineering or technology to add sensors, remote access, or other enhancements. I was well known here, having spent many hours in my first stint here assisting Antonio with the greenhouses, aquaponics, and vineyards. Everyone stopped to speak with me, ask me how I was doing, and welcome me back. As soon as I turned the conversation to plants, Dad was in his element, speaking to everyone he met. Asking questions about varietals and technique, they chatted away like old friends. I pulled back slightly and leaned against a window. Dad had found his people. I smiled, standing back and listening to him talk with Deb about propagation, species selection, companion planting, and espaliering.

"What are these?" Dad asked about the plants growing in one of the internal rooms. "Do you use solely artificial light to grow them? Does it impact productivity?"

"Those are non-photobiotic plants." Deb smiled, seeing Dad was interested.

Dad stared at her. "Truly? I thought those were extinct?"

"No. We have quite a selection, as you can see."

"What are non-photo..." I stopped, forgetting the word.

"Plants that can live without light and can live in total darkness," Dad explained. "They are nearly all parasitic and live off other plants, but there are some, like some species of orchids, that are non-photosynthetic and myco-heterotrophic for part of their life cycle."

"Whoa Dad, back up. All I heard was plant. No light. Grow."

"That pretty much sums it up, sweetheart. How about I come back tomorrow when you are at work?"

"That would be wonderful, Dad. I don't want to intrude on your holiday. I want to show you everything, and I know you can teach the team here so much."

"Sweetheart, we came to see you. Yes, being here is amazing, but I would spend a week in a tiny apartment if it meant I could spend that time with you."

"I see what you mean about needing to expand," Dad said as we finally had a few minutes alone, heading back to the accommodation pods. Dad had seen me tiring and insisted we could cover engineering tomorrow. "Everything here is operating at capacity. It is a good thing you introduced those aquaponics tanks when you did. That adds a great deal of edible food to their harvest."

"Can you review the aquaponics growing? I did the best I could, but I have limited time and nowhere near as much knowledge as you. Antonio learned from me, and if I got it wrong…"

"You did fine. I can make a few minor suggestions, but you did so well. I didn't think you paid attention."

"Well, I did," I fired back cheekily.

"I hate to think where they would be if you hadn't. They barely grow enough with the space they have."

"They lost a few hundred people when the Caspians invaded," I whispered, not really wanting to think about them. "I imagine it was even worse before."

Dad grimaced.

"Did you bring the moss?" I asked.

"As much as I could. We will need to transplant it as soon as possible and keep it wet."

"Dad, it is winter in Canada. Trust me. It is as wet as Scotland. It doesn't matter if the water is infected, does it?"

"No. We have tried both ways, transporting clean water from inside the domes and letting them naturally propagate. It makes no difference. After all, when we found it on Mousa, it had lived only being watered by infected rain."

"Good, so I can drop and run."

"Does that mean you will plant alone?"

"Gio can help. Remember?"

"I do. Please be careful, Catie. You have had one near miss. I can't lose you."

"I have missed you so much!" I threw myself into his arms as we entered the narrow corridor heading toward their temporary accommodation.

"I would love to help you, but we don't know yet if it was successful," Dad whispered, checking that we weren't overheard.

"Oh, Dad. I hope it was. I want that for you. That freedom." Gio had taken careful notes of how much it had taken for him to be immune using my transplanted stem cells and blood donation. I suspected Mum had used his data to inject herself and Dad as I had requested but had no capacity to ask. Gio's data exchange had needed to occur in code, in case the communications were intercepted. After Francesca hacked comms, I was still fearful that she had help.

"I appreciate the gift, sweetheart, but your mother and I have lived thirty years under the protection of the domes. It is our home. We don't mind so much. But if we can help re-green the planet, do our bit to help restore oxygen levels so one day your children can live outside, then I will do it."

"Is that why you accepted?"

"It is. I want to travel, to see you all. But I can help. You and Seraphine planted all those trees around Lewis, and they are thriving. But if I can do that for other communities, then I feel like I should."

"Dad, you can't let anyone know you are immune. Not yet."

"I know, sweetheart. It is still a secret. Only your mother, Illy, and I know. Although I suspect Carmelo knows, but he won't say anything."

"How are Carmelo and Illy?" I asked.

Dad grinned. "I haven't seen her this happy in twenty years. Luca was her soulmate. But maybe she got a second."

"Remind me what he was like." I felt a little awkward asking, but I could never get enough of hearing about him. After all, Luca was my biological father. But Dad didn't take offense.

"He was huge. She is tiny. They were an odd couple to look at. He could scoop her up with one arm and not even try. He was what we used to call a beefcake in the old world. Tall, broad, and enormous, well-defined muscles. I'm tall, but he was far bigger than me. Illy, when I first met her, I thought of her as a budgie. A tiny, sprightly, little bird. Even after all these years, that is still how I see her. Bright and chirpy."

"But he makes her happy? Carmelo, I mean?"

"He does. They are besotted with each other. He treats her like a queen. Only Luca did that. None of the others."

"Others?" I stopped and stared.

"Oh, Illyria had the odd boyfriend or date. But nothing like those two."

"I didn't know she even had boyfriends!" I exclaimed, wondering if Sera knew this.

"None of them were serious. They didn't complement her. She is so bright and bubbly. Luca had a wicked sense of humor. Carmelo is quieter, but he brings out the best in her. He is balanced and loyal. You can rely on him."

"I know," I said, thinking of Carmelo assisting when the Caspians invaded Piedmont. His support of me when I confronted Francesca. Carmelo had been horrified when he learned she was behind my kidnapping. I saw the look on his face before he hid it, but I knew he would have done anything to protect me, even from her.

Dad stopped suddenly as we walked down the passageway. I turned to look back at the puzzled look on his face.

"What?"

"What do they do for pollination? Surely there are no insects or bees inside enclosed cities?"

"None. They pollinate by hand and grizzle incessantly about it. There are no bees, and so no honey. I should have asked you to bring some. It is a high-commodity trading item. Anyone born here has likely never tasted it."

"I remember Giovanni's face the first time he tried honey on toast. I thought he would lick the jar."

"But you will be pleased to know they have a small orchard of maple trees here. The original settlement demanded maple syrup, and even though the trees are enormous and take up a lot of precious space, they are tapped and very productive. The problem is, we don't make enough to sell, just use ourselves."

"This is your place, isn't it? I'm so pleased to see you so settled."

"I love it here, Dad," I admitted. "I feel valued and like I contribute something."

"I can see that. It is a wonderful feeling. Come on. We better find your mother."

CHAPTER 42

GIO MADE PLANS TO show my parents the medical facilities the following morning, ostensibly to show my mother the equipment in other communities.

"Do you need another sample?" I asked over breakfast, knowing the true purpose of their tour.

"Maybe. We have time, *amore mio*. There is no rush."

In my weeks of rehabilitation, the land-bridge project hadn't progressed. Mixed emotions filled me, relief that I would be here to oversee it, but sadness that it was delayed. Even after my short time on Lewis, I wanted the people here to experience life outside.

Gabriel offered to project manage the bridge construction, knowing my hands were full. But he was busy too, and I was frustrated by the lack of progression. Every afternoon when I had spare time, Dad and I started propagating the moss into a large area on the peninsula nearest the pods. In time, we would construct a dome to enclose it and expand the greenhouses outside. Gio sometimes joined us, but more often he was required in the medical clinic. Despite my physical wounds making me slower than I would have liked and frustrating me, I loved spending this time with Dad. Gio had tested him, and Dad was also immune, although we took great pains to suit up before we sailed across the short stretch of lake to the peninsula. Once ashore, we couldn't be seen, so we shed the suits, dug, sowed the moss, and watered it in, chatting and laughing. There was no pressure working with my father. It took as long as it took, and we took regular breaks, mostly for me. Gio had ordered Dad to do all the heavy work. Dad had agreed, looking serious, but had laughed as soon as Gio left us, and we boarded the small yacht we used to access the peninsula.

"Has he met you? Since when did you take anything easy?"

"He cares, Dad. It is a little misplaced, I grant you. But he doesn't want me to take longer to heal than I need to."

"No one wants that, sweetheart." Dad paused as the engine roared into life, and I felt the pain in his next words. "I'm so sorry that happened to you. No one, ever, should be treated like that."

I didn't know what to say to that. For the first few weeks, I had believed I deserved it. After all, I had killed their people. But as time passed and anger took over, I realized I didn't deserve it. Nor did Illy or Gio. None of us. One day, I would meet them again. The world wasn't that big anymore. I could play the long game. I snuggled into his side.

"Dad, you don't need to feel bad. This wasn't your fault. The Caspians are animals. You should have seen what they did to the people in Italy, Canada, and other places. They are merciless, ruthless. They would have always sought revenge. I am grateful I am alive, and I will recover. I know it makes you feel like you couldn't protect me, but no one could. Not from them."

"I kept seeing your mother's face when she came home from Clava the first time. She had a broken nose and cheekbone. Not as bad as yours, but seeing you reminded me of that time. The long road she had to recovery. I wouldn't raise it, and she only mentioned she had told you about her struggles."

"She did, and it means a lot. Knowing I am not the first, not alone, makes an enormous difference. Mum and Illy are the toughest women I know, and if they can survive something as horrific as that, then I can too."

"I don't want you to survive, sweetheart. I want you to thrive. Live your best life. Show those assholes that you can't be kept down."

I loved the weeks we spent together, first planting the moss samples and then erecting the dome above, installing sensors, gutters to catch the water, and reticulated systems. Dad moved in pre-built planter boxes for the seedlings so we could begin growing here immediately, not needing to wait for the moss to take effect. I loved having my parents here, Dad especially. His influence was so calming, and I relaxed, without realizing I had been tense all the time. I jumped less at random sounds and slept better. I still hadn't returned to the lake beneath the city, but I knew I would need to. Mum and Dad were heading home in a few days, jumping to France, and then Summer would collect them from there. Illy and Carmelo had already moved on to Japan, to see Sera and be there for the birth.

"I wish you didn't have to go," I told Mum that night as she and I relaxed on the couch after our final dinner. Dad and Gio were cleaning up and chatting away, washing the dishes.

"Then give us a reason to return." Mum dimpled at me.

"What...? Mum!" I hissed. "It is too early for that."

"No, it isn't. It has been over four months, Caitlin. You are healed, physically. Emotionally is another matter. But the best way to get past this grief is to have another."

"I'm not ready," I whispered, knowing that Stella would have been joining us about now.

"I'm going to give you fifty cents' worth of free advice. There is no such thing as a good time for a baby. They come, and you adapt. People plan for years and never have one. I once said to Illy that they come at the worst time possible. You embrace it and mold your life around them."

"I had another IUD inserted," I whispered, checking Gio couldn't hear, even though he knew.

"So have it removed. You can be fertile from your next cycle. Why do you think we use them?"

"How? I'm the ambassador."

Mum stood and held her hand out to me. "We'll be back in ten!" she called to the guys. "Catie needs to show me something before we head home tomorrow."

Dad looked up from the dishes, perplexed, but we had already slipped out the door before either of them could speak.

"I didn't mean now," I hissed, feeling uncomfortable that this was my mother, and I wasn't ready for this.

"Who else then? I've wiped your bits for years. Besides, you have nothing I haven't seen a thousand times. What makes you think your lady parts are special?"

Heat flooded my face as Mum laughed. "I remember seeing a gynecologist when I was a late teen. I had endometriosis and terrible period pain. So my mum took me to see hers. I was seventeen and mortified that someone would see my most private parts. My mother, who was even more pragmatic than me, told me, 'Freyja, you are like a car engine. They have seen a million vaginas, and yours isn't special. Get over it. He isn't judging yours and won't remember as soon as you leave.' She was right, of course."

"Did it help?"

"You know, it did. I realized he didn't care what I looked like. It was clinical, medical. Like what I do."

Mum led me into one of the medical rooms and gestured toward the bed. I stripped off my knickers and waited, embarrassed. Mum went to wash her hands and find the tool to grip the thread. I sat up, panicked, as she entered the room.

"I can't."

"You can. What are you afraid of?"

I paused, thinking. What was I scared of? "What if I can't have a baby after what happened? Jorja said there was no guarantee. What if I can't carry to term? I don't think I could deal with losing another baby, Mum. It was the loss that was the hardest for Giovanni, too. Feeling so powerless."

Mum sat in the seat beside the bed. "So let's dissect those issues. You conceived once, and you likely will again. The odds of you losing another in similar circumstances are nearly zero, Catie. Spontaneous miscarriage happens but usually in the first trimester. In many cases, before the woman even knows she is pregnant. But let's look at not removing your contraception. You almost certainly won't fall pregnant.

That protects you from the fear of a loss, but you will never know the joy. So what do you want? To not be scared or to potentially be happy?"

"That isn't a fair question."

"You want both. But you can't, darling. There are no guarantees. We throw caution to the wind, and we wait."

"Do it," I said, laying back. "Now, before I change my mind."

Heading to the lower level in the early morning, I felt my stomach tense. I hadn't been down here since I had been abducted and berated myself several times as I walked the long, dark passage behind my parents. Gio was equally quiet as he helped carry their bags.

"Are you alright?" he whispered, checking we were far enough back not to be overheard.

I wanted to lie, to tell him I was fine, but I wasn't, and he could see it.

"It is bringing back memories," I admitted, "and I am not sure I am ready for this. But I want to say goodbye to them. I don't know when I will see them again. I can't let them go without seeing them off."

"We can stop by the wall. I don't want to be near the portal opening either."

Gio gripped my hand tighter, and I was comforted by his presence. His experience had been no less traumatic than mine, stabbed, left for dead, and watching me be taken.

"We do it together," I promised, not just talking about the portals.

We stood back and watched my parents zip themselves into their heat suits and carry the bags to the water's edge. They turned back to where we stood against the outer wall. My heart was in my throat as I hugged my parents and wished them a safe journey.

"We'll come back soon," Mum promised, leaning in for another hug. "Whenever you need us, we will be here."

"We mean it," Dad said, taking his turn. "You will always be our little girl. You need us, say the word, and we will be here as soon as we can. And you," Dad turned to Gio and swamped him in an unexpected hug, "you look after our daughter. And yourself. We think of you as a son. Take care of each other."

The roaring started, and I felt my heart beat faster. Mum took Dad's hand and helped him lower the hood on the heat suit. She smiled at me one last time and, carrying their bags, stepped into the vortex and disappeared. I choked away the tears, not wanting the team to see their leader cry. Gio felt my turmoil and pulled me into a hug. "Wait," he said, feeling me pull away. "I have a surprise."

I looked up at him, puzzled but didn't have time to ask when I saw a silver ball fly out of the portal, followed by another. Gio waited until the swirling waters slowed, and the roar subsided, then helped the travelers stand and unzipped the hoods.

"Joseph!" I exclaimed. "Antonio! I am so happy to see you! Not that I don't love you, but why are you here? Does Riccardo know you are here?" I asked, suddenly concerned that they had come without his knowledge.

"Of course. He knows we need to work on this project of yours. After you showed him the designs, he is desperate to get started on the one in Italy."

"Yes!" I squealed, making a few of the techs stare at my sudden outburst. "That is wonderful news! Let's get you to your apartment. My parents have just left, so there is a spare one."

I turned to Gio. "I can't believe you didn't tell me!"

"I thought you might need a surprise to cheer you up a bit after your parents left."

"This is a wonderful surprise. I am so happy to see you both."

Catching up on the news from Italy, we made our way to the outer corridor, watching the teams moving the crates of freight that had arrived after ours had been sent through. I made a mental note to check the orders. There didn't seem to be quite the quantity I ordered.

"Pete," I called to the logistics lead, "can you count the produce? It isn't the first time we have been short-changed."

Pete made a guttural noise that indicated he had heard me, and that was all I was likely to get.

"What is this?" Joseph asked, picking up a large, tightly packed bundle of brown fiber cloth.

"Oh, I am so glad that came," I exclaimed, taking the deceptively lightweight bundle from him and running my hands over the rough fibrous surface. "That is coconut fiber."

"I thought you ate the inside of a coconut," Gio interjected, touching the coarse fiber blanket in my hands.

"You do. You eat the inside white flesh and drink the milk, but the fiber is wonderful as a scourer, for cleaning. I ordered some for the kitchen and engineering teams to make into scouring pads. I also ordered some bamboo toothbrushes. There was an enormous supply of plastic ones provided here at setup, but these are biodegradable. I'm hoping over time we can learn to make our own."

Joseph's face lit as he stopped to run the fiber between his fingers.

"Does it work?"

"Really well. We had some at home. It comes from New Caledonia and some of the other tropical communities. They waste nothing, like us."

"I would love to try coconut." Gio sighed. Dad and I had told him all about mangoes, coconut, and other tropical fruits. Dad had grown some in the greenhouses on Lewis, but with the bitterly cold winters, they didn't flourish like they had in Australia and warmer countries. I had tasted them, and they were wonderful. The joy of juicy ripe mango was something I desperately wanted to share with him.

"If you play your cards right, I may import some," I teased. "What is the point of being the boss unless you can share the wonders of the world with your people?"

The guys looked at me, spellbound.

"Fine, I did. There is a crate of tropical fruit in that stash. It just needs to be unpacked. Come on." I smiled at our visitors, placing the coir back on the pile of cargo. "Dinner at our place."

"Can you cook now?" Antonio asked, surprised.

Gio guffawed. "No. But the cooks adore her after she sourced all the ingredients they wanted and built biogas cooktops for them as she did at home, so we are fed every night. The food here, as you recall, is very good. Of course, I need to spend the time not spent cooking at the gym, so I don't end up *gigantesco*."

I caught Gio's use of the word home, and a shard pierced my heart. *Would Italy always be home for him? Was this temporary? Would he always want to go back there?* Perhaps stupidly, we had never spoken about it after that day when he told me he would follow me anywhere. I had believed him, but now I felt a little dazed. What if he wanted to go back there one day, and I didn't? Were we bringing children into a relationship destined to fail?

Antonio sensed my discomfort, being the quieter, more sensitive of the two.

"You okay, Caitlin?" he asked haltingly.

I smiled as brightly as I could manage. "It was hard being down there," I said truthfully, not wanting to make this about me. "Not so pleasant memories and saying goodbye to my parents. But I am happy you are here. Everyone will be thrilled you are here. When we came back here from Italy, everyone asked about you."

"They did?"

"Absolutely. You are always welcome here. People still talk about your wedding and the improvements you made here. I can't wait to show you what we have done."

We stopped by the kitchens, and Jodi was thrilled to see our visitors.

"Thank you again for our wedding," they both gushed. "You made it so special. The food was *magnifico*. We told everyone back home about it and the croquembouche!"

That was the best thing to say, of course, and we saw her face beam.

"Jodi," Gio asked charmingly, "our friends are staying for a while. Would it be at all possible to…"

"Dinner for four?" Jodi was levitating at the prospect. "It would be my pleasure. Sunset? The boys will be hungry."

"Thank you," I said as sincerely as I could. "We can't wait to catch up."

CHAPTER 43

IT TOOK TWO DAYS for Joseph and Gabriel to assemble a team of builders, engineers, and other specialists to build the bridge to the mainland. I dropped by several times a day to see if I could offer assistance, but each time watched in awe as Joseph broke the project down into tasks, allocated them out, and set timeframes on them.

"When do you think you will be done?" I asked in a lull.

"Three months, possibly less. But we need Summer. Can you get her here?"

"Absolutely. How soon?"

"Yesterday," he teased, using one of my favorite expressions.

"I'm on it."

All the residents watched with fascination as they started building the enclosed bridge, using cofferdams at either end, and battered piles for the remaining posts. Jake had come with Summer and taught her to embed posts into the lake bed using an aerial crane, which fascinated the children, flocking to the windows every time they heard it rumbling outside. During meetings in the boardroom, I kept one eye on the progress being made outside, sometimes feeling the pod vibrate as they drilled the posts in place. The team had made some minor amendments to our original plans, and I enjoyed seeing how the design had been simplified, allowing for slight movement to accommodate the high winds here. It was still enclosed, like a tube. It needed to be. No one here was immune, and people needed to pass from pod to the biosphere on land without coming into contact with the outside. Joseph and I had speculated how we would connect the pod to the fixed bridge securely, but that still allowed the main pod to be submerged under the bay when powerful storms struck. The problem was, they were both rigid surfaces. The land dome fabric was too flimsy, and we had no way of securing it easily. Frustrated to be stymied, I sent a message to all my family and friends, seeking ideas.

It was Dad in the end who made a suggestion, and Callie designed it. Dad had remembered old airports, those with airplanes that carried hundreds of people. I had seen pictures, even seen some old planes rotting into the ground as we passed abandoned airports. But Dad had suggested we use an air bridge, a moveable enclosed elevated platform that would extend from the aircraft to the airport terminal gate. Initially, Summer went looking for some old ones at airports, but they had disintegrated terribly with years of no use. But Illy persisted, tasking Jake with sourcing some made from metal. Jake carried several to the peninsula, and I saw immediately what Illy had meant. Rectangular metal tubes, large enough for several people to walk through, side by side. They were rigid, strong, yet relatively lightweight. Each end had an articulating mount that allowed the tunnel to seal at either end. The genius part was that the tunnel portions were retractable, so it could be moved away from the underwater pod slightly, ensuring it was never damaged.

"How is it going?" I asked, carrying my lunch down to the engineering pod where everyone was focused on their tasks.

Joseph looked up and grinned. "Very well. This was a brilliant idea of your father's."

"It looks it," I admitted. "How will you retract it? Sensor?"

"Mechanical controls would work better. A switch is easier in a storm, and we would also need to build a manual override. Problem is, no one here knows how."

"Oh, pick me!" I burst in excitement, making Joseph laugh.

"Like you aren't busy enough being the ambassador."

"But I need to get my hands dirty. Please. Let me do this. I have a meeting this afternoon, but I can come down after that."

"We don't need it that quickly!"

"But if I can design it as you install the sections, surely that makes more sense. Retrofitting controls is asking for trouble."

"True. Are you sure?"

"Positive."

"nîpiy!" I called as I headed back into the office.

She popped her out of a storeroom. "Do you need something?"

"Can you reschedule all my afternoon meetings for the next week? On second thought, make it two."

"Planning to go part-time, are we?" she said with a grin.

"Not exactly. They need my help with the final stages of building the land-bridge, linking it up with the pod at this end and the biosphere at the other."

"They need your help, or you offered it?" she asked cheekily.

"Fine. I want to help. But it is important to me. I don't want to spend my life in meetings."

"You can't, not this month. You have a full schedule. Some of these meetings have been delayed for weeks, or taken days to organize, to marry up every-one's diaries."

nîpiy saw my face and relented. "Fine. I will tell them your urgent attention is required elsewhere."

"You are a wonder."

"I know. It had better be worth it. Illyria is coming next month, and I will not be left holding the can."

"You won't," I assured her. "Illy knows all about this project and its importance. I do speak to her, you know."

Pulling long hours, getting up before dawn, and falling into bed late, we worked hard to complete the project. It was built, but we were still working through rigorous safety testing and checking the weight it would hold and its stability during pow-erful wind gusts. We had a goal: for the bridge to be ready for Illy's arrival. nîpiy made arrangements for an opening ceremony, ribbon cutting, and speeches. As I watched her organize people and catering, I real-ized she rivaled my Aunt Di as an event planner. Di had been so kind to me during my rehabilitation on Lewis, bringing me baked goods and flowers. I sud-denly longed to bring her here, with Aunt Sorcha, to see this place. Like Dad, Di loved anything to do with plants and horticulture, and I was certain she would leave her own mark on the techniques used here.

"Goodness, I never get to see you anymore," Gio grumbled as I tumbled into bed, my eyes already closing as I pulled the quilt up.

"Temporary," I yawned, curling into his warmness. "Besides, you still wake me every night."

The bridge opening was a full community event, scheduled the day after Illy's arrival. All the ambassadors were here, except Sera, who couldn't travel so soon after the birth of her son Raidon. I met him via videoconference and was surprised that the pain of seeing her child was not as great as I feared. He had a full head of dark hair, which made me laugh since Sera, like our mother Freyja, was platinum blonde.

"Matt can't deny that child," I teased as I made her hold him up for me. "He is simply divine, Sairs. I can't wait to meet him in real life."

"We might need to wait until he sleeps through the night," she yawned. She looked exhausted with dark rings under her eyes and her hair greasy and limp. "He wakes every two hours for a feed, and they take half an hour. What no one told me was that feeding is timed from start to start, so I barely get an hour's sleep at a time. Honestly, it is the worst torture imaginable." As soon as the words left her mouth, she clapped a hand over it. "I'm so sorry," she hastened to say, stumbling over her words. "It is just an expression. I don't for a second think that..."

"It's okay. I am not that sensitive. I know what you meant. But, I do need to go. Love you."

Knowing I was expected to host and greet all the ambassadors and other dignitaries, I relented and wore my most formal suit. The Canadians were so proud that they had the first land-bridge, and all the other communities were jealous, desperate to build their own. The ambassadors and Illy as Chief were taken on the first tour landside, escorted by Joseph, Gabriel, and myself. We knew the bridge could safely hold up to fifty adults, but had set a limit of twenty-five, just to be safe. Riccardo's face was priceless as he stood on solid land again for the first time in over thirty years. He was tentative with his steps, and I tried not to watch, smiling as bliss lightened his face. Nasir had lived in an above-ground community for years before taking on the role in France, so while he was pleased for his new community, the experience wasn't so novel. Yellowstone had not yet joined the ACC but had sent a representative, a woman who was awed by the bridge and the biosphere. Caspian had not been invited, having cut off all communications with the remaining communities. The three more recently discovered forty-fifth parallel communities were also here as Illy tried to convince them to join the ACC. Representatives from Croatia, Mongolia, and China were spellbound, both by the technologies here, but now also that we could grow on land. Illy was very attentive, I noted, showing them around and answering all of their questions. She called me over to assist the delegation, and I found myself answering questions spanning the construction, the moss we used to rehabilitate the earth, and the varieties planted here. She really was exceptional at her job, I noted, wishing I had the people skills she did. I was prouder of the construction achievement, a legacy I could leave for future generations.

Like Lewis, the ground was uneven, and I watched the younger delegates struggle with the feel of uneven ground. Illy smiled over at me, proud of me, as she watched the awestruck faces, feeling the fresh wind blow through the fabric.

CHAPTER 44

"**CAITLIN, IT'S TIME WE** had a chat."

"What? Have I done something wrong?"

Illy smirked. "Quite the opposite. All I hear are reports about how wonderful you are. Fair, reasonable, listening and seeking to understand all aspects of an issue before you make decisions. Everyone loves you. I watched you with the delegates from Yellowstone and the new communities. You were the perfect mix of hospitable, engaging, and informative, without giving away any secrets."

"Then what?" I asked, suspicious at how perky she seemed.

"It is time, Caitlin; I want to retire. At least partially. I am happy to stay on in a support role, an advisory capacity, but I want to hand over control. After the incident at Caspian, I realize how quickly life can be ripped away. Carmelo would have been devastated to lose two wives, especially to lose me so quickly. I've faced my share of challenges. I want to enjoy my life."

That was a shock. I thought she had only come to attend the land-bridge opening. She would be a significant loss. I tilted my head. "Who has the Collective decided to take over? Mum? She is the second-in-command. Does she want the job?"

"You."

That took a moment to register. "Me? Who on earth wants *me*?"

"Do you recall we had an in-camera session after the meeting last week? We told you we were conducting performance appraisals? Assessing your performance in the role? Which we did, by the way. After that, I tabled my intention to retire, and a transition strategy and a succession plan were discussed. Your mother was asked as a matter of courtesy, and she declined, as I knew she would. She isn't much younger than me, and she still wants to focus on orthopedics, not governance. So we discussed our options. We all agree we need someone younger with the energy to take over. The role is even bigger now, and I need someone I can work with and train. We want to keep the relationship with Caspian neutral, at least not antagonize them. We also want the other four communities to join the ACC. They see the benefits, but they need to adhere to our charter. That will take some negotiation and require the right person. All the ambassadors were assessed, and your name was raised. Not by me, in case you were wondering."

"By who then?"

"Riccardo suggested you. There was a robust discussion. It was agreed that we needed someone younger who had the energy and passion to move the ACC forward. All potential candidates were discussed, and a vote was taken. You are it, if you accept."

"I can't. I have no experience. I'm too young."

"You are not too young. Age is just a number. You have proven to be a leader in every sense of the word. You are innovative, fearless, and strive to achieve the best outcome. You are fair and hard-working. You form bonds with people from all walks of life, all cultures. You are respected and liked. They all voted for you, Caitlin."

"They did?"

"What are your concerns?"

"I don't know what to do. You led projects and teams before you took on the role. I haven't."

"What do you think you have been doing here for the last year?"

"Acting on behalf of the Collective. Facilitating trade, helping this community find ways to expand and share technology and resources."

"So what is it you think I do?"

I paused, thinking. I had never really given much thought to what Illy actually did. She chaired meetings and seemed to have a lot of discussions with people.

"I'm not really sure," I admitted.

"What I do is your job but on a larger scale: ensuring all communities are given equal opportunities, building linkages between them, and troubleshooting issues. But in many ways, it is easier when you oversee all of them. You place competent people in each community as your eyes and ears, people you trust, who are fair, and who get the job done. A good manager is one who enables their team, gives them the skills and support to get the job done—not one who does all the work themselves."

"But I can't," I protested. "I have too much to do here."

"Wouldn't it be wonderful to offer those opportunities, these amazing projects you are implementing, across all communities?"

"I guess. That was always the intention, to pilot them here, and then roll them out everywhere, if they are willing."

"That is what we want, too. All the successes to be replicated, and the lessons learned shared. So what else is stopping you?"

"Would I need to travel?"

"Sometimes, yes. You can achieve a lot via video-conferencing and using your person on the ground, but relationships are key and need to be built face-to-face. You have been to many communities already, but you would need to visit all of them over time."

"I can't," I whispered. "Bad timing."

Illy cocked an eye at me, assessing. Then her face lit with joy.

"Are you?"

"I think so. Very early, though. Maybe five weeks."

"Does Giovanni know?"

"Not yet. In case I'm not, I didn't want to get his hopes up. He wants this so badly, and I'm scared of letting him down."

"Have you had an ultrasound?"

"No, but I know I should. All the signs are there."

"Can I come?" The pleading on Illy's face was quite unlike anything I had seen before. Although she had met her first grandchild, Sera and Matteo's little boy Raidon, she hadn't been in Japan for most of the pregnancy. Likely, Summer and Ally would never have children. They loved their independence too much. Alasdair had a male partner, which, while not impossible to have children, made things slightly more difficult. Unlike my mother, who was surrounded by Louis' children, and soon would have Xanthe's baby to enjoy, Illy never really had the ability to play grandmother. I softened and suddenly wanted nothing more than to share this with her.

"Of course. I might not be."

"You are. I can feel it."

"Really?" I whispered, unable to believe it might be true.

"Now?" She stood and held her hand out to me, her face alight with anticipation.

Illy dragged me down the corridors to the medical pod. She paused just outside the door.

"Are you sure you don't want to wait for your mother? She will be back in a few weeks."

Part of me was desperate to wait for Mum, but I could see the desperate need etched into Illy's face. "No, come on. Mum won't mind. She would be too busy playing doctor to play grandmother."

Gio was in the clinic and greeted me with a kiss, and after a pause, Illy too.

"Are you alright?" he asked cautiously.

Illy turned to me. "Can I ask?" she pleaded.

"Go on."

"My lovely daughter here thinks that you two may possibly be expecting. I need to know. Please."

Gio's face lit up, and I hastened to warn him. "I may not be..."

"Come on."

We followed him into the darkened room used for X-rays, ultrasounds, and CT scans. The MRI was in the adjoining room. Even seeing the horrible white plastic machine made me shudder, and I hoped never to be in one ever again. Gio closed the doors, blocking the view before he lowered the bed and assisted me on as I pulled up my top.

"How far along do you think you are?" he asked in his doctor's tone, switching on the machine and pushing random buttons. I poked him in the belly.

"Well, you should know," I teased, making him blush. "You were there."

"Been practicing, have we?" Illy taunted, making even me blush. "Good to see you followed orders."

"Orders?" I asked blankly.

Gio flushed, and Illy cackled wickedly. "I told him that as soon as you were medically cleared, he needed to get on the job. Not only do I want more grandchildren, but the best way to heal a loss is to focus on a new life. So I told him to get on with it."

"You didn't!" My mouth hung open at the thought of Illy dictating my sex life.

"She did," Gio confessed, unable to look at me.

"Bloody fucking hell!" I seethed, turning on Illy.

"Oh, come on. You enjoyed it," she teased, making me fire up even more.

"Stop that now, or I will ask you to leave," Gio ordered in a mock threatening tone.

"Silence from me," she hurried to say, and I looked at her derisively.

"Seriously? When have you ever been quiet?"

Illy drew her fingers over her mouth in a zipper motion, and I rolled my eyes at her.

Gio started tracing the wand over my stomach, and I had flashbacks of the last time he had done this in our apartment. Then Jorja doing the same, telling me one of my ovaries was irreversibly damaged. I tensed and held my breath. He stopped. My eyes flew open.

"What's wrong?"

"I was about to ask you the same thing. Am I hurting you?"

"I just remember the last time you did this," I whispered, remembering the joy of being told I was pregnant with Stella.

Illy clasped my hand in hers and gripped tightly as Gio resumed.

I peered at the screen, black and white and grainy. I wasn't sure how he could see anything on that. It looked like a snowstorm in the dark outside the glass windows of the pod. Random spatters of black, white, and gray.

"Look." He pointed at the screen. Like last time, I really couldn't make out anything other than a tiny blob that looked like a broad bean.

"Is it?" I asked, fearful of the answer.

"About six weeks at a guess," he said, clicking at various points and taking measurements on the screen.

"You are pregnant!" Illy squealed, making my eyes fill with tears.

"I think so."

"I know so," Gio said but screwed his face up as he continued to squint at the monitor.

"What is it?" Illy asked, also seeing the look of alarm on his face.

Gio fell silent, moving the wand, pushing on my stomach to get a clearer image, then moving again.

"Is there something wrong with the baby?" My throat closed over, and Illy gripped my hand so tightly that my fingers tingled from lack of blood flow. Not that I had any mind for that. Gio's face went blank, and turned to me. His mouth opened and closed.

"I can't…"

"What?" Illy gulped, her fingers pressing uncomfortably into the back of my hand. I stopped breathing, waiting for him to speak.

"I can't remember the word in English."

"Ectopic? Miscarriage? Heartbeat?" I squeaked.

"*Gemelli*," he whispered.

"Twins?" Illy gasped.

"Twins," he agreed, breathless. "We are having twins."

My mouth fell open as Illy's expression lit like the sun after a storm, sheer joy crossing her face as Gio and I stared at each other in disbelief.

"Identical?" I asked.

"I can't be certain, but it looks like they have their own placenta."

"So fraternal," Illy questioned. "Two eggs?"

"Is it even possible? Twins?" I whispered, unable to process what he was saying.

"Apparently, yes."

I turned to look at Illy blankly. "I can't..."

"Now, we need to talk about light duties." Gio regained control of himself and took command once more. "There will be no drinking, no lifting. No caffeine. We will need to speak to the kitchen team about your diet, especially as this is a multiple birth."

"Oh, come on. I am barely pregnant. I feel fine."

Illy spoke over me. "What are the potential implications for Cait's injuries, particularly her pelvis? She could get quite large with twins. I was enormous, and they needed to induce me. The added weight on her reconstructed knee can't be good either."

"She should be fully healed, but we must schedule a c-section. A natural birth could impact the stability of the pelvic girdle. We will also need to watch her size and potentially induce if she gets too big."

"Hello! I'm here! Talk to me, not about me, please!"

"Sorry." Gio kissed my forehead as I sat up.

"Do you want to tell him your other news?" Illy twinkled.

"Bloody freaking hell, you are the worst person for keeping secrets!" I was irrationally cranky, feeling pressured into telling him now, his eyebrows raised in inquiry.

"What?"

"The ACC has asked me to be Chief," I muttered.

"But you are Chief?" He looked at Illy, confused.

"I want to retire or part-retire. Though this may slow my retirement plans a little. Perhaps we could have a slow handover?"

"You can't still want me? I can't travel with two babies."

"No, but the role can be performed from anywhere. What if we do a quick visit to all the communities in the next few months, and then you can choose where you want to work from. You won't want to travel once you are six months or so. It gets too uncomfortable. But you should be fine before that." Illy looked up at Giovanni for confirmation, and he shrugged.

"In theory, yes, she is fine to travel, but..."

"So all you need to decide is where you want to live," Illy finished.

"You are so goddamned pushy! You barge in, tell me I am the new Chief, demand I get an ultrasound, and now you are scheduling me for the next three months!"

"What is your point?" she twinkled at me.

I looked to Gio for support. "I'm not sure I want this. Chief, I mean. I want the babies, although I admit I wasn't expecting two."

He reached for my hand. "You always told me you wanted it all. Now you have it."

But that was before, I wanted to say. Before I was abducted, beaten, and lost my child. Now, I was a different person.

"You aren't, you know. Different." Illy spoke quietly.

"You know how you used to really piss Mum off when you read her thoughts? Well, she was right. You are a pain in the ass. I can't wait to tell her what a bully you are."

Illy laughed and held my other hand.

"Sweetheart, we can get you help with the babies. You can work part-time, or Gio can take time off. You have a fantastic assistant here, but we can find you one wherever you choose to live."

"Where do you want to live?" I asked Giovanni. We had already lived in Italy, Scotland, and now Canada. We had spent several months in France. We could settle anywhere.

"I told you I would follow you anywhere. Do you remember?"

"I do."

Illy stood, squeezing my hand. "You have a lot to talk about. I will leave you with it. But congratulations. Both of you. You know I won't tell anyone until you are ready."

Gio leaned to kiss her again, his face alight with the news that he was to be a father.

"I was hoping for a quiet afternoon," he joked after Illy had left and we were alone.

"Are you happy?" I whispered, suddenly unsure.

"I can't believe you even need to ask me that. Is this not what we have wanted for months? And two children? While that will be hard work in the beginning, I can't help but feel…"

"That we are being gifted with two lives to make up for the one we lost? I know we can never replace Stella, and I never want to, but I never expected this." My head was spinning.

"I worry about you, the impact on you physically and emotionally, but yes, I am thrilled beyond words. Besides, with all the time we have spent together, I am surprised there aren't a lot more of them in there. This is wonderful. But are *you* happy?"

"I am, but I am so confused. I have suspected for a little while but couldn't bring myself to believe it. Then Illy forced me, of course, to come here."

"What are you confused about?"

"Stella," my voice dropped. "I don't want to forget her."

"We will never forget her, *amore mio*. She was our first child, and we will tell these children about her. How they had a big sister who is in the stars, watching down over them. Protecting and guiding them. She will always be a part of our lives wherever we go. She will stay with us. Always."

"Where do you want to go?"

"My home is wherever you are. But this is as good a place as any. You are loved here. People value you. So unless you want to live in Scotland or Italy, I don't see why we would leave. Although we might need to ask for a larger apartment."

"I desperately want to finish these projects," I said, my head still spinning with the knowledge that we were expecting not one but two babies. "Maybe I should find someone else?"

"No, my love. They are yours. Your passion projects, as you call them. They will be your legacy when we leave this place. The link you build between this community and the others, the land and the community. You, and you alone, must do this."

nîpiy's speech about orenda flitted into my mind. While I wasn't sure I believed that I had spiritual energy, I knew from Gianni and Charlie that I could make a difference in the lives of others. This bridge could potentially change many lives for generations to come, expanding the community not only physically but emotionally, reducing the impact of the darkness.

"We stay," I announced.

SNEAK PEAK OF BIFROST

(THE 45TH PARALLEL, BOOK 3)

ILLY PUSHED HER CHAIR away from the table with a contented sigh and rested her hands on her perpetually flat stomach. "That was sensational. I don't remember when I last had a meal that good."

Gio rose, adding her empty bowl to the stack he was juggling as he moved toward the kitchen, beaming at the compliment. Cooking was his passion. He loved preparing meals for family and friends, often experimenting with traditional Italian cuisine, adapted to what foods we grew here.

"I don't think I can move," she groaned, her head rolling back in exaggerated discomfort.

"Well, you don't have far to stagger. Best get moving." The natural cheekiness of my childhood flowed, jealousy filling me, watching her feign being bloated, and I regretted it as soon as the words escaped my mouth. I wasn't trying to be rude. I was exhausted and didn't want them to stay all night, as much as we loved the company and the conversation, which was always entertaining and usually ended in hysterical laughter.

Illy didn't appear to have taken offense as she sighed again and took a healthy sip from her wine glass, which I desperately wanted to snatch from her and knock back in one gulp.

"We have something we want to discuss before we leave."

"I thought you said leaving work in the office was important."

Illy peered over her small, black-rimmed glasses, her eyebrows raised at my suspicious tone. "This involves both of you, or I would have already discussed it with you."

Matching her expression, I lifted my chin, indicating she should continue.

"We have a proposal for you."

My smirk morphed into a grimace as I stretched awkwardly in my chair, waiting for Gio to return from the kitchen. My back was killing me now that I was the size of an elephant. Well, what I imagined an elephant would look like. Like everyone born in the last thirty years, I had only ever seen pictures. Mum had told me there was a protected breeding facility for animals in England somewhere, to ensure that no species became extinct. She had visited when she was still a vet before she retrained as a surgeon.

"Whaaaat?" I tried not to let the skepticism infuse my words, but I couldn't help it. I knew Illyria better than anyone. Plotting, scheming, or simply running a million scenarios through her head to assess the best outcome, Illy got her way. Every single time.

Illy twinkled at me. "It involves all of us."

My shoulders slumped, and my head rolled forward, heavy. *Of course it does. The master manipulator strikes again.* Glancing around the table, I evaluated the assembled party. Illy was glowing, her blue eyes brilliant and sparkling, betraying her wit and intelligence. She looked like she had pulled off a monumental coup before speaking a word. Beside her tiny birdlike form, Carmelo was beaming, little crinkles appearing next to his warm brown eyes, but then again, he was perpetually happy. Carmelo was much like my father, always willing to help anyone, no matter how inconvenient it may be to himself. A bear of a man, he was more than twice her size, yet we all knew she was in charge. Carmelo was full of light. It was almost like his heart was so full of love that it overflowed and infected everyone in his world. They glanced at each other, and my stomach dropped further, realizing we were being set up. Clouds of suspicion darkened Gio's chiseled face as he crossed the room, his brow furrowed. He dropped into the chair beside me, facing Illy and Carmelo. The pile of dishes could sit in the sink for now.

"What?" Gio echoed my question as his hand slipped onto my thigh, giving me a gentle, reassuring squeeze under the table. If we both objected, perhaps we had a chance not to be railroaded into another of her grand schemes, the last of which had seen us end up here. *Please, please don't relocate us now.* Gio's tense posture beside me belied his similar concerns. He didn't trust Illy's grandiose plans either.

Illy peered over her glasses at Carmelo, obtaining his final consent. An infinitesimal flick of the eyelids, and she turned back across the table to us. Making use of her flair for the dramatic, she took a deep breath, pushed her glasses back onto her nose, and paused. My heart sank further.

"Promise you will let me finish. I will explain the offer and our reasoning. But let me speak first."

Gio's eyes met mine, and his fingers squeezed my thigh again. We had both endured a lifetime's experience of Illy's proposals by now. Even after all these months of working jointly as Chief, occasionally I was still surprised by the creativity of her schemes. She always achieved her goal. Illy had a talent for getting her way—every time.

"Speak," I warned, a touch gruffly. Illy had a knack for grating my cheese, always knowing how to annoy me to maximum effect. Besides, it was late, and I was exhausted. Watching the three of them lingering over a delicious-smelling wine was the final straw.

Continue following Caitlin and Gio's adventures in Bifrost, the third novel in The 45th Parallel series.

BOOK CLUB QUESTIONS

1. Can trauma irrevocably change a person?

2. Justice versus revenge. What is the difference? Is there a place for both in our society?

3. When taken captive, Caitlin is put in a no-win situation: sacrifice her beliefs and values or sacrifice her life. Is there ever a scenario where it is acceptable to sacrifice your values?

4. Caitlin recognizes that immunity is a gift but also a threat. Would you want to be immune?

5. Would you prefer to live in an aboveground community or an underwater habitation? Why?

6. Why do you think Bronwyn (Charlie's mother on Orkney) is scared of Freyja? Is this justified?

7. Why is it Gianni who appears to Caitlin while she is delirious in captivity on Caspian?

8. Which character do you resonate with the most? Why?

9. *Orenda* is a First Nations Iroquois belief that all natural objects and people possess a mystical energy. It is the force that allows us to effect change in the world, embrace our values, and manifest transformation in our lives. Do you believe you have this power? How have you used it to improve your own life or that of others?

10. Caitlin describes Gio, saying: "He is the first man who treats me like I am valuable and challenges me to be the best version of myself." What other elements are essential in a lasting relationship?

11. Caitlin says, "People always fear what they don't understand." How true is this?

AUTHOR BIO

T.S. SIMONS IS AN Australian-based author of Scottish heritage. Living in the alpine region of Australia, she believes in the values of integrity, sustainability, and community in a world where we place greater value on possessions than people. She enjoys posing philosophical questions that make readers think and reflect on the world we live in.

The Antipodes series is a unique science-based series that poses philosophical questions about how we live and the decisions we would make if the world as we know it irrevocably changed. Readers are challenged to consider their choices, values, and priorities as they share the characters' struggles with science, engineering, and the complexity of human relationships. The original Antipodes series is extended by the 45th Parallel series, a futuristic look at what could happen if society doesn't address the mistakes of the past.

She holds Bachelor and Master's degrees, post-graduate qualifications in governance and management, and is an accredited company director.

She is an Australia Reads Ambassador and enjoys reading, traveling, mythology, and snow skiing while attempting to live as sustainably as possible with her partner and children. She is owned by a standard schnauzer and three rescue cats who co-manage her household. Recently, she added a fox-red labrador puppy to the madness.

The Antipodes series comprises Project Hemisphere, The Space Between, Infinity, Circle of Protection, and Sessrumnir. The 45th Parallel series comprises The 45th Parallel, Orenda, and Bifrost. She is working on the fourth book in this series, Triple Helix, and a prequel to Project Hemisphere.